Australian author **Ally Blake** loves reading and strong coffee, porch swings and dappled sunshine, beautiful notebooks and soft, dark pencils. Her inquisitive, rumbunctious, spectacular children are her exquisite delight, and she adores writing love stories so much she'd write them even if nobody read them. No wonder, then, having sold over four million copies of her romance novels worldwide, Ally is living her bliss. Find out more about Ally's books at allyblake.com.

Hana Sheik falls in love every day, reading her favourite romances and writing her own happily-ever-afters. She's worked at various jobs—but never for very long, because she's always wanted to be a romance author. Now, happily, she gets to live that dream. Born in Somalia, she moved to Ottawa, Canada, at a very young age, and still resides there with her family.

Also by Ally Blake

A Week with the Best Man
Crazy About Her Impossible Boss
Brooding Rebel to Baby Daddy
Dream Vacation, Surprise Baby

Also by Hana Sheik

Second Chance to Wear His Ring
is Hana Sheik's debut title

Look out for more books from Hana Sheik
coming soon

Discover more at millsandboon.co.uk.

THE MILLIONAIRE'S MELBOURNE PROPOSAL

ALLY BLAKE

SECOND CHANCE TO WEAR HIS RING

HANA SHEIK

MILLS & BOON

First Published in Great Britain 2021
by Mills & Boon, an imprint of HarperCollins*Publishers* Ltd,
1 London Bridge Street, London, SE1 9GF

www.harpercollins.co.uk

HarperCollins*Publishers*
1st Floor, Watermarque Building,
Ringsend Road, Dublin 4, Ireland

ISBN: 978-0-263-29989-2

08/21

MIX
Paper from
responsible sources
FSC C007454

This book is produced from independently certified FSC™ paper
to ensure responsible forest management.
For more information visit www.harpercollins.co.uk/green.

Printed and bound in Spain
by CPI, Barcelona

THE MILLIONAIRE'S MELBOURNE PROPOSAL

ALLY BLAKE

MILLS & BOON

At its heart this is a story about home.
Not only the roof beneath which you sleep at night,
but the city, the people, the music, the memories,
the sensations, the spaces that make you feel safe,
and comfortable, and most yourself. So, I dedicate
this book to whatever it is out there that
makes you feel most at home

CHAPTER ONE

FACE TILTED TO the bright spring sky, Nora Letterman absorbed her daily dose of Melbourne sunshine as she moseyed her way along the beaten-up Fitzroy footpath.

A tram rattled past, rails screeching, sparks shooting skyward from the wires overhead, drowning out the music playing through Nora's earbuds. She danced out of the way of a smiling couple as thcy all squeezed between a lamppost and a young girl walking four small fluffy dogs.

As moments went, it was pretty perfect, actually; one of a zillion lovely mental keepsakes she'd tuck away for when she left this little pocket of wonderfulness behind.

Which she would do. Any day now.

The eighteen months she'd spent there were the longest she'd stayed in one place. Ever. And she loved it dearly. But at her core, Nora was footloose and fancy-free. It even said so, in faded, scrawling script on the inside of her right arm, alongside a delicate dandelion, petals breaking away and drifting with the breeze.

"Nora!"

Nora looked back over her shoulder as Christos the fruiterer threw her a mandarin, which she swiped out of the air. Spinning to walk backwards, she put a hand over her heart.

Christos called, "The Tutti Fruiti website is such a hit,

Nora. Lots of compliments from customers, which I accept on your behalf. Are you sure I can't pay you in fruit?"

"Not unless the phone company accept payment in kind," Nora called back.

Christos grinned. Then he shot her a salute before turning to flirt with the next customer.

Cheeks full with smiling, Nora meandered on, absorbing the cacophony of sensory delights that made this patch of Fitzroy infamous: incense and coffee, flowers and pre-loved clothes, street art and graffiti, multicultural foods and the lingering scent of smoked herbs that might or might not be legal.

Sure, there was a chain chemist or two along the strip, an American burger behemoth on the corner, but for the most part the shopfronts were generational, mum and dad stores, or young entrepreneurs stepping out into the fray. People having a go. Which was why she'd fitted in so quickly.

The fact that so many of them had readily snapped up the services of *The Girl Upstairs*—Nora's fledgling online creative business—for a website dust-off, virtual assistance, or a vibrant social-media overhaul was yet another reason her time in this place had been so golden.

Gait loose, mind warm and fuzzy, her time her own, Nora slowed outside Vintage Vamp.

Misty, the elegantly boho business owner who'd refused to hire Nora as she believed the internet would cause the downfall of civilisation, mumbled under her breath as she reworked a clothing rail full of brightly coloured kaftans flapping in a sudden waft of breeze.

"Hey, Misty!" Nora sing-songed.

Misty turned, her eyes lit with genuine fondness, before she remembered herself and frowned. "Thought you'd have left us in your dust by now."

Nora rolled her eyes. "Do you really think I'd go without saying goodbye?"

"Good point, Little Miss Sunshine. Not a chance of that. Now, help me. Do I retire these things?" Misty waved a hand over the colourful kaftans. "Or leave them here, in memory of our Clancy?"

As one, both women blinked, breathed out hard sighs, then looked across the road, to the row of terrace houses on the far corner.

Some facades were overgrown with weeds, paint peeling, fretwork rusting; the tenants mostly students and artists who had gravitated to the area. Other properties had been meticulously renovated till they were worth an utter mint. But Nora's and Misty's gazes were caught on the cream-and-copper-hued terrace house right in the middle.

Neither dilapidated, nor pristine, Thornfield Hall—as it had been lovingly dubbed by its long-time owner—was tidy and appealing. It was also the house in which Nora had been lucky enough to live as the single upstairs tenant for the past year and a half.

Its downstairs sitting room was well known around the area as a safe, warm space for book clubs, widows' groups, and a widows' book club. Always open for a quick coffee, a listening ear, a place to grieve, to vent, to go for laughter and company.

Though it had gone quiet in the days since Clancy Finlayson—eighty-something, raucous, divine, and the owner of Thornfield Hall—had fallen ill. She had passed away before any of them had had the chance to ready themselves for the possibility.

"Any news?" Misty asked. "About the new owner?"

Nora shook her head. "Still no word."

It was all anyone had asked since Clancy had passed.

Knowing Clancy as she had, the house might have been left to some distant relative, or the local puppy shelter.

While Nora had kept Clancy company during her final days at home, she had no more of a clue than anyone else. She'd focussed, as she always did, on the good not the bad, the happiness not the suffering: reading *Jane Eyre* aloud, telling funny stories she'd picked up in the neighbourhood, playing Clancy's favourite records, and making sure Clancy's hair and nails were *en pointe.*

After Clancy had passed, the lawyers had been frustratingly tight-lipped about it all, citing privacy laws, and Nora didn't know where else to turn.

Which was how she'd found herself in her current state of limbo, ready to move on but unwilling to walk away and leave the beautiful old house untended, abandoned to fate, local squatters or graffiti gangs.

There was also the fact that she'd promised Clancy as much.

In those quiet, final hours, with Nora no longer able to hold back the ache that had been building inside her from the moment Clancy had announced she was sick—her insides crazing faster than she could mentally patch up the damage—in a rare fit of poignancy she'd promised Clancy that she'd take care of her beloved house till the new owner took over.

Clancy might not have been lucid, might not have heard a word, but Nora had been on the receiving end of enough broken promises in her life, a promise *from* her was as good as placing her beating heart in someone's open hands.

So she would stay. Bags packed. Money put aside to cover her interim rent. Ready to hand the house keys to the new owner the moment they showed their face. And only then would she move on, leaving behind nothing but warm feelings and pleasant memories.

After all Clancy had done for her, it was the very least she could do.

Misty cleared her throat and shook herself all over. Pathos was not her natural state of being. “Loved the woman to bits, but I’m never going to move these damn things without her.”

Nora dragged her gaze and thoughts back to the rack of floaty, wildly coloured garments now flapping in a growing breeze, the Melbourne weather having turned on a dime as it tended to do.

“May I?” Nora asked, bringing out her phone to take a photo.

Misty waved a *whatever* hand Nora’s way.

Nora stood back, found the best angles and took a slew of photos, which she’d edit, filter, tag and post later on her *The Girl Upstairs* pages, which had gathered followers like lint on felt from near the moment she’d set them up as a showcase for her clients. If a half-dozen kaftans weren’t snapped up within the day she’d eat her shoes.

Thus distracted, she was too slow to move when Misty grabbed a moss-green kaftan with hot pink embroidery and purple fringing and thrust it up against Nora’s person. “You must have it. And when you wear it, you’ll think of Clancy.”

Beneath the sway of the lurid pattern, Nora’s hemp platforms poked out from under her frayed denim flares. If she ever wore such a thing, she’d more likely be thinking she looked like a seventies boudoir lamp.

Nora caught Misty’s eye, and the gleam of commerce within, then handed over the twenty bucks anyway. It was Nora’s mission in life to leave any place, conversation, and moment brighter than when she entered it and if selling a kaftan made Misty feel a little happier, then so be it.

Kaftan draped over her arm, Nora backed away. “Friday night drinks?”

"If you're still here."

"If I'm still here."

With that, Nora waited for a break in the meandering traffic and jogged across the road.

When she reached the front gate of Clancy's old house, she ambled up the front path; past the Japanese myrtle, to the front patio, its fretwork dripping with jasmine, pale green buds just now starting to show. The elegant facade was a little worn around the edges, but still strong and purposeful, like a royal family who could no longer afford servants, but still wore tiaras to dinner.

Using her key, she jiggled the old lock till it jerked open, then stepped inside.

Dust motes danced in the muted afternoon sunshine pouring through the glass panels in the front door. In the quiet it was easy to imagine Clancy's Chloé perfume on the air, Barry Manilow crooning from the kitchen speaker, the scent of Clancy reheating something Nora had cooked on the beautiful old Aga.

A slice of sadness, of *loss*, whipped across her belly, so sudden, so sharp she let out a sound. Her hand lifted to cover the spot but it took its sweet time to ebb.

This… This was the biggest reason why she had to get the house sorted and move on as soon as possible. As strongly as Nora believed in the deliberate collection of happy moments, she'd made a concerted effort in her adult life not to put herself in situations that might bring on sadness, emotional pain, the sense of missing something, or someone.

Connections, friendships, and traditions felt nice, superficially, but they were so dangerous. They made a person feel as if such things might actually last. Shuffled from foster home to foster home as a kid, promises had been made to Nora, hopes raised, then summarily dashed, again and again.

There was no room for hope, or guilt, or expectations, or regret; not if she wanted a happy life. That lesson had been learned, until it was as indelible as any tattoo. And Nora *really*, *truly*, *deeply* wanted a happy life.

And so she woke up smiling, worked hard, kept little in the way of possessions, was nice to people and expected nothing in return, so that when she moved on, no part of her was left behind. Only a fond lustre, like the kiss of the first cool breeze of autumn at the end of a long summer.

The sudden clackety-clack of toenails on the hardwood floor split the silence, then stilled, snapping Nora back to the present.

"Magpie?" she called, her voice wavering just a smidge. "Pie?"

Pie was a bad-tempered, one-eyed, silky terrier; the latest in a long line of dogs Clancy had fostered in the time Nora had lived there. He'd been due to go back to Playful Paws Puppy Rescue around the time Clancy had passed. But after hearing the news, they'd said it was no rush getting him back.

This wasn't their first rodeo.

So, she was not only stuck looking after a house that wasn't hers, but also a dog that didn't much like her. Which mucked with her head more than she liked. This had better get sorted…and soon.

Nora reached slowly into her tote for the baggie of dried meat she'd picked up at the whole-foods market. "I got you a little treat, Pie. Want some?"

She earned a distant growl for her efforts, before the flap of the doggie door gave her reprieve.

Stepping deeper inside the house, her foot caught on the mail that had been slipped through the mail slot in the front door.

A couple of department store mailers, Clancy's subscription to *Men's Health* magazine—for the articles, she'd always claimed—and an official-looking envelope. The latter was thick and yellow, the Melbourne address of a London law firm etched into the top left corner.

And it was addressed to Nora.

Heart kicking till she felt it in her neck and in a flush across her cheeks, Nora moved to the steep stairs leading up to her first-floor apartment, and sat, popping her tote and new kaftan beside her. Then she opened the envelope without ado.

As expected, it was news of Clancy's will, as it pertained to one Nora Letterman.

She knew nothing would be left to her; she'd made Clancy promise after the older woman had made noise about leaving her a sideboard she'd admired. Unless it would fit in her rucksack, it would only be a burden. From what Nora could ascertain from the legalese, Clancy had listened. Apart from a few charitable bequests, the house and everything Clancy owned had been left to one Bennett J Hawthorne.

An answer. Finally!

Though while she felt the expected relief, hot on its heels came a wave of uncomfortable tightness in her belly.

Bennett J Hawthorne. *Bennett.* It had to be Clancy's adopted grandson who, from the little Nora had gleaned, had lived with Clancy from when he was quite young.

Poor guy. What rotten news. And to find out his adoptive grandmother was gone while so far away. Actually, where was he again?

The dozen odd times his name had come up someone had always changed the subject, so she'd never heard the story behind his adoption. Since mere mention of Bennett had always made Clancy maudlin, which was the opposite of Nora spreading sunshine wherever she went, and in her experience "family" was as often considered a dirty word as not, she'd happily let it be. And never thought more of it.

Now she wished she'd pressed. Just a little.

Rubbing a finger and thumb over her temple, she searched her memory banks for the times she'd heard mention of his name.

Once a month or so, Clancy would answer the phone, her face pinched, her shoulders tight, and she'd quietly take the phone to her bedroom. One of those times Nora had heard Clancy say, "Bennett" just before the bedroom door snicked shut.

Was that it?

Then it hit her.

Bennett. *Ben.*

Deep into the night, near the end, perhaps even the very last time Clancy had been in any way lucid, she had muttered, "Ben." Then, louder, more insistent, "*Ben?* Is that you?"

"*Ben?* Ben who? Would you like me to find him?" Nora had asked, not realising at the time Clancy had meant Bennett, the prodigal, *hush hush* adopted grandson. "Ask him to come?"

"No," Clancy had shot back, her face twisting as if in pain. "Leave him be."

Leave him be. As if asking a guy to take the time to visit his ailing grandmother was too great a burden.

Nora shifted on the stair, the skinny plank of wood with its threadbare patch of old carpet biting into her backside, her initial feelings of *poor guy* having morphed into *what the heck?*

This was the person Clancy had left her beloved Thornfield Hall to? Seriously, what kind of man treated a person that way? Never visiting, calling but rarely. Especially someone as vibrant and loving and wondrous and accepting as Clancy?

Nora allowed herself a rare moment of indulging in feeling all the feelings—the gutting sorrow, the flutters of rage—letting them stew till they coagulated in an ugly ball in her belly before she sucked in a deep soothing breath and reduced them to a simmer.

It took longer than she'd have liked to let it go. But she managed. Letting go of ugly feelings was something she'd long since learned to do with alacrity and grace.

Happiness over suffering.

This was the news she'd been waiting for, unexpected outcome or no. Bennett Hawthorne could come and grab the keys, she'd politely talk him through the vagaries of the old home—the upstairs window that had been painted shut, the noisy downstairs pipe, the wriggly front door lock—then she could draw a nice clean line under what had been a wonderful chapter of her life.

Before the place got its claws into her any deeper. Before this pile of bricks, this street, these people, began to feel like something as insidious and treacherous as *home.*

Nora lifted the papers in her hand, flipped the page and read on, hoping to find a timeline as to when Hawthorne might finally show up so she could be ready.

But then she reached a section that left her a little stunned, as if she'd been smacked in the side of the head.

While the house would go to Bennett Hawthorne, Clancy's will also declared that one Nora Letterman, aka *The Girl Upstairs*, had the right to stay on in the house for a period of up to two months from the date of Clancy's death.

A cleaner would be paid for by the estate. All upkeep and utilities as well. And Nora was not to pay a cent of rent.

The house was not to be open for inspection, put on the

market, or in any way renovated during the time Nora was in residence.

She was—of course—welcome to leave sooner if she desired. But the rooms were hers, for two months, if she needed them.

All of which, apparently, suited Bennett Hawthorne, as the reason the letter was from the Melbourne office of a London law firm was because the guy was London-based and thus would not be able to inspect the property in person any time soon.

"Oh, Clancy." Nora breathed out audibly, the letter falling to her knee, her gaze lifting to glance into the kitchen.

The kitchen said nothing in return. Though, in the silence, the clackety-clack of tiny doggy claws echoed somewhere in the big empty house.

Clancy *knew* Nora was a wanderer. They'd often chat about where Nora might end up next; Clancy wistfully sighing over Nora's stories of camping out on other people's sofas, slinging coffees in a train station café for a day in order to be able to afford the fare to get her to the next place, as if that life were something to aspire to rather than a case of needs must.

So what had she been thinking, sneaking this into her will?

Nora felt the slightest twinge tugging on her watch-out-ometer, as if she'd somehow found herself swept up in some larger plan. But she quickly shook it off. Clancy didn't have it in her to be so manipulative. She'd been good, through and through. The best person Nora had ever known. And now she was gone.

"Dammit." Nora rubbed a hand over her eyes, knees juggling with excess energy as she mentally gathered in all the parts of herself that were threatening to fly off into some emotional whirlwind.

Breaking things down into their simplest forms:

Clancy was simply being kind.

But staying was impossible.

So this Bennett guy *had* to come back. Now.

Irresponsible or no, on the other side of the world or not, whatever the story, he was one of Clancy's people. And Clancy never gave up on her people. He'd know what this house meant to his grandmother. And would take care of it.

If not…

While Clancy had loomed large in Nora's life these past months, had treated her with such kindness, respect, and fierce support, she wasn't family. So, it was actually none of Nora's business.

Ignoring the latest twinge *that* brought on, Nora grabbed her phone and searched for Bennett Hawthorne, but she had no clue what he might look like and, since he was adopted, she couldn't even look for a similarity to Clancy. A plethora of images and articles popped up, all the same, most regarding the sweet-looking, elderly mayor of some small town in America who'd tried to make it so that dogs could legally marry one another. Ah, algorithms.

Figuring it mattered little—the guy was who he was—she popped her phone away, grabbed the legal letter, took it upstairs, turned her Taylor Swift playlist up nice and loud, and emailed the lawyers.

CHAPTER TWO

"MR HAWTHORNE?"

Bennett Hawthorne lifted a quieting finger towards the voice at the office door while he listened, hard, to the message left on his phone by the head of his insolvency division…

Dammit.

Word on the street had been that simply by signing with Hawthorne Consultancy, Metropolis Air was set to be released from their involuntary administration order, the firm's brand of zealous forensic accounting and future planning as good as a golden ticket out of bankruptcy.

The street had been misinformed.

Bennett felt the dig of his short blunt fingernails in his palms, and slowly unfurled his fingers.

It was a blow. Time now concertinaed, the team would need to be scrappy and smart to pull this off. But hard work wasn't the problem. He relished the physical and mental satiation that came with hard work; the kinds of days where he fell asleep the moment his head hit the pillow.

It was just that this week, of all weeks, he could have done with an easy win.

If he closed his eyes, he could still hear the exact timbre of the attorney's voice, dry and sober, as she'd sat on the other side of his desk and read from a sheet of paper.

"Clancy Finlayson passed peacefully in her sleep a week ago Friday. Cause of death, cancer of the pancreas. Cremation took place three days later. No funeral, by request of the deceased."

A wash of pity had passed over the attorney's face at the last, as she apologised, prodigiously, for the delay in passing on the news, assuring him that the timing had been stipulated, in unflinching detail, in the will.

It had been written that he was *not to be disturbed.*

Disturbed.

They'd had their issues, he and Clancy, but he struggled to accept she'd actually believed that was how news of her passing would affect him.

Then again, *disturbance* could account for his wandering mind, the fitful sleep, the fact he'd listened to the rumours about Metropolis Air and believed them. All reverberations from that initial hit. He only wished he knew when the aftershocks would end.

Bennett pressed finger and thumb into his temples.

No. Likelihood was, he could do with a day off. To see daylight while outdoors rather than through the floor-to-ceiling windows in his office suite high up in The Shard. To watch something more diverting than the Bloomberg channel.

But with the volatility of the current market, finance was fast, furious, and fragile. Cowboy investors and workaday drones, old apparatuses and new technologies, government turnovers and special interest groups were all scrambling to find their feet in the new order. If he stepped off the treadmill, he'd lose traction and never catch up to where he was today.

Clancy's voice echoed in his head. "Life is change, kid. Making hard choices on the fly is all we can do. It's also short as hell. Don't you dare mourn an old lady who had a good run; worry about your own life."

"Mr Hawthorne—?"

Ben rubbed a hand over his face, tossed his phone onto the couch beside him, and looked to the younger man hovering in the doorway.

Every year Bennett hand-picked a bunch of the first-year employees and put them on an assistant/mentee rotation with the heads of departments. Meaning Damon had been in the room when Clancy's lawyer had dropped her bombshell. The kid was keen, canny and discreet, and Ben couldn't have been more grateful Damon's turn had fallen into this quarter.

"What's up?" Ben asked.

Damon held up a tablet. "You wanted me to let you know when we heard back—"

"I just got word," said Ben with a dismissive shake of his hand.

Damon shook his head. "Not the Metropolis Air hearing. The lawyers. Apparently, there's an issue regarding Nora Letterman."

Ben raised an eyebrow.

"The girl upstairs from your grandmother's—"

"Right," said Ben, cutting him off. The last thing he had time for right now was managing the feelings of one of Clancy's band of merry acolytes.

Damon glanced over his shoulder, towards the bustling workplace outside the door. "I think you need to see it."

Ben waved Damon into the room. The kid was smart. Didn't need the whole office listening in. Work was work. Private life was private. Compartmentalising the two kept things clean. Tidy. Efficient. If numbers were his thing, high drama was definitely not.

Ben stood, buttoned his suit jacket, and moved to sit in

his big leather office chair. The desk—with its smoky glass windows and imposing view of London from his corner office—was a better spot from which to make important decisions.

He began, "So, you mentioned an issue."

Damon landed with a lanky *kerflunk* in the chair on the other side of the desk and tapped the tablet. "Paraphrase?"

"Please."

"Cool. So, she's sorry for your loss. But while Nora is appreciative of Clancy's offer, she'd actually rather not stay."

Ben waited. Realised he'd have to keep on waiting unless he spoke. "That's it?"

"In a nutshell. She also looks forward to you 'coming home', so she can 'hand over the keys in person', which was a promise she made to your grandmother 'on her deathbed'." Damon didn't hold back on the air quotations. "That's pretty much the gist."

Ben sat back in his chair; the absorbers sighing as it rocked him gently in place, his mind no longer wandering.

While the lawyer had winced when reading the subsection of the will regarding the tenant, Ben had been relieved. The existence of a grey-haired, sparkly-eyed, slightly stooped woman keeping watch over the house seventeen-thousand-odd kilometres away gave him breathing space; a good month or two before he had to make any decisions regarding the estate. Before he had to really think about it at all.

Turned out the universe was not about to give him a break this week, at all.

Done with his wandering mind, or any excuses for anything less than his usual mental acuity, Bennett grabbed a sharpened pencil from the stash kept in his World's Best Boss mug on his desk, opened a fresh notebook to the first page, wrote *The Girl Upstairs* on the title page, and readied to tackle the issue at hand.

"She'd rather not stay," Bennett repeated, jotting down the words, then letting his fingers scribble, sketch, and shade, his mind following.

It seemed odd. Why would Clancy make the offer if it wasn't fait accompli? Was this woman simply being polite? Was she looking for solace? Was she angling for a better deal?

Ben looked down at the page to find a series of zigzags. "The stairs."

Years back, in the before, he'd tried to get Clancy to sell the old terrace house because of the dodgy old staircase. She'd laughed at the very thought. She'd finally agreed to move into the downstairs section, after he'd paid to have a second bathroom put in.

"The stairs?" Damon asked.

"Too small for my feet, even as a kid," he muttered. "They'd be a hazard for old knees. Have the lawyers let Ms Letterman know she's to use the ground-floor rooms only. And look into liability on that score."

Damon blinked, a smile tugging at the corner of his mouth, as he reached over the desk and handed Ben the iPad.

"There's more?" Ben asked.

Damon shook his head. "I don't think *old* knees are the problem."

The tablet was open to an Instagram page.

Ben's gaze skipped over photos of what looked like a row of dresses hanging on a rack, a fruit and veg platter, the shopfront of a florist bursting with arrangements. Glaringly bright, a cacophony of colour, the page was an assault to eyes that were used to the more subtle nuances of a London winter.

"What am I looking at?" Ben asked.

"Nora Letterman."

"Where?" Was she hiding behind a cantaloupe?

"The whole thing. It's her page."

Ben looked up. "She's on *Instagram*?"

Clancy had refused to even have a smartphone, sticking with one of those flip things, a clamshell phone, even though she jumped every time it snapped shut. At least, that was how she'd been a couple of years back, at the time of his last visit. Before everything went to hell.

Damon leant back in the chair, a definite gleam in the eye. "Keep scrolling."

Bennett—who most certainly did not have time for *this*—scrolled with speed through the feed.

More colour-rich photos of café menus, a clutch—compendium? flurry? sneeze?—of orange kittens that made him itch just to look upon them, and street art that was so indicative of the kitsch, anti-establishment mien of Fitzroy he'd have recognised the place even without the slew of energetic hashtags.

For all that they were a violation of the retina, the photographs were quite good. The thematic nature also ticked his liking for symmetry and consistency.

And then his thumb came to a sudden halt, pausing to hover over the screen as his gaze snagged on a picture of an actual person.

A young woman, mid-twenties, tucked up on a chair by a window. Long blonde hair in loose braids tumbled over a soft-looking cardigan, the rest of her swamped by what looked like pyjama pants and fluffy socks. A shaft of sunshine hit the side of her face, lighting up a neat straight nose, a smattering of freckles, and huge blue eyes that smiled over the top of a cup as big as a soup bowl.

The heading beneath the image: *My job is better than your job ;)*

As a whole, the image was cosy and appealing, offering the viewer a glimpse into someplace warm and inviting. Artless. Enviable. Private.

But it was the wallpaper behind her that had the wheels in Bennett's mind spinning with crystalline precision for the first time in days. Dark green, it was, and covered in massive brown moths. The woman in the picture was sitting in Clancy's upstairs bedroom.

The next picture showcased what he could only assume were her knees and a goodly part of her bare tanned thighs, poking out of the bath in the upstairs bedroom—the one with the peacock wallpaper. The water very light on bubbles while she read a paperback covered in wet thumbprints… purchased, apparently, from some local bookstore.

Then an image showed her sitting before a massive cheesy pizza at Brunswick Pizza—the décor hadn't changed in twenty years—elbows on the table, chin propped in her palms. Again those eyes, looking through the camera. Right at him.

He scrolled slowly back to the top of the page, which was entitled *The Girl Upstairs*, leaving him in no doubt that Damon had found his new tenant.

Running a hand over his chin, Bennett breathed out hard. Who was this woman in his grandmother's home?

"So what do you think?" Damon asked.

"I think she is unlikely to struggle with the stairs."

"Not so much."

"Did the lawyers send you this?"

Damon shook his head. "I went looking. First thing I'd have done, if I was in your shoes. First thing I ever do before a job interview. Or a blind date."

Ben shot the kid a look, and Damon sat back, hands lifted in surrender.

Ben wasn't on social media. Not personally. He'd outsourced to a brilliant company to look after that side of things for the business, but did not see a single reason why anyone needed to see a photograph of his dinner, or where he went on holiday—if he ever took holidays. It was akin to forcing people to look at one's vacation slideshow, only now people chose to watch on purpose.

What Bennett did with his life was serious. Consequential. Forensic accounting was about uncovering the raw data, the raw truth, from beneath the tangles and fog of human interference. It was more cathartic than yoga—he knew, he'd tried it.

Social media was the antithesis of what he did. All show and no substance. Hooks and tricks and filters and curation; people showing only the side of themselves they thought people would like. And by the tone of the comments and the eye-popping number of followers, Nora Letterman was clearly good at it.

Which had the hairs tickling at the back of Ben's neck.

He'd last spoken to Clancy a month before. Or, thinking back, it might have been closer to two. That was right. It had been her turn to reach out, and she hadn't. Refusing to chase her up, he'd planned to wait until it was his turn again—the deal they'd put in place after the fallout, and he was a man who lived by his deals—but then…the lawyers had shown up.

For the hundredth time since that morning, he wondered: had Clancy sounded unwell the last time they'd spoken? No. She'd sounded…the same: bolshie, impatient, contrite. Talking ten to the dozen in an effort to cover up any discomfort that might arise between them.

Never once had she mentioned feeling off. Or having a tenant. A girl upstairs.

Why was that? Because she knew he'd have asked why. She'd resisted the idea as long as he'd known her. Was she worried he'd have realised something was wrong?

Or had this person, this girl upstairs, been the one to stop her from telling him? Had she seen in Clancy an elderly woman in need and used it to get free rent? If so, it made sense that she'd be keen to scarper, now a new landlord was on the scene.

"I'm afraid your find has opened up more questions than it answered," Ben lamented.

"What would you like me to do?" Damon asked. "Get back to the lawyers? To Ms Letterman? I could slide into her DMs. Get the lay of the land."

Unlike some who found themselves in a position such as his, Ben *liked* to delegate. The same reason he liked to rotate his assistants. He surrounded himself with self-starters. Go-getters. People who didn't require gentle handling. People like him. It was why his success rate was so high.

But this wasn't business. It was personal.

And, incongruently, the thought of anyone sliding into the DMs of the blue-eyed woman curled up on the chair in the sunshine made him feel strangely uncomfortable.

He shook his head. "Good work, though."

Damon unfolded himself from the chair. "No probs. Wanna keep the tablet? Research purposes."

Ben thought of those big blue eyes, the cosy set-ups, the artlessness he didn't believe for a second, and shook the tablet at Damon. "Ms Letterman is neither a job interview nor a blind date."

"Right." The kid grinned and nabbed the tablet back, tucking it under his arm before lolloping out of the room.

Leaving Ben to ponder his next move.

Get the lawyers to tell Ms Letterman she could move out at her pleasure, then ask Clancy's Melbourne firm to have a rental agency let it out? That would mean strangers living with Clancy's furniture. Her books.

Not ideal. Neither was boarding the place up in order to keep it safe till he could figure out the next right move. Which, if he was at all honest with himself, he'd be happy to put off for a very long time.

While Ben couldn't deny the frisson of concern sparking in the back of his head, keeping the girl upstairs *upstairs* might give him time to figure out her angle, while also holding at bay any necessity as to deciding what to do with the house.

For now.

CHAPTER THREE

NORA LAY ON her bed, staring at the ceiling, random songs from musicals playing in her ears, when her phone quieted a beat as it pinged with a notification. Nora pushed herself to sitting and slid her thumb across the screen to find a new email from Hawthorne Consultancy.

"Here we go," she said, crossing her legs and dragging her laptop onto her lap. Her legs were jiggling by the time she opened the email.

Dear Ms Letterman
Pursuant to your queries regarding your temporary residence at Thornfield Hall, Fitzroy, Victoria, Mr Hawthorne's responses are as follows.

1. As per the stipulation in Ms Finlayson's will, no rent is owing, so please do not allow any concern on that matter to colour your decision to stay in Thornfield Hall for the allotted time.

2. Please forward any and all copies of invoices regarding upkeep of the house to this email address so that future accounts are paid from this office forthwith.

3. While Mr Hawthorne is delighted that you'd care to meet in person, he has no immediate plans to return to Australia.

4. No smoking.

5. No pets allowed on the premises.
Regards.
Damon Davidson
pp Bennett J Hawthorne
From the desk of Bennett J Hawthorne, Hawthorne Consultancy
Forensic Accounting, Financial Regulation and Compliance, Insolvency and Restructuring

Nora paused the music she'd kept running in the background, the silence only heightening the fact that her brain had gone into a kind of *pffft-cough-splutter* mode.

Flinging her hands out to the side, she blurted, "What the heck am I meant to do with that?"

When she'd promised Clancy she'd look after the house till she put the keys into the new owner's hands she'd meant it. Her intent had been precise, never imagining that the new owner would fob her off onto some lackey, who'd declared the guy might not bother turning up at all!

And as to no *pets*—did the guy not know his grandmother *at all*? Not that Pie was a *pet* so much as a kind of grumpy, temporary house guest who had not warmed to his host at all.

The point being, this house deserved better. This community deserved better. The memory of the woman who'd helped raise him deserved better.

Nora had only a shadow of a memory of her own father, an artist and musician who'd tried to take care of her after her mother had died, but whose own demons had led him to letting her go. But she feared, now that that memory was mostly an amalgamation of the revolving door of grim-faced foster parents who'd taken her in, found her "too spirited, too needy, too much", and one after another blithely sent her on her way.

She'd have given anything to have a woman like Clancy in her corner. To have that kind of consistency, that support, that love.

Nora's right knee began to jiggle again. A few slow breaths usually calmed that down, but she didn't feel like being calm. She felt offended on Clancy's behalf. That her adopted grandson had grown too selfish or too lazy to take up his family responsibility.

Meaning Nora was caught between the proverbial rock and a hard place: her *mission* to sprinkle sunshine wherever she went, to be helpful without being a nuisance, without pushing too hard, or being "too much", and her *need* to fulfil her promise to Clancy, to repay Clancy for all of her kindnesses so that she could leave this place with not a skerrick of regret.

Both knees now jiggled, and her fingers flicked at the ends of her thumbs, as the solution came to her. Like a big bright light bulb flickering to life overhead.

Clancy's heir might not yet know it, but she was about to help him in a big way.

Nora was going to charm Bennett Hawthorne into coming home.

Once the decision was made a preternatural calm overcame her. She could do this. It would take finesse, and restraint, and careful choices. But she could do this.

First step: make it past the assistant to the man himself.

She reached for a notebook on the bedside table, grabbed a pen, and opened it up to a fresh page. In her neat, blocky handwriting she jotted down the few random things she could remember people saying about him before Clancy had shut them down.

Then she stretched out her fingers, pressed *reply* on the email, and began to type.

Dear Damon
So nice of you to get in touch! Though I was rather hoping to connect with Mr Hawthorne himself.

Despite Clancy's truly gorgeous offer to have me stay in her beautiful home, I am sure Mr Hawthorne is keen to visit the house that has been left to him as soon as possible without some stranger in the way.

The house in which he learned to play "Baby, One More Time" on the trumpet. The rooms Clancy decorated in black wool spiderwebs the year he decided he wanted to be Spiderman when he grew up. The kitchen where he danced to celebrate the first morning he'd not wet the bed. So many warm, wonderful memories.

Rent is not the issue. I'm happy to go with his wishes either way on that score, as he is the new owner of the property. And I will move on without a fuss the moment he arrives and takes the front door key from my hot little hand.

Perhaps you could mention that to him next time he pops his head out from behind his "desk"?
Cheers!
Nora

She added her mobile number, her Instagram handle, along with several other ways in which he could get in touch. Then, after a beat, she deleted her usual *The Girl Upstairs* signature footer and added:

From the desk of Nora Letterman, the Girl Upstairs
Lover of Dandelions, Dragonflies and Rainstorms on Summer Afternoons.

Sassy, yes. But she could live with that. Before she could edit, or change her mind, she hit *send*.

Then, feeling full of energy all of a sudden, she decided to get a head start on the next day's jobs.

The Ambrosia Café down the street was having a two-for-one coffee promotion that Nora had agreed to hawk all over their social media pages and hers, and, unlike some people out there in the world, Nora did not make a habit of letting people down.

A dank drizzle had settled over London earlier that week, creating a permanent oppressive gloom, but now the rain was coming down so hard, it pelted against the glass of Ben's office windows and smudged any effort at a view.

"Mr Hawthorne."

Bennett blinked, and turned away from the window, to find Damon hovering in the doorway. Again.

"I heard back. From Nora. The girl upst—"

"Yes, I know who she is." Her face had popped into his mind at the most inconvenient moments over the past day or so. Likely, he figured, because he was wishing for just a smidge of the shard of sunshine that she'd captured so cleverly. "All settled, I hope."

"Not exactly. She's still determined to leave."

"Seriously?" Dammit. Dammit. *Dammit.* "Is she fishing for something, do you think? A payment? A share?"

Damon blinked, as if it had never occurred to him. "I don't get that feeling. I think she just wants to speak to you. Directly."

"Why?"

"Ah…there was mention of your particular connection to the house. Spiderman decorations, Britney Spears and…other things."

Britney Spears? Bennett reached for his phone as

Damon said, "I've forwarded it to your personal email as it felt a smidge, well, personal."

Damon moved *into* the room, after silently shutting the door. It was becoming a habit.

Bennett scrolled through the personal account he rarely used to find emails from a gym he no longer frequented and juice bar newsletters he didn't remember subscribing to till he found the one in question.

And read it.

What the ever-loving—?

"I did *not* wet the bed," he growled.

Damon held up both hands in surrender. "Know my mum five minutes and she'll tell you I used to eat dirt and wanted to be a turtle when I grew up. We all have a past."

Bennett grunted. "You know way too much about me. I may never be able to let you leave this room."

Damon only grinned. "She's feisty, though, right?"

"I think the term you are looking for is passive aggressive."

"Tom-ay-to, tom-ah-to." A shrug, then, "I like her."

Those big blue eyes swam back into Bennett's consciousness, as well as the strange sensation that she could see to the bottom of his clouded, grey soul. Whatever Damon saw on his boss's face, he lost the grin.

"Okay. So what do we know?"

Bennett refocussed. This was his wheelhouse; he took messy situations, broke them down to their origin, and fixed them.

"She wants out. No one is forcing her to stay. So what's keeping her there?"

"Perhaps," said Damon, "*you* could ask her."

Dealing with a house on the other side of the world was one thing. Dealing with Clancy no longer living in that house required space in his head he simply couldn't commit to right now. Except a spanner in the works, by the name of Nora Letterman, was not going to let it be.

"Just saying," Damon said as he backed out of the office, leaving Bennett to stare at his phone, while running a hand over his mouth as he decided how to approach this.

He took messy situations, broke them down, and fixed them.

The very first question he had every employee ask every client who walked through their door was: who are you, and what do you want? Often times they didn't know themselves until Bennett had found their pressure points and given them a little squeeze.

Ben felt *something* was going on with the woman in Clancy's house, he just couldn't put his finger on it. But the deeper truth was, he didn't want to put his finger on it. Not now. Not yet.

So his next step was to find out who Nora Letterman was and what she wanted.

To: Nora Letterman, The Girl Upstairs
From: Bennett J Hawthorne
Dear Ms Letterman
My assistant Damon passed on your details after your recent correspondence.

Please advise your leave date and I'll call Clancy's lawyers and have them collect any and all keys at your earliest convenience.

Until then, know how deeply I appreciate the fact that someone Clancy trusts so implicitly is taking care of her home until other provisions are made. As you said yourself, Thornfield Hall was very important to her.

If there is anything you require in order to make your stay more comfortable please let me know.
Sincerely
Bennett Hawthorne

To: Bennett Hawthorne
From: Nora
Dear Bennett—or do people call you Ben? Benji? Benny-Boy?
I'm Nora, by the way. Just Nora. "Ms Letterman" sounds like the admin officer at a strict all girls' school.

Pleased to finally "meet" you! Though meeting you in person will no doubt be even better. I have so many stories to share about Clancy's last months: the people she helped, the havoc she caused. Passing those stories on to you will be cathartic—for us both.

If it's concern over the work to be done—finding, sorting, collating and donating Clancy's things—which is hindering your immediate return, please let me know if I can help. It must seem such a daunting task.

If you'd prefer me to leave it all be, then of course that's what I'll do. I can keep to my little cave upstairs, leaving Clancy's private corner of the house just for you.

Other than that, there is nothing I need. Easy-peasy is my middle name.

Thank you for asking.
Cheers,
Nora

PS Apologies for the bed-wetting thing. I'm almost sure I was thinking of someone else.

PPS My middle name is actually Betty. I know. I sound like I ought to be Clancy's grandmother. My dad was a muso and named me after the last two songs he'd heard on a jukebox in the Irish pub in which he was playing the night I was born.

PPS What does the J stand for in Bennett J Hawthorne? John? Jeremiah? Jehoshaphat?

To: Damon Davidson, Hawthorne Consultancy
From: Nora
Damon,
Thanks so much for nudging your boss into connecting. Whatever magic you sprinkled, it worked.
Cheers,
Nora xxx

To: Nora Letterman, The Girl Upstairs
From: Bennett J Hawthorne, Hawthorne Consultancy
Dear Nora
Bennett is fine.

Please do not concern yourself with sorting or collating. It's not an immediate concern. I am in the midst of a deeply complicated case at work and I simply cannot get away.

As to any concerns, are you satisfied with the security measures? It took some convincing for Clancy to allow me to put in the alarm, but I would be happy to organise security cameras as well. Whatever it takes to make you feel comfortable and safe in the interim.

The J stands for Jude.
Regards
Bennett

To: Bennett
From: Nora
Bennett Jude! Not only do we have Clancy in common, we have musical leanings to our names. I'd love to hear the

story of how that came about. Something we can save for when you arrive to take over the house, perhaps.

There's an alarm? Huh... I had no clue. BRB.

Yep. Found it! Behind a plant in the front hall. Any clue what the code is? Probs best if I don't guess. Might bring a fleet of those little hatchbacks to the door. Firefighters, on the other hand... ;)

Actually, don't worry about the code. If I've been fine till now I'll be safe enough during the short time I'm here before you make it back. Anyway, the back door doesn't exactly lock right; I nudge a chair against the handle at night. That plus a copy of *Wolf Hall* on top. At six-hundred-odd pages the thing is overwhelming, but as door wedges go, it's the perfect fit.

Are you a reader like Clancy? If not I'll make sure to pop it back on the shelves before you come. The thing is seriously intimidating.

Cheers,
Nora

To: Nora
From: Bennett
Nora,
Please pass details of the security company to my assistant, Damon, so that a new password can be organised.

At six foot five inches, feeling intimidated by size is not a concern of mine.

Jude was Clancy's father's name.

Regards
Bennett

To: Bennett
From: Nora
Six foot five? Yikes! How on earth did you ever navigate

Clancy's stairs? I have to take care not to trip up the things every day and I have unusually dainty feet.

As for the alarm—I've always slept with a stump of wood under the bed. If anyone does break in, they're in for a rude shock. So don't bother Damon with it. I'm sure he's busy enough, getting your extra-long suits dry-cleaned and bringing you hot, black, single-blend coffees all day long.

I have clearly picked up my vision of what an assistant does from Nancy Meyers movies!

Unless you're really as swamped at work as you intimated, meaning you probs don't have time for entertainment-type things. Just in case, movies are like newsreels, only made up, books are words on pages all bound together that hit you in the face as you fall asleep reading, and music is the thing your phone's ringtone is based on.

You're welcome.

N

PS What on earth is Forensic Accounting, Financial Regulation and Compliance, Insolvency and Restructuring in plain English?

To: Nora
From: Bennett
Nora,
I would feel better knowing the house is fully secure, lump of wood under the bed aside. Next time Damon brings me a coffee—cream, three sugars—I'll ask him to get in touch.

As to my work: I take struggling companies, figure out where they went wrong by following the numbers, help them create new business practices, and restructure them so that they might live to see another day.

Take care on the stairs. Please.

Bennett

To: Nora
From: Damon
Nora, hey!
Mr Hawthorne has asked that I grab the details of the security company in charge of your alarm. If you could send me the deets, that'd be great.
And I'm also to remind you to please take care on the stairs.
Damon

To: Damon
From: Nora
Aw… Both of you reminding me to take care on the stairs makes me feel so…so certain you are unsure of your liability if I'm hurt.
I hereby release the Boss Man of any blame if I'm a goof on the Thornfield Hall stairs. That do? Great.
As to the other thing… I'm all good.
Cheers!
N
PS Does your boss really take three sugars in his coffee?

To: Bennett
From: Nora
You help companies so that they "might live to see another day"?
That's impressive.
Might I even suggest…heroic?
N

To: Nora
From: Bennett
It's satisfying work, yes. But I can attest to the fact that

I have never—not once—walked around at work feeling particularly heroic.
B

To: Bennett
From: Nora
Have you tried wearing a cape?

To: Nora
From: Bennett
Do you know how hard it is to find a cape to match your tie?

To: Bennett
From: Nora
Ha! Yeah, I can see how that might be a problem. Something you can get Damon onto, perhaps? Give him something to do other than buff his nails and flirt with the other assistants. Just spit-balling here...

In case you're wondering, but are just too polite to ask, I also have my own business. *The Girl Upstairs.* I manage social media pages, build manageable websites, act as virtual assistant to work-from-homers—that kind of thing.

I might not wear a cape, but I feel I make a difference. That I am of use. Which is a really nice thing.

Actually...do you ever do what you do for smaller companies? On the quiet, there are a couple of local businesses who I'm sure could do with a sprinkle of your expertise. Ones who need more than a new website and shareable self-promotion to stay afloat.

Maybe when you come—you know, to grab the keys and take over the house—I can nudge a few of them your way? Yes? Really? Excellent!

From your partner in spreading goodness all over the world,
Nora

To: Bennett
From: Nora
Hey, all okay?

To: Bennett
From: Nora
Hope I didn't offend you with my assumption that you need an assistant to buy your capes, when, in fact, you are world-famous for your cape-buying abilities.
N

To: Bennett
From: Nora
Hi! Remember me?
I know you're busy saving the world, one corporation at a time, but if you could assure me you didn't manage to find a cape to match your tie only for it to get caught in the engine of your private jet and strangle you, that'd be great!

Unless…gasp! Are you currently en route? About to arrive at my—aka your—front door with a flourish?

See, I now can't imagine you without a cape! Not that I've imagined you…
Yours
Nora

To: Nora
From: Bennett
Dear Ms Letterman
Apologies for my lack of response. Things have rather blown up at work.

I humbly request we put our correspondence on the back burner—at least until I am able to put the current situation to bed.

I continue to appreciate your taking care of Thornfield Hall.

In the meantime,

Sincerely

Bennett Hawthorne

Ms Letterman?

Nora reeled away from the laptop with such speed she nearly hit her head on the headboard.

Really? They were back there again? After a week of emails back and forth, of her bag remaining unpacked, future plans unplanned? She'd been certain she'd made headway; softening the guy up, getting Damon on side, giving him a dozen reasons to come home.

Now she had the awful, cheek-warming, neck-tingling, stomach-dropping feeling he'd been stringing her along, knowing he had all the power and could cut her loose without a word.

Dammit. Damn all six feet five inches of him—if Bennett J Hawthorne was *really* that tall. Guy was probably shorter than her. And compensating.

Without taking a single extra moment to think, Nora pressed *reply*.

To: Bennett

From: Nora. Just Nora

Dear Mr Hawthorne

I'm afraid "putting our correspondence on the back burner" does not work for me. In the meantime or any time.

In case I've been too subtle, or you are immune to my clever ploys, or you're a tougher customer than I had thought, here goes: COME HOME AND TAKE CARE OF YOUR GRANDMOTHER'S HOUSE.

Appreciate my presence here all you like, but I am only here for Clancy. I promised her I'd look after the place till the new owner came, and I take promises and responsibilities seriously.

I'd appreciate it if you'd stop taking advantage of my good nature and come home.

If, in fact, you know all this, deep down beneath your big and tall suits, perhaps the fact you do not feel heroic isn't down to your lack of a cape.

The ball's in your court.

Nora

CHAPTER FOUR

NORA SAT ON a barstool at Shenanigans, nursing a warming gin and tonic and fiddling half-heartedly with filters for an Instagram post about the bar, while the Friday night crowd laughed and danced and flirted and hustled at her back.

Her gin was warm, and her mind wouldn't settle, for it had been three days since she'd last heard from the disappointing Bennett Hawthorne with his "humble requests" and his "appreciation". Three days since her inglorious "the ball's in your court" email.

So much for charming Bennett Hawthorne into coming home.

She'd started out so well—delightful with a hint of optimistic coercion; it was her MO, after all. But she'd soon found herself swept up in his rhythm: wry, dry and a little sly. Used, as she was, to writing upbeat, engaging, client-centric verbiage, engaging in a little light snark had been a kind of relief.

High on sass, she'd taken a misstep somewhere. Only when he'd stopped responding did it hit her that she'd pushed too much, or tried too hard. The realisation had tipped her usually well-restrained sensitivity into umbrage and she'd gone off half-cocked, screwing up all the lovely headway she'd been making.

For all that she favoured being footloose and fancy-free,

she wasn't just one thing. Her spectrum ranged from Sunshine Mode Nora to Survival Mode Nora. She'd been at the sunshine end for so long, she'd forgotten how intimately entwined both ends actually were.

Of course, there was the very good chance that while she'd been plying him with her greatest hits, he'd seen her coming from a mile off and played her like a violin.

"Nora the Explorer," said Misty as she appeared at Nora's elbow. "Drinking alone?"

"Just getting a head start," Nora said with a smile. "What'll you have?"

"The same," said Misty, waggling a hand at Sam, the young bartender she had her eye on. He smartly kept his distance, nodding his response. "Was half hoping, for your sake, the wind might have finally swept you off to more exciting climes, like a ladybug on the breeze—"

"A dandelion on the wind." Nora turned over her wrist to show the scattered dandelion tattoo thereupon. "Let's just say, my plan isn't coming together quite as I'd hoped."

"How so?"

"I found out what's happening with Clancy's place. She left it to her grandson."

"You mean *Bennett*?" Misty asked, eyes near popping out of her head.

"That's the one. What was the story there?"

"I didn't live around these parts at the time but apparently Clancy adopted him when he was, like, five. She always called him her grandson rather than her son as she was already in her fifties at the time."

"Well, that's nice." To five-year-old Nora it would have been the dream. And eight-year-old Nora, and thirteen-year-old Nora… "He's her only family, right? So why didn't everyone assume she'd leave the house to him?"

"The Great Falling Out, of course."

A dark little corner of Nora's usually determinedly chipper psyche unfurled itself. "Falling out, you say?" It would explain the shushing.

"Clancy never said anything?" Misty intoned.

Nora shook her head. "Do you know what it was about?" Translation: what on earth did the guy do to upset Clancy so badly? It must have been huge as Clancy was the queen of second chances. And third. She was basically unoffendable.

"We all knew *when* it happened. Bennett was the light of her life, then, boom, he stopped visiting and a chill seemed to come over the room anytime anyone brought him up. But she refused to give up why."

Nora turned on her seat, warming up to this new development. Anything that might make her feel better about her bad feeling about the guy could only help. "Did you ever meet him?"

"Sure. Plenty."

"What's he like? Cold-blooded? Shark-eyed? Slovenly? A diminutive sociopathic troll?"

Misty blinked. "You've searched him on the internet, right? That's what you young ones do nowadays."

Nora's mouth twisted. "Half-heartedly, back at the beginning. With no luck. Why?"

"First tell me why you're so interested in him."

Misty's gaze turned predatory as she turned to face Nora on her stool. If Nora weren't so stuck on the subject, she'd have changed it. Fast.

"Well...we've been emailing." *Had* been emailing. Past tense.

"Really? *Sexy* emails?"

"What? No! Jeez."

But they had been playful. At first. Sarcasm, irony, verbal acerbity—they were her secret catnip. She'd found herself reaching for her phone the moment she woke up in the morning, in case there'd been a new email overnight. It was how he'd lulled her into a false sense of security before ghosting her.

"They were…frustrating."

Misty's eyebrows waggled. "Sounds sexy to me."

"We emailed about his *grandmother*." Nora's voice dropped to a respectful whisper as she lifted her eyebrows and added, "His *dead grandmother*. I…I kind of promised Clancy that I'd look after the house till the new owner came. And Mr Stuffy McBusiness Suit is taking that to mean he can go on ignoring his responsibilities!"

"Wow," said Misty, blinking Nora's way. "I'm not sure I've ever seen you this worked up. You're always so chilled I had floated the idea you had some kind of dopamine imbalance."

Nora rolled her eyes, then glanced around to make sure no one was listening in. "Look, being 'chilled' doesn't exactly come naturally to me. The bastion of sunshine you see before you has been diligently cultivated. Over many years."

After the third foster home that had sent her back for being too loud, too noisy, too demanding, too much, she'd taught herself to pull back, to be helpful, a force for good, while not taking up too much space, and leaving nothing of herself behind.

"Being 'chilled'," she admitted, "is hard work."

"Oh, honey," said Misty, on a rare kick of empathy. Then added, "I *like* this side of you. Sassy, sharp, a little groundswell of rage."

"Thanks?" Nora laughed, then rewarded herself with a goodly sip of warm gin.

"Now, you know helping people isn't my thing, but, in the spirit of trying new personalities on for size, I'll give it a go this once."

With that, Misty dragged Nora's phone towards her, and slowly typed letters into a search engine. Unlike Nora had, however, she typed in *Hawthorne Consultancy.*

Clicking the *About Us* page, they found pictures of accountants, and lawyers, and financial advisors. The images were effortless, elegantly casual: people laughing over coffee, or twirling a stylus, or working hard at a laptop.

For a company that sounded as dry as burnt toast, the site had a modern, holistic *trust us, we've got you* vibe. Despite herself, Nora loved it.

"Wait for it," Misty murmured beside her as she continued to scroll through the images—

Whoa, Nelly.

Right at the very bottom of the page, almost an afterthought, was the largest image of all. Beneath the picture it said *Bennett J Hawthorne, Founder of Hawthorne Consultancy.*

Peripherally, Nora noted the Millennium Wheel, an out-of-focus smudge over one shoulder, and the sun glinting creamy gold off the Thames. But her eye was stuck on the man.

Acres of broad-shouldered wonder filled the frame, hard angles wrapped up in a dark suit and a snow-white shirt. His hair was a tumble of thick, chocolatey waves. Strong jaw, freshly shaven, but with a look that said the stubble wouldn't be kept back for long. Intelligent dark eyes looking just off camera.

Thank goodness. Because she wasn't quite sure what she might have done had they been looking at her.

"Not so much a diminutive shark-eyed troll, then."

"Mountainous, in fact. With the eyes of a matinee idol. Pity he's so frustrating."

"Right," Nora murmured. "Pity." Then, "Do you think he's looked *me* up?"

"Ooh. Good point. Did he flirt in your not-sexy emails? Even a tiny little bit?"

Nora thought back to the cape-and-tie comment, the sense that he'd been laughing *with* her. "There were moments where he wasn't entirely exasperating."

"Then he's looked you up for sure. Ooh, I love this song!" With that Misty leapt off the barstool and carved a path to a space in front of the jukebox and began to dance while Nora found herself very glad she hadn't searched deeper before she'd sent her spate of emails. Knowing this was the man she'd been flirting with—not flirting, cajoling—she might well have sent nothing but drool.

Thumb moving slowly, surreptitiously, she clicked back to her search page and under *Images* typed *Bennett Hawthorne Consultancy London.* She found pictures of him at some international symposium, his expression stormy, his shirtsleeves rolled at his elbows, sporting longer hair and a beard—oh, my. There was another with Bennett in a group shot at some charity fundraiser at the Royal Albert Hall, where he stood a half-head taller than everyone else. This time those eyes of his looked directly down the barrel of the lens; darkly intelligent, and stunning.

Mouth suddenly dry, yet somehow also watering, her skin clammy, yet overly warm, Nora put her hand over the screen.

So what if he was gorgeous? It didn't negate the fact that Clancy had fallen ill, had died, had been buried, and he hadn't been there. While Nora would literally have given a kidney to have been adopted into a family, *any* family, much less one of Clancy's calibre, if she'd been given half a chance.

And, despite her setback, she still had a promise to fulfil.

Maybe the problem was the medium. Perhaps her sunshine had got lost in translation over the great distance between them.

If she were to get through to the man, to encourage him home, and at the same time show him what he'd missed by not being there for Clancy, it would be worth it.

It would take subtlety. Savvy. Self-will. And, as Misty had pointed out, if she had to tap, ever so slightly, into the parts of herself she'd spent years holding back—the sass, the spirit, the stubborn refusal to believe no was even possible—then so be it.

An hour later she was home, a little tipsy, but determined.

She opened her laptop, took a deep breath, and typed.

To: Bennett
From: Nora
Ben
Remember me? Nora the delightful?

Now, I know I said the ball was in your court—clearly it always was, and I was just being cute suggesting otherwise—but here I am again. With a tap dance and an apology.

The fact that I haven't heard back from you makes me think that, despite the fact we do not know one another at all, you noticed that I kind of lost my cool.

My reasons, though, were entirely altruistic.

For I believe, deep down inside, that wherever she is Clancy's heart would be breaking at the thought of seeing this place empty. Abandoned. Left to dust.

And I promised—literally promised—I wouldn't let that happen.

I have wondered, since we began to chat, if she knew you wouldn't come running. Perhaps that's even why she put the provision in her will that I stay.

Maybe she wanted me on your case, hoping I'd be able to out-stubborn you, and convince you to come home.

I don't know what happened between the two of you, she never said, but perhaps all of this is her effort at giving you closure, whatever that might mean for you.

Perhaps she wanted you to come home to say goodbye.

Nora

The massive streak of coarse grey fur huffed and puffed and pulled so hard on the lead, Nora could no longer feel her fingers.

"Anyone would think you've never walked a dog before," called Misty as the huge dog dragged Nora past the Vintage Vamp.

"I haven't!" Nora managed, waving as she passed, before using both hands to grip the lead.

None of the families she'd been sent to live with had been the warm and fuzzy types. Which should have told her all she needed to know before she'd let herself get her hopes up about any of them falling in love with *her*. Benefit of hindsight.

She'd visited Playful Paws Puppy Rescue to talk to them about coming to pick up Pie, and somehow been roped into fostering yet another dog, claiming Cutie—that was his name—might draw Pie out of hiding. She should be taking lessons on making people do her bidding from them.

The fact that Mr Stuffy McShoulders had said "no pets" might have been a slight sweetener. Especially since she'd woken to still no response after her *very* nice email overnight.

The breath oofed out of her as Cutie took off across the street. She managed to angle him towards the front gate, up the path and through the front door once she'd managed to jiggle the key in the lock.

Her phone rang just as Cutie bolted, bumping into the walls, sniffing everything, lead following behind him like a manic snake. She could only hope Pie's hiding spot was a good one.

She grabbed her phone, slid her thumb over the answer button, and sing-songed, "The Girl Upstairs!"

The pause was so long, it had to be a telemarketer. She nearly hung up.

Until a voice—deep, rough and definitely male—eventually intoned, "Ms Letterman?"

There was no way she could be certain the voice belonged to who she thought it belonged to. All he'd said was her name, and yet…the way it was said—low, rumbling, with a burr at the edge. *Whoa.* The hairs stood up on the back of her neck. And every cell in her body slowed to a grinding halt.

"That's me," said Nora, her voice a little tight, breathy. "I'm Nora Letterman."

"Bennett Hawthorne."

Her breath left her lungs in a whoosh.

It was him. On the phone. Which was excellent! Her conciliatory little email must have made a difference. Yay her!

Only she wasn't ready for him. Not in the least.

If she'd known he was going to call, she'd have prepared. Done some deep breathing. Plastered a smile on her face then drowned him in kindness till he agreed that she was right and he was wrong.

"Ms Letterman?" That *voice.* It was like molten chocolate. Like promises made in the dark.

"Yes," she croaked. *Water.* Most ailments could be solved by a drink of water. She hustled into the kitchen. Filled a glass an inch and skulled it. "Sorry. Hello! Well, this is unexpected."

"Quite," he responded.

She tapped the phone onto speaker and poured herself another drink. "I'm glad, though. Glad you called. There's a lot to discuss. Unless you're calling to tell me what time to pick you up from Melbourne airport?"

"Ah, no."

"Sigh. Then what can I do for you this fine afternoon?"

Another beat slunk by. "Fine, is it?"

"Mmm-hmm. Sunny, blue skies. Prefect spring day here in Melbourne. You?"

"Cold. Dark."

"Dark? It has to be, what, eight in the morning over there?"

"Seven. And it's raining hard enough I can't see anything beyond my office window."

"Man, you need a holiday. And I know just the place."

Hang on, was that a *laugh*? And had she just called him "man"? Whatever had just happened, he found it necessary to clear his throat before saying, "I am calling to apologise."

"Oh." Oh, indeed. She hadn't expected a phone call, or a chat about the weather. But the number one thing she'd not have expected from this man was an apology.

He went on. "I seem to have said something to upset you in our original email exchange, which was never my intention."

That stopped her with a glass halfway to her lips. "You *seem* to have? According to whom?"

She heard his hesitation. Got the feeling that for Bennett J Hawthorne it was a highly unusual occurrence.

"My assistant, Damon, pointed it out."

Nora cocked a hip against the kitchen bench and said, "I knew I liked Damon. Right from the outset."

"Mmm," he intoned, his promises-in-the-dark voice dropped, deepened, which she would not have thought possible. "Then you'll be happy to know he's quite taken with you too."

"Not surprising. I am actually very likeable once you get to know me. You can tell him I'm taken with him too."

After that came a stretch of silence. Not thin and chilly, the way it had felt after his last email. Loaded. Weighty. Filled with waiting.

He's stubborn, her subconscious piped up in a panic. *Clever. Disloyal. His interests do not align with yours and you are being super-shallow. You would not be acting this way if you hadn't seen his picture.*

Before she could fully convince herself, the guy had to go and say, "What if I told you Damon had no skills in co-ordinating ties and capes?"

Nora felt a definite something flicker inside her; the surety the man was flirting. Yes, she'd seen his picture. But they'd toyed with one another, just a little, before she'd had a single clue what he looked like.

She swallowed. "I'd feel shocked. Bemused. Totally off my game."

"Well, we don't want that, now, do we?"

Nora's mouth opened and closed again. She felt as if she'd stumbled into some kind of alternate universe. One in which their emails had gone down a very different path. One in which she and Bennett J Hawthorne were on very different terms.

One in which he wasn't simply a person who she was certain had wronged one of the few people she had ever loved. He was also a person who'd recently lost his grandmother and was struggling to know quite how to deal with it.

Nora gently cleared the tickles from her throat. "Did I imagine it, or did you mention something about an apology...?"

"I did." A beat, a collecting of thoughts, a shift of tone that she could all but hear, then, "Hence the phone call. Text can easily be misconstrued. In my work, subtlety and nuance often breed misinformation and misunderstanding. So, I'm afraid my correspondence tone has, over time, become rather blunt. Which I acknowledge is not conducive to civil conversation outside the business realm."

"I see," said Nora as she tried to navigate the meander back into corporate speak. His comfort zone, she figured. "And?"

"And?"

"And *I'm sorry, Nora*?"

Oh, yeah. That was a definite laugh. Gentle, rough, but there. She felt it skitter down her spine, and land in the backs of her knees.

"And I'm sorry, Nora," he said, his voice quieter now too. More intimate. As if he was trying not to be overheard. As if his words were not for anyone else but her.

Nora held the water glass to her cheek, which seemed to have come over a little warm. "Do you call all the girls you offend over email? Or should I feel special?"

She squeezed her eyes shut; hoping he might not pick up on her own flirty tone if she couldn't see herself doing it.

This time the chuckle was louder. She heard what sounded like the squeak of an office chair. She imagined him leaning back, cocking a foot over the other knee. Running a finger along his full bottom lip—

"Special," he intoned. "Most definitely special."

Nora might have been in danger of losing *all* feeling in the backs of her knees, except a thump from down the hall had her spinning to watch out for a blur of grey fur.

Cutie. Cutie was out there somewhere. As was Pie. Neither of whom she was allowed to have, according to her new landlord. Who was on the phone right now.

Her landlord who had responsibilities here. Which he was shirking. To her detriment!

But still…

This *was* progress.

"I hope you accept my apology too."

"For?"

"Calling you out. I may have been a little touchy. This whole thing has been rough. Clancy's passing, waiting to find out what would happen with the house… Taking it out on you was indefensible. And very much not like me."

Again with the pause. As if the man was deliberate in his choice of words. As if nothing he ever said was said by accident.

Nora closed her eyes again, this time against the fact she kept revealing herself to this man. First via email, gushing about how much she loved her job, how helping people made her feel good about herself. Now this…this vulnerability. Talk about not like her!

"So-o-o?" he said, drawing the word out in that cavernously deep voice of his.

"So?"

"I'm sorry, Bennett?"

Nora felt a smile start deep in her belly before it moved, warm and slow, like molten treacle, up her throat and into her cheeks. "I'm sorry, Bennett."

At that the man made a sound in the back of his throat. A deep, rough hum that had her leaning over her phone so as to catch it. Subtlety, nuance and all.

Her feelings just a little raw, and exposed, she found herself saying, "I'm sorry about Clancy too. For your loss. She was a wonderful woman. Possibly the best I've ever known. It must be hard, being so far away, at a time like this."

When her words brooked no response, she quickly

added, "That wasn't a tactical manoeuvre, I promise. I meant it."

When she heard a distinct *woof* echo from deep inside the house, she pulled herself upright, grabbed her phone, took it off speaker and jammed it against her ear. "Look, I have to go. But thank you. For the call. And the apology. And keeping the lines of communication open."

"My pleasure."

"But don't think you got off that easily."

Laughter. Absolutely no doubt that time. The kind that sent golden sparks down the back of her neck, which met the warmth in her cheeks and the erratic *ske-bump* of her heart until she felt utterly discombobulated.

"And why's that?" he asked.

Woof-woof. Deep and wall-shaking that time. Definitely Cutie. She only hoped he was standing still. Either that or she'd be spending every cent of her savings on new furniture and hoping Ben didn't notice the difference.

"Because, Ben Hawthorne, one way or the other I'm convincing you to come home."

With that she hung up.

She'd unpack the conversation—the chuckles, and the warm, deep voice, and the complete lack of stuffiness, and her reaction to it—later. Or maybe she wouldn't. Actually softening towards Ben Hawthorne was not an option. Not while there were so many reasons to be disillusioned with the guy.

Pretending she had, on the other hand, might be something she could learn to do.

First, she had to track down the critters who were now running amok in her house.

But it wasn't her house.

It was his.

CHAPTER FIVE

BEN STARED INTO the takeaway container filled with some kind of meatless rice dish Damon had brought in, insisting the "slow-release energy" and "superfood content" was a necessity for "a man with his workload".

As if a week of blocked avenues, stalled agreements, and lack of progress on his current deal was any different from every other client in the same kind of deep mess as Metropolis Airlines.

As if, for some reason, this one was taking a toll.

Scoffing at the very thought, Ben tossed the dish to his desk and picked up his phone. To check his emails. And… other things.

The phone just happened to be open to Instagram. Damon had set him up and bade him follow a few sites—local news, NASA, Celeste Barber. *The Girl Upstairs.*

He'd been aware from the very first email what she was trying to do. She had the subtlety of a velvet-covered sledgehammer. What he should have done was made himself clear, from the outset: he wasn't coming. Not any time in the foreseeable future. His life was here. His work was here. That place—the memory of the last time he'd seen Clancy—was something he wasn't prepared to relive.

But he'd found himself looking forward to the ping of his phone, in case it heralded another message from her.

Ben sat back in his chair, his thumb swiping slowly down Nora's page. Past a picture inside a bar, everyone out of focus aside from one dancer in the middle, hair flying. Another of a group of women laughing and clinking champagne glasses while painting matching cacti in some kind of class.

His thumb hovered over the screen, no longer scrolling when she appeared on the feed. Hair down, decked out in a long green dress that clipped behind her neck and left her lean, golden-brown arms bare, she leant against a tall menu board, drinking some kind of fruity drink from a huge plastic cup. A dimple popped in one cheek, her face lit with half a smile.

New pictures, all. He knew. It wasn't the first time he'd given up a few minutes of his day in that space.

At first he'd gone back to her page to get a fix of the old area. A place he didn't know he'd been missing. It helped a little, dealing with the fact that he hadn't been there; not just at the end, but for a really long time.

But soon he'd found himself lost in the bright chaotic colour of *The Girl Upstairs* feed, and it felt like sorbet for his brain. There was a vitality to her page—her words, the way she cut to the quick—that he found crisp, bracing, refreshing. A relief from the standard long days and bitterly cold nights.

Ben's phone buzzed and he actually flinched. As if he'd been caught doing something untoward.

He checked the screen to find a video-chatting app flashing a notification at him. Some other thing Damon had no doubt installed in a fit of enthusiasm. The caller was someone by the name of Dandelion.

Ready to put it down to spam, a little twitch in the back of his head made him pause, before tapping the answer button.

Big heart-shaped glasses covered half a woman's face, sunny blonde waves tumbled over her shoulders, lips the reddest red there ever was sucked on a paper straw above a milkshake three times the size of her hand.

Nora Letterman; as if he'd conjured her out of thin air.

"Nora," he said, his voice rough.

"Why hello!" she sang, tipping her glasses slightly forward with a single finger sporting chipped orange nail polish. "If it isn't Bennett Jude Hawthorne himself. I figured I had about a twenty-three per cent chance you'd answer. Even then I was pretty sure I'd be looking at the delightful Damon. But there you are!"

Those big blue eyes of hers, half hidden behind the sunglasses, told a story all their own.

There was an unhurried quality to her, ethereal even, the kind that had made him wonder if the woman he'd imagined he'd been talking to was a figment, a construct. But the easy sway of her shoulders, the gentle clamp of her teeth on the straw, the glint in the small part of her big blue eyes that he could see—she was so real her life force near leapt off the screen.

A wave of attraction sluiced over him, like the water of an outdoor shower on a summer day. It unmanned him. And woke him up.

What was he doing stalking this woman's Instagram, calling her to apologise, just so he had an excuse to keep the conversation going? All he knew about her was that she'd somehow ingratiated herself with Clancy in the final months of her life, and was now trying to do the same to him.

He didn't have Clancy's Pollyanna positivity, he never had—from the moment his mother had left him, he'd been wary, untrusting, and it had served him well—and he didn't know her from Adam. He honestly did not have time for any of this. Or the head space. It was time to demand all future correspondence remain between their respective lawyers.

Instead he found his mouth forming the words, "Twenty-three per cent seems a little high."

She laughed—a light, happy bark—as her head tipped back and her mouth stretched wider than a human mouth ought to stretch. Her phone wobbled as she shifted position. She sat cross-legged on some kind of bench with enough light and colour flashing all around her it looked as if she might be in an arcade.

Then she put down the drink beside her and pulled the glasses right to the end of her nose.

His determination to put an end to their correspondence was no match for the riot of sensation that stampeded through him as he got a load of those eyes. Damn, they were something. Dusky, blue, and tilted in a way that made her look permanently amused.

Nora Letterman had the sort of eyes that made sailors dash themselves against rocky shores. And gladly.

Ben cleared his throat. "What can I do for you, Ms Letterman?"

"Oh, no, we're not going back there again. Not after our heartfelt apologies the other day." Her hand went to her heart, the move tipping the thin strap of her floaty top just off her shoulder. "I'm Nora. And you're Ben. And that's that. Unless you think we're up to the nickname stage… B-Boy. Benny and the Jets. Franklin as in Benjamin."

Ben blinked.

"No? Fine. Ben and Nora, it is." The phone swung sideways. Lights and music buzzed and blinged all around her head. Then she lifted a handful of popcorn and tossed it piece by piece into her mouth.

Ben found himself leaning in. "Where on earth are you?"

"I'm glad you asked. I am having dinner at the night

market down the road from your place. It's new since you were last here. Super swanky." She took off her glasses and tossed them into a net bag at her side. "Wanna see?"

Before he had the chance to answer, she switched the phone away from selfie mode and gave him a virtual three-hundred-and-sixty-degree tour of what looked like a 7-Eleven store mixed with an arcade mixed with a cinema candy bar. Swanky? It gave him a sugar headache.

Rubbing his temple, he called, "Nora." Then louder. "Nora!"

It switched back to selfie mode. And once again he found himself struck, as if he'd been hit in the back of the head. Those eyes. That inner light. That smile.

"Cool, huh?" she asked, before her lips once again puckered around a straw.

"That's your dinner?" he asked, unable to keep focus. "Popcorn and a shake."

A grin. A shrug. "Veggies and dairy. Boom." She turned her head, beamed at someone passing by. "Hey, Ross."

"Hey, Nora," said a deep male voice before a face popped into view, bussing a kiss to her cheek.

"Ross," she said, jabbing a thumb at thin air once the man had moved on. "Owns the local florist. One of the businesses I'd mentioned to you who could really do with your professional heroic eye."

Ben ran a hand up the back of his neck, gripping it tight, and tried not to wonder what else Ross might mean to Nora. It was none of his business. *She* was none of his business. In fact, she was a thorn in his side, a pain in his neck, and a dangerously disruptive influence in his heretofore tightly engineered life.

All of which she managed from the other side of the planet.

Imagine what havoc she might cause if he actually went home—

Not home. Melbourne. Home was London and had been for a number of years. In fact, he'd likely spent more hours in this office than he had in Thornfield Hall. He was exactly where he was meant to be.

"Why are you calling, Nora? Is there an issue with the house?" he asked.

He could have sworn her left eyelid flickered, before she said, "Nope! Everything's perfect."

"Then what can I do for you?"

Her hair bounced as if she was now kicking the wall of the counter on which she sat. "Do I really need to say it?"

Ben knew what she wanted. She wanted him to get on a plane, grab a cab to Fitzroy, and take the keys from her hand. He shook his head.

"Okay, then. So what do you think of the night market, huh?"

"It's giving me a tension headache."

She laughed, and it made her face even lovelier than it already was. "Fair enough. But remember, this city… it offers every kind of fun under the sun. Culture, food, sport, beaches, relaxation, games. Give me a chance and I'll find that one thing that makes it impossible for you to stay away."

Ben's next breath in was deep as he stamped down a ridiculous thought as to one thing that might induce him to pack up and fly halfway across the world. And Nora, she watched him with a sudden woozy fog in her gaze.

She shook it off. And the bright bubbly sunshine girl was back. "Till then, consider this the first of my now daily check-ins!"

I'm about to get this on the daily? he thought, and something fast and furious, something that felt as if it ought to come with a warning, flickered to life inside him.

"Unless," she said, head cocking to the other side, "you hopped on a plane today. Took the house off my hands. Then you'd never have to hear from me again."

Her smile stretched slowly this time, giving him a flash of tongue before she once again wrapped her lips around the straw.

"Not happening," he said.

"Then I'll talk to you tomorrow." She appeared to slide off the bench, the phone shaking before the connection was lost.

The next afternoon, the new short-term rental agreement Nora had asked Damon to put together landed in her inbox. Despite any stipulations Clancy had put in her will, or Ben's lack of concern about rent, not paying her way just felt wrong.

After their last couple of conversations, it somehow felt even more imperative that when she passed over the keys, it would be a clean break. No ripples, no regrets. Everything on the up and up.

She moved to scrawl her digital signature, before glancing to where Cutie and Pie slept in the corner of her room.

When the Playful Paws crew had suggested Cutie might encourage Pie out of the shadows, she'd thought it was a ploy. But it had totally worked. They were inseparable. She'd let the foster home know, so they could pick up the pair. Soon.

For now, her top teeth snagged on her bottom lip as she looked back at the part of the contract that stipulated no subletting, no smoking, no illegal activities, no pets.

Officially, they were not her pets. She was only fostering them. Loophole? No. She really should call Ben. Tell him about the dogs. And Clancy's personal patch of happy herbs that still grew in the backyard, which were not illegal so much as they might be a surprise to their new owner.

Tucking her legs up onto her desk chair, Nora grabbed her phone, using the camera as she ran a finger over her teeth, gave her hair a quick fluff. Then she pressed *call*.

When Ben's face snapped onto the screen her breath caught in her throat, as it did every single time she saw the guy. Clean-shaven, eyelashes slightly tangled, dark hair swept into a kind of businessman's quiff—the man really was all kinds of beautiful.

"Hey!" she called, unable to control her goofy grin. So much for only pretending she was softening towards the guy. She could barely keep the warmth from her face, much less the rest of her.

"Nora." A short, sharp, single word of greeting, yet there was a definite smile tilting at his lips. As if maybe Mr McStuffy was softening towards her too.

"Where are you?" she asked, unable to see much behind him bar a grey-tinted window.

"Work."

"What you doing?"

A beat, then, "Work."

"What are you wearing?" The second the words were out of her mouth she regretted them. Then, to press her lack of self-control home, she added, "Have you heard the percentages on how many people who have online work meetings rarely wear pants?"

"I have not."

"Newsreaders do it all the time. Business up top, party on bottom."

Ben's blink was slow, and did things to her insides that made her breath hitch.

"Are you asking me if I'm wearing pants, Ms Letterman?"

"Pfft. No," she scoffed, then ruined the brief moment of cool by saying, "But are you?"

Ben's eyes darkened, just a fraction. Then with a "you asked for it" lift of an eyebrow, he moved his phone slowly down his body.

Past a snow-white shirt, the buttons straining against the broadness of his chest. A conservative red-and-navy-striped tie that fell rakishly to one side. Once he hit the bottom of his shirt, he paused, and Nora held her breath.

Then he swiped the phone over a belt—black, shiny, the buckle brushed silver—and past a pair of very nice suit pants to socks and shoes, the former covered in Batman symbols.

Nora let out her breath in a huff that was half laugh, half relief. What was she expecting? That he was about to put on a peep show? That his socks might be boring? That he might find her assertiveness affronting? That he'd find her, altogether, too much?

Nora was still riddled in discomfort at that last thought when Ben lifted his phone and there was that face again. All rugged angles and dark bedroom eyes. And since her mind's eye was still dealing with the sculpting of that white shirt, the slightly loosened knot of the tie, all the strength that the suit pants beheld, it was a lot.

"Right," she managed to say. "All seems in order, then."

Ben's mouth kicked up at one corner, as if he was fully aware of how flustered she was. And liked it.

That would all come to an end as she was about to tell him about the dogs. And the weed in the garden. And the strange smell coming from the washing machine since she'd washed the dog's blankets.

But first…

"The reason I called, apart from asking when you're coming home…" She waited expectantly.

He gave her a look that made her insides curl and her toes warm.

"Nothing? Okay. Well, I'm about to sign our new rental agreement—"

"Your new what?"

She swung her phone around and showed him the contract on her laptop. "I had Damon draw it up. I insisted. People find me pretty persuasive. Present company excluded."

When she swung her phone back, he looked pained. No, he looked stormy. His voice was preternaturally calm as he demanded, "Show me that again?"

She did as asked. Heard his voice bark, "Were you Clancy's only tenant?"

Funny, she thought, Ben never called Clancy his grandmother. Was it because she'd adopted him? And so late in life? Though, vivacious and vibrant as she was, "grandmotherly" wasn't the first adjective Nora would have used to describe her.

"Nora?"

"Sorry. Yes, I was her only tenant. I rented out the top floor—bed, bath, home office beneath the window. I don't take up much space."

"And *that's* what you were paying?"

When she swung her phone back around, he looked exactly as she'd imagined he might after his first round of emails. Cold, hard, disapproving. The earlier frisson of discomfort felt like mud settling in a hot, heavy ball in her belly, as she felt a confrontation coming on.

She searched her databanks for sparkles, for sunshine, and so unprepared had she been to need it, she came up blank. "Pretty much. Though I asked Damon to up it a little now that I'm not cleaning the place any more. Which is nice. Though who doesn't clean a house before the cleaner comes in, am I right?"

"You asked—" Ben looked ready to pounce, but then he blinked. Blink-blink. The earlier disapproval gone, in a flash. "You were *cleaning* the place for Clancy? As in *cleaning* cleaning?"

"Is there any other kind?"

When he ran a hand over his mouth, and said nothing, she filled the silence.

"I also did the shopping. Looked after the garden. Cooked dinners. Helped host her various community nights. Clancy had company and help, I had affordable room and board. We had eighteen-odd months like that, and it suited us both beautifully."

As her discomfort faded, it made room for indignation. "Which you'd have known if you'd talked to your grandmother more."

"We talked," Ben gritted out. "She simply never mentioned you."

"I find that hard to believe," Nora scoffed, knowing she was pushing things, but just so glad not to be on the receiving end of bad opinions for a bit.

Ben shifted on his chair, the phone swinging to show a little more of his office. Pale cream walls, huge bookshelves, massive windows—definite Master of the Universe stuff.

"How long?" he asked. "How long was she unwell?"

"What do you mean how long? When did you last speak?"

"A few weeks ago."

"Oh."

Oh, Ben. It had not, not once, occurred to her that *he didn't even know Clancy was sick.* However that miscommunication had come about, whatever their relationship had been, this was *his* family they were talking about. His loss. It was on her to be kind, and gentle, and leave the conversation on even better terms than when she'd started it.

"Not long," she said, her voice softening. "Not long at all. A few weeks. It was… It was really fast. But when the time came, she was ready."

Nora's words drifted between them, like a cloud of smoke after a fireworks display, till Ben broke the silence. "That must have been hard. For you."

His eyes caught on hers, so dark, so deep. It took every bit of willpower she had not to look away. "It was hard. But it was also…a gift. To be there. To the last."

Ben breathed out, his gaze drifting off to the side.

She wondered what he was thinking, what he was feeling, what she might do to make him feel better. But she didn't know him nearly well enough to ask.

"It seems I need to apologise to you, yet again."

"Nah," said Nora, the queen of conciliation. "This is all weird. For both of us."

"Weird is no excuse. I was on the verge of raking you over the coals for taking advantage of an old woman."

"I would never!" Nora spluttered. "I… That's not how I roll."

"I know," he said, his voice a murmur. Then, again, "I know. And I'm sorry."

Nora absorbed those words, that tenuous, unanticipated thread of trust, in that deep rumbling voice; tucking them away in the most special secret memory box she had.

"Clancy, on the other hand—"

He stopped, ran a hand over his whole face, then shifted so that his phone was leaning on something on his desk. On anyone else the angle would give a double chin but Ben just appeared big, and strong, and as if his cape might start fluttering behind him at any moment.

Nora leant elbow on desk and chin on palm and all but sighed.

"I'm not taking any money from you, Nora. If you send the contract back, I'm telling Damon to tear it up."

"It's digital."

Ben breathed out slowly, his expression long-suffering but in a way that didn't set Nora's alarm bells ringing. Instead it felt sort of…intimate. Special.

"Then he will do the digital version of tearing it up."

Nora opened her mouth to reason with him—she really was very good at it.

But then Ben ran a hand through his hair and it reminded her of the times—the many times—people looked pained when she expressed her opinion, or told her she really was too much, and could she just tone the excitement levels down. So she bit her lip and let him be.

"Will you do this for me?" he said.

"Fine," she agreed. "But I will not live here indefinitely. I have plans too, you know!"

"What plans?" he asked, sounding genuinely interested.

"Well, not so much plans as plans to have plans. But I will not overstay my welcome. So you need to get off that pert tushy of yours and get yourself the heck down here!"

Ben's expression stilled, his eyes gazing into hers. "What makes you think my tushy is pert?"

Oops. Um… "I looked you up?"

"Did you?" he drawled. "Chat tomorrow?"

What could she say but, "Count on it!" before quickly hanging up the phone.

Feeling like an emotional taco—tough-looking on the outside, but one bite and her insides would spill out everywhere—Nora let her head fall to the desk.

And promised herself the next time they talked she'd not mention his backside, or his pants.

CHAPTER SIX

"WHERE ARE YOU?" Nora asked Ben, without preamble, when he answered the phone a few days and a couple of calls later.

"Work," he said, his phone on speaker.

"Work, work, always work. Why no video?" Nora asked. "Does my expression of disillusionment at the fact that *I am still here* make you feel guilty that *you are not here*?"

Ben, who had been reading a scathing email his legal team had drafted to the mediators stalling on one small contract negotiation that might tip a fifty-year-old airline into insolvency if it wasn't sorted in the next twenty-four hours, clicked on the camera, and angled the phone against the stapler on his desk.

The screen flickered a moment before Nora's face beamed at him.

Her hair was back off her face, only a couple of loose blonde curls skirting her cheeks. Long, lean golden-brown arms poked out of a white sleeveless T-shirt knotted above her belly button. His next breath in tasted like springtime.

"There you are," she said, with such delight in her voice, in her eyes, he felt it as an ache behind the ribs. Another reason he'd chosen not to use the video.

For things were getting rambunctious between them. *Double entendres* running thick and fast. And he was getting far too used to looking forward to seeing her face. Hearing her voice. Tangling with her wit.

Nora added, "I figured maybe you were, I don't know, getting changed. Or in the shower. Or doing your daily calisthenics and didn't want me to see you in your unitard."

Ben shot her a look, saved the email to draft—he'd finish it later—then grabbed the phone and held it at arm's length, giving her a view of his regular Tuesday suit.

"Ooh," she said, eyebrows waggling. "The money shot."

Ben's laughter was loud enough he looked to the door, to make sure Damon didn't burst in to check he was okay. The kid had been all over him of late. Making sure he was eating. And going home at a reasonable hour. Ben had wondered out loud when he and Damon had married, because he couldn't remember the ceremony, which Damon had thought was the best thing he'd heard all week.

"Where are *you*?" Ben asked.

Nora turned the phone, showing off big silver washing machines and a clean-looking blue-and-white checked floor. "Laundromat."

"Does Clancy not have a washing machine?"

"Did you see the ambience of this place? It's hopping!" she said, glancing away and biting at her bottom lip, a move Ben had come to know was her tell when she was prevaricating.

Ever since Clancy, and the great lie of his life was uncovered, his number one rule in all of his dealings—with employees, clients, friendships—had been honesty. Nora's unpredictability should have provoked him more. But she was just so blatant, his shackles barely quivered.

"Clancy's washer," he repeated.

"Are you asking as my landlord?"

"I am not your landlord; you are staying in Clancy's house as a guest, remember?"

"Good. Because I don't want to tell you how I broke the washer. Not yet."

She pulled her phone closer, till her eyes seemed to fill half the screen. They were a guileless blue, but with just a hint of smoke, much like the woman herself.

Then she said, "You always call her that; did you realise? Clancy. Not Grandma. Or Granny. Was that an adoption thing? Your choice? Hers?"

Ben looked to his office door, suddenly hoping Damon *would* burst through.

Nora continued. "Sorry. That's extra nosey, even for me. Just I… I was a foster kid. Never made it to the adoption phase. Blah-blah-blah. So that kind of thing is seriously fascinating to me."

Despite the fact that her voice was lilting and cheerful, and her eyes were smiling, he caught the yearning beneath. Recognised it. Understood it. Felt another thread of connection to this bright, unusual, relentless woman on the other side of the planet as physically as if a creeping vine had wrapped itself around his middle.

"Forget I asked," she said, her phone shaking as she waved a hand in front of her face. "But give me something. Tell me about the Clancy only you knew?"

Ben sat back in his chair. Hell, maybe if he just came out with it, the whole damn story, she'd understand why he didn't want to go "home". Maybe she'd stop trying so hard to mend things.

Then again, if she gave up on him, he'd never hear from her again.

"She made sure I was well fed," he said, the words coming from some untouched, unbroken place deep inside, "and well read."

Nora's spare hand slapped against her chest. "She constantly plied me books. Though I did the plying with food part."

Something snagged on Ben's subconscious.

Clancy had been a great cook. And she hated people fussing about in her kitchen. Add that to the fact she'd let Nora do the shopping and the gardening…

"*You* cooked for her?"

"I'm quite the amateur foodie. Baking especially, because yum, but I can make a mean main."

Ben nodded, all the while his mind reeled. "Did she ever make you her chilli con carne?"

"Clancy? Are you kidding? She couldn't stomach spicy food. As for cooking, I never even saw her boil an egg."

The snag gave way with a massive yank.

"You said Clancy only found out she was unwell a few weeks ago."

"That's right."

"And how long ago did you move in?"

"Eighteen months or so." Something pinged in the background. "Ooh, washing's done!"

Nora angled the phone against a shelf and proceeded to drag what looked like a set of dragonfly-patterned sheets from the dryer and dump them into a big pink washing basket, leaving Ben to mull over the disquiet that had been whispering at the edges of his mind since he'd seen how little rent Nora had been paying.

Clancy knew. She knew she was sick long before she let on. She'd have hated having a nurse, so instead she opened her home to someone young, and fun, and overconfident. To help. To take care of her. Without giving Nora any warning as to what was to come.

Dammit.

She'd done it again. Lied, outright, to serve her own

needs. Without any consideration as to how it might impact the other person. For the rest of their lives.

If he could see Clancy one more time, he'd have some choice words to impart.

Which was likely why she'd never mentioned Nora in their stilted monthly phone calls. The irony too rich, even for her blood.

While Nora continued to empty the dryer, singing something about "a mind at work" under her breath, Ben madly scrambled as to what to say. How to say it. *Whether* to say it. Which made him feel all twisted up inside, as it made him complicit.

"Done!" Nora said, her eyes bright, her hair a little mussed. "Talk tomorrow?"

Ben nodded and Nora hung up.

The image of her grinning at him, soft and sweet and sassy—and totally in the dark—stuck in the back of his mind the rest of the day.

Late the next night, Ben landed on the couch in his lounge with a thud, so spent he didn't even bother taking off his coat.

The apartment was quiet, bar the gentle swoosh of the heating. The double glazing of his wall of windows keeping out the sounds of the city, as well as the rain banging against the outer panes.

He picked up the TV remote and stared at the blank screen, before tossing the remote back onto the coffee table.

Then he glanced to his phone sitting beside him on the couch. It wouldn't ring. *She* wouldn't. Once a day, she had promised, and that was how it had been. And she'd already called that morning.

Yet he found himself waiting for it. Willing it. Wanting to see her face as she flirted up a storm. Or told him stories of the neighbourhood as if it might light up some latent poignancy deep inside him. Or demanded he "come home".

Ben picked up the phone, turned it over and over in his palm. Checked the time in Melbourne. Then he knocked his head against the back of the couch. Once. Twice. Three times. "It's just a phone call. You're a grown-up. You want to call the woman, call her."

And, since she was on the other side of the world and therefore it meant nothing more than a port in a storm, he called.

Nora picked up after several rings.

For once, no bells or whistles or crowds or music added to the show that was Nora Letterman. This time, it was simply her. And, as was becoming habit, her utter loveliness took his breath away.

"Where are you?" he asked without preamble, using the opening line that had somehow become a thing. Their thing. *Port in a storm, my ass.*

She took a beat to take the bait, a beat in which Ben wondered if he'd overstepped. If maybe he was the only one who'd noticed they had "a thing".

But then her face broke into a soft smile. The kind that made his next breath in a little harder to manage.

Her voice was low, unusually subdued as she said, "Home. You?"

"Home."

"You're here?" she asked, clearly not meaning it.

"London. Apartment. The place in which I live. You know, home."

"Ah. That home. Go on, then, give us a look."

"I didn't actually turn the lights on when I came home so all you'd see is the rectangle of light from the microwave clock. Just imagine a minimalist aesthetic. Then take away half the stuff."

"Done," she shot back. Then, yawning wide enough he had a fine view of her tonsils, she tipped onto her side, the phone now taking in a pillow and a dragonfly-patterned sheet over her shoulder.

"You're in bed."

"That I am. While you walked in the door. Sat on the couch. And called me."

Ben was too tired to come up with a better story. "Pretty much."

Again with the soft smile. Again with the tightness in his chest.

"I'm calling because I wanted to make sure you got my package."

"If by package you mean the big, burly dude from the security company who banged on my front door at six this morning, scaring me half to death, to the point I spat out my cornflakes, then yes, I got your package."

He slid down a little lower in the couch, let his feet rest on the coffee table, shoes and all.

"Wait," she said, "I didn't mean *my* front door, I meant *your* front door. I'm just keeping the place warm for you, till you come."

That, Ben thought, had to be the most apt, and loaded, statement of his life. Him here, the heating only just starting to take the edge off the chill of the night. Her, all the way over there, the living embodiment of sunshine.

"So, the package," he said. "It came with a dude?"

"It came with a dude."

"And did that dude fix the alarm system and set you up with a new pass code?"

"Maybe. I didn't ask. I just invited him in and gave him a bowl of cornflakes. Nice guy. Lactose intolerant, though."

"Nora—"

"Yes. Well. That was the plan. But apparently there's

an issue. So he couldn't do it, but he'll be back. I told him there was no rush."

Ben rolled a shoulder and let out a sound that felt something between deep frustration and...whatever this feeling was he always felt when he was talking to Nora. Restlessness. Edginess. As if everything he wanted to say and do was just out of reach.

"Hey, Ben," she said, her mouth mid-yawn, the rough languorous notes in her voice scraping against his insides.

"Yes, Nora."

"I like it when you growl at me."

Ben stopped fidgeting. "Do you, now?"

"Uh-huh," she said, on an outshot of breath, her phone suddenly moving every which way, flashing wall, and wood, and more wall, as if she was changing position. "I do. I do like it."

"And why's that, Nora?"

"Because, Ben, it shows you care."

"Is that right?"

She smiled. Shrugged. And stirred again, the view through the phone flashing and tumbling as she settled into a new position.

Ben ran a hand over his mouth in the effort to wake himself up, and shifted his legs to make room for a sudden telling discomfort.

It was his own fault; allowing her to control the narrative. She might look as though butter wouldn't melt, but she was astute, and savvy, and not afraid to push his buttons for her own ends, which were different from his own. Something he could pick from a mile away, thanks to Clancy.

That ability had put him light years ahead of the game when starting his own business, but had made interpersonal relationships trickier. He considered himself fair and direct, but had been accused of being hard, cold, unforgiving, his people too in awe of his reputation to offer an opinion contrary to his own.

Which was how he'd let Nora in. She was the antidote. In fact, she'd begun to feel…essential.

"I do care, Ms Letterman," he said, keeping his voice neutral. "I care that the 'dude' I hired will do what I've paid him to do. And can only hope that you were kidding about the cornflakes, in case he's some psycho killer. I'd hate to come home to a crime scene."

"You're coming home?" she asked, her voice husky and laced with hope.

She'd said the same words a thousand times, it was practically the soundtrack to their relationship. But whether it was the darkness of the room, the city lights creating a shimmer out of the corner of his eye, or the slumberous note in her voice, Ben found himself blanketed in the warmth of unexpected, unwarranted, unsought intimacy. And want.

"You're a pushy broad—you know that, right?"

Nora scoffed. "To think I was just starting to like you."

She settled deeper into the pillow till half her face was buried in its softness, her hair now tumbling over her shoulder. His mind went to wondering what it would feel like to be lying there beside her rather than on his stiff couch, mattress sinking beneath him, her warm skin mere inches away.

Bennett breathed in, then out, fully aware that he was well past beginning to like her too.

"Sorry if I've been a little off my usual game," she said through another yawn. "The cornflakes were more of a late-night snack than early brekkie."

Yawning even wider, she covered her mouth with the back of her hand, her palm curling softly towards the phone. It was such a vulnerable thing, the inside of a woman's palm. Secret and warm and intimate. He imagined himself capturing her hand, turning her palm face up. Tracing her lifeline. Pressing his lips to it.

Ben dragged himself back to sitting, the phone pointing at the floor to give himself a break. And he asked, "Big night?"

"A little rough actually."

"How so?"

"Don't worry about it."

"I have nowhere else to be, nothing else to do, but sit here in my big, empty apartment, and listen."

He heard the ragged letting-go of her breath before her voice came to him, monotone and dry. "Matt, one of my foster brothers, called; head in a bad space. I kept him on the phone till his partner was home from her night shift. It's not easy for some, coming from where we came from. Struggling to form relationships, to trust, to believe they deserve to be happy. I'm one of the lucky ones. *Totally* well adjusted."

Her laughter was soft, self-deprecating. Raw.

Ben pressed a thumb into his palm and closed his eyes. For all of her light and loveliness, this was the Nora he found hardest to deny—candid, genuine, vulnerable. If she asked him, right now, to come home, chances were he'd be on a plane by morning.

He turned his phone so that he could see her face once more. His voice was like gravel when he said, "I should let you get some sleep."

"Only if I'm keeping you," she said, her voice coming to him like a memory. "Do you mind if we keep talking for a bit? I don't know why, but hearing your voice somehow makes it seem like everything's going to turn out okay."

Ben nudged his shoes off with his toes, grabbed a cushion and popped it behind his neck as he lifted his legs onto the seat, and lay back. "I can bore you to sleep, if you'd like, by telling you about my day. A day filled with meetings and financial statements and cold takeaway for lunch."

"That sounds just perfect."

And so, Ben kept Nora on the phone, talking about the raindrops slithering down his apartment window, about a girl in the coffee shop downstairs from the office whom Damon had his eye on, about why he liked working with numbers: the clarity, the truth.

"You got a girl out there, Ben?" Nora asked, when Ben stopped talking for a minute.

"No one special," said Ben, his voice starting to grate from overuse.

"Mmm..." Nora murmured, the sound sending waves of sensation rolling through him. "I bet there are plenty who wished they were. The clever ones, who see past your stubborn, grumpy outer shell."

"Dozens," he deadpanned. "Maybe even hundreds. Did you want me to make a list?"

"Sure. Have at it."

A few moments later Nora's phone dropped to the side and all Ben could see was ceiling. All he could hear were her soft even breaths.

And if Ben kept the phone line open for a few minutes while he closed his eyes and let himself rest, and breathe, and be, as he felt the tension of his day slip right away too, no one ever had to know.

CHAPTER SEVEN

BROW TIGHT, SHOULDERS tense as he navigated the heavy crowds spilling out of the shops, Ben took a quick bite of the beef and salad roll he'd nabbed from the Marks & Spencer downstairs, when his phone buzzed in his pocket.

Please let this be good news.

Damon had been instructed to call if they heard from the lawyers, after having put together a tight, last-minute plea to extend credit and hold off a final decision on Metropolis Air's involuntary administration for another six weeks.

Tucking the food under his arm, he juggled the umbrella staving off the misting rain and pulled his phone from his inner jacket pocket. Despite the fact it wasn't the news he was after, warmth skidding through him when he saw Nora's name.

He knew he needed to keep the phone line clear; his thumb still pressed *answer.*

"Where are you?" she said, in a voice of pure sunshine.

"Walking the streets of London."

"No video today? I wore a new hat and everything. Picked it up from Vintage Vamp. It's very fetching."

Ben's cheek tugged. "I can imagine. But while I might have Instagram now, walking and video chatting feels a step too far." He stopped under an awning at the edge of a hidden underground car park, lights flashing as a truck pulled slowly up the driveway. "What can I do for you today, Ms Letterman?"

"Well, Mr Hawthorne, for once this is not a personal call."

The way she said the word *persona*l made the warm feeling sizzle a little. Till his wool coat, his double-layered scarf, felt too heavy.

"Business?" he asked. "Or pleasure?"

"Why, Mr Hawthorne," she chastised. "Business, of course."

He imagined her sitting in the swing chair in his office, the view of the Thames a blur behind her, legs crossed, hair tumbling over her shoulders, wearing her new hat, and not much else. Maybe he should be trying to get her to visit him, instead.

"Mate," a voice called behind him, jostling him back to the here and now. The crowd behind him pressed forward and he stepped back into the rain.

"So," Nora's voice continued to sing in his ear. "You know how we talked about you helping some of my locals with your business amazingness?"

"I remember *you* talking about it."

"Excellent," she said. "The Fleur de Lys florist. Family owned. Their gear is gorgeous. But their rent is astronomical, a deal they put in place a decade ago. I thought, perhaps, you might represent them in their renegotiations."

"Unfortunately, my team has to turn more clients away than we are able to take on."

"Really, Mr Big Shot?"

"I'm not tooting my own horn, Nora. I'm merely pointing out my business model. I don't offer myself to clients, they come to me."

"Huh. And there I was, thinking you were some ambulance chaser. Was it the cheap haircut, perhaps? Or the polyester suits?"

The feet ahead of him kicked dirty puddle water onto his Savile Row suit pants, yet he couldn't help smiling. Laughing really, at his own hubris. Nora had a way of making everything he'd ever believed about himself shift. Just a little. Just enough. To think that maybe there might be, could be, more out there than the life he'd built.

"Then there's also the local restaurant," she went on. "Ambrosia. I think their chef enjoys the fact he's spending other people's money. Last time I spoke with the owner he looked like he'd aged a hundred years. When I mentioned I knew a guy who was a whizz with finances he practically fell to his knees in gratitude."

Ben turned the corner, the entrance to The Shard in sight.

"You'll do it, right?" she asked. "I can send Damon their contact details? Hmm? Hmm? Dust off that invisible cape of yours?"

Before he could reiterate the impossibility of her request, Bennett was bumped from behind, his wrap knocked free, landing half open on the ground. Phone pressed against his ear, he scooped up the mess and tossed it into the closest rubbish bin.

"Ben?"

"I'm here," he said. "I'm just…" Wet, filthy and hungry. Lost. "Just wondering what the weather's like there."

A beat, then, "Well, I'm looking outside my little office window in the apartment upstairs, and it's around ten o'clock-ish at night here. So it's dark. But clear. Clear enough I can see a couple of stars, despite the streetlamps and the night lights from all businesses across the road. How about where you are?"

Ben, now an island amidst a churning sea of wet, grumbling Londoners, tipped his head back and his umbrella with it, letting the misting rain soak him through. But he also caught the sun, its weak glow shining beyond the smear of grey covering the sky. The same sun that would beam down on her, blue and sunny and warm, in a few short hours.

The urge to say, *I'm booking a flight today* filled his throat. Right alongside, *What the hell am I doing getting wet like this? I must be going mad.*

He closed his umbrella and ran the last few metres till he was under the protection of The Shard's entryway. "I'm fine," he said. Then adjusted it to, "Send me those details, okay?"

"Really? Oh, my gosh, Ben. You are the best. The absolutely most wonderful best. I could just kiss you! Or maybe hug you. Or shake your hand vigorously at the very least. When might that be possible, do you think?" she asked, her voice suddenly a little husky.

"The shaking of my hand?" he asked. The doorman smiled politely as Ben passed, as if he didn't look like a drowned rat.

"Sure. That."

The air-conditioning bled through his wet suit, hitting his skin like a sudden snowstorm. "The florist and the restaurant. Let's start there."

"Okay."

There was a pause, then Ben stretched his ears to hear her say, "Bye, Ben."

"Goodbye, Nora."

When the lift doors closed he was surprised to find a bedraggled giant looking back at him, with a moony grin on his face.

Nora sat on one of the upholstered cane chairs in the sunroom at the back of the house; a blanket over her knees, sipping on her first cup of coffee of the day.

When her phone rang, Ben, her first thought was: *Better than coffee.* Which, even in the depths of her early morning state, she knew was a problem.

"Where are you?" he asked, the moment she pressed *answer.* Lights flickered behind him; city buildings through a rainy window. His face was all hard-carved shadows in the darkness of what she assumed was his apartment late at night.

"The sunroom." Nora checked to make sure Cutie wasn't nearby—she hadn't quite got around to sending him back or telling Ben—then panned the camera around the room.

Sunshine poured through the white shutters, sending shafts of creamy gold over the soft wood floor, the chairs, the jewel-coloured throws and cushions.

"Go back," Ben's voice commanded from the speaker of the phone.

"What? Which bit?" she asked, with a flare of excitement that something about the house had caught his curiosity.

"To the bit that looked like your underwear drying in the corner."

Nora turned the camera back to her face. "Seriously? There's nothing to see. It's basic boyfriend undies in whatever colour is on sale."

"Eye of the beholder," Ben said, waggling his eyebrows.

Nora snorted. The guy was in a good mood. It suited him.

"So how about you?" she asked.

"You want to see what underwear I prefer?"

"It's okay. You can just tell me. Y-fronts? Chastity belt? Woollen tights?"

"Why not commando?"

At that Nora burst into laughter. Ben really was in a mood. And it really was better than coffee. Just thinking his name made her blood warm, and her skin tingle. She was long since past the realisation that she'd developed quite the crush on Ben Hawthorne.

The fact that he lived a million miles away? The best kind! Ben *wasn't* coming home, not any time soon, so she could indulge in all the lovely daydreams, but none of the hope, or the heartache. A crush on Ben Hawthorne was safe as houses.

"What exactly is it about me that makes the thought of my going commando so hilarious?" Ben asked.

"You are kidding, right? I'd be more likely to go commando than you. In fact, I have, more than once, when I've waited too long for laundry day. And why do I keep telling you things that I would never tell another living soul?"

There was a long pause. "I feel like this conversation has spun a little off topic."

"Oh, so you *didn't* call so that we might talk underwear?"

"Shockingly, no."

The lighting changed as he switched on a lamp. No, he'd opened the fridge door; his face all angles and beauty in the cool light. Nora's heart thumped and shimmied in her chest.

"Just quickly, I've been talking to some of your friends," said Ben, his eyes roving back to hers. "The restaurant. The florist."

Nora sat up so fast the blanket on her knees fell to the floor. "Ben! Oh, my gosh. Could you help them?"

"I believe I already have. Now, it might surprise you to find I am not a fan of the social media."

"No?"

"But the upswing in custom both businesses saw after taking you on was marked. You're very good at what you do. So I've told them they need to do whatever it takes to keep you around."

Nora's belly flipped. Then flopped. It might have been one of the nicest things anyone had ever said to her, but it had a heartbreak chaser. Staying wasn't an option. A girl couldn't be footloose and fancy-free if she had connections all over the place, constantly tugging on her heart.

"I concur, I really am quite amazing. But still, it's nice of you to say."

"My pleasure."

"But just to be sure, you have other ways to help them, right? You're not relying entirely on me—"

"You can park the panic, Nora. I have. I will."

"Right. Great."

There was a pause. A pause in which she held her breath, waiting for him to sign off, yet hoping he would not. Not yet.

Then he said, "I think this might be the longest time you've gone without asking when I'm coming home."

"When are you coming home?" she asked, her voice deadpan.

His laugh was a deep, sexy rumble. And then he rang off.

Nora kept the phone cradled in her hands as if it might help keep the warm, fuzzy feelings tucked all around her.

Crushes were nice, she decided. She might even do this on the regular. With other people. Once the whole Ben Hawthorne saga was done and dusted. Though when she tried to picture someone, anyone, she'd ever met filling that void, she came up blank.

It was bizarre to think that when Clancy was alive, Ben had barely registered as a person in her head.

Then he'd morphed into the bad guy in Clancy's tale. A terrible grandson; selfish, ungrateful, even cruel. Somehow worse, in Nora's mind, because he'd been adopted, when she'd never had that chance.

But now when she thought of Ben—and she thought

of him far more often than was in any way sensible—she knew that he was many things. Wry, generous, conflicted, strong-minded, too handsome for his own good, a workaholic. A man who'd dedicated his life to getting people out of trouble. A man, she was beginning to believe, who was rather lonely out there in the big city.

A confidant.

A friend.

Whatever had happened between him and Clancy no longer felt as if it had quite so much to do with her. She'd surprised herself by discovering she had room inside her for liking them both.

But still, it was just a crush. Nothing so perilous, so terrifying, as actual feelings. Her heart had been far too beaten down by rejection to ever let that happen.

Late Friday afternoon, the stay on the Metropolis Air insolvency had been granted.

It meant Hawthorne Consultancy had breathing space: six weeks in which to plug the leaks, make a plan to repay creditors, and create the bones of a new business model that would keep the airline's staff in employment and their planes in the air.

Nora was right: cape or no cape, helping people did feel good. Turned out the joy in what he did wasn't just about the numbers, after all.

Speaking of Nora, when he'd heard the news she was the first person he'd wanted to tell. Part of him was thankful it was the middle of the night in Melbourne, forcing him to pull his head in and make plans with his team, instead. That had to be his focus, now.

And yet, come Saturday morning, Ben once again felt restless. So restless he'd tossed and turned all night. Which was how he found himself heading into the office late

Saturday afternoon, his head filled with mad plans he couldn't possibly air.

When the lift doors opened on the twenty-fifth floor, he paused at the sound of chatter. Peering around the door, Ben found the place abuzz, with several desks in use.

Carly—a go-getter, second-year paralegal, and the assistant he'd had on rotation just before Damon—saw him and stood to attention, hair in a high ponytail, decked out in running gear. Her gaze widened, dropped and lifted; she was clearly discombobulated by the sight of the boss in jeans, jumper and coat.

"Mr Hawthorne!" she cried, and a ripple went through the place, heads popping out from all over, the chatty noise hushing. "We didn't think we'd see you till Monday."

"I could say the same about you. What's going on?"

"Um…"

"Why's it so quiet in here?" That was Damon, heading around the corner with phone in one hand, a coffee in the other. "Oh. Hey, boss. Didn't think we'd see you here till Monday."

"We've done that bit already."

Carly leapt out from her cubicle. "Don't blame Damon. When he came to us, asking if we'd be keen to get some extra experience on a big account, by helping the Metropolis team get a head start on the grunt work, we leapt at the chance."

Another paralegal added, "You work so hard, Mr Hawthorne."

Carly nudged back in front of her second and added, "And it's come to our attention that, while HR insists *we* take our leave in a timely manner, none of us have seen you do the same. Which doesn't seem fair."

Ben looked over the crowd of young faces, before he

found Damon once again, at the back of the small crowd, leaning against a cubicle. "It came to your attention, did it?"

Damon lifted his coffee in salute.

Carly popped up onto her toes. "The next couple of weeks are all about data processing, collation, reporting, finding discrepancies and obvious areas of improvement. The grunt work. Right?"

"That's right." Funnily enough, it was exactly what he'd been thinking all night long.

"*We* can do that," Carly insisted.

"I know you can," Ben allowed. "It's why I hired such a bright, self-motivated, energetic team, after all."

Carly grinned at her counterparts, who all grinned back.

Damon—who had ambled over to the group of eight or ten staff who had now collected around Carly's desk—added, "Leaving you free to swoop in like Superman and save the day at the last."

Carly turned and glared at Damon. Then looked from boss's assistant to boss, as if only just figuring out she was a pawn in someone else's game. "This is not a coup," she said, "if that's what you're worried about."

"Well, it hadn't been..." said Ben, finding himself laughing. For a strange feeling of lightness had come over him. A mix of relief and possibility. "Truly, though, you guys have blown me away. Now, you can all go home, enjoy what's left of the weekend, and come back fresh and ready to tackle this on Monday. You, on the other hand—" Ben pointed a finger at his assistant "—come with me."

Ben made a beeline for his office, where he went straight for the safe tucked behind a picture of a sailing boat on his wall. And he didn't much care for boats.

A designer had chosen it. The same one who'd decked out his apartment. And he'd let them. As it allowed him to live like an automaton. Work, home. Work, home. Too busy working, proving himself, building a reputation for honesty and impeccable work, to even pick a comfortable couch.

He'd built a fortress of self-protection. As if getting *comfortable* would leave him open to attack, vulnerable to having his life tumbling down around his ears. Again.

And it was a lonely place to be.

"You might be looking for this."

Out of the corner of his eye, Ben saw Damon holding out Ben's passport. And a dossier.

Damon wandered into the office. "List of daily flights to Melbourne, a map of Melbourne with the address of your grandmother's house circled in red, some Aussie cash, and your passport. I've had it ready for the last week."

Ben carefully took the dossier from Damon's hand. "I'm not sure if you're the best assistant I've ever had, or if I should change the locks."

Damon grinned. "Figure it out later. After your holiday."

Ben's fingertips pressed hard into his palm, as if trying to alert him to the fact he might be about to do something uncalculated. With too many variables to control. Something bonkers.

He uncurled his fingers, knowing all of that and wanting to go anyway. Needing to go. It was time. "Set up a meeting with the heads of department for Monday."

"Emails are drafted, letting them know you're taking time off. No meeting necessary. I press *send*, you're good to go."

"So, it is a coup."

Damon grinned. Then followed Ben out of the office door.

In between staff members calling out, "Have a good break!"

"Get a tan!"

"Bring back some sunshine!"

Ben told Damon, "I might be out of town, but I still require constant updates. You be my firewall. Filter as you need to. I trust you."

Damon's next smile held none of its usual cockiness. "Thanks, boss. Fair warning, there might be a slight bump in doughnut purchases to keep this ragamuffin bunch going, but with my new title and company card I can take that on."

"And what title is that?"

"Permanent attachment to the Desk of Bennett J Hawthorne."

"You want to *remain* as my assistant?" Ben asked as he moved into the lift, slapping the dossier against his palm, feeling the telling bump of his passport.

"For now. So I can learn at the feet of the master. Because in the long term, I plan to *be* you. I'll keep your seat warm while you're gone."

Ben's laughter echoed as the lift doors closed.

CHAPTER EIGHT

NORA'S EYES HAD just started to drift shut, the Harlan Coben book she was reading tipping precariously towards her nose, when she was startled awake at the sound of a knock at the front door.

A few woozy blinks and a glance at the clock on her phone told her she still had a couple of hours for a last tidy before the cleaner came. It was likely someone selling electricity plans.

Having stayed up way too late re-watching the entire second season of *Fleabag* for the zillionth time, then spending the morning preloading a bunch of content for a couple of local businesses before tying off their contracts, a nap was necessary.

She rolled over, laid her arm over her eyes and—

Knock-knock-knock.

"Argh! Okay!" she shouted, sitting up so fast her head spun.

Dragging herself out of bed, Nora tugged at her vest top—it would do—then grabbed a pair of ancient cut-off denim shorts from the top of her clean-clothes pile and dragged them over her undies.

Knock. Knock-knock!

"Sheesh. I'm coming!" Nora called, twirling her wild

hair into a messy bun atop her head as she jogged down the precariously skinny stairs.

At the door she checked to make sure Cutie wasn't about—he had a habit of licking door-knockers half to death—then she opened the front door a crack.

Only to swing it open wide when she found Bennett Jude Hawthorne standing on Clancy's front porch.

"Oh, my God. You're here!" she blurted.

"That I am," he said in a voice that—up close, in person—was, if possible, deeper than over the phone. Lit with a loose, lackadaisical drawl.

The backs of Nora's knees began to tingle, while her feet felt as if they weren't quite attached to her body.

Because *he* was there. He was really there! He wasn't merely a warm voice on the phone, or a two-dimensional image on a screen, or some impossible crush she could happily indulge as he lived on the other side of the planet.

He was here. He was real. And, boy, was he beautiful.

There was no other word for it.

Misty hadn't been kidding when she called him mountainous, for the man was tall. With serious shoulders filling out a brown suede jacket, all kinds of heft filling out dark jeans, and if his boots weren't kidding his feet were huge. Add thick, dark, wavy hair with a perfect smattering of silver over his ears she'd never noted before, and those intense eyes; the man oozed fire-crackling, log-cabin-on-a-winter's-night deliciousness.

Nora shook her head, feeling as if she were coming out of a trance. "When did you get in? Did I miss a call?"

"The decision was made. I got on a plane. I am a man of action. When I want to be." With that came a smile. A lazy kick at one corner of his beautiful mouth.

Holy moly. Nora was tingling so hard it was a miracle she didn't set on fire.

"Come in!" she said, a small measure of sense finally finding a way through the fog that had overcome her. "*Mi casa, su casa.* Literally."

With that, her mind stuttered back to reality. She remembered the kitchen she was yet to clean before the cleaner came, the clothesline still covered in undies and bras she'd set up by the sunny window in the sunroom out back, the dogs—

The dogs! She'd yet to tell Ben about the dogs. Or, you know, make sure they didn't live here any more, as per his landlordy stipulations.

She cocked an ear, but couldn't hear the telltale tick-tick-tick of Pie's claws on hard wood, or Cutie's desperate whimpers. Meaning they must be out back stalking a bird or digging up the garden. For now.

Still, what could she do but step back, swoosh an arm towards the hallway like a game-show host, and wait for him to pass?

The scents of the outdoors came with him as he entered the house, jasmine and myrtle, as well as something other. Something warm and rich and wholly delicious. Him.

Nora shut the door and leaned against it, using its solidity to keep her grounded as Ben Hawthorne filled the entrance. With his bigness and his elegance and his delicious scent.

He didn't go far, the back of his head moving as he seemed to take the place in. Fair enough too. Everything he saw was now his.

Well, not everything. Not *her*.

"Has the place changed much, since last you were here?" she asked, her voice sounding not at all as if she had lemonade in her veins.

"Not a bit," said Ben, his voice gruff.

Then he turned, shooting her a quick smile. When his

eyes caught on hers, they darkened all the more. All the air seemed to disappear from the room.

Nora's stomach swooped. Her heart thudded in her throat.

Ben.

He was *right there*. Within touching distance. Big, overwhelmingly beautiful, smelling like the woods in springtime, and looking at her as if he was rather taken by the fact she was within touching distance too.

"It seems I've caught you unawares," he said, a definite hint of humour lighting his velvety voice.

"What? No. It's all good. I'm fine. I was just—" She turned, flapped a hand towards the stairs, and her messy bun flopped sideways, a hank landing in her eye. She swished it back over her shoulder and held a hand to her face. "I have pillow marks on my cheek, don't I?"

"Pillow—?"

"I was napping, see. Yes, in the middle of the day. Because I can. I'm decadent, that way. One of the joys of being footloose and fancy-free." By habit she held out her arm, showing off her tattoo.

His eyes followed the move, took it in, before they dropped to her bare legs, slid smoothly over her tank top, under which she remembered she was not wearing a bra, then back to her face.

Nora pulled her arm across her belly, suspecting her distraction-by-sunshine move might not have near the same impact it usually did. Not with this man. This astute, acute, grown-up man.

"This is weird, right? I mean, I'm not sure whether I should shake your hand or..." *or throw myself into your arms, bury my face in your neck and breathe you in till I faint* "...or hug you."

Ben breathed in, breathed out, and said nothing.

"So it's just me," she managed. "Good to know. If you don't mind, I'll duck up and get dressed."

"Not at all," he said. Though something in his voice made her think he'd prefer she stayed. Just as she was.

Breathless, light-headed, in need of a moment to reset, Nora moved past him, quickly breathing in his warm rich scent—like a sip from a sneaky flask at a dry wedding—before bolting up the stairs.

"Coffee machine is on!" she threw over her shoulder. "I baked, late last night, so there are snacks. I won't be a minute!"

She hit the bedroom at a run, caught sight of herself in the mirror. Face pink, tiny curls framing her cheeks, eyes overbright. Nipples saying, *Why, hello, Ben...* beneath her thin white vest.

Oh, good gravy.

She found some floaty linen pants, a loose top, a bra, and hustled them on. She gave her hair a quick finger-detangle before twisting it into a loose side plait. Swiped on a little lip gloss. Tidied up her mascara. Gargled a minty mouthwash—

Then stopped.

She closed her eyes and breathed. Told herself to calm the heck down.

Ben was not here *for* her. *Maybe* something she'd said had helped him make the decision to come home, to claim his inheritance, but that was the extent of her involvement.

But he was here. Meaning her promise to Clancy had been fulfilled. She could grab her bag, right now, do the rounds of the neighbourhood, say her goodbyes, and go.

Anywhere. Land where she landed. Find a small patch of space for herself in a share house, or a motel. And start over. Start fresh. No expectations.

But something inside her tugged. Something unfinished.

If she gave herself just a *little* more time, maybe she could do more. Help Ben make peace with his wonderful grandmother. Then she could walk away from this whole experience, truly free and clear.

Nothing left undone. No regrets. No looking back.

On the way out of the door she spotted Cutie and Pie's day bed in the corner. She grabbed an old throw from the back of her office chair, tossed it over the dog bed, and headed downstairs.

Ben didn't move.

He could hear Nora moving around upstairs—footsteps, drawers opening, taps turning on and off. But he stayed where he stood, his hand gripped tight to the handle of his suitcase, his shoes glued to the floor.

For his senses were being bombarded with memories of his sneakers squeaking on the dark wood floors, counting the blown bulbs in the ancient chandelier, running his hands over the wallpaper every time he walked into the kitchen…

Despite Nora's belief Clancy couldn't boil an egg, the galley kitchen, with its wooden doors and dark green marble bench tops, was the room in which Clancy had spent much of her time while he was growing up: cooking Vietnamese salads, American burgers, Italian pasta sauces from scratch. He could almost smell the herbs, even now.

But then his throat tightened, the backs of his eyes gritty, as he remembered the first time he'd braved asking Clancy about his birth parents. She'd gripped the kitchen bench, her eyes haunted, her voice reed thin as she'd asked: wasn't he happy there with her? Hadn't she given him a wonderful life?

"Hey," a voice called from behind him.

Ben flinched so hard his shoulder tweaked.

He took a moment to centre himself before he turned

to find Nora at the bottom of the stairs, a hand resting on the railing.

From the moment he'd had his passport in his hand, he'd been on a forward trajectory. Book flight, pack bag, connect with heads of department to make sure they all knew this wasn't a fortnight in the Bahamas. He was contactable. He was on the clock.

Then suddenly he was standing outside Clancy's gate. The scent of jasmine near overwhelming. He'd been so cocky, so gung-ho, he hadn't considered how it might feel to be back, knowing Clancy wasn't there, and never would be again.

He'd walked to the front door on legs of lead. His arm not feeling like his as he'd knocked.

Then Nora had opened the door, and everything else had just melted away.

A vision of long brown limbs, sleep-softened face, and joy. Behind the surprise, she'd been truly happy to see him. Knowing it, feeling it, some deep, lawless part of him had unfurled under the regard of those big blue eyes. At the sight of a bare foot running up and down the back of her calf. The way her breaths had become deep and hard won.

It had occurred to him in that moment, the hold she had over him. The place she had made for herself in his head. If he wasn't careful, he could get into a lot of trouble for this woman.

"Okay!" she said, clapping her hands, her eyes not quite meeting his. "Let's start over, get you settled in. As you know, I have the apartment upstairs, but can move my stuff out in five minutes. Or the spare room beside the sitting room is made up. Or there's Clancy's room—"

"Spare room is fine," he gritted out. His old room. Clancy had assured him when he'd first moved out, to go to university, it would be called "Ben's room" until the end of time. Another equivocation in a long line of them.

"Okay, then," said Nora.

Her eyes finally found his and a frisson of electricity, of heat, seemed to arc through the air. Connecting them. As if the bond he'd felt from, oh, so far away had been amped up to eleven.

She took an audible fortifying breath as she slid past him, as if that might negate the disrupting crackle of attraction. His feet finally moved, following hers.

When she hit his old bedroom door, Nora nudged it open, then stood in the doorway, her hands tucked behind her, her body at one with the doorjamb.

As Ben moved past Nora, he could feel the air around her shift. Could taste citrus at the back of his throat. Could feel a burst of sunshine on his wrist closest to her.

Thus unnerved, he entered the spare room to find small aeroplanes swooping over dark walls. The ceiling pale grey with fluffy white clouds. The chest of drawers sporting a small collection of stickers saved from the apples he'd eaten over the years. It was a time capsule, after all.

"I'll leave you be—" said Nora, her voice tugging him back from the brink of near desperate discomfort.

"No," he said, tossing his suitcase and jacket on the single bed and running both hands through his hair in an effort at keeping himself in the here and now. "I'd rather stay awake. Fight the jet lag. How about a tour?"

"Of the house?" she asked, eyes narrowing. "Trying to make sure I haven't done off with the family candlesticks?"

"If there are any, you're welcome to them."

Her laughter was bright, and big. "Nah. I'm good."

Nevertheless, she bowed to his request, taking him through the house, telling charming tales about her time there, and using the chance to talk up Clancy: how beloved she was in the community, her wild style, her wicked sense of humour.

The fact that she was as transparent in person as she was over the phone eased something inside him. She was the woman who'd drawn him here. Who he'd hoped to find when he'd stepped up to the front door.

"Keeping in mind you gave me no time to tidy up, you're welcome to check out the apartment upstairs," she said, suddenly finding her fingernails fascinating.

"But, Nora, we've just met."

Her gaze lifted to his, a wild spark glinting within the smoky blue. "Ha-ha." Then she took the first step, then the second, all but daring him to follow. "You've already seen my underwear, so I have nothing to hide. Come on up if you dare."

Ben dared, having to turn his feet at an angle so as not to trip.

Once upstairs her bravado faltered as she quickly swept him past her unmade bed—he felt himself smiling at the sight of the dragonfly sheets. One pillow sat neat and trim at the head of the bed, the other at an odd angle, comforter askew, as if she was a restless sleeper. The bathroom smelt of fruity shampoo, and soft soap, and skin. Of Nora.

"So that's it! Shall we…head back downstairs?" she asked, her voice lifting at the end, as if there was an alternative.

Ben took the initiative, moving out of the door, but not before sending her a feral grin that made her cheeks pink, even as she rolled her eyes.

Halfway down the stairs, his big feet turned so he didn't fall off the edge, Ben stopped, turned, checked to see she was coming.

She was. Right behind him. With a loud, "Whoop!" she

tried to stop her descent, her hands landing on his shoulders to steady herself.

But gravity had its own ideas.

Ben's big feet, not having purchase, slipped down a step, or two. Ben grabbed her, spinning so that they didn't both tumble down the damnable stairs. Even so, they landed awkwardly, her body sprawled on top of his, his face buried in her hair.

In the quiet that followed, Ben did a quick mental scan, assessing the damage to body and limb. Her breath washed over his ear as she huffed out a laugh, sending goosebumps shooting down his neck, and it was all he could feel.

"You okay?" he asked, his voice rough, his hands moving over her shoulder, her skull, swiping her hair from her eyes.

She nodded, her hair sliding through his fingers. Her body shifting, rubbing up against him in a most unfortunate way if he wanted to get out of this with his dignity intact.

"Are *you*?" she asked.

"I'm fine," he said, his voice rough.

Her eyes flickered between his before her gaze dropped to his mouth. Meaning she didn't miss a syllable as he growled, "Now you have me here, what do you plan to do with me?"

Her eyes shot back to his. Wide. Filling with heat, with smoke.

"In Melbourne," he qualified, shifting a little to ease the feel of a step digging into his back, only to have the length of her slide more fittingly over his. "It's been your mission to get me here. I'm here. So now what?"

"I can feed you," she said, her chest rising and falling, eyes once again locked on his mouth. "Or we can head out for a bite."

"I could eat," he said. "Either way."

When her eyes moved back to his, her pupils had all but swallowed the oceans of blue.

"Unless," he said, barely in control of his own voice any more, "you have something better in mind?"

Later, he couldn't be sure who moved first, but next thing he knew her mouth was on his. Hot, wet and wanton.

Somehow they moved, till she was lying back on the stairs, Ben over the top of her. Her hands were tugging on his shirt till she found skin. Splaying across his back, kneading, hauling him closer, waves of heat rocketing through his body while his hands were buried deep in her silken hair as they kissed. And kissed. And kissed. No teasing, no testing; wet, lush, exquisite.

When his tongue swept into her mouth and she groaned, he saw stars. Moons. Distant constellations.

As if the weeks of conversation, flirtation, of building sexual tension, of play, of talking late into the night, falling asleep to one another's yawns and husky goodnights, had been long-build foreplay that had funnelled them here, to this moment.

Then Ben's knee hit a stair, sending a sharp shot of pain up his leg, right as he heard something of hers hit the wood with a loud *thunk*. Her elbow, he realised when her head dropped back to lean on the stair and she dragged her arm between them to give her elbow a rub.

Ben shifted, giving her room. Himself too. Even as he found himself in all kinds of discomfort—from bumps and bruises and tightness in the front of his pants. Her eyes were scrunched closed, even as she laughed, the sound husky and raw, and sexy as all get out.

"What were we thinking?" she asked.

"I wasn't."

More laughter. He did love her laugh.

The pain eased from her face and her eyes fluttered open. "This kind of thing always looks so hot in movies."

"Which movies? Tell me their names."

Nora laughed again, and it felt as if diamonds were exploding behind his ribs. It was ridiculous. Reckless. Irresistible. His fingers of his right hand were near enough to her wild braid, he let them get lost in a loose curl before giving it a light tug.

Then her knee shifted, sliding between his legs, making contact with a gentle insistent nudge. Before he had the chance to draw breath her body followed, undulating into him, all soft curves and bumptious invitation.

It was enough to bring him back to reality.

Giving her one last smile, he carefully pressed himself to standing then held out a hand to help her do the same.

She took his hand and curled herself upright. Standing two steps above him, she was nearly eye to eye. This woman, a walking, talking peril.

"I knew these stairs were a danger. I'd asked Damon to look into my liability in case anything happened."

"This what you had in mind?"

He'd not had *any* of this in mind back then. Not an unplanned trek to Australia. Not facing Clancy's legacy. And certainly not Nora Letterman.

She reached out and tugged the neckline of his shirt back into place, her small light hands running over his chest. Then she grabbed a hunk of shirt and tugged him towards her.

Her vivid gaze remained glued to his. Her tongue darted out to wet her top lip before her teeth dragged over the plump lower lip. Slowly, incrementally closing the gap; this time, giving both of them the chance to decide if this was a mistake.

By the time her lips met his she was trembling. Hell, maybe it was him.

Either way, if their first kiss had been an explosion of flint and steel, this was a slow, soft exploration. Her lips dragging over his. Again and again. Finding where she fitted best. His arm slid around her waist, bringing her closer, as if in slow motion; so that when her body finally lined up against his he could almost feel the house sigh in relief.

Eons later, when she pulled back, her eyes were closed. Ben turned her till her back was against the wall; his hand braced beside her head, determined not to let the stairs, or gravity, get the best of him.

She lifted her hand to her lips, then she murmured, as if to herself, "I've been wondering what that might feel like for the longest time. You feel like lunch yet?"

Lunch. Ben needed a moment to fathom the meaning of the word.

"Or," she said, lifting her head, to whisper against his ear, "we could go back upstairs."

The hand against the wall curled into the wallpaper. Hell, this was fast. He'd been in her vicinity fifteen minutes, tops. But the truth was, they'd been a snowball rolling down a hill, gaining speed and momentum, since their very first conversation.

Yet, he was no savage, prone to act on a whim. He made decisions based on reason, evidence, fact. One of them had to try to take control of this thing.

"We should slow down," he managed.

"Why?"

Good question.

"I'm a big girl, Ben. And you are most certainly a big boy. Whatever worries are bouncing about inside that big brain of yours, let them go. I am the one thing in your life that you never, ever have to worry about. I ask nothing of you but this. Now."

She took him by the hand and moved a step higher, tilting her head towards the upstairs apartment, towards her big, soft bed, giving him that slow, languorous, wider-than-should-be-possible smile, and he thought, *To hell with it.*

He was on holiday, after all. For the first time in more years than he could count, he was responsible for no one but himself.

At the letting go Ben felt something shift inside him. Something big and cumbersome and weighty. He felt a hook slide into the new-found space, right through his centre, tugging him wherever Nora chose to take him.

Which was up the stairs, and into her bed.

Skin still slick with sweat, bones lax, muscles no longer of any use, her entire body drifting on a blissful fog, Nora stared at a spot on the ceiling where a small patch of paint was flaking away, as her thoughts threatened to spin out into crazy town.

She'd just taken Ben Hawthorne to bed. Literally taken him by the hand and led him there! What had she been thinking? She *hadn't*. That much was clear.

And what happened to helping Ben make peace with his wonderful grandmother so she could walk away, no regrets?

One thing she hadn't considered when letting her feelings for Ben have free rein, while they'd flirted, and teased, and talked about things she never talked about with anyone, ever, was that within the word *crush*, crushing was implied. *Being* crushed. The heaviness she felt in her chest sure felt as if it was heading that way.

When Ben moved beside her, all big and warm and

strong, Nora whimpered; the urge to curl into him, absorb his warmth, absorb *him*, was rich and lush and terrifying.

She flopped her arm over her eyes, as if that might quell out the tumble of concerns fast bubbling up inside her.

"Nora," Ben murmured, in that deep, rumbling, bone-melting voice of his. "Everything okay over there?"

"Mmm-hmm," she said, her voice coming out an octave too high. "Everything's super-duper!"

Nora felt Ben's fingers—oh, God, those fingers—curl around hers, before he gently lifted her arm away from her face. She gave herself a moment, or three, to brace herself against the onslaught of that face before she opened her eyes to find him leaning on one elbow, looking down on her.

Her heart *kerthunked*. Her head swooned. His heartbreaker face was just so serious, and earnest, and lovely, it made her ache.

"That was my fault," she blurted.

"How so?"

Excellent question. "Okay, maybe it was your fault for smelling so good."

His mouth kicked ever so slightly at one corner, as if he was laughing at her—no, as if he was *delighted* by her—and it was possibly the most beautiful thing she'd ever seen.

"If so," he said, lifting a hand to his chest, his beautifully sculpted chest, "then I take full responsibility."

Nora smiled. Dreamily. Then shook her head hard enough her brain *thunked* against the sides of her skull. "See, now you're looking at me as if I'm adorable. But you should know, I'm this delightful to everyone. So don't think you're special."

"I wouldn't dare."

"Actually," she went on, as if he hadn't spoken, "maybe

not *that* delightful. The falling-into-bed part was new. An aberration. A hiccup."

"A hiccup," he repeated, though he didn't seem at all perturbed by her summation. Instead his fingers curled around a lock of her hair. Then he leaned down and placed a kiss on her cheek, then another at the edge of her ear.

Her eyes closed and she let out a sigh, her body shifting as waves of pleasure scooted through her. If she wasn't careful, if she didn't get control of herself, she'd be hiccupping again before she knew it.

"The cleaner!" she cried, eyes flying open.

"What about her?"

"Him. He's due soon. Any minute."

"Okay." His lips moved down her neck, dragging against the skin till she felt feverish.

"He has a key!"

Ben's mouth halted. He laid one more kiss on her collarbone, as if he was marking his place with a promise, then he sat back up.

Nora did the same, bringing the sheet with her. The rest barely covered Ben, hip to thigh; his huge feet hung off the end of the mattress.

Oh, now you're all demure, a devil on her shoulder intoned. *Five minutes ago you were riding him like a—*

"As I was saying," she blurted, "what happened, just now, was the result of a number of factors."

"My smell, your adorableness…"

"Yes. And hanky-panky can be wonderfully…ah…*distracting*."

He blinked, his long-angled lashes sweeping against his cheeks. The move devastating to any kind of balance she might be trying to regain. "Distracting."

"Sure. We clearly both needed a good…distraction. From how much we both miss Clancy."

At that, Ben reared back, his brows coming together, forming deep burrows in his forehead. Seriously? How could forehead burrows be so sexy? But, gosh, they were.

He ran a hand over his face, before saying, "Don't do that."

"Do what?"

"Negate what happened by making it about Clancy." His voice sounded weary. None of the delicious, teasing burr that had kept her enthralled as he'd whispered all the things he'd imagined doing to her during their late-night phone calls, then followed through.

"Sorry," she said, and meant it. "It's just… All this time, I wasn't actually sure that you even liked me."

The moment the words came out of Nora's mouth, she regretted them. Letting such ignominies slip in front of Ben over the phone, in the quiet, the night crowding in around her, had been one thing. But in person? It left her defenceless, and her defences were her lifeblood.

Ben breathed out hard and fell back on the bed beside her, the mattress bouncing with him. For he was a big guy, in all the best possible ways.

He was quiet for a moment. A long moment.

She risked a glance to find he'd tucked one big, strong arm loosely behind his head. The other rested on top of the covers, which only came to his waist, leaving his stunning torso bare, his profile a study in manly beauty.

To think she'd traced the lines of his ribs with the flat of her hand. Felt his muscles contract under her touch, while he'd tried to stay in control. Followed the trail of dark hair that came together in an arrow leading—

"I *like* my coffee sweet," said Ben, as if he'd worked hard on his answer.

"Hmm? What now?"

Ben tipped his head. "I *like*," he reiterated, "my avocado smashed. My socks to be one hundred per cent cotton."

"Could you be more preppy?"

"You're determined to put a label on this."

Her eyes snapped back into focus to find him looking deep into her eyes. "Labelling things helps me remember where the landmines are buried, and where I've yet to map. It's a thing of mine."

"A thing of mine is that I do not put you in the same category as avocado on toast or cotton-rich socks."

Nora's next breath in stuttered. If Ben noticed, he let her be.

Deep down, she so wanted to be liked. She craved it. Having been told, over and over, that she wasn't enough, or was just too much, she'd learned that being affable, easy-going, helpful, of use—*happy*—made her likeable in a way that she could control.

Unlocking her Sunshine Mode had been like tapping into some magical power. It put her in the driver's seat, no longer at the whim of anyone else's opinion or desire.

Ben, for all his Ben-ness, would be no different. He'd tire of her. Or become distracted by some other shinier, easier thing. And that was okay. It was life.

And so she would do as she always did, and leave while she was ahead. Before she was pushed. His liking her or not, her liking him—or more than liking, as was clearly becoming the case—couldn't and wouldn't play into that decision.

"All that talk of avocado toast has made me hungry," she said. "You hungry? There's a pub across the way. They do a mean steak. Unless you're bushed. And just want to go to bed."

The glint in his eyes gave her ideas. So many ideas.

She rolled her eyes in order to break eye contact, lest

she give into those ideas. For, despite all of her fancy self-talk, she was not impervious. Not to him.

Then she smiled her sunshiniest smile, and sing-songed, “Steak it is! Now get the heck out of my bed, big boy, get dressed, and let’s go!”

CHAPTER NINE

AS NORA PRESSED through the Shenanigans crowd she instantly wondered if she'd made a huge mistake.

Her plan had been to show the place off—it was infamous for great food and atmosphere far beyond the borders of Fitzroy—and have him meet some of the younger locals. Make him see this was a place a successful guy from London could fit right in.

But as she angled her way through the early-evening crowd she noted the number of people who stopped talking as they looked Ben's way. Maybe they knew who he was. Or maybe they'd figured out sooner than she had that beneath the stuffed-shirt stubbornness lurked the dark charisma of a bit of a bad boy.

Because the stairs. And then the wall. Then the top of the stairs. Then her bed. Rolling around, clothes flying, hands everywhere. All salty, and hot, and reckless. And then there was that thing he did with his—

Nora tripped. Over nothing, bar her own metaphorical tongue.

Ben's hand reached out and captured her elbow, steadying her.

She glanced back. Caught his questioning smile. And even though all that warm, hard male skin was hidden away behind a chambray shirt and dark jeans, spot fires still popped up all over her body.

She spun front in the hopes he might not notice the blood rush to her cheeks, but could still feel him behind her; all big, and broad, cutting a swathe through the place like a hot knife through butter.

Nora breathed out in relief when she caught Sam the bartender's eye as they approached the bar. "Hey, Sam! I heard you aced your uni results. You're killing it."

Sam lit up; her sunshine working its magic.

"By the way, this is Ben. Clancy's grandson."

Sam's eyes lit up. "Clancy was great. My ma was in her book club. We miss her heaps around here."

Nora glanced back to see Ben take the note with a smile. But only a quick one that didn't quite reach his eyes. None of the bottomless warmth and subtle humour that had filled their depths when it had been just the two of them. Alone. In her bed.

Nora, cheeks starting to hurt from fake smiling, said to Sam, "We sure do. I'd love a cider. Ben?"

"Sounds good," said Ben.

"Sam, can we grab a spot for early dinner?"

"Sure. Take the corner booth," said Sam, popping the tops off a couple of ciders before sliding them across the bar.

Nora took a swig as she checked out the corner booth. It was big and secluded. The kind of booth in which you could get away with all kinds of things under cover of near darkness.

"Any other tables available?" Nora asked.

"Nope. Have a couple of groups coming in. All booked up."

"Cool. Cool, cool, cool." When she caught Ben's gaze,

she was rewarded with the slow, sexy rise of a single eyebrow that threatened to short-circuit her brain.

"No-o-o-ra?" Misty said, the vowel suggestively elongated.

Groaning inwardly, Nora turned to find Misty slinking up to their little group, and tried desperately to convey with wide eyes and gritted teeth that Misty should please behave. "Misty, you remember Ben, right?"

"Of course. Bennett Hawthorne, back in the flesh."

"Hey, Misty," Ben said, his deep voice creating hot skitters up and down Nora's spine. "How's tricks?"

"Tricks are fine. So, Clancy left you the house. Were you surprised? After what went down between you?"

Nora coughed on her drink.

Ben's arm reached out to slide across Nora's back, giving her a light rub that sent sparks shooting in every which direction. It was followed by a hearty thump. His way of saying thanks so much for bringing him here.

Nora shot him a glance of apology only to find him looking cool, and unfazed, and unutterably handsome. And his hand didn't move. It stayed, his thumb making slow circles over her spine.

"Menus," said Sam handing a pair across the bar.

Misty snapped them up. "Super, I'll join you."

Ben pulled out his phone and paid for the drinks, then he held an arm before him, and the ladies led the way.

An hour, a drink, a steak dinner later, the bar was hopping. And the corner booth was the place to be.

Christos from the fruit shop had pulled up a chair. Maryanne who ran the vintage book shop joined them, along with the twins who worked the coffee machine at Ambrosia. When Janey from the florist realised Ben was the very man who'd helped them renegotiate a brilliant new lease agreement, she threw herself bodily at him and hugged him tight.

So many drinks had been shouted, eventually Nora had to make a move to the ladies' room.

Wanting to get back to Ben—only so she could act as mediator and bodyguard—she peed faster than she'd ever peed in her life. Wiping her clean hands down the sides of her boho skirt as the bathroom had run out of paper towel, she banged into Misty in the dark hall.

"Whoa!" cried Misty. "What's the rush? Your man is doing just fine without you running interference."

Nora scoffed. "He's not my man."

"Honey, if you haven't spent half the night imagining crawling into his lap and nibbling on whatever bare skin you can reach, I'll eat my shoes."

Nora leant against the wall to let a couple of women pass, and said nothing.

"If it helps," Misty added, "he's been watching you as if he's never seen the sun shine so brightly before."

Strange that something could feel really nice but not help a bit. Under cover of semi-darkness Nora heard herself say, "I may have nibbled a little already."

"Atta girl." Misty put up a hand for a high five, which Nora bluntly refused to meet.

She moved to glance round the corner of the hall, and found Ben surrounded by intrigued locals, all of whom were hoping to find a little spark of Clancy in him. He absorbed their stories, their loss, with grace and kindness. But even from here she could see the tightness around his jaw, the exhaustion creating creases at the corners of his eyes.

And it hit her, he was grieving too. Whether he wanted to admit it or not.

And *that* was her job here, not to nibble on the guy.

Not to give the man hidden pieces of herself. Not to find solace in him.

She'd had her fun. Now the real work had to start.

The night air was brisk, but sweet compared with the spate of sludgy, grey days Ben had left behind in London. The streetlights stymied any view of any stars, but managed to create their own kind of whimsy all the same.

There was no denying the feeling of home with a dash of unreal, Nora ambling beside him; her hair, long and loose, caught by the slight breeze, sending tendrils of spun gold floating about her face.

Nora shivered. And without overthinking it, Ben moved closer, put an arm around her shoulder and said, "I like your friends."

She stiffened a moment, shooting him a look of surprise, before allowing it. A pragmatist at heart. "Did you like them as much as you like avocado on toast?" she asked.

His laughter was swept up by the night.

Then, just as they'd found a rhythm, their steps, their breaths in sync, they neared the house. Nora took him by the hand and untwirled herself from his side, let her fingers slip through his, then hastened up the steps to unlock the front door.

"The alarm?" he reminded her, when she sashayed inside the house.

"Ah," said Nora, spinning on one foot, giving him a look that was full of mischief, before backtracking to the door, "the alarm. Sure."

She walked up to the big plant in the corner, moved back a bunch of fronds to reveal a small, dust-covered panel. She wrenched at it till it opened, then said, "Beep-boop-boop-beep."

"Beep-boop-boop-beep?" he repeated.

She turned back to him with a beatific smile, with a definite impish spark. The power of it hit like a smack between the ribs.

Then something came over her face, a kind of soft, breezy calm. It was as if the woman who had grabbed him by the shirtfront and kissed him on the stairs, the woman who'd refused to give up on him, had called him daily to get him here, had been replaced by a bright, airy, translucent version of herself.

And he felt a flicker of discord deep in his gut. A match to the flicker he'd felt when she'd come back to the table at the pub. Something…off.

"Coffee?" she asked, her tone light as she tossed her keys into a small bowl on the hall table and bounded towards the kitchen. "I have plenty of sugar. Or decaf if you're worried it'll keep you up."

"No, thanks. Thinking I should hit the sack. You?"

Her face half turned. Enough for him to see the colour rise in her cheeks, the heat flare behind the smoky blue, before she extinguished it as patently as if she'd stuck her head in a bucket of water.

"Glass of water for me. Hydration is an excellent cure for jet lag too. Keen?"

"Sure. Why not?" he said as he watched her fuss about in the kitchen, humming beneath her breath like some cartoon princess.

If not for the fact that they had all but torn one another's clothes off a few scant hours before, he might have believed he'd imagined the pull, the gravity, the connection he'd felt across the phone line. That he'd misread the signs.

Or, worse, been played.

Ben ran a hand through his hair. She had no reason to lie to him. It was this house—old ghosts playing tricks with his head. Yet for all that, he couldn't discount what his gut was telling him: for all that he was drawn to her, he didn't really know her.

Perhaps her suggestion that they were finding solace in one another's arms wasn't so far from the truth. Or, in fact, a bad thing. Yet, at the very thought, a wave of exhaustion swept over him, making his eyes feel heavy and his legs a little loose. "Look, I think I'll just—"

"Oh, no." Nora looked up from the sink, neither airy nor translucent. As if the latent energy she'd been keeping in check had spilled free; she practically glowed.

While Ben reeled from the impact, she quickly glanced over her shoulder, towards the back of the house, and said, "Um—look, I'm really sorry, but—"

"Arooo!"

Ben stilled. "What the hell…?"

"Arooo!"

Yep, it was definitely a howl. A howl of desperation and psychic pain.

Nora shot Ben a look before she fled into the darkness towards the back of the house. Towards the God-awful sound. And he heard the sound of the door creaking open. The back door that didn't lock.

"Nora!" he called, moving after her, his hand unerringly finding the hallway light.

A desperate whimper filled the air, followed by Nora's voice, stage-whispering from a room beyond, "Hello. I know. Good boy. Are you okay? Did you get stuck? Poor darling. Down. Yes. Good boy. No, down!"

"Nora?" he bellowed. "What the hell's going on?"

Her murmuring stopped, and she slowly edged around the laundry door. Her face was alight with pure guilt—which, he realised with a flicker of concern, he much preferred to the blank sweetness. A huge, scruffy grey dog pulled against her grip while with all of her might she hugged it between her knees.

"This big galoot knocked a planter over, blocking off the doggy door. So they were *stuck* outside. All afternoon. And this one is afraid of the dark, you see."

"They?" Ben asked, right as, out of the corner of his eye, he spotted a small fluffy dog, with only one eye and a notch taken out of one ear, standing on the kitchen bench. Growling at him.

He leapt back, a hand over his heart, and swore to blue heaven. "What the hell is going on here?"

Nora glanced from the dog wriggling between her legs to the one on the bench. It would have been funny if not for the fact he could practically see her brain trying to come up with a likely story.

"Nora," he said, his tone brooking no argument. "The truth."

He saw her waver. He saw her decide. As if truth was a thing to be metered out, not cut and dried as it was to him.

"The truth," he reiterated.

"Of course," she said, shaking her head. "This one is Cutie. He's here to befriend Pie. That one's Pie. Pie doesn't like people. Clancy was fostering him when she…when she died."

When Clancy died. And Nora was there, looking after her house, her foster dog, the cooking, the cleaning. Looking after Clancy, while Ben had been going about his life, busy working, arrogantly sure he had a handle on his life, when he hadn't had a clue.

"It's been a whole thing," Nora went on. "And I'm sorry I didn't tell you about them, but I… This is going to sound so stupid, but they are foster dogs, and I was a foster kid, and I've felt like a hypocrite, wanting to send them back."

Ben swore beneath his breath. And took a moment as his

heart began to recover from its caveman-about-to-battle-a-sabre-tooth-tiger rate.

There was truth and there was *truth*. And Nora, as was her way, had hidden the small and gifted him the big. More than he'd asked. More than the timing of their relationship deserved. Unless they were more than strange bedfellows after all.

Ben looked to the small offender on Clancy's bench. All battle scars and patchy fur. It stared at him with its one good eye and he felt a strange echo rush through him. As if he was staring down a canine version of himself, the day he'd arrived at this very house.

"Pie, is it?" he murmured, taking a step towards the bench, keeping eye contact with the ball of scruff. "How's tricks, Pie?"

Pie huffed out a long-suffering breath.

"Like that, is it?" Ben asked, his voice gentling all the more as he approached. Then he held out a hand, palm down, a good foot away from the dog's mouth.

"Wait!" cried Nora, shuffling closer with the big dog still stringing between her knees.

Ben curled his fingers and turned his hand over and let it stay there, near the smaller dog's nose. "For?"

"Aren't you allergic? Or, traumatised somehow? Humans might not be so good at telling if someone doesn't really like them, but dogs can."

Ben baulked. "Who doesn't like dogs?"

Nora baulked back. "People. People who live in minimalist apartments. People who wear ridiculously nice clothes they don't want to get dog hair all over. People who say 'no pets' in their lease agreements."

Ah. Now they were getting somewhere. "Did I say that?"

"Ah, yes! Way back at the beginning. In your first email. Don't you remember?"

Ben shook his head. "It is a common rule for renters. Yes?"

"You mean you just threw it in there as an aside?" Nora rolled her eyes. "Jeez, Ben! I've been terrified about you finding out about these two. Now you're telling me it didn't matter?"

"Oh, it matters, Nora," said Ben. "It matters that you hid it from me. I don't appreciate being lied to."

She nibbled at her bottom lip. "Sometimes it's necessary to fudge the truth a little. To stave off hurt feelings. To make your stories a little more exciting. To avoid overdue library fees. But that's not what you mean."

Ben shook his head even though he got that she'd had her mixed-up reasons, reasons that made it hard for him to feel truly aggrieved.

Nora cleared her throat. "Then I'd better tell you that's how I broke the washing machine. Washing the dog blankets. There was so much fur. And maybe a tennis ball caught up in the folds. And a stick. And the old engine couldn't cope."

Ben's gaze shifted from the little dog and back to Nora. To those big blue eyes. And that face. Wide open. So lovely it made his gut clench.

But he knew Nora was feeling bad for having been caught, not having done the deed in the first place. In Ben's world, the difference was everything.

"Anything else?" he asked.

"Probably."

Ben laughed, unable to hold it back even if he'd tried.

Trouble, he thought and not for the first time.

And while that should have sent him to bed, alone, with a big caveat as to how much of himself he'd open up to this foxy, conflicting, singular woman, he moved in, placed his hands on Nora's cheeks, tilted her lovely face to his and kissed her.

It was the only way to be sure that no more fudged truths fell from her lips. For now.

Her mouth opened on a soft sigh of surprise, before one arm, then the other reached up to wrap around his neck as she lifted onto her toes and pressed her body against his as if she'd been waiting for eons to be able to do so again.

It was over before it started as they were joined by a bag of muscle and bone, with a tail like a leather whip, as Cutie jumped to join the embrace.

Nora pulled away laughing, her face flushed, her eyes bright, as she held the dog at bay with gentle shushing. Then, after shooting Ben a quick look of apology and bemusement, she dragged Cutie towards the laundry room.

Pie—who had somehow found a way down off the bench—now stood at Ben's feet. Looking at him. He reached down, slowly, and gave it its own scruff behind the ear.

After a beat, the dog harrumphed, turned, and headed into the laundry room as well.

When she came out, after having fed and locked up the dogs for the night, Ben was leaning back against kitchen bench. Whatever she saw in his face, she stopped, her hands clasped together in front of her.

"We should talk."

"Sounds ominous."

"Quite the opposite," he said, adding a smile. "There's no room in my life for fiction. Or secrets. Covering up is how my clients get themselves into trouble in the first place. And while I'm not prepared to talk about what happened between Clancy and me, suffice it to say it lies down that path."

Nora listened. Her expression was neither Stepford

Wife–blank, nor mischief and trouble. It was wary. Considering. And he wondered if he was finally getting a glimpse into a side of her she rarely showed.

Nora in her truth.

Ben pushed away from the bench, not letting the weight of that stop him in his current path. "I live in London. Soon you'll be heading off as well. The one thing bringing us together will be at an end and we'll likely never see one another again. Still, while we are here, together, I'd like to spend time with you. And I'd like to know how you feel about that."

Ben didn't move as he waited for her answer. For a breath, or three, while thoughts too fast to discern raged and stormed behind her eyes, he believed it might be a no.

"Temporary," she eventually said. "With the end in sight. Agreed upon. By the both of us."

He nodded.

"One condition," she said, her voice more strident now. "So long as I'm here, you continue helping out the locals with some financial advice."

Ben's right eye twitched. "Behind that sweet face of yours is the mind of a mercenary."

Her eyes narrowed.

"Fine," he said. "Then I have my own addendum. You stay as long as I need help sorting out Clancy's things." He looked around, felt the buzz of the past biting him on the back of the neck. "Truth is, I'm finding the idea a tad… overwhelming."

Her narrowed eyes softened, before filling with purpose. A smile nudged up a corner of her sweet mouth.

Say yes, his inner voice begged, *so I can kiss that spot as soon as humanly possible.*

"Deal," she said, then held out her hand.

He took it, using it to tug her to him, before lifting her

off her feet and into his arms. Kissing her till the world outside their door began to melt away.

"Where are you taking me?" Nora asked as he began to walk her down the hall.

"Your bed," he said. "Mine's too small for the plans I have."

"Promises, promises," she said, pulling back, to hold a hand to his cheek, her gaze following, before it landed back on his.

No guile therein. No faux innocence. No blank sweetness. No secrets. No lies.

Just Nora. The Nora he'd crossed oceans to find.

At the top of the stairs, he shoved her bedroom door open with a foot, and tossed her onto the bed. Both of them laughing. And he knew; if she could forgive him for not being there in what had to have been some of her darkest days, he could forgive her for hiding the truth about the dogs.

In the grand scheme of things, their ledger wasn't even close to even.

CHAPTER TEN

THE NEXT DAY, after he'd spent a couple of hours going over Damon's updates on the work done on the Metropolis account in his absence, making note as to where the team might put more eyes, Ben stood outside the sitting room, gaze pinging off the walls of books, overstuffed couches, floor rugs, throw cushions, baskets of dried flowers, knick-knacks on every surface, trying not to settle on any memories in particular lest they drown him.

"I've set up a few bags and boxes in the entrance, labelled donate, gift, sell, keep." Nora pulled up beside him, hands rubbing together, her voice bright, excited. "So, you want to start in here?"

Ben turned to her, slid an arm around her waist, pulled her close. "I'd rather start here," he growled. And then he kissed her.

Laughing against his mouth, she started to pull back, before her body stilled, softened, and rolled against his and she kissed him like a woman drowning.

And soon Ben was lost in far better memories—the taste of her skin, the way her body moved, lithe and fearless, the sounds she made as she fell apart in his arms.

"No," she said, slapping him on the chest. "Not now. Later. Consider it a reward for a job well done."

"Fine. How about you move your stuff first so it doesn't get mixed up?"

"My stuff is all upstairs. Fits into a single suitcase and a small backpack."

"Seriously?"

"Mmm-hmm. Can't be footloose and fancy-free if you're weighed down with baggage." She ran a thumb over the tattoo on her arm, as if it was some kind of touchstone. And proffered him one of her gentle smiles—the light, easy, unassuming type. The one that made him feel as though if he reached out for her, she wouldn't actually be there.

But if he was going to get through this today, and the next, he needed the real thing—the raw, dark, slippery smile he'd only ever seen her offer him.

"Should I be worried?" he asked. "Are you on the lam? Ready for a quick getaway? If you try to vamoose before I get through this, I will find you and bring you back."

At that she laughed, the sound low yet enormously compelling. "I'm not going anywhere." A shadow passed over her eyes. Then she shrugged. "I had to pack fast, a lot, as a kid. Circumstances tended to change quickly."

"A skill you might not have picked up otherwise," he said, happy to shift focus from himself for a moment. Or for ever.

"Correct! I also taught myself how to cook, knowing it would mean I'd always get fed."

"Brilliant. What else?"

"I can shape-shift to fit into different situations—loud, wholesome, alpha, nerdy. It really helps put different clients at ease."

That, Ben thought, a frisson of edginess creeping back in, that was the feeling he'd had the night before when he'd all but seen the masks slip into place. Cheeky and honest and brave. Sweet and sparkly and inoffensive. She was a chameleon.

Everyone was to some degree; Nora, perhaps, more than most. So long as that was all it was. Not that she was faking everything.

"Now," she said, before the silence grew awkward. "Let's do this!"

She padded into the sitting room, and stood in the middle, arms outstretched. All lanky legs and mismatched clothes. She looked so right, so part of the room, Ben's chest tightened.

Or maybe it was the fact that he'd delayed enough. He had to go in there. And clean up Clancy's mess.

"You could rent the house fully furnished. Or there's a local domestic violence shelter I've done some pro bono work for who would love anything you could give them. How about we focus on the keepsakes first? Start small. Tell mc, what do you remember most about this room?"

Ben's throat began to tighten, his mouth filling with the sharp tang of stale anger. He'd just come back from having drinks at the local pub with a couple of old school mates, when he'd found Clancy in this room. It had been summer, the fire grate empty. The room lit by a single lamp. She'd been holding a piece of paper. Tears pouring down her cheeks.

But when she'd looked up, he'd not seen sorrow in Clancy's eyes, he'd seen dread.

"Ben?" Nora weaved her way back to him.

When he didn't respond, his throat now thick with anger and regret, she reached out, curled her fingers into his.

"If I'm going too fast, or being too chipper, let me know," she said. "I told you, I'm a shape-shifter extraordinaire. Whoever you need for me to be, I can be."

Whoever he needed her to be.

The irony was suddenly so bitter he could taste it in the back of his throat.

Ben yanked his hand away. "I've got to go."

"Oh?" She blinked, confused. "Okay. Where?"

"Out." Away from here. Away from her.

He could feel her need to help, to fix, as if it were a physical thing. But he also felt as if he might stop breathing if he didn't get some air. If he didn't get out of that damn house.

He mumbled something about being back soon, and burst out of the room, out of the unlocked front door, and down the street, not even caring which direction he was going.

Nora sat staring out of the window from her upstairs bedroom. It was late afternoon and she'd heard nothing from Ben for hours.

She'd tried calling him with a bland excuse at the ready, only to track his ringtone—classic, no pop song for him—to the spare room. His suitcase sat neatly against the wall. Nothing unpacked. As if he didn't want to leave an impression on the place. She knew that move intimately, and it did not bode well.

He'd said he wasn't ready to talk about Clancy, but it had become clear there was some crack inside where that was concerned; unhealed, buffed over. Even now—if the look on his face was anything to go by—he was out there, in pain.

When she realised she was rubbing the heel of her palm over her ribs, right over her heart, in fact, Nora whipped her hand away.

This wasn't empathy she was feeling. It was something else entirely.

Despite his pretty words, his bold suggestion they "spend time together" until their job here was done, and despite her belief in that moment that she was fine with that, she'd been hasty.

She liked the man. More than avocado on toast. More than any man she'd ever known. She liked his smile, his laugh. She liked his self-awareness, his arrogance, his self-containment, his focus. She liked the way he looked at her, the way he kissed her, the way he never baulked whenever she was accidentally vulnerable.

What she didn't like was that, despite all that, he had the ability to hurt her without meaning to, or wanting to, just like the rest of them.

Either way she couldn't sit around waiting for him to come back. It was driving her nuts.

Padding down the stairs, she found Pie sitting at the front door, his little nose twitching as he stared at the patch of sunshine slicing through the mail slot. Turned out she wasn't the only one waiting for Ben to return.

Her heart—unguarded, unprepared—gave a twitch. Then a thump. And didn't quite go back to the same spot it had been before.

Muttering under her breath about toughening up, for Pete's sake, about keeping a clear head and staying the course, she shucked her feet into a pair of sandals, instructed both dogs to stay put, and headed out of the door.

Across the road, Misty was sitting on her stoop, blowing bubbles, as if that might bring in custom. Misty lifted her chin in greeting. "You guys disappeared like old smoke last night. Was sure I wouldn't see either of you for days."

"Funny. On that note, you seen Ben, by any chance?"

"Why?"

"He just… He went out in a bit of a hurry. And I want to make sure he isn't…lost, or something."

"Lost? A man that huge can't get lost." Misty stopped,

mid bubble blow, her eyes dancing over Nora's face. "Why did he leave in a bit of a hurry?"

"Ah… He's starting the clean-up of Clancy's stuff today. I'm helping."

"He's down with that?"

"Me helping?"

"Going through Clancy's stuff."

"I…hadn't asked." Nora remembered again the look on his face just before he'd left, and her heart squeezed in her chest. "It can't be fun, for anyone, but I truly believe this whole process will be good for him. Cathartic."

"Don't know about that. Some people like to reminisce. Others like to burn the past to the ground. You know what's truly cathartic? Those glowing cheeks of yours, the lopsided stride, the hickey on your neck."

Nora's hand went straight to the spot on her neck that Ben particularly liked to nibble.

Then Misty's eyes narrowed. "Looks like the man knows how to lead. Are you letting him do that? Or are you spreading your sunshine all over the place and hoping he'll do as he's told?"

Nora blinked. Gawped. Struggled to find an apt response.

Misty shook her head. "You're a smart cookie, Nora, and ridiculously compassionate. But you're a nuffy when it comes to the big stuff."

Nora crossed her arms. Then uncrossed them, not wanting to appear defensive. Or feel that way, to be honest. "What big stuff?"

"Ben Hawthorne is a big, important guy. He sorts out multinational conglomerates, business empires, small countries. He did not come all the way over here to sort out his grandmother's dress closet."

Misty waited, as if Nora might suddenly click her fingers and say, *I get it*. But she did not. Could not. Would not. Forcing Misty to shout, "Honey bun, the man came home for *you*."

Nora waited for the bluster and fluster of outrage to come over her. Instead, Misty's words uncurled beneath her defences, like a cat waking up and stretching after a long, luxurious nap in the sun.

"So take care," said Misty, "and give the man some credit, that's all I'm saying. Drinks tomorrow?"

Nora gave her a thumbs up before she turned and walked back towards home. Clancy's home. *Ben's* home. Not hers. She'd been a tenant, but now was merely a guest, at the mercy of Ben's pleasure. His choice, his decision, his lead.

Add the feelings she was feeling for the guy, feelings swirling through her, bumping into one another, making her feel hot, and flustered and nauseous, and she hadn't realised how little control she had over the whole situation until that moment.

Misty might have been right about some things, but she was wrong about the sunshine. Nora had thought she was deep in Sunshine Mode, but she'd been skirting the edges, letting Ben's ease, and strength, drag her towards the centre.

If she was going to get through the next couple of weeks in one piece, it was time to ramp things up.

Ben walked for hours, past new stores and old pubs, in search of air, space, and perspective. Or, at a pinch, a teleportation device that could take him back to London, a month or two before, when his life had been logical and straightforward and steady.

Before Clancy had died. Before he'd ever heard of *The Girl Upstairs*.

Hell, maybe he'd go back further, a couple of years

even, to before he'd found Clancy reading the letter over the empty fire grate in the sitting room. The letter telling her that Ben's birth mother had died.

Ben's birth mother who, as it had turned out, had also been Clancy's daughter.

Aida.

Aida, who'd left Ben on Clancy's doorstep when he was five years old. Aida, whom Clancy had told if she walked away she'd never be allowed to return. Aida, who'd been living in the world, for twenty-something years, without Ben's knowledge.

All of which he'd only discovered a week after Aida had died.

Clancy had lied to him. Outright. For years. Calling him her "adopted grandson", which, she'd later argued, was mostly true. The grandmother part, not the adopted part. As if that justified what she'd done.

She'd taken from him the chance to meet his mother. Even when he was a grown man, she'd kept it from him. She'd been so stubborn and sure of herself.

By the time Ben finished walking, the sun had begun to set and the early evening chill started to cut through his clothes. The streetlamps created pools of golden light up and down the block and the house—his grandmother's house—looked down at him, all but daring him to make a decision already.

Sell me. Rent me. Move in. Give me away. Burn me to the ground. Walk away and never look back.

The only decision Ben made was to go inside, as Nora would be there, and that was as far as he could think.

Music played softly from Clancy's old radio in the kitchen. The dogs lay splayed out on a blanket in the entrance—the little one's tail wagged as it saw him, the big one snored through.

Nora sat curled up on the big, soft couch in the sitting room; a blanket wrapped about her shoulders, a book in her lap. The fire flickering behind the grate sent long shadows about the room, making her skin look warm to the touch.

Even at this distance he could feel her in the air. As if she mucked with his perspective on a cellular level. Despite his assurances, to her and himself, there was no way he was getting out of this thing unscathed. The only part of the story left untold was whether it would be his doing, or hers.

He must have made a sound as she spun on the chair and looked up, those big blue eyes of hers luminous in the low light, and shadowed with worry. For him. The guy people came to when they were in trouble. It was a hell of a thing.

"Hey," she said, her voice soft, rough from under-use. Then she closed her book gently, using her finger as a bookmark. "Want a cuppa?"

"No. Thank you. I'm good. I grabbed something when I was out."

She uncurled her legs, as if to make room for him. He moved into the room, for the first time in over two years. And he sat. The ancient springs tilted them both towards the centre. Towards one another.

Smiling still, all sweetness and light, she held up her book. *"Jane Eyre."*

"Ah."

"Have you read it?"

"I have, actually. A long time ago. Rite of passage, growing up here. All a bit dramatic for my taste."

Nora laughed, the sound simplifying everything and creating a quickening inside him, all at once. "I know, right? But Clancy adored it. Was it the drama, or the house, or was there a tragic love affair in her past; a Rochester of her own?"

He was aware Nora was making conversation in order

to alleviate whatever tension had sent him running in the first place, but she had no idea she'd just stumbled over the exact reason he'd wanted to be anywhere but here.

Clancy. Love. Affairs. Family. The lies binding them together.

Nora moved, the blanket dropping away to reveal a loose T-shirt hanging off one shoulder. He knew how fast he could lose himself in that soft warmth of her neck. How it would make all of the noise in his head disappear.

Wanting her because he wanted her was biology. Using her to block out the ghosts in his head was an ass move. He sat forward instead, letting his head fall into his hands.

"Dammit," she said, her voice velvet soft, a little edgy. "I was trying so hard not to push. But it's what I do. You don't have to tell me anything. Or do any of the things I suggest. I have thick skin, Ben, so please, don't be afraid to tell me to shut up. Or back off. Or leave."

"Don't," Ben said, the word busting out of him.

"Don't...ask?"

"Don't leave. Not yet."

He heard Nora's sharp intake of breath beside him, before she eventually whispered, "I'm right here."

Then she reached out, her hand landing on his knee, in nothing but comfort. But the scent of her, the warmth, the sincerity, the complexity, knocked about the empty spaces inside him. Begging to be let in. To fill him up. To help him forget.

He clenched his jaw hard enough he heard a crack.

"If you're keen on sticking with the strong, silent thing," she said, "more power to you. You wear it well. But the best thing about me is that I'm nothing to you. A firefly flittering past in the night. Whatever you tell me goes with me. If that helps at all."

Ben lifted his head from the cage of his hands and turned her way.

She was so still. So calm. Her focus, complete. The power of it, of her, when she wasn't putting on a show, when she was simply being, was staggering. And she had no idea.

"You are not nothing, Nora."

Her recoil was infinitesimal, but he felt it. "I'm sorry?"

"You, Nora Letterman, are not nothing."

Her eyes sparked with defiance. "*That's* not what I meant. Of course, I'm not *nothing*. I'm amazing! What I meant to say was, in the grand scheme of things, I'm unimportant to you."

Ben slowly sat up straight. "I'm not sure where you're getting your news, Nora, but you are *not* nothing, and you are not unimportant to me. If you were, you would not be sitting here, beside me, in Clancy's house, with your hand on my knee."

She pulled her hand away as if burnt.

He caught it; brought it back to his side of the couch. Cupped both of his larger hands around hers. Felt her fingers curl into his palm.

She shook her head, but didn't pull away. "Everything's coming out wrong. My point is, none of this is meant to be about me. This, me being here, sticking around, this is all about you. Helping you."

For a long fraught moment her eyes remained stuck on his. He felt as if he were falling into her, till he could feel all of her parts—the fire and smarts and savvy and insecurity, the sensitivity and the blinders, the damage and the heart.

Eventually, she said, "I'm sorry, but I'm struggling here. You won't tell me what happened between you and Clancy, but you want me to trust that you're a good guy in all this, even though Clancy is…*was* one of the loves of my life. You want to stay, to help, but now you don't want that? What is it you want from me, Ben?"

"Nora, just give me a minute."

After a moment, Nora gently tugged her hand free and tucked it back, safe, into the folds of her blanket and said, "Okay."

Ben coughed out a humourless laugh. He didn't do this—talk, share, self-examine. But somehow this complicated creature had unravelled him without even trying. Forced him to think about things he'd kept locked up for years. Clancy, his mother, his loss, on both counts. Till the ropes that held him together felt frayed, and untethered, unrecognisable.

He had to let some of it out or he'd explode. Could he tell her about Clancy? About the falling out, or the feeling he had as to why Clancy had taken on a tenant for the first time in her life, his suspicion that she'd known she was sick a long time before she let on?

No. It would break Nora's heart. And he knew her enough to know there was a very good chance she'd shoot the messenger. Perhaps he could lead her there, gently. Help her figure it out on her own. It wasn't a lie. He was protecting her.

And if that wasn't the most ironic moment of his entire life, he wasn't sure what was.

He glanced across, found the fire playing over her hair, her face, her eyes, like a rainbow caused by sunlight slicing through a crystal. Her eyes were bright, restive. If he felt laid bare, it was clear she did too.

He held her gaze as he said, "It's been a rough few weeks."

"Yep."

"But through it all, you've been the lighthouse in the

storm. A warm voice at the end of some bitterly cold days. The cream in my coffee."

She swallowed. "And there I was thinking I was a pain in your ass."

"That too." A smile settled on his mouth. She did that. It was a gift. He bumped her knee with his, then left it there. "If you really want to help me, Nora, I don't need advice, or a nudge, or to be pushed. I can do what needs to be done. If you really want to help, all I need is for you to be you."

She pressed her knee more fully against his, and said, "That might just be the most spectacularly lovely thing anyone has ever said to me." Her brow furrowed before smoothing. "And that's not me being cute, or sassy, or… whatever. I mean it."

He smiled.

She smiled.

Then her blanket slipped again, tugging her top with it so he got an eyeful of warm creamy shoulder, a whole lot of décolletage and the truth colouring what *else* he wanted from her twisted all over again.

Ben pressed his hands to his knees and stood. "With that," he said on the back of an old-man groan, "I'm going to head to bed early tonight. I am officially dead on my feet."

Nora wrapped the blanket tighter around herself as she stood, her bare feet curling into the rug, the glowing embers creating dips and shadows on her lovely face. "Sure. Good plan. Smart. I'll head up too. Alone. To my room. Keep the place quiet for you. Goodnight, Ben."

"Goodnight, Nora."

With that she ducked out of the room, her voice calling softly for the dogs to follow. Which they did, the little one giving Ben a forlorn glance, almost as if it was disappointed in him for not following as well.

I hear ya, buddy, he thought. Then he trudged down the hall to his old room, running both hands over his face as if trying to make the skin fit.

He nudged off his shoes, tugged his jumper over the back of his head, ready to fall on top of the bed and sleep for a year. Then, when he turned on the bedside lamp, he saw a book on the side table.

A copy of *Jane Eyre*, sporting a Post-it note reading, *Read me!* with a little picture of Alice in Wonderland sketched into the corner.

He recognised it instantly as Clancy's copy. The spine faded, pages all but falling apart. He opened the book to find it soft, well-read, dog-eared, with notes in the margin, in Clancy's tiny handwriting; exclamation marks, smiley faces, sighs. A big circle around the first mention of Thornfield Hall.

He could picture the book on side tables, in Clancy's gnarled hands, face down on the hall table. Could feel Clancy's love for high drama, for romance, for her friends, for this house, and for him, as patent as if she were right beside him.

With no plan in mind, Ben headed back out into the hall and through the kitchen to find Nora at the bottom of the stairs, the blanket still wrapped around her shoulders. One foot was on the floor, the other crooked, as if she was heading down and not up.

Her eyes were huge, luminous in the low light as she whispered, "The book."

Ben held it up.

Her sweet face fell. "Of course, I put it there *before* you said all you said about not wanting my brand of help." She let her hovering foot fall to the floor beside the other one. "But I still feel like a goose. I'm so sorry."

Ben took another step her way. "You have nothing to apologise for."

"I'm pushy."

"You're wonderful. And I'm a cranky bastard. And you're wonderful."

Her mouth fell open in a half-smile. "You might have mentioned that already."

"Bears mentioning twice."

Her throat worked. Her eyes were dark and beguiling. A tug of war being fought behind their depths. When they caught on his, they captured him whole.

"Ben, can I…?" She took a step his way, her hand trailing over the wallpaper. "Can I ask you something? Just one small thing. Something Misty said today—"

"What's that?"

"Actually, forget it."

Ben ambled several slow steps closer, his blood hastening in his veins at the way she watched him. His breaths deepening as he neared. "Nora, not all that many minutes ago I heard myself call you the cream in my coffee like some spotty seventeen-year-old writing bad song lyrics in his bedroom. There is nothing you can say that will top that."

She laughed, the sound husky and raw. "Don't be so sure. Misty suggested today that the reason you've yet to do any of the things I thought you came here to do is that you didn't come back here for Clancy's sake. That you actually came back here for me."

Her eyes fluttered, full of tenderness and doubt. The readiness to be shot down. The complete lack of faith in her own drawing power.

The people in her past, who'd had the chance to know her, to love her, but instead made her feel so unworthy, deserved to be quartered.

Clancy had given him *that* at least. Safety, laughter, and confidence, and the assuredness that whatever he wanted to do with his life, it was his for the taking.

He slowed to a stop. Maybe he couldn't give her the dirty truth, but he could give her this. "You know how little I wanted to be here."

Her nostrils flared, ever so slightly.

"You know I'd have let the place sit, untouched, unwatched, for who knows how long, before I found the wherewithal to deal with it. So then, you must know, the only reason I'm here, now, at all, is because of you."

Nora's eyes were now huge in the half-light. "Ben—"

Ben stepped into her space, reached out, trapping her cheek in his palm.

She leaned into it, her eyes dropping half closed, her brow furrowing, before she seemed to gather herself, lifting her face free from his touch.

"Just… The reason I asked… I can't…"

"I know," he said, his voice gentle. He didn't want to spook her. He wanted to kiss her, and hold her, and exalt her.

"It's not you. You're gorgeous. And successful. And so sure of yourself. While I'm… I'm stronger than I'm sounding right now. But it's taken work to get here. I know I'm not nothing. I do. But I *have* nothing to offer. Apart from this. Being here. Helping you find a way back to Clancy."

Ben reached out for her hand, turned it over so he could see her tattoo. Ran his thumb over the words: *Footloose and fancy-free.*

She believed it too. She'd have to, in order to engrave it into her skin. Problem was, seeing her curled up on the couch, by the fire, book in hand, all rugged up in a soft blanket, dogs at her feet, to Ben she'd looked…

She'd looked like home.

Ben tossed the book onto the nearby hall table.

When he looked back at her, the blanket was falling from her shoulders as she was all but vibrating.

"So, you think I'm gorgeous, do you?"

She rolled her eyes. "I don't become pen pals with just anyone, you know. There's gotta be something in it for me."

"Stop your sweet nothings," he murmured, moving closer. "I might get ideas."

Her hand lifted to rest against his chest. Right over the now thunderous beat of his heart. She was close enough he could happily have drowned in the clean tangy sweetness of her scent. In the silken fall of her hair.

Her eyes lifted heavily to his. Drugged with heat. Need.

"So we're clear. It can't mean anything," she said with a half-hearted press of her hand.

Too late, thought Ben. *It already does.*

He kissed her and she threw herself into his arms. Bodily. Up on her tiptoes, her hands flung around his neck. Her eyes slammed closed and she kissed him back.

He felt the shudder of her breath. As if she'd heard the words he'd not been able to say and they'd loosened all kinds of things inside her. As if she needed him to hold her together, just as she'd been holding him together.

Bending, he slid an arm behind her knees and swept her off her feet, literally, and carried her up the stairs to her tower.

When he slid her gently, preciously, to the floor, she pushed him back onto her bed.

The old mattress bounced and shifted beneath his weight as Nora crawled on her knees towards him.

He let her think she was in control, till she was over the top of him, her hair sweeping the pillow beside him. Then with a growl he flipped her over, catching her laughter with a kiss that sent bursts of something that felt a hell of a lot like pure and simple joy right through him.

And then, after a day of trying to find something, an answer, a path, a plan, he gave up, gave in, and lost himself in her, all night long.

Nora was mindful to remember herself as they continued making their way through the house. Tidying. Cataloguing. Bagging. Stopping if Ben looked as if he might implode, such as when they happened upon Clancy's well-thumbed collection of *Men's Health* magazines. Or when Nora had found a box of cookbooks in the back of the pantry.

Nora started putting out feelers as to where she might end up next. And made sure to spend decent time on finalising her local client work, and posted plenty on her own Instagram page—fun, friendly shots for the Pizza Place, dark, moody, come-get-me vibes for Shenanigans, a most adorable picture of Ben nose to nose with Pie while tagging Playful Paws Puppy Rescue. Because how could she not?

And while, in that one inexplicably lovely moment, Ben had said "all I need is for you to be you," she knew, in her heart of hearts, what they both needed was closure.

So Nora told stories from the last couple of years, trying, gently, to fill in the blanks, to build a bridge back to wherever things had fallen apart between Ben and his adopted grandmother.

In an immensely satisfying move, Ben started telling stories of his own. First there was the calculator he'd found on her bookshelves. He told her how he'd loved the thing so much he used to sleep with it at night. Then there was the fire poker with the missing tip. A fight between Luke Skywalker—Ben—and the Emperor—Clancy—was to blame for that one.

Then there was the subtle easing of his furrowed brow.

The way he whistled when making their morning coffees while she buttered their toast. He even spent one whole day in his striped flannelette pyjamas. Man, he looked fine in those things; especially when he ditched the top and padded around barefoot in only the pants.

There was also the lack of hesitation in taking her hand and curling her in for a kiss any time they ended up in the same space for longer than a minute. The way he lingered when kissing the top of her head as he passed her in the kitchen, his arm slung around her shoulder, almost as if he were breathing her in.

A small part of her wondered if it all had more to do with her than the house, but there was no point in going down that path.

When night fell, they often ate in, Nora cooking, as she was good at it and loved the way he hummed when he ate the things she made. Ben, on the other hand, was no cook. "Like grandmother, like grandson," she'd said, to which he'd smiled a little tightly. But it was still nice to discover he wasn't brilliant at everything.

And while every day that Nora stayed was another day on the wrong side of leaving, every day also added more strands to the web from which she'd have to disentangle herself when she eventually did go.

She consoled herself with the fact that the memories she was making, and tucking carefully away, were the kind that would keep her warm for a long, long time.

CHAPTER ELEVEN

A KNOCK SOUNDED at the front door.

Nora looked up from her spot at her laptop by the window to find rain creating rivulets down the window. Huh, it was the first time she remembered seeing rain in weeks.

Ben—asleep and snoring on her bed, arms akimbo, big feet poking out the ends, which had made her inordinately happy for some bizarre reason she had no plan on going into—didn't stir.

Another knock, and what sounded like a "Yoo-hoo!" floating up from downstairs, had Nora leaping from her chair, wrapping a cardigan around her shoulders, and padding down the stairs, Cutie and Pie in tow.

The dogs disappeared into the back of the house—Pie in search of a hidey hole, Cutie in cahoots with Pie—while Nora found a cacophony of older women piling into the foyer. Umbrellas dripping, shaking water droplets all over the floor, they forced Nora back up the stairs.

"Uh…ladies?" Nora said, gripping the railing.

Phyllis—the holder of the spare key, and Clancy's oldest friend, as well as being the doctor who'd been with Nora during Clancy's last days—gave Nora an apologetic smile. "Sorry, love, you weren't answering the door. And there was really no stopping them."

Beryl gave Nora a mutinous glare. "It was Clancy's turn, you see."

"So here we are!" Janet added, waving a book and a bottle of wine.

Sylvia followed. Then Carol. Misty came last, shut the door behind her and shooed everyone deeper into the house.

"Widows' Book Club," Nora realised.

"Yup," said Misty. "Do you still have that bottle of Scotch Clancy opened last time we were here?"

Nora muttered, "A heads up might have been nice."

Misty shrugged, rubbed her hands together, and grinned. "Where's your dastardly landlord?"

It took all of Nora's powers not to glance towards the stairs, where she'd left Ben, face down, naked atop her sheets.

"You okay, honey?" asked Beryl. "You look a little flushed."

"I'm fine. Just great." She angled herself behind the noisy group and hustled them into the sitting room, a couple already sitting on the couch on which she and Ben, just the night before, had—

The women stopped as one, eyes lifting, as if sensing a shimmer in the air, a rush of testosterone flowing through the house, just before Ben's heavy footsteps sounded on the stairs.

"Nora? I thought I heard—" Ben walked into the entrance to the sitting room still tugging his moss-coloured Henley T over his jeans.

"Oh, if it isn't little Ben Hawthorne!" said Phyllis, breaking the loaded silence, her arms stretched out as if for a hug. "They said you were back but I didn't believe it!"

Ben—whether by way of politeness, or habit, or instinct—held out his arms and gathered her in. "Hey, Dr Rand."

Over the top of the doctor's head, Ben's gaze caught on

Nora, eyebrows lifting at the situation in which he found himself. Nora simply shrugged. Not enough fairy dust in the world to help him now.

"That man ain't little by any stretch of the imagination," a dismembered voice whispered somewhere behind Nora.

"I hear that," murmured another.

"Who is he?" asked the whisperer.

"Clancy's grandson."

"Oh. I thought they'd fallen out after he found out she was—"

"That's the one."

"Ladies!" said Phyllis, making Nora jump as her ears had been so attuned to the whispers behind her. She'd told herself Ben and Clancy's past was none of her business. But clearly her curiosity was still piqued.

One arm still around Ben's waist, Phyllis said, "Everyone, this is Ben, Clancy's grandson." With that she did introductions all round, finishing with Nora. "Nora, you know Ben? Of course, you must. You're staying here. And he's staying here."

"Um, yep."

Phyllis's eyes opened a fraction wider before glancing towards the stairs. "And… I think it's time we eat?"

Food. If anything was to distract a room full of octogenarian widow book-clubbers from possible sexual intrigue, it was food.

"Settle in. Leave it to me," said Nora, most glad to slip out of the room, with all the unspoken questions hanging over her.

"I'll help," a deep voice rumbled behind her.

She made it into the kitchen before she turned to find Ben standing before her. The top buttons of his Henley were undone, a shadow of dark hair peeking out of the top. Her favourite jeans of his moulded to his strong legs. His feet were bare.

"Hi," she said, her voice barely more than a breath.

"We have visitors."

"The Widows' Book Club. It's Clancy's turn to host."

"Of course it is." His face creased into a long, slow smile, still soft with sleep. With stubble covering his jaw he looked good. He looked happy.

"Teacups!" she said, her voice cracking. "Trays. Do you remember where Clancy kept the—?"

She turned to find Ben with a pair of Wedgwood platters in hand.

"It's all right with you if they stay for a bit?"

"Of course," he said, moving to kiss her, lightly, as he slid a hand under the centre of the tray of cookies she was holding and took it out of her hands. "I'll take this in before they start eating the furniture. I've come to like that sofa and would hate to see it disappear."

The flush flowing through her turned her up to eleven, even as he left her alone in the kitchen.

By the time she collected herself, and enough plates and napkins for the group, Ben had settled into the single armchair in front of the fire.

Nora perched on the edge of the sofa near the entrance, as glasses and cups were raised to Clancy. Then the Widows' Book Club moved on to talking about the books they'd read: everything from self-help, to horror, to young adult romance.

Before long, the women began to creak and groan and rearrange themselves in their chairs, and start muttering about heading home, making her wonder if they'd come for tea and cake and books, or if they'd come to check out little Ben Hawthorne.

Nora, with Ben's okay, told them to raid Clancy's bookshelves, to take as many as they liked.

Phyllis gave her a hug on the way out. "Again, apologies. Lovely to see you looking so well though, love."

Nora felt the tears burning the backs of her eyes all too late. "Thank you."

"Bennett," Janet said, her voice carrying. "Your falling out was the one great regret of Clancy's life. Well, that and losing Gerald, of course."

"Thank goodness for Nora," said Beryl. "Gave your grandmother such joy in the last couple of years. A distraction from her broken heart."

Nora glanced back to find Ben seemed to have developed a tic in his cheek muscle. He murmured something conciliatory, but Nora missed the details as Misty stepped in her path.

"Hey."

"Hey."

"Nice book club."

"Thanks?"

"Shall I stay and help clean up? Or do you have plans for the leftover whipped cream?" Misty tipped her head sideways, in Ben's direction.

Nora held the front door open wide. "There was no whipped cream."

"Check again," said Misty, bringing a tube out of her bag and forcing Nora to take it.

Nora whipped the whipped cream behind her back as they turned to find Ben in the arch of the sitting room, arms crossed, big body holding up the wall.

"Being good, Hawthorne?" Misty asked.

Ben grinned. Nora swooned. Misty turned to Nora with a grin, blew her a kiss and was gone.

Nora slowly shut the door behind her, then turned, leant

back on the wood, closed her eyes, and breathed out. She opened one eye, then the next, to find Ben still leaning in the doorway to the sitting room. Looking at her in a way she hadn't seen before.

As if he were seeing her for the first time.

"They're lovely," she said, "but, gosh, they're a whirlwind."

"You held them hostage with muffins."

"I did not. You're making me sound like Little Red Riding Hood."

He clicked his fingers at her as he followed her into the kitchen. "That's exactly it. You head off into the woods, muffins in tow, looking after everyone—the widows, the local shopkeepers, Misty. Does it occur to them that you might need someone to bring muffins to you once in a while?"

"Why would I need muffins when I'm perfectly capable of making my own?" said Nora, wondering how they'd suddenly become so caught up on muffins.

Ben plucked a tea towel from the bench and tugged it through his fingers, again and again. "You're missing the point."

"Which is?"

Ben paused, as if considering whether or not to go on. Whatever he saw in her face decided it for him. "You wanted to help me make peace with Clancy. I want to make sure, when you leave, you don't let the next lot take advantage of you."

Nora shot Ben a look. "Excuse me?"

Ben ran a hand over his face. "I'm going about this all wrong. It's just, watching the dynamic in that room, watching you with Clancy's friends, I wondered, and not for the first time, if Clancy treated you the same way."

Nora coughed out a breath. Then, trying really hard to

tap into her well of sunshine, she came up empty. Which meant the only place to turn was Survival Mode.

"If I'm Little Red Riding Hood, surely Clancy was the sweet old grandmother. So that only leaves the big bad wolf."

"Come on, Nora. Clancy was no sweet old grandmother."

Ben was right. Clancy was mad and obstinate and opinionated, but she balanced that out with the ferocity of her support. *But what if...?* Nora suddenly thought. *What might make her take that support away?*

"Why didn't she tell you she was sick?"

Ben breathed out hard through his nose.

"Because you didn't call her, right?"

"It was her turn to call me."

"That's your excuse. It was her turn? Who takes turns calling family? If she missed a call, why didn't you reach out?"

"You don't think I've asked myself the same thing every damn day since?"

As Ben's words echoed in the kitchen, Nora's ire dropped a good ten degrees.

This was *Ben*. Lovely Ben. Measured Ben. The man she… She trusted, and respected, and liked a hell of a lot. Like-liked. Was *like-like-liked* a thing? It should be.

"How did this go from muffins to a battle?" she asked.

Ben gave her a measured look, and said, "Clancy. That's how."

"I know you guys had issues, but Clancy was good to me. She didn't take advantage of me. We found one another at the perfect time in our lives and I'd not change a single second of it. Not even those final weeks."

"Do you have any idea how sweet you are?" said Ben, turning to face her.

"Pfft. I'm not sweet. I'm tough. I'm smart. I choose my actions. I choose my responses. I'm in charge."

He tossed the tea towel to the bench and held out both hands as if about to hold her by the upper arms, but instead he hovered, just out of reach. "Why didn't you get the alarm on the house sorted?"

"What does that—?"

"The alarm. When I asked you to send Damon details of the alarm company so we could get it connected, why did you resist?"

"Because it was unnecessary. I was fine!"

"I've done a lot of walking since I've been back and this area is riddled with graffiti. I've seen baggies beside bins in the park. Sirens whiz by three times a night."

"That's life in the big city."

"The back door doesn't lock properly."

"No one knows that, except you."

Ben shook his head, ever so slightly, a glint of something warm, and tender, yet serious, behind his bottomless dark eyes. *Like-like-like-like* pulsed through Nora's head like an anthem.

"I know you are no pushover, Nora, but that doesn't mean you have to act as if you're indestructible. That if you own up to even a modicum of fragility, you'll be hit from all sides by a fleet of Mack trucks."

If only he knew he was the Mack truck. That she was struck, and continued to be struck, every day she knew him.

"Can't a girl simply like muffins?" she asked, grateful to find words that didn't make her look like the puddle she'd become.

As if he knew she needed a little extra fortification, he laid his hands on her, resting, warm and secure on her upper arms. Then he pulled her in, his arms sliding around her shoulders. Hers—oh, so naturally—slid around his back.

"I didn't mean to upset you, Nora. I just want you to know that you deserve more than people in your past might have led you to believe you deserve."

"I know."

"Promise me you'll learn to say no."

"No."

His laughter rolled through her like a summer storm, fast and invigorating.

Nora tilted her head so the side of her face pressed up against Ben's chest. She'd have pressed deeper, pressed till all of herself was up against all of him if it were physically possible.

Because while it was something she'd spent her entire adult life telling herself she'd never crave, never need, never find, she knew what *like-like-like-like* meant. And now she'd felt it, now it was a part of her, she knew she had to hold on to it as tightly as she could, soaking up every skerrick, until it was taken away.

When Ben lifted his arm, she might have whimpered just a little. When he used a finger to tilt her face, when he smiled down at her before laying his mouth over hers, the whimper turned into a sigh.

Later, as she lay back in Ben's arms in her big, soft bed, her leg curled over his, her fingers making tracks through the hair on his chest as he checked his phone for work emails, her mind tracked back over the conversations of the day.

Little Red Riding Hood amongst other things. Ben lounging in the doorway. Ben tensing any time talk strayed to his relationship with Clancy. Ben intimating that he thought Clancy might have taken advantage of her good nature.

He cared. He felt protective towards her. That much was clear.

But some bigger part of the conversation felt undone. As

if she'd missed an opportunity to get to the bottom of it all. For while Ben had seen to the very heart of her, over and over again, been witness to every one of her insecurities, she still had no clue why Ben and Clancy had fallen out.

It had to be intentional. Was he just that hard to crack? Or was it that she wasn't the kind of person people ever let close? Not when she was pushy and brazen, or since she'd learnt how to be sunshiny and soft.

While she'd spent years telling herself it didn't matter, that it was okay, that she could cope, it turned out she was lying to herself the whole time.

It hurt. It hurt so bad.

Nora yawned, scrubbing some life into her scalp as she flicked through her morning emails. When she opened the third, her jaw all but dislocated when it fell open in shock.

It was a job offer, by way of a competition she'd entered. Six months working at a resort in Far North Queensland on a social-media takeover. She'd be paid, and pretty well too, for experiencing every adventure the region had to offer, and posting about it.

It was the opportunity of a lifetime for a fledgling social-media sort like her. And it started two weeks from now.

Nora glanced quickly towards the en suite when she heard the shower turn on. And had the strange sense that it was something she ought to discuss with Ben.

But no. No discussions. This was her thing. Alone. And the timing could not have been more perfect.

Because she had fallen in love with Ben Hawthorne.

He, on the other hand, clearly had no clue, trundling around the house with the exact same comportment as the day they'd met: with grace, and strength, and a locked box where his heart should be.

She must have made a noise, or was sending anxious

waves into the universe, as Cutie lifted his head from his position on the end of her bed. Pie, snuggled up beside him, slept through, not giving a jot as to Nora's cares.

"It's okay," she said, and Cutie cocked his head. "In fact, it's brilliant. The universe has pointed the way to my next adventure. Great news, huh?"

Cutie shook his head and snuffled—a goodly amount of saliva flying across the room and landing on the wall, the floor, a lamp—then he lay back down and closed his eyes.

She shook her head too, managing to keep all saliva locked away, then read over the email one more time.

The packing list was laptop, beachwear, and a six-month supply of sunscreen. Even less than her usual minimalist fare. And she already owned a kaftan! Slow lifestyle, sunshine, impermanent population; it was the polar opposite of the bustling community that she'd spent her last year and a half falling in love with. The perfect cathartic cleansing.

A sound came from the bathroom. It was Ben. Humming. No, *singing*, in the shower—"Blue Moon", no less—that hot, deep, sexy voice of his terribly out of tune. And she had to admit, he wasn't *exactly* the same man he'd been when he'd shown up at Clancy's front door. He walked the place in bare feet, eating peanut butter from the jar, lying back on the too small couch with his feet over the arm rest. All things happy people did. People who felt content. Comfortable.

But still, not lovesick.

Meaning her job here was done.

She pressed *reply* and began to type an effusive yes, but then stopped herself. There was no need to be rash. First she'd read the fine print. Figure out her finances. Check if there was a non-compete clause. Would she be able to keep *The Girl Upstairs* going at the same time? The exposure would be fabulous, but she didn't want to leave her current clients in the lurch.

With that, slowly, achingly slowly, she closed her laptop. Stood. Wiped dry palms down the sides of her shorts.

When Ben's phone lit up the caller was listed as *World's Best Assistant*. Damon. *Ha.*

When Ben started up "Smoke Gets in Your Eyes", after a half-second hesitation, she answered.

"Hey, Damon."

A beat, then, "Nora? That you?"

"'Tis me."

"Well, what do you know? The boss man around?"

The humming from the shower continued. "He's indisposed. Can I pass on a message?"

"I guess. But first where is he, and why are you answering his phone?"

"None of your business, boyo."

"I know you say that, but I feel as if I was a big part of getting the two of you together—"

"We're not together." They weren't. They really weren't. But the thought of *actually* leaving him made Nora's heart clutch.

"Right," said Damon, the tone of his voice making it clear he didn't actually believe her either. "My message is twofold. First, he wanted the name of some local real estate agents. Do you have a pencil?"

"Ah…"

"Long sticky-looking thing you can write things down with?"

"Got it." Nora grabbed a pencil, while her mind quietly spun about in even more frantic circles.

"Okay, this company had the best rep when it came to honest valuations," said Damon, naming a local group.

Valuations? Valuation meant *selling.* Was Ben selling

Thornfield Hall and hadn't mentioned it to her? *Just like you planned to move to Far North Queensland without discussing it with him?*

"Not the same thing."

"What's that, now?" Damon asked.

"Nothing. I've got it."

Yeah, she got it all right. Ben was selling Thornfield Hall and he hadn't deemed it something she might like to know. Just as he'd made a concerted effort not to tell her why he was still so upset with Clancy. Damon knew the former. Everyone else around her seemed to know the latter. Leaving her on the outside, looking in. Again.

"What was the other thing?"

Damon paused. "You know what, I'll save that one for when he calls back."

Nora's phone rang. She glanced at it as she said, "Are you sure?"

"I'm sure," said Damon. "Thanks. Make good choices!"

"You bet," she sing-songed before hanging up, out of habit rather than any real sense of sunshine, as her well seemed to have completely dried up.

Her phone rang again. She answered, "The Girl Upstairs."

"Hey, Nora? It's Gemma from Playful Paws. Good news! We've found a home for Cutie and Pie! A young couple on the Peninsula. Big yard. Near the beach. She has a small business making baby food, works from home."

Nora slowly sat on the bed.

"Oh!" said Nora, her gaze flicking to the patchy, scratchy, bitsy dogs curled up on the end of her bed.

Gemma went on, "The photo you put on your Insta went crazy. We had so many expressions of interest we were able to pick and choose where they are going. Though, it has to be said, several of the phone calls were expressions of interest in the guy."

The guy being Ben. Eyes crinkled, huge smile on his face, as he crouched down to make eye contact with Pie. Cutie in the background, head cocked. *The Girl Upstairs* knew how to sell "likeable" like no one else.

She ran a hand over her eyes, as they suddenly felt gritty and so very tired. "I'm so happy. They sound…perfect."

Suddenly the singing stopped. Then the shower. Then Nora's heart seemed to give up right along with it.

She smacked herself in the chest. Then said, "Sorry, I have to zoom. Message me the details and I'll make sure they're ready to go when you're ready to take them."

"Will do. Thanks again, Nora. You're the best. We literally could not have done this without you."

Nora hung up without saying goodbye, her throat too tight to form anything other than some kind of strangled grunt.

To think that where she used to hear, "You're a lot, Nora. Too loud. Too much," now she heard, "You're the best. We literally could not have done this without you." So why did it feel like the same thing?

"Nora?"

Nora jumped out of her skin.

"You still here?"

She bit her lip to keep the ever so slightly hysterical laugh to herself, then managed, "Yep. I'm still here."

"Good. Now take your clothes off, because I have plans!"

The door swung open and with it came a waft of steam, and Ben; towel slung low around his waist, a pair of water droplets sliding down his buff chest, water making his eyelashes tangle and curl.

Her heart squeezed at the sight of him. At the love that swirled about her insides like brandy on a cold night. She'd never imagined love could ache like this. But when it was only one way, it hurt like crazy.

If only she'd never made that promise to Clancy that she'd look after the house till the new owner took it off her hands. She would have never heard of Ben Hawthorne. Never have reached out. Never have emailed, or rung, or video-chatted. Never have cajoled him into coming back. Never have met him, kissed him, snuggled up to him on the couch, made love to him. Seen him in that towel.

Never have spent the last few weeks with a pair of butty dogs, and a house to call home and…and the man she loved sleeping in her bed. She'd never have lived the dream she'd never dared have.

Or lost it all in one fell swoop.

"Why are you still dressed?" he asked.

And when he lifted an eyebrow, his mouth quirking adorably, Nora burst into tears.

CHAPTER TWELVE

NORA THOUGHT IT safest to let Ben think her meltdown was about the dogs.

At which point he took over. Completely. Which, actually, was a blessed relief as the afternoon had completely sapped her. She could barely remember what sunshine even felt like, much less conjured up enough to put on a brave face.

Ben gave them both a last bath—Cutie in the yard, Pie in the laundry sink, his eyes glinting lovingly at Ben the entire time. He gathered their toys, washed their bedding, didn't get upset when the newly fixed washing machine broke once again. Not once did he look at her sideways, or make a big deal of the fact that she sat on the floor watching and crying. Crying as if she might never stop.

Then it was over. Gemma came around in a cute little pink van with the Playful Paws logo on the side. And—with Ben and Nora's help—loaded Cutie, Pie and all the paraphernalia they had collected over the past few weeks into the back.

"I travel lighter than they do," Nora managed.

Ben stepped up beside her, put a strong, warm arm around hers shoulders, and kissed her atop her head. "You're not giving them up," he said as Gemma beeped the horn and raced away. "You were a warm, kind, protective space, readying them for their for-ever family. They'd never have found one another, if not for your patience and your kindness."

Her love for the guy doubled, just like that.

When, later that night, Ben fell asleep in front of *The Sting*, her hands playing with his hair, her gaze tracing the contours of his beautiful nose, his tangled lashes, his strong jaw, she told herself the only reason she hadn't yet told him about her job offer, or Damon's phone call, wasn't because she was keeping things from him,

But because she'd only burst into tears again, and this time not have a safe excuse.

"Nora!" Ben called, his deep voice curling its way up the stairs.

"Ben," she muttered back, lifting her head a smidge from where it had been resting on her forearms on her desk. She felt as if she was coming down with something. Was there a tablet to cure the doldrums?

She heard Ben's feet taking the stairs two at a time. She winced as she waited for him to trip—but no, the man was too lithe for that to happen unless she was the one tumbling into him. Taking him down.

"Why didn't you tell me Damon rang yesterday?" he asked as he burst into the room.

Nora nibbled at her bottom lip. "I forgot?" Yeah, okay, so the lilt at the end of her sentence made it clear that wasn't entirely the case.

She prepared to bat her lashes his way—she couldn't quite muster the energy to do much else—but in the end she gave up and put her head back on the desk.

"Hey," he said, his voice dropping. She felt the air shift as he moved her way. "What's going on? Is it the dogs? Gemma said we could visit any time." He put a hand on her forehead. "You haven't been yourself the last couple of days."

Not wanting to be a bother, she pressed herself to sitting and turned on the chair, leaning her arms across the back. "I'm fine. While you've been a busy boy."

"It's the house," said Ben, moving to sit on the end of the bed.

"I can't believe you're selling it, after all the progress you've made here."

"I'm considering my options. And what do you mean by progress?"

"With *Clancy*," she said, throwing her arms out to the side. "You seem to have made so much headway, telling stories about her without my having to nudge, no longer frowning when her name is mentioned."

"Nora, sweetheart, come on," he said, reaching for her.

"Don't sweetheart me!"

Ben pulled his hand away, his expression wary, as if she were about to go rabid. Which she just might.

She knew that tone all too well. It was the I'm-about-to-disappoint-you tone.

"You're upset," he said.

"You think? I'm furious." And she was. Suddenly she was pacing, back and forth, at the end of her bed. "I'm furious with myself. I've been such a fool."

"Regarding?"

"You!"

She waved both hands in his direction, and his hand lifted to rub against this mouth, as if he could sense what was truly front and centre on her mind. As if she could tell him the truths he'd assured her he'd always want to hear.

But she baulked. Deflected. "You didn't want to talk about Clancy, so I left it alone. Let you set the pace. That's not what I do. Why? Because it always bites me on the ass. All this time, all this work, and you're just going to sell the house."

"I'm just considering it. You want me to tell you about Clancy?" he said, his voice rough, a muscle ticcing in his cheek.

"Are you kidding me?"

Ben shook his head. "If it's that important to you, I'll tell you anything you want to know."

"Anything?"

He nodded.

And for a second, a brief suspended moment in time, with his dark, serious, warm, kind eyes locked onto hers, she once again felt as if she *could* ask him anything. Did he have feelings for her? What scared him most in the world? Would they ever see one another again?

But her self-protective instincts had been slumbering of late, basking in the warm glow of having Ben near, and now, as familiar feelings of being pushed into a corner ramped up inside her, it was almost a relief to feel those instincts come back to life.

"Tell me about Clancy," she demanded. "Tell me what happened between you. Because it is eating me up inside to think the two of you, two people whom I…respect and admire, were so at odds that it ended the way it did, and I can't take it any more."

There, that felt better. No more pussyfooting around. It was time they had this out. Because time was running out.

Nora had no clue she was crying again until a tear fell past the edge of her lip, the salty taste touching her tongue. She swiped it away, her gaze fierce, hoping he couldn't see in her eyes the ache that whatever it was they'd shared these past weeks was coming to an end.

Ben dropped his face into both hands and sat there, his

gaze faraway, his skin stretched tight over his bones. He looked ravaged, and it had happened so fast.

It was nearly enough for Nora to drop to her knees, to take his hands in hers and tell him to forget it. To spend what time they had left snuggling and eating homemade tacos and making love.

But then he said, "I wasn't adopted."

"I'm sorry?"

"Clancy did not adopt me. She was my actual grandmother. My mother's mother."

Knees losing functionality, Nora sat gingerly on the corner of the bed. "I don't understand. She said—"

"I know what she said. I know what everyone said. How selfless she was for taking in a quiet, serious five-year-old kid. At her age."

"But she was your mother's *mother*? For real?"

Ben breathed out hard once more. "She was. You asked me once if Clancy had a Rochester of her own. She did. My grandfather."

"Gerald," Nora whispered, the name coming back to her from overheard stage whispers between the widows.

"He was a war correspondent. Clever guy, quite well known in his time. Died, overseas, when Clancy was pregnant with my mother. They hadn't married, but turned out he'd changed his will, leaving her this house. His family tried to fight it, but Clancy stood strong. She had a child to raise, after all. Aida Hawthorne. My mother."

Nora's head spun. What a thing to discover. "But surely that's a happy lie?"

Ben's gaze seemed locked in the past, as if he wasn't seeing the room in front of him at all. "When my mother left me on Clancy's doorstep, she told me she was going away for a while, but she'd be back. The one time I asked Clancy when that might be, she told me my parents were both dead. The truth was she'd told my mother that if she walked away, she was never to darken the door again. I figured that's why the adoption ruse—Clancy was ashamed at what my mother had given up. The only reason I even know that much is because I happened upon Clancy when she was told the news that Aida had died."

And Ben. Oh, Ben. *That* was why the armour. The desire for truth. The slow, measured, deliberate decisions. Poor guy was always waiting for the axe to fall.

Clancy, what were you thinking?

"How are you so functional?" she mumbled. "How are you so together?"

His dark gaze swung to her and her heart went off; beating like crazy for this big, clever, generous man with his big, beautiful broken heart.

"I was," he finally said, his gaze travelling over her face as if committing it to memory. "I was functional, I was *fine*, till you dragged me out here to rehash all this stuff."

His cheek twitched; a smile, even now. Another sign of his immense fortitude. His wonderfulness. His determination to protect her from his baser feelings.

But she didn't need protection. Not from that. Not from him.

"I'm so sorry," she said, her voice gravelly. "I'm sorry for forcing you to come here."

"I'm not."

Heat flashed in his eyes, leant weight to his words. And had her fingers curling into the blanket.

"Besides," he said, "I'm the one who needs to apologise to you. For not being there to look after my imprudent grandmother when she was sick. That should never have fallen to you."

"It wasn't your fault. No one knew."

Ben shook his head. "That's the thing. Clancy did. She knew she was sick, long before she let on."

Nora's mouth dropped open, but she didn't know where to start. Ben's words made no sense.

Ben clasped his hand behind his neck, the muscles tight. "I suspect Clancy knew she had cancer for some time."

Nora shook her head. "No. That's not right. She might have felt *unwell* on occasion, tired easily, but she didn't get an actual diagnosis until a few weeks before she died."

"She knew. She knew before you moved in."

"Before...?" Like a combination lock clicking into place Nora realised what Ben was suggesting. "No. I don't believe you."

"Those recipe books we found at the back of the pantry. They were hers. She was a great cook. Her dinner parties were what originally brought people to the house."

"Are you saying she took me in, as a tenant, knowing she was unwell? That I paid rent for the privilege of taking care of her?"

Ben nodded.

Nora's hand shook as it covered her mouth. The first person, the *one* person, she'd ever let herself believe loved her for her, and it was all a ruse. "She saw me coming from a mile away."

A tear slipped down her cheek, then another.

"Nora, honey, don't cry. Dammit. I never wanted to ruin your good opinion of Clancy, which was the only reason I kept it from you. But you just seemed so determined to know. And I didn't want to hide anything from you, not any more, as I know how that feels. And..."

Ben swore beneath his breath, his expression even more ravaged than it had been before. "Look, if it's any consolation, if she saw you coming from a mile away it wouldn't have been due to any desire to dupe you. She'd have never wanted a nurse. Or sympathy. She'd have taken one look at you, felt your youth, your vitality, your assertiveness, and figured that's how she wanted to spend her last days: alongside a fearless young woman who carries muffins through deep dark woods, despite any and all danger to herself."

Ben shifted closer, waited till her eyes snagged on his. "For all that I wish she were here now, so I could have a piece of her for what she did to you, I understand that want. The urge to soak in all that you have to offer, all that you are, even temporarily. You are a force, Nora Letterman, whether it feels like it right now or not."

Nora knew he was trying to make it better, but all she could do was shake her head. It was too much. The dogs, the house, the rewriting of the past. Her feelings for Ben all tangled and hard.

Ben reached out to brush a strand of hair behind her ear, as if she was right there beside him, when really she was outside her own body, leaving room for him to add, "I might have been able to forgive her for not telling me about my mother, but I'll never forgive her for what she did to you. Never."

Nora came back into her own body with a whoosh.

She was mortified. And pissed. And embarrassed as hell. But she'd been on the receiving end of so much bad news over the years, she knew that, while it felt immediate, and sharp, right now, she'd live.

But Ben. Ben looked changed. As if telling her had taken something from him. As if he was honestly more upset about Clancy duping her than lying to him.

Meaning everything she'd done to help Ben reconcile with Clancy—staying, reaching out, opening up, giving up so much of herself to the cause that she'd fallen in love with the man—it would all be for nothing.

He *had* to forgive Clancy. And the only way that was possible was if he let it all go. The house. His anger. And her.

While her tears dried on her face, a sense of clarity came over her. Not the clarity of sunshine, but the clarity of survival.

This was no different from any other time she'd hit a crossroads; it was time for her to jump before she was pushed.

Before she could change her mind, she wiped away one last tear, steeled herself, and blurted, "In some better news, I got a job."

"A job," he parroted.

"Well, an amazing opportunity, really," she said, doing a mighty fine job of not sounding as if she was paddling like mad beneath the water. "A social-media takeover at a resort in Far North Queensland. It starts in a little under two weeks, but I can head up there as soon as I please. Yay."

Ben reared back as if she'd taken a swipe at him. "When did this happen?"

"I applied a while ago. I got the news yesterday."

His eyes roved over her face as if looking for something. A way in. Or a way out. Then something seemed to shift. To dislodge. Leaving him open. And with a flash that felt like a knife between the ribs she saw his hurt. Deep, cavernous, ancient and immediate. If they looked anything like this when Clancy had ripped off the Band-Aid regarding her truth, she'd never have forgiven herself.

"So, you're taking it?" he said. "Just like that. Please tell me this isn't some knee-jerk reaction to what I just told you."

"It's not. It's real. And I can hardly say no."

Something in her words snagged him. She saw it in his eyes. A flicker. A sense of hope. "But is it what you want?"

"Sure. I mean, it sounds fine. Great, actually. A once-in-a-lifetime chance."

What did it *matter*? He'd come to Fitzroy for her. She'd stayed in Fitzroy for him. And it had been magical. But now she had to go. And he had to let her. So he'd forgive Clancy. And so she could move on, knowing she'd done all she could to leave the situation better than when she'd found it.

"Come on, Ben, we're almost done here. And you're leaving anyway." Ugh. She'd almost made it through before her voice broke on the last word.

"Are you saying…you want me to stay?"

Did she? Yes. *Yes, yes, yes.* Could she? Not in a million years. Even while the thought of walking away from him made her feel as if she were tearing out a rib, she bit her tongue and said nothing.

People weren't to be trusted with their own feelings. Look at Nora: when the going got tough, she left. How could she ever expect Ben not to do the same?

"Look, we'll talk later. I have to meet Misty. Promised her I'd do a thing. So, I'll see you in a bit, okay?"

Eyes welling, she quickly turned, went downstairs, headed out of the broken back door to find it was no longer broken. There was a new lock. With a key on the inside. She used it to scurry through the back garden and out into the alley behind the terrace houses.

And she walked. She walked and walked, away from their little street. Past houses she'd never seen, parks she'd never traversed.

It was all so unfamiliar it felt as if she'd already moved on.

When Nora came home later, the house was quiet bar the murmur of Ben's voice from his room as he spoke to someone, probably Damon, probably about work stuff. The important stuff in his actual life, back in London.

When he didn't come to her bed that night, she lay awake, imagining his long frame curled up on the small single bed downstairs. Wondering if he was lying there in the dark, thinking about her too, till it became too much so she got up and started to pack.

And while she wished she could turn back time, and redo that entire hot mess of a conversation, she consoled herself with the fact that, right now, she was exactly where she'd hoped to be at the very beginning.

Ben had faced his issues with Clancy. And she finally had a way out.

Yippee.

Nora's two small bags were sitting at the front door early the next morning.

In a brief flare of insight, she wondered when having so little had become a kind of flag to wave when really it only served to make her appear smaller and less of an imposition. As if that were the best gift she could give those she left behind.

In the end it was a lie. Because the memories she'd collected in this place filled ten times that much space. Her heart clutched so hard at the thought of walking away from them all, she rubbed the heel of her palm into her chest.

Speaking of people, Nora turned to find Ben leaning against the kitchen doorjamb in a Henley T and soft jeans. Barefoot with a little stubble on his usually clean-cut cheeks, a tuft of hair sitting not quite right, as if he'd tossed and turned as much as she had.

"Running away from home?" he asked.

God, he was beautiful. And kind. And forgiving. While she couldn't be sure how long it would take her to get over him, to get over this whole place, and everything that had happened here, he'd be so fine.

She mustered a wobbly smile. "Despite appearances, I wasn't going to leave without saying goodbye. I'm staying at Misty's for a couple of days. Something I probably should have done earlier. To give you the space you needed to focus on what was important."

Something hot and dark flashed behind his eyes. "And what is that, exactly?"

"Reconciling yourself with your grandmother, of course. Last night you seemed to make some giant leaps in that direction. Leaps you might have made sooner without me pressing and prodding in all the wrong places, or making you lose focus on what mattered to you. I fear my being here made things…muddy."

"Muddy, you say."

"I do. I do say that. I can be a lot. Sunshine or no sunshine, I can be a lot. And while I'm slowly becoming more and more okay with that, you need to just be alone here. To say goodbye."

His chest lifted and fell. Then his strong arms folded over his chest. "I've never much liked goodbyes," he said.

"Me neither. But they are a fact of life." She shrugged. What more was there to say? "Anything you need me to do, before I go, just let me know."

"Don't go," Ben said, his eyes serious. His words harking back to another time he'd said nearly the same thing. "Not yet."

With a soft shrug she gave him one last part of herself. "For years, I'd wake up every morning, waiting for someone to tap me on the shoulder and tell me I didn't belong there. The thing is, I *knew* I didn't belong there. I don't belong anywhere, and I've always been okay with that. But here? With you? I forgot. I forgot myself. I forgot my limits.

"I've been living someone else's life and it's time I start living mine again."

She grabbed her backpack and slung it over her shoulder. Then took her battered old suitcase and held tight to the handle.

For a breath she thought they might move as one towards the middle; she could all but feel him in her arms. But neither moved.

She gave him a smile and reached for the door handle. Then turned at the last.

"Clancy called your name, the second last day, maybe the third. Did I ever tell you that?"

Ben shook his head, slowly.

"I think she thought I was you. Looking after her. At the end."

Ben's chin dropped, the muscles in his neck tensing, and he said, "She didn't need me. She had you."

"She needed you, Ben. She loved you. She missed you. She just didn't know how to tell you."

Nora wondered if Clancy had seen that in her too. If part of her appeal was that they were both useless when it came to expressing how they truly felt. If she'd felt she needed someone, at the end, who wouldn't judge. Would simply hold her hand.

"Thank you," Nora said. "For telling me about Clancy. For trusting me with your story. For not protecting me from mine."

She locked eyes with his, saw way too much understanding therein. He knew how she felt. Knew why she had to leave. He had to.

For the first time ever, she'd met someone who was too much for her.

With a watery smile, she grabbed the door handle, walked out onto the patio and was gone.

CHAPTER THIRTEEN

BEN STOOD ON the threshold of the sitting room at Thornfield Hall, eyes glancing off the fireplace, the ottoman, the bookshelves that had been well cleaned out by the Widows' Book Club, and found himself in an unfamiliar position.

He had not a single clue what he should do next.

For as long as he could remember, from when he woke up in the morning to the moment he finally fell asleep, he felt sure of his actions. As if he had some kind of moral divining rod in his subconscious that let him know he was on the right path. If, at one point, that metaphorical rod had spoken with Clancy's voice, well, then, it was what it was.

But now? Nothing. Take a step forward? Step back? Scratch his nose? Clear his throat? Give up or go hard, book a flight back to London tonight and put the damn house on the market or stay a few more days and finish what he'd begun?

It was as if the divining rod had turned its metaphorical back on him right as he felt as if he were in the centre of some centrifugal vortex. Now whatever he decided to do would spin him off in a direction from which he'd never return.

The *spinning* had begun the moment Nora had left, with her backpack and battered little suitcase. Her tilted chin and brave smile no match for the heartache and disenchantment written all over her face.

For a moment, he'd believed that heartache had been all his. That her feelings for him might even come close to matching his own for her. But she'd never been one to hold back, so he'd had to assume he was projecting.

So, London. Surely his next move was London. They were just fine, for now. The Zoom meeting he'd set up moments after Nora's departure, so that he had something to do other than stare at the door and will it to sweep open with her on the other side, had seen Damon and the team tumbling over one another like puppies to get out the good news about how much work they'd been able to achieve.

But they'd need him soon. Him and his cape.

Twelve-hour days, meetings and working lunches, falling asleep on the couch with his coat on, alone, seemed like a different world. A different life. And yet getting back to work would be a welcome distraction from the constant low-level ache that had descended over his body after Nora had walked out of the door. Surely.

For she'd left. She'd really left. After all she'd done to get him here, she'd actually walked away.

Sure, she'd *told* him she would, from the very first time they'd spoken. It hadn't come out of thin air. And yet he hadn't seen it coming.

He'd been far too busy loving her. Distracted entirely by the falling, the surprise of it, the richness, the joy. Assuming all the while that she'd been feeling the same. Maybe not quite so fast, maybe not with quite such easy acceptance, but they'd been falling together. And while he hadn't had a plan, he'd been okay with that. Not having a plan when he'd hopped on the plane to Melbourne had led to the time of his life.

Only now she was gone.

And he didn't know what to do about it.

His first experience with feeling loved had gone to

Clancy. Her version all about control. Hanging on tight. Too tight. He understood now that its origins hadn't given her much room to move, and in the end it had suffocated him.

What choice had he had other than to love Nora a whole other way? By giving her space, and time, and room. By being truthful, brutally so if necessary, but not pressing, not over-sharing. If she wanted to go, then surely, even if it cut him to pieces, loving her meant letting her make that choice.

But, damn, it hurt.

Needing to feel something other than heartache, Ben took a step inside the very room in which he and Clancy had had their God-awful falling out. He could picture himself standing there, he could see her wonderful familiar face, wretched with apology, yet determined that if she'd had to make the same choice, she'd make it again. Because look at him. Look at the man he'd become.

But it was also the room in which he and Nora had watched a dozen movies he could barely remember, as he'd been far too focussed on her fingers making gentle tracks through his hair. The way her eyes crinkled and her mouth hooked when something whimsical happened on screen. The way she'd burst into laughter any time the dogs let off wind in their sleep and raced him out of the room.

Whatever secrets it had kept hidden, this house had always been a safe place for those who felt at sea. But despite Nora's hopes, it wasn't his home. Not any more. The only person who'd made him feel at home in a very long time had walked out of his door. And he'd let her.

She'd made her move. In pure survival mode, she'd left before she could be told it was time to go.

The ball was in his court.

And with that Ben felt a small shift in perception, like a glimpse of sunlight through a rain cloud. Maybe there was a happy medium. He'd read enough of Clancy's book-club reads as a teen to know that love was meant to uplift and illuminate. Maybe there was some way he could hold Nora tight, and also give her space to be whoever she wanted to be.

The ball was in his court.

But he'd asked her to stay. No, he'd said, "Don't go. Not yet"—a very different thing to a woman who'd been asked to leave more foster homes than she could count—when what he should have said was, "If you want this, if you want me, if you choose to come to me, as I chose to find you, if you're willing to take the risk on trusting me, I will love you and never leave you," over and over until she had not a single doubt.

The ball was in his court.

The divining rod inside him was back, with a vengeance.

"Did you hear?"

"Now what?" Nora snapped, not looking up from her laptop as she flicked between reading the contract the resort island had sent for the hundredth time and checking out the many ways she could get out of town fast.

Not that they'd changed in the couple of days she'd been holed up at Misty's, waiting in case she got a phone call from a certain person asking for her help.

"Feisty," said Misty. "Yet you were such a droopy Dora when you turned up on my doorstep, all maudlin after your day of self-sabotage."

Nora rolled her eyes, and twisted her back, sore from having spent a few nights on Misty's couch in the tiny apartment above her shop. "It wasn't self-sabotage. It's called 'putting a family back together'," Nora said, wishing she hadn't told Misty a thing.

But the moment she'd walked into Vintage Vamp, the first tear had dropped, then the next, then suddenly it was all over red rover. Misty had closed the shop and taken Nora up the side stairs, shoved her on the couch, brought her a tub of Jamoca Almond Fudge ice cream and let her cry and vent enough over the past twenty-four hours to drown herself.

At least the lack of sleep had given her plenty of time to mull.

Over Clancy.

Even knowing there was a fair chance Clancy had taken advantage of her good nature, if Nora knew anything to be true, it was that surviving was hard, and people had to do it the best way they knew how. She'd loved living in that house, and if she had to do it all again, she'd not have changed a thing.

She'd mulled over her future. Six months of cocktails and free steak dinners and sand in the crotch of her bikini. It'd be great. Lonely, though, and far away from a whole bunch of people she'd come to like. *Like*-like, in fact.

And she'd mulled over Ben. She'd done that most of all.

Turned out love was not a tap you could simply shut off just because you'd decided it was too hot. Every time she thought of him, it hurt. Every time Misty turned on the radio and Nora thought she heard his voice, it hurt. Every time she imagined how things might have gone down differently if she weren't such a messed-up scaredy-cat, it hurt.

But what else could she have done with a man so stubborn and dry? Who worked far too hard. Who snored, just a little, and couldn't sit through a single romantic comedy.

A man who liked to sleep closest to the door, and who didn't tell her when he was putting in a new lock because he knew she'd protest. Who didn't even blink when a one-eared, one-eyed, raggedy mutt rubbed noses with him.

A man who'd travelled halfway around the world to face his biggest heartache, because he wanted to be there when she faced hers.

Yes, her feelings for the guy had been overwhelming. Because *he* was overwhelming. Her subconscious had been right to see danger where he was concerned. And if she'd thrown every missile she had in his direction, and in the end only shot herself in the foot, okay, yes, one might call that self-sabotage.

But she was who she was. And if he couldn't handle that, then so be it.

The beaches of Far North Queensland it was.

And, boy, didn't she sound excited about the prospect, even to her own ear?

Knowing she'd not absorb a single word once her mind went down this path, Nora breathed out hard and slowly lowered the lid of her laptop. She stood and dragged her hands through her hair. Then, in need of a distraction, she met Misty in her kitchen as she reached up to bang the smoke detector when the toaster set it off.

"What were you saying before?" Nora asked. "Did you hear…?"

"Right. Did you hear, Ben—?"

Nora held up a hand. "Nope. Sorry. But nope. I've dealt with enough rumours and secrets about that man to last a lifetime."

Misty's mouth worked silently, her body rocking side to side as if she was struggling to contain her news, till Nora was hit with the awful feeling she already knew.

"It's about the house, right?"

Misty nodded.

"It's on the market." Ben had probably put the terrace house up for sale the moment she'd walked out of the door. And gone back to London. Without looking back. It was the soundtrack of her life, after all.

"Wrong."

"Wrong?"

"He's given it to us!"

"I'm sorry, what?"

"Ben! Your big, beautiful, mountainous hottie. At first he seemed too serious for me, but now I do believe he's a saint."

"What are you talking about?"

"He's not selling, you numpty, he's giving Clancy's place over to the community. As a community space. He wants us to be able to continue to use it as a place for people to gather, to come together, for free. Book clubs. The Garden Club. Play groups. Puppy play groups. He said you gave him the idea. He's going to fund a mini renovation, make sure it's sturdy and functional, while keeping its cool Clancy vibe. And he's asked if I'll administrate."

Oh. Oh, Ben. That was…beyond. Perfect. Generous. Clancy would have been so proud.

"Hey… Hey… *Hey!*" said Misty, moving in and hovering over Nora, before hugging her awkwardly around her head. "No more tears. Please. I can't stand it."

"I'm not—" Nora swiped her cheek to find it dry. She was done with tears. Truly.

Misty lifted away, a hand moving to Nora's face, before she said, "He said not to tell you."

Nora flinched. "Ben said that? Why?"

"He said if you knew you'd decide to stay, at least for a while. To help get things in order. Because you know you'd be awesome at it. Which he knew too, but that wasn't the point. The point was, you needed to be where *you* wanted to be. No strings. No caveats. No taking care of others. No hanging around to help him, or be with him, or so that he could be with you. If any of us told you, we'd have him to deal with. But since when have I ever done what some man told me to do?"

"Never," Nora whispered, her head spinning.

What was Ben playing at? He *knew* Misty would tell her. That she'd delight in passing on every word.

It was a sign. He'd given her a *sign.*

She looked to her tattoo. *Footloose and fancy-free.* A dandelion on the wind. That was the only signpost she'd followed for years. And right now it could take her to some gorgeous island resort for six months where she'd feel lonely and miserable.

Imagining herself out in the world with Ben, on the other hand—pretending to understand modern art, playing footsies under the table in some café, or snuggled on a couch, slowly turning one another on—made her feel alive, and tangible and just a little scared.

But it was a good scared. The kind born of anticipation.

She was in love with the man. From the desk of, in the bed of, nose to nose, in heated disagreement with, and everything in between. They'd delighted in nights of quiet and weathered emotional storms. She'd cooked while he'd washed up. They'd never once fought over the remote. And even as she'd walked out on him, it had been done with kindness, and generosity and love. On both sides.

Ben had given her a sign. He wanted her to come home.

Only home wasn't any place she'd ever belonged. It was Ben. All Ben.

She moved so fast she banged into Misty's kitchen table, and somehow caught her laptop before it fell to the floor. "I'll be back for this. Some time."

"No more tears?" Misty asked, her gaze far too clever for her own good.

"No more tears," said Nora.

"Atta girl."

CHAPTER FOURTEEN

NORA STOOD OUTSIDE Thornfield Hall, thinking back to the last time she'd really stopped to take it in. The beautiful fretwork, the creeping jasmine. A little love and understanding, and a lick of new paint, and it would truly shine.

"Okay," Nora said, shaking out her hands and rolling her neck. "No more waiting. You're done waiting. You've waited your whole life to meet someone who liked you, and accepted you, just the way you were. So go get him."

A new mantra beating in her head, she walked up the path.

At the front door, she pulled her phone out of her tote. Brought up Ben's number. Took a moment to gaze at his contact profile, a sneaky pic she'd taken of him while he was sleeping: his face half hidden by the pillow, the half you could see enough to make a girl's heart tumble.

Taking a deep breath, she pressed the call button, then shook her hair off her shoulder, put the phone to her ear, and hoped against hope that this time, of all the times, she'd read the signs right.

It was worth the risk.

The ringtone ceased, then came a pause that seemed to last for ever before a familiar deep voice said, "Where are you?"

Nora felt a ball of sunshine spontaneously appear in her

belly. With those three little words she spun back in time to their first phone calls and video chats, when she'd actually believed she'd only been checking in with him daily because it was her duty. When all the while she'd actually been adoring him, wooing him, in her own clumsy way. And he'd never once called her on it. Not once. When it must have been obvious as hell.

"I'm out front," she said, her voice breathless. Despite all efforts to stay cool, there was no stopping the feelings this man brought out in her. The warm delight. The hope. No fairy dust required. "I'm… I'm home."

No response. She looked to the phone to find he'd hung up. She heard footsteps, as if they were coming down the stairs, then the door flew open.

And there he was.

It had been a few days since she'd seen those warm eyes, that face—so handsome it took every effort not to squint in the presence of so much gorgeousness—but it felt like for ever.

"Hi," he said.

"Hi." She wondered if she looked as hungry as he did as he drank her in, eyes tracking her old yellow T with its pink tractor motif, the small hole in the hem covered by the knot at her belly, the long floral skirt Misty had thrown at her when she'd nearly run out of the door in just her T-shirt and undies.

"How've you been?" he asked when his gaze once more connected with hers.

"Crap. You?"

The edge of Ben's mouth twitched, then curled, and then he laughed, the sound so rich and warm and delicious it was all she could do not to throw herself at him, bury her face in his neck and move in.

"Were you upstairs, just now?" she asked, peering about the corner.

He let out a long slow breath, before admitting, "I've been sleeping there. Since you left."

"Smart move. The bed is the biggest in the place."

"It is. But that's not why."

"Oh." To think she'd thought him so dry, so uncompromising, so stubborn, when he was truly the most warm, wonderful, astonishing man. Again, all she could say was, "Oh."

"Mmm," he said, an enigmatic smile on his face.

Then he leaned against the edge of the doorway, his hands sliding into the front pockets of his jeans. He did that—leaning and wearing jeans—better than anyone she'd ever met. He always seemed so comfortable in his own skin it made her breath hitch. Whereas she often felt as if a colony of flying ants were wriggling under her clothes.

Then he said, "Are you okay? I've been worried about you."

Nobody worried about Little Red Riding Hood. She was the bad ass of the forest. It felt…pretty wonderful. Yet still, old habits died hard, and so she asked, "Whatever for?"

"The way I tore that Band-Aid off, while telling you my concerns about Clancy's motives. As well as the fact I kept it from you at all. In the end I did exactly what my grandmother did to me."

"You were trying to protect me. Just as she was trying to protect you."

Ben nodded, and Nora saw acceptance in his expression. "You are very wise for one so young. Now, want to come in?"

"Yes. Thank you. That would be lovely."

He stood back and waved an arm. She slipped inside, catching his scent as she passed—fresh cotton sheets, woods, and clean male skin. She'd missed it. She'd craved it. She never wanted to go another day without breathing it in.

She had to tell him. But how to tell him when she'd spent her whole life shoving such emotions deep down inside?

When she turned in the entrance it was to find Ben standing closer than she'd expected. Close enough her nose came level with the second button on his navy Henley T. Close enough to see a day's worth of stubble covering his swarthy jaw. The sparkles of silver therein.

Her gaze felt heavy as she lifted it to his eyes. All those lashes. All that deep lovely brown. It was too much. He was too much. And she loved every bit of him.

She swallowed, squared her shoulders, just a fraction, and said, "I heard what you've chosen to do with the place."

"Oh, you did, did you?"

"You knew Misty would tell me."

He ran a hand up the back of his neck and had the good grace to appear chagrined. "Yeah. I figured that was a safe bet. I know you said I could call on you, ask for your help, but, after you'd been so determined to leave, it didn't feel right to get in your way. So what do you think?"

"I think Clancy would be beyond proud. And this community will be so grateful."

"I asked what *you* think."

Nora's cheeks warmed under his intense gaze. "I think it's perfect, Ben. I think you're—I think you've been more than generous. Which is not a surprise. Because you're—" Nora stopped a moment. Breathed. Pressed her feet into the ground. She could do this. She wanted to do this. "Ben, you're wonderful."

His smile was slow and inviting and addictive. She knew

in that moment there wasn't much she wouldn't do to bring out that smile.

"I'm glad you think so," he said. "Didn't feel right, having come all this way, to leave before I'd done what I truly came here to do."

"Sort out the house?"

He shook his head.

"Reconcile with Clancy?"

A smile spread across his face, before his gaze dropped to her mouth. "You do realise I could have done all of that from London, don't you?"

Nora blinked. Well, no. It had not occurred to her. "So then why—?"

His dark gaze lifted till it tangled with hers. "I might not have made it as clear as I thought I had, given that brevity is my preferred style of address, but, Nora, you must know by now that I came here, to this city, to this street, to this house, for you."

Nora felt every good feeling she'd ever felt swelling inside her like a rising current, pushing every sadness, every regret, every fear out of the way. Making just enough room for her to say, "And I waited, here, in this city, in this street, in this house, for you."

Ben breathed out hard. As if *he'd* been sweating *her* response.

As if every woman who ever met him didn't drool, just a little.

As if it weren't patently obvious how taken with him she was.

He went to open his mouth, but she stepped in, lifted onto her toes and pressed a finger to his lips. "I have more to say."

He nodded. Her finger moved with it. As she slid her finger away, his nostrils flared, his eyes dilated. And he waited. She knew in that moment he would wait as long as it took for her to get to where she needed to be. This great, hulking, strong, handsome, generous, measured, patient man, whose forbearance deserved awards.

"I walked away. I walked away because that's what I do. I walk before I'm pushed. Walking *always* feels like a relief. Like I've escaped the jaws of a lion. Walking away from you, though… I didn't like it."

"I should have stopped you."

"You tried."

"Not hard enough. I would have told you, asked you, begged you, held you, kissed you, lassoed you, serenaded you, if I didn't *know* you had to choose to stay, all on your own. And, you know, if I'd had any lassoing skill."

"And if you'd had the rope?" she asked.

"And if I had the rope."

She moved in a little closer.

He noticed. A muscle ticcing in his cheek as if it was taking every ounce of power he had not to do the same.

"I have a question," she said.

Ben's eyes crinkled. All kinds of lights sparkled in their dark depths. "Ask, Nora. Ask me anything you want."

Okay. Here goes. "Is there a chance…? I mean… Do you think that you might ever find it in you to—?"

"Yes."

"Yes?"

"Yes. I love you, Nora. I love you. I'm in love with you. I have been since before I even set foot on the plane to come to you. If missing you so much these past few days I slept in your bed doesn't prove that, then let me tell you again. I love you. Don't get me wrong, you drive me around the bend. But it turns out I really like it there."

Nora stood there, mouth agape, as Ben's words rolled over her in waves of luscious loveliness. And while, in the past, she might have closed down in fear that it couldn't possibly last, she opened herself up to every last drop until she felt as if her bones were made of stardust.

"Nora?" Ben's deep voice came to her like a dream.

She blinked up into his gorgeous gaze and said, "Mmm?"

"Did that answer your question?"

"It did. It really did. Lucky for you, I love you too."

The words fell from her mouth with such ease. And she felt a huge weight lift off her chest. As if a hundred pairs of arms that had been holding her down, holding her back, let go as one.

Ben smiled; with teeth, and crinkling eyes, and all. There was no shock in his expression. No surprise. Just a whole load of relief and a joy that she'd finally realised. That she was finally able to feel it. To own it. To share it with him.

Then, as if he could hold back no longer, Ben moved in, sliding his arms around her and pulling her close. Pulling her flush up against him so that not a sliver of sunshine peeked through.

He pressed a kiss to the top of her head. To the top of her nose. To the edge of her earlobe where his lips stayed as he murmured, "You came out of nowhere, like an invading army from the south, your weapons of choice your determined joy, and passion, and bottomless empathy. I had no clue I'd been living in greyscale till you burst into my life."

Then he placed a kiss on her neck, in that spot that always made her knees give way. And they didn't disappoint. Her breath left her in a sigh that was part groan as shivers rocked through her body.

But he was there to catch her, to hold her, to keep her close.

She pulled away, just enough to reach up and place her hands either side of his face. "If I'm an invading army, then you've made me work for every victory. But it was worth it. You're worth it."

With that, Nora tilted up onto her toes and kissed him. She kissed the man she loved. And she felt it, boy, how she felt it.

In the way he held her, as if she was precious and strong all at once.

In the way he followed her lead in the kiss, while also tempting her to follow his.

In the way he seemed to breathe her in, as if making sure she was real.

When they pulled away, breaths heavy, bodies trembling, Nora leant her head against his chest, then turned so her ear could hear his heart. It was nice to find it sounded as erratic as hers felt. "So what do we do now?"

"I have ideas," said Ben, the tone of his voice enough to send skitters of heat all through her.

"Don't worry, we're both having ideas." Nora grinned against his chest. "I mean, where do we go from here? We are both about to be kicked out of here; sooner rather than later, I'd think, if Misty has any say in the matter."

"Did you know she has a law degree? And an MBA? That before running that wild shop of hers she was a pretty famous civil rights attorney, and she still helps out on pro bono cases?"

Nora closed her eyes and breathed him in. "Sounds about right."

"Mmm…" said Ben, holding her closer.

"Mmm…" said Nora, figuring that if a plane fell on the house she'd die happy. Well, not happy, as she really wanted Ben to follow through with those ideas of his.

"I've been thinking," said Ben.

"You're good at that."

"I really am. So, working remotely has been doable in

the short term, but it wouldn't be fair on my team or clients going forward. Meaning I'd have to shut up shop and move it here. Or take a partner. Or sell."

Nora reared back, her gaze dancing between Ben's eyes to see if he was messing with her. He seemed serious. Drop-dead gorgeous, but serious. "What do you mean, *sell*? You can't sell the Desk of Bennett J Hawthorne. It's where I found you. It's a part of you! It's where you earned your cape. And what about Damon and the team? They've come so far."

Ben laughed. "Trust you to think of everyone before yourself."

Nora's nose wrinkled. "Nah. I mean, yes, but I'm mostly thinking of you. *And* me. I took a holiday to Bali a few years ago. Do you think my passport might still be valid? Do I need a visa to go to London?"

"What about your island?"

"My—the *resort*? Are you suggesting you'd move your company to a beach hut on the Great Barrier Reef? For me?"

"I'd move to the moon if it meant I got to wake up to this face every day."

She kissed him again. A kiss that made her see stars.

Before she completely went under his spell, she dragged herself back. "That gig, it's not for me. I'd be spending my days alone, writing puff pieces for some rich dudes. I prefer making a pittance working for people I can look in the eye. People who appreciate it. People who actually need *me*. *The Girl Upstairs* can create content anywhere. And if you're so het up on living on an island, England is an island, right?"

"Again," he said, his thumb tracing the edge of her nose. "So wise. So very wise. Now, are we done with all the talking? Because I'm still having those ideas I mentioned earlier. Ideas that involve getting you naked and horizontal and, since we could be kicked out at any moment, I think it best we get cracking—"

Nora leapt at him then, throwing her arms around his neck. And he caught her, as he always had. Kissing her, and carrying her slowly, carefully, deliberately, up the stairs.

Because they really were precarious for a man with such big feet.

* * * * *

SECOND CHANCE TO WEAR HIS RING

HANA SHEIK

MILLS & BOON

To my family, who love and support me endlessly.

To the Sassy Scribes:
Ann, Ash, Heather, Jade, Jayne, Laura,
Melanie, Nico, Suzanne.

Finally to Nic Caws, the best editor a newbie author could ask for—thank you for taking a chance on me.

CHAPTER ONE

"MANSUR, I NEED your help."

The closing words of his mother's voicemail had kept Mansur Ali awake on the flight and alert on the bumpy ride from the airport to his childhood home.

Manny gripped the roof handle, peering out the truck's dusty, dirt-tracked window. How had he ended up traveling from Pittsburgh to Somaliland in the end, after vowing he wouldn't? He leaned back into the matted sheepskin car seat cover, knowing exactly how. One missed call from his mother was what had done the trick.

She had answered his return call, but her explanation had been vague at best, dodgy at worst. Even so, he'd understood that something was wrong. It was enough of a reason to fly home to her.

Spying the sky-blue gates of his family property, Manny sat up, anticipating he'd get his answer soon, in person.

The driver, a distant older relative, grinned at Manny. The gaps in his teeth didn't dim the sunny gesture. "Your mother will be so happy to see you. For days she's talked about only you."

"Yes, it's been too long," Manny agreed, his Somali rusty from little use these days.

Leaning on the horn, the driver waited for the gates to

be opened by other staff before he eased the pickup onto the spacious driveway.

Manny didn't wait for him to quiet the engine, exiting hastily. Outside, he faced the morning chill. His flight had come in early, though seven a.m. was well past the usual morning hours he kept. He had a self-imposed grueling schedule as CEO of a multimillion-dollar construction and engineering firm, Aetna Builds. Adrenaline kept him upright after zero sleep.

The whole house hopped with activity. One of his mother's new maids closed the gates she'd opened for the truck and Manny nearly collided with another unfamiliar young woman, this one carrying a mop and bucket. Soapy water sloshed out, inches from his expensive handmade Italian loafers.

Though she didn't know how much the shoes were worth, she stammered an apology for blocking his path.

"It's all right," he said.

She had enough to worry about, with the bucket looking way too heavy for her to carry alone. Besides, those wide, startled eyes of hers suggested she knew who he was. As did her sudden urgency to cover her head with the shawl wrapped around her shoulders.

Manny redirected his gaze, allowing her privacy. The bespoke three-piece suit gave him away. He hadn't dressed for his new surroundings. Getting to his mother had been his prime objective. And his mission wasn't over yet.

"Is my mother inside?" Manny nudged his chin toward the entrance the woman had staggered from, bearing her load.

She nodded, still gawking at him.

Manny thanked her, breezing past in his hurry to see his mother.

Frankincense perfumed the air, its sweet, thick tendrils curling around him, calling up childhood memories.

Squinting, he tried to get his bearings, waiting for his vision to adjust. The house had always been dim inside. His mother swore by natural light, despite the electricity working fine. Manny resisted flicking on the lights in the entrance. He crossed the spacious entrance hall to the living room.

"Mansur."

Facing the door, his mother had noticed his entry and now called to him, her eyes as large and disbelieving as the young maid's. The sound of the truck's running motor grumbled in with the cool breeze. The door to the veranda was open, as were all the windows in the tastefully furnished living area.

She shouldn't look surprised. She had known he was coming. Manny had left a message for her before he'd boarded his private jet. He'd figured she must have heard it as she'd sent the driver to fetch him.

Then again, she was likely shocked that he had shown up. She hadn't expected him to heed her summons. And what did that say about him?

That you're a failure of a son, maybe?

He scowled at the thought and fixed his attention on the scene before him.

His mother stood with the help of a woman who had her back to Manny. He assumed it was another maid. That was the wrong assumption.

"Amal..." Manny breathed her name. It felt too long since he'd allowed himself to think about her. A whole year, to be exact.

If he'd known they would cross paths so quickly he would've arranged for his mother to meet him elsewhere. Perhaps in his old bedroom. She'd likely furnished it for him, in the hope that he would opt to stay with her rather than check himself into a hotel.

But it was difficult to think about his accommodation when his mother was approaching him with Amal.

He flinched as they neared, his instinct roaring at him to flee. His heart, a battering ram, drummed so loud he feared that Amal would hear it. That she would know how easily she continued to affect him.

Curiosity kept him rooted. But he was seconds from storming out of the house to spend his first day here in a hotel.

Only the flash of emotional pain in his mother's wet eyes cooled his indignation. Halima Ahmed Adan didn't shed tears lightly. Only two instances came to his mind before this: when his father had died last year and when Mansur had announced his plan to leave for America on a college scholarship at the impressionable age of seventeen.

But she was crying now, her shawl forgotten where she'd left it on the ornately patterned floor cushions.

"Hooyo," she said, and the Somali term of endearment wrapped itself around his heart. It meant *mother*, and by choice he hadn't had one this past year, for reasons he was still ashamed to contemplate.

Moved by her tears, Manny stepped into her open arms and sank into her embrace.

She pressed her mouth to his ear. "I missed you."

"I missed you, too," Manny murmured.

Over his mother's shoulder, he met Amal's eyes. Her face free of makeup, her tawny, reddish-brown skin glowed as if freshly scrubbed. She wore a neutral expression. Her midnight-blue silk veil was styled to match her dress. Snug around her chest and curvy hips, its flowing design was meant to discourage the kind of heated thoughts slipping into Manny's head unbidden.

Squeezing his mother tighter, Manny eased his hold when she gasped and gave a small laugh. He'd almost forgotten he was hugging her.

"Forgive me," Manny mumbled, releasing his mother.

When his hands dropped to his sides again he flexed his fingers, the lingering feel of her warming his gut and falling over him like a comfort blanket. It was easier to hold on to the grudging anger.

Noting where his attention was directed, his mother grasped Amal's hand and pulled her closer. "Have you forgotten Amal?" she asked.

Like he could forget Amal Khalid.

She had become almost like one of his family after the tragic loss of her mother.

Amal and her two younger brothers had been taken in by their kind-hearted grandmother when their father abandoned them. They'd moved in next door as strangers, though that had quickly changed since Manny's mother and Amal's grandmother had been close neighbors and good friends. Naturally he'd grown close to Amal, and to her brothers, as well. And, without siblings of his own, Manny had thought of them all as family.

But that had ended once he'd awakened to his attraction for Amal.

Then she had broken his heart.

Mansur's eye twitched from the strain of holding his composure. Tension thrummed through his body. He wanted to leave, but he'd have to wait. Fleeing this meeting wasn't an option for him. Besides, his path converging with Amal's had been bound to happen eventually. Twelve months was a long enough reprieve. Plenty of time for his head and heart to heal. For him to move on.

"Salaam." Amal held his gaze, her soft voice accented

when she greeted him in English. "Welcome home, Mansur."

"*Salaam.* It's good to be home." If only he believed himself.

Amal's cocoa-brown eyes assessed him. She wasn't smiling, her pouty mouth curling as she frowned. Finally, unable to stand the prickling heat of her stare, Manny snapped, "What is it?"

Amal grimaced, and Manny's mother sucked in a sharp, warning breath.

Manny forced a smile, making a second attempt at polite conversation. He could be civil. "How have your brothers been, Amal?"

"Good."

His smile slipped at Amal's curt response. Curiosity thrumming through him, he wondered aloud, "That's all?"

Amal's sculpted brows swooped down, and her mouth was a long line of displeasure.

This questioning was bothering her. It shouldn't. He wasn't asking anything private. In fact, Manny had kept it light and impersonal on purpose. There was his heart to consider, and he wasn't allowing it to guide him this time. Not again.

Not ever again, he vowed.

Still, his curiosity wouldn't let this go. Amal was hiding something. And, judging by his mother's pinched expression, she knew exactly what. He highly suspected that she wouldn't tell him, though. Both women shared a rapid look, and if he'd been only lightly suspicious before, it only intensified after their furtive glances.

"Is Abdulkadir still working at the travel agency?" Manny queried, tilting his head. He stared hard at Amal, willing her to crack. "What of Bashir? Is he still out of the city at university?"

At the mention of her brothers Amal's gaze flicked to Manny's mother. He didn't miss the panic softening her mouth, parting her lips and widening her eyes.

"Yes, Abdulkadir and Bashir are where you left them," said his mother.

"I didn't ask you, Mother."

Manny's jaw clenched. He paid no heed to his mother's cool regard. Later, she could scold him all she wanted. For now, he wanted answers. And he wanted them from Amal.

When Amal didn't speak, he turned for the door leading out to the veranda. "Follow me," he told Amal. She visibly bristled, her frown intensifying. But Manny needed some explanation, and he had a sense that Amal would follow him if he started forward.

Knowing his mother meant to trail them, he said over his shoulder, "I'd like to speak to Amal alone."

Something was definitely going on. He needed to find out why he had come to Somaliland again, a year after his promise to return home only on his own terms.

These weren't his terms. They weren't even close.

Out on the narrow veranda, Amal sidled past him, her eyes squinting and shifty with suspicion, acting as though he meant her harm.

Stifling his hurt at her reaction, he arranged his mouth into a semblance of a smile. Amal wasn't buying it. She narrowed her eyes, hugging her arms about her middle.

"Is there something you'd like to tell me?" he asked.

"There's nothing." She lifted her small chin, staring at him down her pert nose as best as she could when she stood a head shorter.

Manny might have believed her response, too, if he hadn't noted the trembling of her bottom lip. She was shaking like a leaf out here, and he guessed only some of it was due to the chill clinging to the late spring morning air.

"You're cold," he observed, unbuttoning his suit jacket.

He cornered her then, and saw her lips tightening as she peered up at him, all fierce defiance. The parts of Amal's personality he recognized seemed to be mixed with bits of the new person she'd become in his absence.

Draping the jacket on her, he smoothed the charcoal-gray herringbone wool over her shoulders. The need to touch her was strong. After all, he'd denied himself for so long. How could one moment of indulgence undo the steel encasing his heart? And they had been friends once. Good friends.

But you ruined that, didn't you?

The thought provoked a sneer from him. If only it were that easy. If only he hadn't tried to see her as more. It wasn't enough that he'd lost a whole lot; he had also obliterated their long-standing friendship.

His comfort now was that he wasn't alone in wanting this. Right in that moment she mirrored the same stabbing, hot attraction unfolding in him. It knifed him in the gut. Over and over. Exacting and brutal. Leaving him breathless.

His adrenaline was at a shaky high and his head was full of cotton, so that he almost forgot why he'd risked exposing his still pathetically weak heart by invading her space.

The truth, he reminded himself. Amal was hiding something. And whatever the secret was, it had inspired his mother to say just enough to bring him home again.

He had to know what the reason for them wanting his return was if he stood any chance of regaining the fragile and temporary peace of mind he'd had before reuniting with the one woman who truly battered through his defenses.

The woman he'd once loved with the whole of his being. *Amal.*

Apparently she still had some hold on him. Otherwise

he wouldn't be demonstrating nearly as much patience with her.

Amal arched her back, her smooth neck bared to him where her veil's silky material was slack. Her chest rose and fell fast, and he felt tiny puffs of warm air brushing his tense jaw, his face having pushed closer of its own accord.

His body was running the show. That couldn't be a good thing.

But he needed his answer. And he needed it now. Before he did something he'd seriously regret.

Like kissing her.

"Amal." He gritted her name, hating how the syllables still warmed his blood. "What's wrong?"

Amal's mouth parted, but no sound slipped free. Her eyes shimmered with fear.

Concerned, he cupped her chin and kept their eyes level. She was going to tell him what had frightened her—because he sensed it had nothing to do with him.

"It's her brain."

Manny snapped his head to the side, hissing sharply at the sound of his mother's voice. He'd told her to stay out of it.

He made an effort to give Amal space now they weren't alone. They were single adults locked in what might be misconstrued as a lovers' embrace. Maybe one time he wouldn't have cared… But now? Now, he most definitely cared.

Dropping his hand from Amal's chin as if he were scalded, he gave her space and scrutinized his mother more fully. "What does that mean?"

"She hurt her head." His mother continued with her explanation. "It was an accident at one of her worksites a month ago."

"This is why you called me?" Soaking this new information in and pushing down the useless anxiety prickling over his skin and churning his gut, Manny asked the next logical question. “Is she unwell?”

“She’s healed nicely. The wound itself wasn’t life-threatening.”

Manny’s relief lasted for only a few seconds.

His mother had said a prayer aloud. It had never boded well in his childhood when she did that.

“The doctors fixed her on the outside. But it’s her inside they can’t cure.”

“What do you mean?”

Manny looked at Amal, studying her. She appeared healthy. The veil had to be hiding a scar, but his mother had just assured him the doctors had treated her. A month, he thought, feeling the anguish settling into his bones. Why hadn’t anyone called him then?

The same reason you stayed away—they didn’t want to see you.

Manny clenched his teeth at the thought, annoyed by how much it stung to hear the truth ringing so clear in his mind. It would be easier to concentrate on what his mother and Amal had to say for themselves than to dissect his hurtful self-reflection.

“She’s forgotten things.” His mother shook her head, her brow pleating in sorrow, clearly too overcome with feeling to say any more on the matter.

Amal stared at him with those wild, wide eyes, her mouth set in that grim line again.

Of all the things he’d imagined facing on his return home—of all the things he’d feared—amnesia hadn’t been one of them.

Tired of how they spoke like she wasn’t present, and shying away from their sympathetic looks, Amal hurried for the steps down from the veranda.

She didn't so much hear Mansur as feel his hand circle her wrist, pulling her to a stop. She whirled to confront him, bracing herself to endure more of his sympathy—or was it pity?—head-on.

Amal tugged at his hand to no avail. His grasp was forged of steel. She sensed she'd tire out before he did.

Better that you find out what he wants.

As if peeking into her thoughts, Mansur said, "We're not done talking."

Of course. That was what it was. He hadn't dismissed her, so he'd assumed they were still having this pointless conversation. She couldn't hide or pretend everything was all right now Mansur knew about her affliction. About her amnesia.

"I don't have anything else to say. You heard your mother. I'm not well."

"Still, I'd like to talk," he said. "But not here."

He glanced around, forcing Amal to note the curious maids and the perplexed driver.

They must be making quite a scene, standing so close, their chests nearly brushing. It was scandalous.

"Show me my room."

His husky voice stroked something unexplored and forbidden inside her. Unwilling to explore it out here in the open, Amal chose to entertain his request for privacy.

"It's this way." She gave his hand a pointed look.

Once he'd released her, Amal turned briskly, her skirt and robe swishing as she forged her path. She wasn't going to overthink why she was missing the warm and welcoming pressure of his palm. It should be the last thing on her mind. She needed to be concerned about her fried brain and scattered memories.

Still, she hadn't anticipated the force of attraction she'd feel for Mansur. She had hoped for a personal connection—

hoped his face would free a more recent memory than the few childhood ones that were returning to her more rapidly. But the man before her was certainly not the gawky, grinning teenager she fuzzily recalled.

Amal hadn't gotten the chance to ask Mama Halima much about who Mansur had grown to become, and his arrival had been more or less a surprise to her. It hadn't been until only a couple hours earlier that his mother had pulled her aside and informed her of Mansur's journeying home to them. For her.

She now knew he had no clue that he'd traveled because of her amnesia. Mama Halima had left that part out when she'd contacted him.

If she didn't feel obliged to guide him to the guest room that had been prepared for him this morning, Amal would have scurried off to lock herself in the spare bedroom. Maybe even insisted that she move back next door, although Mama Halima wouldn't have been too happy about that decision. With both her brothers having moved out of their late grandmother's home, Amal lived alone. Mansur's mother hadn't liked to leave her alone after the accident. She had convinced Amal into temporarily moving in with her.

The new living arrangement had worked perfectly. The two women had each other for company. But now, with Mansur home to his mother, Amal felt as though she had overstayed her welcome. Also, it must appear like she couldn't take care of herself.

But it's true, isn't it? You're helpless, weak. You need someone to save you.

No! She didn't need rescue. She was fine.

Forcing herself to concentrate on her steps, Amal closed in on Mansur's bedroom.

"Over here," she said, glancing back at him.

He'd paused at the wrong door, his hand on the brass handle.

"That isn't your room," she said.

Disregarding her, he opened the door and pushed inside.

Amal followed close at his heels. Frustrated that he hadn't listened, and embarrassed by the sight of her messy room, she gestured for the door, hoping he'd grasp her cue.

"I told you—this isn't your room," she said.

"That's where you're wrong." Mansur shifted his attention, his eyes scouring her face. "It used to be my room… long, long ago."

Amal frowned. "Well, your mother didn't tell me," she muttered.

"She didn't expect I'd return anytime soon." Walking toward the bed at the far end of the room, he looked around. "Everything almost looks the same. Except this." He gestured at the headscarves on the bed and the books on the floor.

Amal skirted past him and collected the headscarves. She walked with them to her temporary dresser, popped them in the first drawer. Then she moved to handle the scattered books, just as Mansur lifted a notebook that the scarves had hidden on the bed.

Her journal!

Mansur smoothed his palm over the spiral notebook's cover. "You still journal, then?"

"I try," she replied, accepting the book when he handed it to her. He hadn't even made an attempt to read it.

"And you're reading, too."

He glanced down at her books. She had been in the middle of reorganizing her reading pile. Many of the book covers were worn, hinting at how loved they were. That had to be the only upside of amnesia. Reading the books that she'd enjoyed in the past and getting the ultra-rare chance of reading them like they were new.

So far, her skewed memory retrieval had worked strangely. She recalled some things more clearly now than she had right after her accident four weeks earlier, when she'd woken up in the hospital with stitches to her right temple. But the returning memories were further in her past, which frustrated her more now that she stood before Mansur. Amal had no recent memories of him. The glimpses of the childhood of this man standing with her were hardly enough to assume his personality now. For all she knew, he could have grown to be a terrible person.

Terrible, maybe. Yet still darkly gorgeous.

She wasn't sure how to feel about her sudden and fierce attraction to him.

"It's strange to be back." He drilled his gaze into the side of her head, lips turning down. "I have to admit I hadn't planned to be here."

What he meant was, he'd come back because of her.

Reflexively Amal lifted a hand to her temple. Her scar was tingling and a conflux of noxious emotions was blending in her. She felt her stomach swooping, but she hadn't eaten anything to heave up.

"There's a scar, then?" he asked.

She nodded, felt her mouth refusing to open and answer him.

"Does it hurt still?"

She shook her head.

He scowled, but it didn't detract from his good looks.

"I'm just glad your brothers and my mother were here." The sincerity in his tone softened his eyes and face. "You have to be more careful. I know first-hand how dire accidents on construction sites can be."

"Have you had an accident before?" Amal stared at him,

forgetting that she should not be seeing him in her private space. Suddenly she was gripped by a new worry. For him.

"Not me, personally. Employees. Contractors. Coworkers. When it's bad, it becomes devastating pretty quickly."

Amal should've left it there, but she heard herself wondering aloud, "But you're alone in America. Who watches out for you?"

Without missing a beat, he said, "No one."

"And you're not lonely, Mansur?" Her heart felt pain at the thought of his having no one.

"It's Manny. You used to call me Manny," he replied, after what felt like the longest silence. "Now I should probably head to my room."

He smiled then, and she was surprised to see it. Mansur didn't seem like a man who smiled a lot.

Amal basked in that smile, with a niggling feeling reassuring her that his happiness was due to *her*. Aware of how crazy the thought was, she shrugged his jacket off and held it out for him to take, careful that their hands didn't touch when he took it back.

"Lead the way," he said, trailing her out of her room.

Luckily, she didn't have to spend any more time with him. She saw Manny to the guest room and left him to freshen up and change. Meanwhile, it was Amal's turn to help the kitchen maid. Since temporarily moving in, she had become used to relieving Mama Halima of that duty. And today, especially, she anticipated mother and son wanting time alone.

"What's he like?" the kitchen maid, Safia, wondered aloud. "Nima said he is a gentleman. He didn't yell when she almost washed his shoes."

Safia snickered then, her hand poised over the pot of simmering ground beef as she expertly poured chopped onions in. "I think she's already in love with him. Don't leave Nima alone with him when she's cleaning the rooms."

The housemaid peeked in, hearing her name. "It's not like I'm going to be *in* the room while he's there." She gave them a scandalized look.

"Amal was alone with him."

Safia's arch remark suggested she'd been spying again. She was the youngest and newest member of the household staff. She still had a lot to learn. But Mama Halima had cautioned Safia about snooping before.

Amal was about to remind her when Nima breezed into the small kitchen, setting down the large metal tub of laundry she'd been planning to soap and rinse by hand.

"What were you doing with him, Amal?" Nima asked.

Safia grinned. "Flirting with him, of course."

The girls gossiped as if Amal wasn't there, spinning stories about what had happened between her and Manny. And Amal didn't say anything to correct them. She ducked her head, her eyes blurring from the onions she hastily peeled and diced into a bowl.

She didn't glance up until Nima asked, "You've known each other for a while, haven't you, Amal?"

Mama Halima must have told her. Nima hadn't been in her employ for that long.

The housemaid sighed and eyed her with such longing Amal's chest panged for her. "That's why I'm sure you two will be married."

"Nima…" Amal scolded, but too lightly to convince the girls to cease their gossip.

If they didn't stop, someone would hear them.

As if the girls had conjured him, Amal stiffened at Manny's deep-timbred voice from behind them.

"Ladies," he greeted them, breaking up the maids' giggling. "It smells delicious in here."

Amal had trouble straightening her face after Safia's and Nima's teasing. Her cheeks warmed as she turned and studied Manny.

He'd traded his suit for a collared T-shirt and cargo shorts. The crisply pressed shirt and shorts accentuated his toned arms and legs, and his corded, lean muscles flexed as he moved into the dim kitchen. Even in the weak sunlight, Amal could make out his attractive features.

A smile softened the angular planes of his long face, and at Safia and Nima's giggled greetings he flashed another smile, his straight white teeth popping against his rich umber skin and the short black curls of a beard growing in. It was scruffily sexy—and not what she should be thinking about at all.

"Did you need anything?" Amal prayed he'd say yes. She needed a break from the girls. But Manny shook his head.

"Just looking for my mother. I thought she might be in here. She was always fond of the kitchen."

Amal knew that much even with her amnesia. Mama Halima would be in the kitchen all day if Amal didn't insist on relieving her. "She should be in her bedroom, if she isn't in the living room. I could check—"

Amal made to stand, but Manny gestured for her to sit. "I'll find her myself."

He left as quietly as he'd entered.

Nima and Safia traded knowing looks. The saucier of the two maids, Safia, winked at Amal. "So, when is the wedding?"

Somehow Amal managed to get through dicing the onions for the *sambusa* wraps. Then, discerning the hour, she poured a cup of spiced tea, prepared a plate of sour flatbread—*anjero*—and ladled tomato soup into a bowl.

She ignored the maids' teasing about her organizing Manny's late breakfast. It was only right she fed him; Mama

Halima would have expected Amal to see to the comfort of any guest.

It was one of the things she loved about the older woman, aside from her abundant patience, kindness, and generosity. Mama Halima didn't treat her like an invalid. Amal's amnesia was a concern to Manny's mother, but she didn't handle her like she was fragile, expensive china. Quite the opposite. She believed Amal should be helping Safia and Nima with the household duties. And it was a great relief that she was allowed to be...*normal.*

Which was why the maids wouldn't stop her preparing and traying Manny's breakfast. On reaching his room, Amal noted the heavy oak door was ajar. She was about to set the tray down and knock when she stilled. Sharp voices spilled out, the words clearer now she was listening for them.

"Think about what you're saying!" Mama Halima's displeasure pulsed in each word. "You're going to abandon us now, after you've traveled so far?"

"I don't know what you want me to do. I'm no doctor. I can't help her."

Amal flinched at this brusque statement, her hands tightening painfully on the tray.

"I'm of no use to you and Amal. Better I leave. I have business in Addis Ababa anyways."

Manny sounded exasperated and at the end of his rope. Amal knew it was because of her. They clearly hadn't anticipated her hearing, or else they'd have shut the door.

"Mansur, please," Mama Halima begged.

Amal hated it that Manny's mother had to do it on her behalf.

"Please, don't do this. Don't leave us."

"If it's money you need I can wire it to you as usual. But I won't stay here!" Manny stressed.

After that exclamation, the silence inside was deafening. It spilled out into the foyer, washing over Amal. She was nearly knocked down by the force of the burden she'd become on people who were her family, of sorts.

Family she'd forgotten. Family she was hurting unconsciously.

Unable to stand around and contemplate why she should feel so humiliated by her injury and uncertain recovery, Amal acted quickly. The watery heat burning her eyes hurried her movements. She wouldn't cry—not openly, for anyone to happen on her tears.

Setting Manny's breakfast tray to one side of the door, where he'd be able to find it and not step on it, Amal hurried away.

"Amal?"

She froze at Manny's imploring tone. She'd lingered too long and he stepped out, catching her fleeing.

"Amal," he said again.

When he called to her Amal rounded on him. She knew he could see her tears. His lips stretched into a grave line and his dark eyes were steely. They held zero comfort for her.

It was all she needed to hear and see—all she needed to know. Mansur was leaving. He wanted nothing to do with her. She'd overwhelmed him, and he was washing his hands of her memory problem, like most everyone had. It wouldn't be too long before Mama Halima gave up hope, too.

"I have to go," Amal said, her voice sounding choked by the tears she'd tried so carefully to hold at bay.

This time he didn't stop her leaving.

CHAPTER TWO

NOTHING SHORT OF Manny finding Amal and begging her forgiveness would satisfy his mother, and she left him in a flurry of long black skirts and robes. She refused to speak to him until he apologized to her precious Amal.

One of her comments in particular circled his mind like vulture on carrion.

"Do you not care for Amal?"

Manny had flinched when his mother had hurled the question at him, her accusatory tone laced with bitter disappointment. There had been one other time when she had looked at him like that—after he'd missed his father's funeral, nearly a year ago.

Manny hadn't been too warm on his father, and he hadn't cared to lay a stranger to rest. In hindsight, he regretted showing up at all. Maybe if he hadn't he wouldn't feel the relentless remorse of having failed his mother again. Only now his failure concerned Amal and not his father.

In the end, he hadn't been able to answer her. So his mother had departed his guest room with her dramatic ultimatum: either he fixed what he'd broken with Amal, or he could leave Hargeisa and never bother contacting her again.

She was willing to sever her relationship with him for Amal. As if *he* wasn't her biological child. Her *only* child.

Manny gnashed his teeth, frustrated to have been put on

the spot like that. Halfway through dragging his suitcase to the bedroom door, prepared to catch his mother out on her bluff, he grasped the brass doorknob and froze.

Despite his resolve to leave after his mother's stinging dressing-down, he couldn't do it.

Manny smoothed a hand over his weary face. He closed his eyes and touched his forehead to the cool, solid oak door and counted his inhalations and exhalations. What he needed, moving forward, was a clear head.

Several thoughtful breaths later, he opened his eyes and confronted what had been staring at him all along. In that moment he relinquished some of the barriers around his hardened heart to the sharp pull of culpability. He had played a role in pushing Amal away. The least he could do was leave when they were on a neutral footing. Though he struggled to admit it, he didn't want Amal to hate him.

Grunting, he turned from the door and dragged his suitcase back over the worn carpet, setting it by the guest bed. He hadn't touched the breakfast Amal had prepared for him, though he'd carried it inside. The tray rested, forgotten, atop the crisp, freshly scented bedspread. It was only one more reminder of the daunting task before him.

Did he not care for Amal?

He cared for her plenty—obviously. Or else he wouldn't be leaving this room hungry and annoyed, with guilt gnawing at his insides, doing exactly what his mother would have him do.

Satisfied the foyer was empty, and that no one would witness his short walk of shame to Amal's bedroom, Manny resisted barging in and dredged up enough patience to rap on her door. He gave her three biting warnings with his knuckles before he turned the doorknob, pushing the door open cautiously.

There was no need for caution. Manny faced her empty bedroom.

Stepping inside and closing the door, he looked about, as if preparing for Amal to burst out from under the bed or pop out of the stately wardrobe that had once belonged to him. It was different seeing her belongings in the space he'd called his own through much of his childhood. Worse, they looked so natural there. Like they always were meant to claim this room.

He hardened his jaw and scowled at the memories in the room, looking at Amal's new touches.

The scarred pale yellow walls and the old wrought-iron single bed had once been his, and now they held Amal's books and her headscarves. Her journal was now tucked away somewhere he couldn't see, so he couldn't be enticed to riffle through its secreted pages. Had she ever mentioned him in there? What were her thoughts of him now, with her amnesia?

Manny stilled his hand, stopping shy of opening the single drawer of his old nightstand. It took considerable strength to pull back, calm his itching fingers. Even when she wasn't present she tempted him.

Recognizing lingering snatches of the fruity notes of Amal's perfume over the sharper, spicier frankincense trailing in from outside, Manny caught himself soaking in her aroma. It took great effort to stir from the side of the bed, stalk from the room and from the main house to the kitchen, adjacent the side entrance. There he hoped he'd find answers for Amal's disappearance.

The temperature outdoors was beginning to warm as morning crept over the blue, cloudless sky. He stepped in from the sunlight, his eyes adjusting to the change in lighting within the dim kitchen, and startled the housemaid who'd been carrying the mop and bucket earlier. She gawked up at him from her stool. It appeared she hadn't gotten used to his presence yet.

"Is Amal around?" he asked, moving to a door near where the shocked housemaid sat before the charcoal stove.

The roomy pantry was empty. Disappointed, he turned and discovered the other maid was joining them in the kitchen. She was the one who had originally sat in front of the stove with Amal.

Manny repeated his question to her.

"She left for work," the kitchen maid said in Somali, leading Manny outside. She obviously trusted that he understood her, not slowing her rapid speech. "You might be able to catch her. Ask Abdi for a ride." She pointed out the small guardhouse in the corner of the gated property.

Manny had to round the dirt-caked truck that had brought him there to find the driver, his much older relative. Once he had the other man's attention, Manny asked, "Can you drive me to Amal's workplace?"

"I can," the older man replied, a carefree smile at the ready. He pushed himself off his worn mattress, tucked his phone away and made for the driver's end of the pickup.

As Manny climbed into the truck he acknowledged the lengths he was going to for Amal. But the sooner he found her, the quicker he could be done with his apology, be back on amiable terms with his mother, and the faster he'd be able to leave Hargeisa.

Reaching for the seatbelt, he paused, remembering that it was broken. Gripping the roof handle, Manny girded himself for yet another teeth-rattling, bumpy ride like the one he'd endured from the airport.

Unfortunately, he hadn't thought to grab an antacid from his suitcase. Not that he truly believed an antacid would reverse the heartburn creeping up on him. Intuition warned that it had to do with his impending meeting with Amal. And until that was done he'd have no relief.

Amal looked out her office window at her firm, AK Designs Architecture.

It still floored her that she *had* a firm, even though she now remembered having purchased this fourth-floor office for her business. At one point, a few weeks ago, she hadn't even been able to recall that she owned a business.

Progress in her amnesia.

It gave her hope that she'd eventually regain what she had lost, and all would be as right as the heavy rains that would come as soon as spring changed into summer.

She looked away from the bustling world down below—the traffic, the people, the wandering goats, all under the morning sun's golden blanket. She moved from the window to her desk, stroking her fingers over the smooth cherry oak surface.

This was all hers.

Amal sat in her office chair, picking up where she'd left off in trying to make sense of the technical drawings on her laptop. Only now it wasn't because she was worried that she'd forgotten her job skills, but rather that she couldn't tap into the right emotions for a project that should have been near and dear to her.

A hospital in Hargeisa. One that actually had up-to-date medical technology and the right crop of professionals with the training to handle the equipment.

As Amal now understood, it had been on the worksite of the hospital that she'd had the accident that had led to her amnesia. She had no recollection of having ever set foot on the construction site. But those newer adult memories seemed lost to her at the moment.

"Or forever," she said, with a weighty sigh whooshing out of her.

She leaned back in her office chair, tipping her head up to the ceiling, her mind straying to Mansur, of all people.

She snapped her head down, annoyed at herself. She was in the middle of giving her head a good shake when a knock stirred her into grasping the perfectly timed deflection.

"Come in," she called, standing and waiting for her visitor.

She sucked in a sharp breath when Mansur opened her door, his height and muscled frame filling the doorway. Somewhere behind him Amal could hear the impatient snap of her office manager and friend, Iman.

"Excuse me, sir! You can't go in there."

Iman's annoyance thickened her accented Somali. She was practically growling when Mansur stepped into the room, and Amal could see her glowering on the threshold of her office. The women exchanged a look and Iman rolled her eyes, crossing her arms, waiting for Amal's signal to call some of their junior technologists—all young men who would be happy to drag Manny out of the building for them.

As amusing as that might be—especially after her last interaction with Mansur—Amal gave Iman a little shake of her head. She had this covered. Seeing that she wasn't needed, Iman offered one last frown and then swiveled on her tall heels, disappearing from the open door.

Mansur's intense stare had stretched on throughout Amal's silent communication with her office manager. Now he said, "We need to talk."

Those four words had her even more on edge than when she had lived through his discovery of her amnesia.

Amal gulped softly, and stammered, "D-Do we?"

She hated it that her wariness was so apparent to him. She wanted the advantage of at least appearing unaffected by his sudden arrival at her office. She'd come here figuring she was safe from the hurt and dismay that had chased her once she'd learned he planned to leave Hargeisa immediately—when he'd all but stated she was a hopeless cause.

"I think we do," he told her. His eyes tracked over her features. "I'd also like to apologize if I've offended you."

She looked from him to her computer screen, and the schematics for the hospital that were still throwing her a bit. She had thought to add some alterations to the technical drawings, but she'd require all her focus for that. And she wouldn't be able to concentrate much on her work now her thoughts were preoccupied with Mansur.

"If you're all right with it, I'd like to have breakfast with you," he said.

"Now?" she asked, staring up at him.

He nodded. "I'll understand if you're too busy, though."

She knew that he would, given his own high-powered job.

"Amal, don't feel pressured to come with me."

Hearing her name from his mouth did it for her. He spoke with a kindness that had been absent in his tone when he and his mother had been discussing her amnesia.

"All right," she said. "But it'll have to be a quick breakfast."

"I can do that," he agreed.

Manny needed this breakfast to be his closure with Amal. She'd already surprised him by agreeing to join him. The relief he'd felt had been eroded quickly when he'd realized how affected he still was by her, emotionally and physically. Case in point: Amal moved ahead of him, her steps short but fast, her thick hips swishing from side to side, whipping up more of that unwelcome desire in him.

Concentrating on the dusty beige world around them,

instead of Amal's sensual curves, Manny marveled at how the only pops of color came from the garbage bags that were like tumbleweed in the downtown marketplace. The concept of trash bins didn't exist here. Sure, there was some waste management, but not nearly enough effort to keep the streets free of pollution.

A pale, thin goat snacked on a piece of cardboard. The animal lifted its head on their passing, its black, glassy eyes tracking them. More livestock wandered aimlessly alongside the beggars on the street. Young and old, male and female, sick and healthy. They all had reasons to be asking for loose change.

Amal paused for a thin, sickly woman and her trio of small, wide-eyed children, and then again for an elderly man rolling his wheelchair.

She doled out more donations, her heart as generous as he remembered it being. When she paused for a shirtless, sad-looking boy, Manny rooted out an American twenty-dollar bill. The boy grinned wide before he sprang off with the money, as if his benefactor might change his mind.

"You're still stopping for them?" he wondered aloud, not expecting a response.

Her frostiness had suggested there would be no conversation until they reached a restaurant. So, he was taken aback when she said, "I try. There's only so much I can do, though."

She looked both ways and crossed the street, marching ahead. Manny shadowed her, his hand bumping her arm when a minibus stopped inches from collision, the driver honking wildly and shouting for them to clear his path.

"That was dangerous," he observed, his fingers itching to grasp her wrist. He was worried she'd hurt herself, navigating directionless traffic. It was one of the many things he hadn't missed about Somaliland.

Amal didn't respond until she paused before a fenced construction site. "The hospital," she said.

He studied the leveled ground and the deep hole. The foundation was still in progress. Only it appeared the construction site was abandoned. Glancing around, he imagined it should be filled with workers at this early hour on a weekday.

"A project of yours?" Manny asked, not questioning how she'd remembered the hospital. It was becoming clear her amnesia was fickle about what she recalled and what she didn't. And that didn't set him at ease at all.

Amal nodded once, her attention dead ahead and her voice soft and disconnected. "It was supposed to be a new hospital, but the development of the infrastructure was stopped after my accident." A frown furled her eyebrows. "It happened here. I hit my head somewhere on site. I don't recall it, but that's what everyone's been telling me." She touched her temple. "The government has since pulled their funding. As I understand from my employees, it wasn't too supportive of this project to start with." She dropped her hand and balled it into a fist. "They're all greedy politicians who want to line their pockets rather than care for their constituents."

Manny regarded her profile. Could she be thinking of her mother when she looked at the abandoned grounds and the would-be hospital? He had been eleven and Amal only eight when she'd lost her mom to childbirth complications from eclampsia—the baby had died, too. But he recalled how his mother had said the hospital had been ill-equipped to cope with the medical issue.

Grief-stricken, Amal's father had admitted that he couldn't care for his surviving children, and without any other relatives willing to feed three extra mouths he'd dumped them on his mother-in-law—Amal's maternal grandmother.

That was when Amal and her brothers had moved in next door. And that was how Mansur had gained three childhood friends.

But Amal's amnesia must have robbed her of those few memories of her mother, too. Mustn't it?

"My mom..." Amal trailed off, as if she'd taken a peek into his mind and now answered his doubt. Her throat fluttered, undulating with quiet but powerful emotions. "A new hospital could help someone like her."

"You remember?"

Manny frowned, his mind whirling. Did she or did she not have amnesia? He knew it was a complicated, loaded query. And this wasn't some daytime melodrama. It had to be more complex than whether she'd lost all her memories or not and would regain them in a plot twist.

Shoving off the selfish unease building in him, he stumbled on the tail end of her soft explanation.

"I'm recalling more of my childhood, if anything. My adult memories—they're the ones I can't fully access yet." She sighed, forlorn. "Sometimes I wake up not knowing who I should be. And wondering if it was that way before the amnesia."

"You aren't having problems at work, though," Manny said, suddenly driven to wipe the despondency from her pretty face. She'd looked confident and at home in her office.

"Not with my skills, no. They did need a bit of brushing up, but my procedural memory's been good to me. Thankfully. I wouldn't have known what to do if I'd had to cancel all my clients' projects and close the firm."

"Small blessing," he murmured.

Sympathetic was what he was. Being CEO of an in-demand, top-earning company meant there was added pressure on every delivery to a client. He imagined it was the same for Amal, running her own company.

The fact that they had both succeeded in their respective and similar careers hadn't gone over his head. It reminded him of the dreams they'd once shared as children. How they had both wanted to rebuild Hargeisa, usher the lively city into new infrastructural heights and brighten the futures of its citizens.

He'd ended up leaving for the States, but she'd stayed. She'd continued living their dream.

"Do you love what you do?" he asked out of the blue.

"It's all I've ever wanted to do."

"I know," he said, nodding and looking at the excavation site and beyond it, to what it could be if Amal's vision came to life. "We've both studied in similar fields, and now we're building our dreams into reality. Despite being in the industry for nearly a decade, the feeling of being at a ribbon-cutting ceremony and seeing the final product can't be beat."

She smiled. "The faces are what I remember most. What I *love* most. Seeing how happy clients are with the reveal."

Manny chuckled. "How could I forget?"

She laughed lightly then, her eyes sparkling, the hint of gloominess from earlier gone. He wished he didn't have to ruin the peaceful moment. But time was pressing, and they couldn't stand around reminiscing all day. Soon she'd want to return to her office, and he still had his piece to say.

"Amal, what was your doctor's prognosis for the amnesia?" he asked. Saying her name was tripping him up. It sounded too familiar on his tongue. Like coming home. But he was undeserving of the happy relief that welled up in him.

As for this amnesia business—he couldn't shake the absurdity of it.

Her memory loss was perfect for him, and yet terribly painful, too. Perfect in that it saved him from explanations and reliving heartbreak, and painful because he was going through it alone.

She had no recollection of their long-distance conversations about building a future together, let alone his marriage proposal and her hasty rejection.

In her mind, it seemed their long-distance romance had never existed. While he recalled—*and* replayed, clip by clip—how their friendship had blossomed into…more. Something he'd had no name for until she herself had shyly confessed to liking him romantically.

No, she said she loved me.

And he had asked for time to process it.

Process it he had—and that was when he'd come to her, closing the seven-thousand-mile gap between them with a diamond in one hand and his heart in the other. He'd planned to offer her both—and he had. But she had shocked him with her refusal.

How could she not remember?

Did it matter, though? He knew it didn't alter the situation they were in now, standing and facing off like strangers. He'd do better to focus his energy on what he *could* change. Like having her consider the options of medical treatment elsewhere.

"The doctor said I could regain my full memory."

She folded her arms over her chest. Her new posture wasn't offensive so much as it was defensive. Protective, even. Like that alone was enough to hold at bay the everyday problems of the world and her extraordinary problem of amnesia.

"There's also a possibility that I could stay like this forever."

She shrugged and lowered her arms. She shifted so that her body faced the fencing of the empty worksite. It looked more like a war zone than the start of what could be Hargeisa's premier hospital, for rich and poor alike.

"The timeline for my recovery is uncertain," she said softly, defeat beating at her words.

"And yet you could seek better medical care and technology elsewhere," he said.

She snapped her bemused gaze to him.

"I know you heard my mother and I speaking," he said.

Amal opened her mouth, closed it, and frowned. Smart of her. No point in wasting time and breath arguing about her eavesdropping. Actually, right then he appreciated it. It saved him from explaining what he'd already told his mother. That he had business in Ethiopia.

"Why not join me? You could visit with a doctor in Addis Ababa, and we could try for a second opinion."

"'We'?" she echoed, lifting her brows. First one, and then the other. Speculation and disbelief collided and mingled in her arresting features.

Manny understood why she might not trust him. To her, he was a stranger now. But even if she possessed full command of her memory she likely wouldn't give him the time of day, given how they'd parted ways. A year was a long time for him to expect her to wait for an apology—and he wasn't even certain why he should apologize.

An old, earthy grudge swelled in him. Stuffing it down, knowing that *now* wasn't the time to pick and unseal scabbed wounds, he tackled her question.

Of course he'd heard it, too. He had hoped she'd missed his slip of the tongue, but he wasn't that lucky.

"What I meant is that *we* would be going together," he

said lamely. "And *I* would be happy to show you Addis, as well. It'd be your first trip out of Somaliland, wouldn't it?"

He knew it for a fact, and yet he waited for her answer.

"Yes, it would be—but I can't just leave. I have work piling up."

She hugged her arms around her middle again. Back to being defensive.

Avoiding his eyes, she murmured, "I can't go with you, Mansur."

"Manny," he amended instinctually. "Can't or won't?"

In her surprise, she looked at him again. She tucked her bottom lip between her teeth and, worrying at the soft flesh, appeared distraught. Lost. *Cornered.*

He hoped not by him and his offer. Though he *did* want her to strongly consider it.

Again Manny regarded the would-be hospital, the construction site frozen and forgotten...but not by her. Never by her, given the strong, unspoken feelings he'd sensed in her when she had been talking about her accident and how it had come to stall the construction of the hospital.

Her dedication demanded admiration from him, and he gave it to her readily. Which was why he said, "Do it for the hospital, then."

"Pardon?"

"I said do it for your hospital. For Hargeisa, even. For the tens of thousands—no, *hundreds* of thousands of patients who might be saved because of your choice right now."

Dramatic, yes. The over-the-top, boardroom-worthy pitch would have roused even his most dour-faced directors, and his board had *plenty* of that type. Old fogeys who clashed too often with Manny, their new, young CEO and president.

The hyperbole worked, though. Amal's bemusement melted and a clarity brightened her eyes. She, too, stared at the site of what would be her hospital someday soon, and she smiled.

Manny's heart thudded at the radiance of her smile and the sharpness of each heartbeat alarmed him. Clearly he'd underestimated the mystical power she continued, unknowingly, to wield over him.

Mouth dry, he said, "I know my mother orchestrated my arrival, and I know you played no part in her good-intentioned deception."

Amal didn't seem to notice the break in his even, confident voice. She waited silently for him to finish. Riveted was what she was. Beautiful and still and curious.

And very disrupting, he surmised.

"Word of advice: if you choose to join me in Addis, make the choice for yourself. Not for my mother's sake, or because of what others think of you."

"For myself?" she repeated.

"Yes, for *yourself*," he emphasized. "Ultimately, you know what course of action is best for you."

She was quiet…thoughtfully so. "It's a tough decision."

"It's *your* decision either way." And he promised himself he wouldn't interfere in her choice.

Instead of choosing, though, she asked, gazing almost shyly at him, "What would you do, in my place?"

"If I thought it'd make a difference, I'd go."

"And if I strongly believe it might not?" she whispered.

Manny didn't know what to tell her. He suspected that no matter what he said she'd march to her own drum. So he said, "I had a choice not to be a CEO. I could've easily stepped aside and allowed another candidate to sweep the title."

"Why didn't you?"

He palmed his beard. "Because I felt I was the best for the position. I still feel that way." He lowered his hand from his jaw and recalled how hard he'd worked to be where he was professionally. "I make sacrifices. I work day and night. And my social calendar suffers even more these days."

He'd lost a few friends when it had become obvious to them that he couldn't be bothered to maintain friendships. But he'd also done the same to his family.

"I haven't seen my mom in a year," he confessed. Not since he'd had to travel home to see how she was doing after his father's wake and funeral.

"But you talk to her on the phone."

Amal spoke matter-of-factly. It was amazing she couldn't see the worst in him. He hadn't been a good son to his mother. And when he'd heard his mother say *"Hooyo"* he had felt an earthshattering guilt for not calling her as often as he should have.

"I call her when I can," he replied.

Amal smiled and nodded. "You had to make a tough decision, too."

It was a tough call. She gets it.

Manny stuffed down the balmy calm that her empathy brought him.

He understood that he might not get an answer right then. She had a lot to consider. Even though he'd advised her to think of herself alone when making a decision, he knew how improbable that was. Amal didn't live in a bubble or a vacuum. Besides, she'd always been more considerate than he. Sensitive to others and generous to a fault. If she had a flaw, it was that she was too good. Too kind. Too thoughtful.

Too spellbinding, he mused, finding some humor in his startling weakness for her.

He didn't expect her to make her choice right then, and he certainly wasn't waiting for her to pack her bags and come with him. Manny was prepared to stake his net worth on her refusing his offer. The only upside being that this time he wouldn't be blindsided when it came—unlike when he'd asked her to be his wife.

So Amal surprised him when she nodded. Firmly. Decidedly.

"All right. I'd like to go," she said.

Like a candle wick, resolution flickered to life in her eyes, the flame gleaming more brilliantly with every passing second. Some switch had been flipped on inside her, and she was transformed by incandescent light and beauty.

By her decision to go with him.

Now he had to make certain that that light wasn't dimmed and she didn't regret her choice.

CHAPTER THREE

ALMOST AS SOON as they were in agreement that Amal would be joining him, Mansur looked at his vibrating phone. He sent a reply to the message-sender. When he met her eyes again, his phone tucked away, he offered news that would turn everything around and make her rethink her hasty decision to travel with him to Addis Ababa.

"It seems we'll be leaving sooner than I intended," he said, grim-faced.

The sudden change in him ruffled Amal.

"Sooner?" she squeaked, feeling more and more like a broken record.

She'd been parroting him since they'd left her office—but that was because he kept shocking her. First with his offer for her to go to the capital of Ethiopia with him, and now this. This about-face in their timeline.

When Amal had agreed, she'd assumed they would stay longer in Hargeisa. Long enough for her to get her work-related affairs in order and sort everything else out. She still had to tell his mother, too. And pack for the trip.

The to-do list was staggering, and her anxiety shot up at the realization of it. She was almost afraid to ask, but she had to. "How soon?"

"As soon as possible, ideally," he said, confirming her

unease. If she still planned to tag along they'd be leaving sooner rather than her much-preferred later.

"I'll be heading back to my mother's to gather my luggage. I suggest you join me and pack, as well," he informed her, all business as usual.

She was beginning to sculpt a clearer picture of him, and it wasn't favorable. And yet he'd given her this opportunity to seek a second opinion. A second fighting chance at besting her amnesia. These opposing sides to Mansur were throwing off her impression of him. Did he mean her well, or was there more to his offer than he'd revealed, along the lines of doing her a favor on his mother's behalf?

Amal knew mother and son were close from how happy Mama Halima became whenever she mentioned Mansur. It wasn't happiness Amal felt when she was around him, though. Far from it. More like a giddiness. A fever in her blood she couldn't rid herself of. She'd say she was sick, but this illness required no doctor and no diagnosis. Just a simple acceptance of the fact that Mansur was a *very* good-looking man, and if she hadn't been attracted to him before her amnesia, she was *very* much developing a crush on him now.

"What about breakfast?" she wondered softly, letting her mind linger on her attraction for him and at the same time hoping they could discuss some wiggle room in their looming departure.

He flashed her the faintest of smiles. "We'll get to enjoy breakfast. Only not in Hargeisa."

"As promised—breakfast," he announced, two hours later.

Manny believed himself a man of his word. And, although he knew that his expert and well-paid flight staff wouldn't fall short of his expectations, he puffed up with pride at their display of an in-flight meal. They hadn't disappointed him. And *he* hadn't disappointed Amal.

"It's too much!" was her first exclamation, followed closely by, "But it looks delicious! I couldn't let it go to waste."

"*We* couldn't let it go to waste," he amended, lifting his fork to tackle a fluffy omelet.

Mirroring him, Amal grabbed for her utensils and surprised him with the vigor of her hunger, considering that only a few minutes ago, after their plane had leveled off and they'd reached cruising altitude, she had still appeared wan with airsickness. Now she dived into the American-style meal and even drizzled more amber maple syrup over her perfectly golden waffles. Apparently his fears for her had been for naught.

When the last piece of halal turkey bacon was plucked off the middle plate by Amal, and Manny's fingertips brushed hers, he felt his body ignite from the simple touch while she crowed at having been quicker.

"I think that piece was the yummiest," she gloated, laughing at the face he pulled.

"It's my plane. I could fetch more for myself and myself only," he said, fighting his own grin.

Amal shook her head at his light threat, an easy smile on her soft-looking mouth. "Go ahead." She sat back in her seat, her hands folded over her stomach. "I'm full! I couldn't eat another bite."

"I take it you're satisfied, then?"

Amal nodded and yawned. "But now I'm sleepy. I shouldn't have eaten so much."

"I'm sorry," he said, not knowing how else to respond.

The awkward misplaced apology made her open her eyes wide. "Why do you have to be sorry? I'm the one who lost self-control. Also, I don't regret it. It was a meal fit for royalty. A once-in-a-lifetime feast. Overeating was to be expected." She tilted her head, her shy smile making his heart race. "I wouldn't have gotten to enjoy it if you hadn't talked me into this trip. So, thank you."

"You're welcome."

Her contentment pleased him more than he would have anticipated. More than he liked to admit, even to himself. Only *she* had ever been able to do that to him. Lower his guard. Give him these indescribable, intangible...*feels.*

Nostalgia brushed the periphery of his mind and crept over him, and it carried a sparking storm of nebulous feelings. He tripped a mental alarm, warning himself away from naming any specific emotion.

This is how it starts, he thought bleakly.

This was how he opened his heart again and risked his sanity.

I can't do it.

He wouldn't do it.

"Where's the restroom?" Amal clasped her hands over her seatbelt, popping it off.

"This way." Manny stood, and then froze at Amal's protest.

"I can go alone," she said quickly—too quickly.

She avoided his eyes, her embarrassment all too plain. What did she think he was going to do? He felt a similar flush of mortification flutter through him. This was exactly what he'd feared. Encounters like these. Misunderstandings that would get him in trouble again.

He clenched his jaw, then unclenched it to say, "It's straight down, toward the back of the plane. The left bedroom and bathroom are roomier."

"You have two bedrooms?" she asked, standing when he sat down and looking shaky on her legs.

Fighting the urge to offer his arm for support, he shifted

in his seat and forced himself to get comfortable. Because he wasn't budging. She didn't want his help, and that was more than fine by him.

"Yes," he said, realizing he hadn't answered her. "There are two bedrooms. So if you'd like to lie down, feel free."

She blinked.

He stared, his brows slamming down and then hiking up. "What is it?"

"Nothing," she murmured.

Her large, soulful eyes and drawn features told another story, though. A flare of annoyance fluttered through him. "Is something bothering you?"

She lowered her eyes, and for a moment he thought she wouldn't respond, but then she said, "It's just all of this… It's your success, isn't it? It's a lot…but it says a lot, too. I can see why your mother is proud of you." Amal lifted her chin and met his eyes. "And she has every right to be."

Like a trigger, her words fired his ego. His head could have burst from the sudden and sharply rising pressure. His heart swelled from the rush of it.

He heard his own voice through the filter of rushing blood roaring in his ears. "It's not much."

She smiled wider. "Let me be the judge of that."

She left him with a short nod, her careful steps guiding her away from him. Manny sat there, his fingers clawing into the armrests and his body buzzing from the tidal emotions crashing in him.

Amal was dangerous to him—he knew that. She posed a threat to his renewed sense of calm. For a year he'd believed he had worked her out of his system. How wrong he'd been. In less than a day she'd unwound his security and his self-control. Worse, she had no clue what she was doing to him.

Unlike that night, he thought bitterly.

Like a stone skating over the surface of standing water, a memory from twelve months ago rippled to the fore. Before he could fight it, it dragged him under…

"Amal—wait!"

Whipping her skirt around, her abaya snapping as sharply as her flashing dark eyes, she pegged him with a full-blown scowl.

"What more could you say, Mansur? What could possibly explain how...how rude you were in there? You know it hurt your mother, and yet you didn't do anything to change it."

Her mouth curled with disappointment and her eyes shimmered with unshed tears.

His heart had to be in his throat, expanding it, and the burning sensation was making it hard to explain himself. Explain his absence from the wake. He'd missed the funeral, too, choosing instead to catch a later flight to Hargeisa and check on his mom.

Manny had seriously thought no one would notice. But she had.

Of course she had.

Amal could see his heart.

See his living, breathing anger and his undying grudge against his father.

"I'm..." He couldn't bring himself to say sorry. He just couldn't. Instead, he blurted, "I love you."

She gawked at him, eyes round now, her anger temporarily subdued.

Fearful of losing this tenuous reprieve, he lowered to one knee and retrieved the ring box nestled close to his heart in an inner jacket pocket.

"I love you," he repeated, snapping the ring box open and revealing the shining solitaire inside. It gleamed in the

twilight like a fallen star in his palm. "I love you, Amal, and I never want to lose you."

She stared from the ring to him, her shock morphing into nothingness as she herded her emotions behind a steely expression.

"Will you stay?" she asked quietly.

When he didn't respond, she reached for the ring box and closed it, leaving it in his hand. Unaccepting of his token of love.

"Your mother needs you," she said then, "and you won't stay for her."

Finally, Manny gritted, "I have a business to oversee, Amal."

He couldn't throw away his life in America. He'd built too much there. Hargeisa, beautiful as it was, held too much pain for him. And now his father was buried here, too.

"I can't," he said again, imploring her to understand, to be reasonable with him.

"I know."

She nodded, smiling with a sadness that sank his heart to his stomach. No. It obliterated it, that sorrowful smile of hers.

"It seems we're too different. I can't change you, and I don't want to hold you here. Trap you into being with me when I know you'll only resent me for it."

Manny launched to his feet when she turned to walk away from him again. "Wait!" he panted, breathless from his heartbreak.

Pathetically, he held the ring box out to her. He had to ask. He nearly bit his tongue off in dreaded anticipation. But he had to know for his peace of mind and his heart.

"Is that a no, then?" he asked, his voice a hoarse whisper.

"It is," Amal said softly. "Goodbye, Mansur."

She left him standing there, his arm thrust out, his fist squeezing over the small box that seemed to hold his whole world inside.

Manny surfaced from the memory breathless and perspiring. His chest was tight. His eyes wide and stinging. In that moment, he embodied sheer panic.

The only positive was the fact that he had no audience. Amal hadn't returned yet. That she hadn't witnessed his uncharacteristic meltdown soothed him greatly.

They were nearly upon Addis. It wouldn't be long before the pilot announced their landing...before Manny's real trial started.

Staring at Amal's vacant seat, he accepted that it wouldn't be easy. There was incontestable chemistry between them. And he had residual feelings for her that he hadn't laid to rest.

Now he had the opportunity to do that. To define their relationship in a way he could live with. Once and for all. Even if that meant losing her forever—*again*.

Amal returned, still astounded by the glamour of the aircraft's amenities, and discovered Mansur had cleared all evidence of their breakfast.

He held a tablet in his hands, his finger flipping pages of the document he was reading. She hovered nearby, slowing to a stop, curious to watch him while he didn't yet suspect her presence.

It bothered her that she couldn't recall him. She burned with frustration and the longing to demystify the enigma that he was. She might have asked him straight up, but a strange niggling sensation cautioned her against it. Strange because she didn't know what kind of man he was.

He's generous.

Or she supposed he was. He'd allowed her to join him in Addis Ababa, and he was correct about her chances at receiving better medical care there.

He wouldn't have helped if his mother hadn't intervened.

True, Mama Halima must have gotten through to him. Perhaps that was what was bugging her? Causing this restlessness to uncoil in her roiling stomach? It was either that or her breakfast wasn't sitting well with her. She didn't think all that good food was the problem so, grudgingly, she conceded that it was her lingering distrust in his motivation to invite her.

She didn't know him. Didn't *remember* him.

But she could start changing that now. They were alone. She had his attention until they landed, so long as he wasn't too busy working, and it couldn't hurt to re-establish a relationship with him even if he wouldn't be with her for too long.

She approached him, feeling like she'd played voyeur and spied on him long enough.

He looked up at her passing. "Find everything all right?"

Mansur lowered the tablet to his lap and gave her his full attention. The intensity that had been focused on whatever work he was doing was now bearing down on her.

She resisted fanning her heated cheeks.

"I did. Not that I almost didn't get lost. The plane's much bigger than I imagined."

She fidgeted in her seat, convincing herself she was getting comfortable. The truth was she couldn't squelch her attraction to him. It took everything in her to meet his eyes and wipe clear any evidence of the turmoil inside her. She fought against the instinct to look away. Prey had to feel much like she was, when facing down its predators. And Mansur was big game. Apex. At the top of the social and economic food chain.

"Am I interrupting you?"

She glanced at his tablet, the screen darkened after lack of activity. There wouldn't be any point in talking to him if he had work on his mind. She knew what that could be like. Being consumed with the passion of your career. *She* hated disruptions when she felt most inspired. And Mansur had appeared absorbed in whatever he'd been doing before she'd returned.

"It's work, but nothing I can't do later." He drew out the retractable table and placed his tablet atop it, facedown. "You have something on your mind?"

His perception surprised her. Was she that obvious?

"What business do you have in Addis?" she blurted, curiosity running away with her. She'd held it in for long enough.

He rubbed his beard, his hand molding to his jaw as he stroked thoughtfully. "My father left me an inheritance and I've been placed in a position to claim it."

What he said captured her interest, because it wasn't the kind of business she'd anticipated. And then there was his flat delivery of the information to consider…

His late father had to be a sore topic.

A year after his father's death had to feel like nothing.

Amal knew and understood. Any thoughts of her beloved grandmother, even with her memory loss, never failed to stir up melancholy in her. Death and grief and loss in some form or another were all difficult subject matters. Especially when her twenty-nine years had been steeped in it.

"I'm sorry for your loss," she said, her eyes stinging a little already.

"Thanks," he said coolly.

Mansur thinned his lips and hardened his jaw. A muscle leaped in his left cheek from the tension that dripped off him. There was a question in his dark, probing eyes.

She had no doubt that the tables would be turned, and they were. Promptly.

"Do you remember him?" he asked, one brow raised sharply.

"Your father? No. But I'm aware that he passed away. And even though it's been a year, I'm sorry for it." She watched for signs of sadness. They didn't exist. Manny either held his cards so close to his chest that he'd perfected detachment or—and much more worrying—he truly wasn't concerned in the slightest.

The latter provoked a chill in her. Even the notion that he could be so cold-blooded perturbed her immensely.

Changing tack, she asked, "How long are you planning to stay in Addis Ababa?"

"If I'm lucky, it won't be long," he replied.

Amal's heart sank at his response. What had she expected, though? He was there to do business. In fact, he might not even have invited her if he hadn't had to stop by Addis in the first place. It was a stark reminder that she wasn't his priority.

More like a chore, she thought glumly, recalling how Mama Halima had pleaded on her behalf with Mansur.

"What's it like living in America?" she asked. She wanted to forget that she was his obligation, and that he was being a dutiful son to his mother and nothing more.

"It's nothing special," he said.

Amal tipped her head to the side. "It's different than life in Hargeisa, isn't it?"

"Of course—but that's a given."

At first, she truly believed he would leave it there. But then Mansur cleared his throat and continued.

"Pittsburgh is a good city. I don't explore it as much as I should, but when I manage to get out of my office I find there's never a lack of something to do."

Amal gripped her armrests as the plane shuddered against some turbulence. Gritting her teeth, she implored, "Describe it to me, this city of yours."

Again, she'd expected him to stonewall her. But he shocked her with his reply.

"Skyscrapers that appear to touch the heavens on the streets of Downtown. Bridges and rivers as far as the eye can see. It's a historic and diverse city full of music, art, sports and soul. And the food..." he said with a small but warm smile. "You'd have to taste it yourself, but I'd say it can't be beat."

Amal closed her eyes as the plane swayed violently again. She pictured his city instead, hoping she wouldn't upchuck the tasty breakfast as her stomach swooped with her rising fear. She wouldn't have stepped on this jet if she had known how scary it was to be tens of thousands of feet above ground. They were helpless against the turbulent winds and pressure up here.

"Are you all right?" Mansur's silkily deep voice asked.

"Just a little queasy," she confessed. It was her first time flying. She hoped he'd cut her some slack if she did wind up vomiting in his ritzy plane.

"Would you like a sick bag?" he asked, concern roughening the timbre of his voice.

"Maybe that'd be a good idea."

And while he had someone fetch it for her he calmly told her more about his beloved American home. "Moving to Pittsburgh was difficult at first. I'd grown used to studying and living in Boston. But I don't regret the move now that I've called it my home city for nearly a decade."

"Do you have many friends?" she asked, once a flight attendant had tapped her arm and delivered the sick bag. She opened her eyes and found Mansur studying her.

"Those sacrifices we spoke of...well, I've lost some friends along the way."

His candor humbled her. Very softly, she said, "I was surprised when not many people visited me in the hospital. I've learned that not all my friends cared enough to check on me."

She would've hung her head, embarrassed, if Mansur hadn't spoken up again.

"They weren't your friends if they weren't by your side."

"No, I suppose they weren't," she agreed, smiling when he nodded.

He picked up his tablet and began working again as they lapsed into a natural quietness. After some time, he glanced up and announced, "We should be landing soon."

Amal followed his cue and buckled her seatbelt, renewing her taut grip on the armrests of her chair.

Not too long after, the pilot's voice crackled over the intercom to inform them of their descent.

Amal practically swallowed her tongue as she felt the plane dip. Lower, lower. Down, down, and down.

They were descending at a pace she began to feel. Soon they'd be on the ground in Addis Ababa. And, as much as this last leg of the flight rattled her, it wasn't as unnerving as wondering what the Ethiopian capital held in store for her and Mansur.

What else might she learn about the temptingly handsome tycoon who had invited her on this adventure?

That last thought challenged her most of all.

CHAPTER FOUR

"So, this is Addis..." Amal whispered the words to herself.

Alone in the cavernous hotel suite, and astonished at the luxury all around her, she walked through double doors out to the balcony. She soaked in the fresh air, not knowing she'd needed it until that moment. The city noise was nowhere as shatteringly loud when she looked down from her eighteenth-floor view.

She grasped the cool balcony railing, a sudden spell of lightheadedness rocking her. She'd really done it—traveled for the first time, braved flying in Mansur's jet—and it had been worth testing the boundaries of her strength and the limitations of her fear.

Amal turned her face up and slightly angled it toward an easterly wind. The sweet kiss of cool air was a pleasant change from the heat of day.

The sweltering near-summer temperature in Addis Ababa was similar to that of downtown Hargeisa—where her architectural firm was located and where the beige grainy sands were all she could taste in her mouth some days, so she experienced a smidgen of the terrible drought that sometimes struck.

A shortage of rainfall there decimated smaller and poorer dwellings. And everyone suffered the disaster of extreme heat and crop destruction—from farmers to merchants, beggars to businessmen, some worse than others. It was a time when hospitalization increased. And she'd looked on helplessly, dreaming of her hospital, wondering if its completion and opening would overturn many unnecessary sicknesses and deaths.

Why did she have to hit her head? She'd had the project approved by the corrupt local government at last, but instead of withstanding their continued disapproval of the hospital's construction she'd bared her throat and they had torn at her jugular. No, at her very heart!

Her amnesia had ruined everything.

Some days she didn't know how she could ever make peace with her ravaged memory. Those days were beginning to become more and more a staple of her life.

"Don't cry," she muttered, feeling a familiar heat lashing at her eyes and the tears falling anyways.

She clung to the guilt of having let down the countless faceless patients who would have benefited from her forgotten hospital. And then she envisioned Mansur, his words to her resounding in her head.

"Do it for your hospital. For Hargeisa, even. For the tens of thousands—no, hundreds of thousands of patients who might be saved."

Thinking of him was enough to make her wipe at her wet cheeks and blink back any remaining tears. She knew without a doubting bone in her body that if he'd been in her shoes right then, he wouldn't bother with crying. Mansur possessed the traits she desired for herself. Stout confidence. A healthy ego. Visionary results.

She knew all this from observing him in the flesh. And also because she'd scoured the details of him in the one place accessible to her and most of the world: the Internet. The Wi-Fi at the hotel had hooked her phone up to the online sleuthing she'd wanted to do all along.

He'd told her of Pittsburgh on the plane, and he had even hinted at losing some friends to his career success, but Amal yearned to learn more about him. And she shied away from asking him for fear that he'd see her as being nosy.

So she had settled for the Internet, but her search had proved to be fruitless. His professional accomplishments were all she'd been able to find. Barely any mention of his personal life. Oh, there was the occasional shot of him on a charity gala red carpet, or at the podium of some business symposium. But no hint of any slips and cracks in his professional mien. And no suggestion of a woman in his life.

In the end, her efforts to sleuth were stymied by Mansur's lack of a virtual footprint.

A doorbell chiming indoors placed her firmly in the present. She followed the musical chime to the entrance and opened the door.

Mansur pushed away from leaning on the doorframe. His hair was wet, darker from his shower. Gone was his suit. He wore black slacks and a fitted white T-shirt. His red sneakers were the brightest thing on him.

"May I come in?" he asked, his voice rumbling but polite.

She stepped aside, gesturing wordlessly for his entry. He passed her and led the way to the living area. Claiming a leather armchair with an ornate wood frame, he crossed his ankles and drummed his fingers atop the armrests. There was a lurking frustration in his gaze.

He smothered it as he blinked and said, "I'm sorry I left you alone for as long as I did."

"It's fine. You had business to oversee," she replied.

And he had, by the sounds of it when he'd answered the call that had ultimately pulled him away. He had seen her to her suite and gone next door to his. Knowing the challenges of running and managing a company, she understood why he'd disappeared for a couple hours.

"I hope it wasn't anything too urgent."

He stilled his fingers, frowning. "Unfortunately, it was."

She sat across from him, realizing that it was awkward standing beside the sofa that faced his armchair. It sounded like he had something to say and being seated for it would be nice, especially as her curiosity had weakened her knees.

Softly, she wondered, "Oh? What happened?"

Amal believed she'd nailed a casual tone, but his arched brows knocked her confidence.

"My lawyers discovered a hiccup in my father's will," he reported, "and an unforeseen one. I'd hoped I would be lucky and be done quickly here, but my luck's soured. I'll be staying on longer."

"For how long?" she asked.

"I can't be certain, but longer than I planned for."

She clasped her hands in her lap, forcing a stillness she didn't feel into her overly strung body. "It makes you unhappy to stay longer?"

"Yes, it does. I hadn't scheduled for it. So I'll have to do some adjusting. That takes time and sometimes—if I'm truly unlucky—it costs money, too." He lifted a hand and curled his fist under his chin, his elbow perched on the armrest. Cocking his head, he studied her quietly and then asked, "Is the room to your liking?"

She couldn't complain, if that was what he was wondering. "It's exquisite. Excessive, but luxurious." She took a break from looking at him to survey their surrounds. "I'd be lying if I said I was feeling at home. I feel like I shouldn't be here."

She felt like an intruder. This glamorous world wasn't hers, but Mansur's. Even dressed down, he appeared comfortable with the high-end amenities and furnishings in her suite. Simply put, she didn't belong.

But that wasn't what he'd asked. So she continued, "I like it. It's perfect."

"But you're uncomfortable?" he remarked, his brow curving into a brooding frown.

"Not uncomfortable," she lied.

"We could change hotels."

His suggestion snatched at her breath. She had to remind herself to breathe when her chest ached and her lungs cried out. She was certain he didn't care about her beyond their connection through his mother, so she couldn't make sense of why he was going out of his way to please her.

Maybe he wants to look good for Mama Halima.

She didn't know what to think, though. Because she didn't *know* him. And it felt unfair to judge him prematurely.

"No, I like it here just fine," she said, realizing he was waiting on her response.

"Good. I made lunch reservations for us at the hotel's restaurant, but I hadn't anticipated business interrupting."

No lunch together, then.

"That's fine," she murmured. The kitchen in her suite was stocked with everything she could possibly want. She wouldn't starve, if that was what he was worried about.

"Instead, I was hoping we could dine here, in your suite." He pushed his chin off his closed fist, moved his hands back to grip the armrests of his chair. "If that's all right with you?"

Hearing that he wanted to spend time with her was shocking. She hadn't imagined he'd stick around with her once they arrived in Addis Ababa. In fact, a part of her had been prepared for him to say as much now. Not tell her that he hoped still to lunch with her despite the change of venue. He looked serious, though. And he was awaiting her reply.

She gulped, her throat rippling. "All right."

"Good. I'll order now, then."

Without a backward glance he walked away from her with his phone pressed to his ear, and her eyes tracked his back as he took the call out on the balcony. His deep, steady voice drifted to where she sat.

She buzzed with giddy energy when he returned, sitting up straighter and widening her eyes as his stare locked onto her. Her belly cramped in a pleasant way when he offered her a small smile.

"I just realized that I ordered for us without asking if you'd like something specifically," he rumbled, adding, "I hope that's okay?"

"I trust you," she said, face flushed.

He stared quietly at her, and then he dipped his chin, his smile gone and his face impassive. "I hope your trust isn't misplaced."

She didn't know what to make of that.

Taking his seat once more, Mansur hooked his ankle over his knee and leaned into the high-back armchair. There was an intent gleam in his eyes and she felt sweat forming along her brow under her headscarf. She swore her scar from the worksite accident sparked at the pressure of his stare.

"What is it?" she croaked softly. Worry had slurped the warmth from her belly.

"About going to the hospital..." he said, and his words sank her spirits. "I was wondering how you'd like to proceed. You did, after all, come here for a second opinion. I wouldn't want my schedule to throw your plans."

"Throw?" she echoed.

"Disrupt," he amended. His jaw set more firmly, he continued, "I'll be tied up after lunch. But I was going to suggest you confirm an appointment with the surgeon."

"Surgeon?" That would be the second time she'd parroted him in the span of a minute, if not less. Flushing from embarrassment, she stammered, "I—I don't understand. What surgeon?"

She dug crescents into her palms with her nails. It was just all too much. Mansur was talking a mile a minute, it felt like, and she couldn't keep up. And she hadn't ever thought they'd be discussing her medical plans for the amnesia—and so frankly.

"I have a connection with one of the premier hospitals in Addis. The neurotrauma surgeon there, awaiting your approval for a consult, is at the top of her game. She's renowned in her field." He blinked languidly, dropping his ankle from his knee and shrugging. "But if you feel like I've overstepped by contacting the doctor, stop me at any time."

He couldn't hide the hard shift of his jaw under his short beard. Yet he kept his emotion from leaking onto his face. With no tells to direct her, Amal had to rely on him once again. Because the offer of a consultation with a surgeon whom Mansur had pulled strings to tie down couldn't be passed up.

But before she accepted, there was one thing she needed to know. "When did you call the hospital?"

"Not too long ago," he answered, no hesitation in his tone.

"Before you were speaking to your lawyers?"

"After. I had time, and I wanted to ensure that at least one of us finishes what we came to accomplish in Addis Ababa." He leaned forward, his elbows resting on his knees now, his dark eyes probing her. "If you're not comfortable accepting the offer, please know you won't be hurting my feelings. You must do what's best for you, Amal."

She could've sighed with pleasure at the way his resonant voice spoke her name. It was hard to predict what she'd feel next with Mansur. And she'd be lying if she claimed she wasn't daunted by his mastery of her emotions.

She couldn't lean on him forever, though. Despite what he'd told her about being set back in his inheritance, eventually he'd head home to America. He would be gone, and she'd be alone again. She could only fully rely on herself. Not that it didn't warm her heart that he'd gone out of his way to help her. She just had to be careful.

With that last thought in mind, she steeled her spine and opened her mouth. "No, I'm happy that you did. I'd like to accept."

He held his phone out to her, saying, "I have the hospital programmed as nine. They'll want your explicit approval to book you in for tomorrow."

"Tomorrow?" she squeaked in surprise.

"It's either that or a few months down the road. The doctor's schedule is filled well in advance." He shrugged again, his piercing eyes slicing through her. "It's your choice, ultimately."

She bit her lip, staring down at his phone, her hand crushing it in a death grip. Finally, she sighed and tapped nine. She didn't wait long on the line before Reception answered and she confirmed her appointment. Swiping to cancel the call, Amal glanced up to find his eyes on her. She'd felt them appraising her the whole while.

Once more, a skitter of pleasure skated up her spine. She resisted trembling in front of him, even as her body flushed under her layers of clothing. Suddenly the controlled temperature which had been perfect in the suite felt stiflingly hot. She adjusted her headscarf and watched his eyes tracking her every movement. Hawkish was his gaze, and she had the distinct sense that he knew *exactly* why she was becoming hot and bothered.

He was attractive. And she was letting her emotions get tangled up in her appreciation of his good looks.

Silly, she chided.

Passing his phone to him, and ignoring how his fingers brushed along hers, Amal said, "I should get freshened up before lunch."

She excused herself, and Mansur let her leave without a word on his part. She sagged against the closed door of the bathroom, flattening a hand to her chest. Her thundering heart felt as though it would leap out of her chest and into her awaiting palm.

"Stop it," she whispered to herself.

There was no point in working herself into a feverish state over someone who would never see her in the same light. The chances of Mansur feeling the same desire was slim to nil. She had to keep her head on her shoulders. Fantasizing about him would only muddle her feelings when he departed for America. And that was an eventuality she couldn't overlook.

Mansur's life wasn't in Somaliland anymore. He belonged elsewhere, and she was a guest in his world for but a moment. She needed to accept that, swallow the bitter pill that it was, and move on.

This was how she would protect what mattered most: her heart.

Manny sensed Amal approaching him from behind. He didn't know how, exactly, only that the atmosphere had changed around him and he was compelled to turn and face her.

Leaning his back against the balcony railing, he followed her every move as she neared him.

She flicked her eyes down to where his hands grasped the railing. She thinned her lips. “Careful,” she warned, her face contorting with concern.

“Nothing wrong with living a little dangerously,” he said, but he heeded her cautionary look and pushed off from the railing.

He didn’t have a death wish. He was just a little floored at the sight of her. She looked radiant—stunning in a floor-length dress, the colorful vertical stripes of the skirt pairing well with the blouson bodice. She had on a burnt orange cardigan and a pale pink headscarf. She wore makeup, but she’d kept the colors soft and muted. A perfect palette for her outfit.

He couldn’t help wanting the extra support of the balcony railing.

Mansur swallowed with great difficulty, his mouth drying and his heart racing. But more troubling than his reaction was how he’d kept time in her absence. Half an hour she’d been gone, and he’d noted every minute—to his utter distress. This obsession with her was growing to be a dilemma.

If he wasn’t careful he might do something ridiculous.

Like fall in love with her again.

He scowled at the possibility, even as his heart juddered faster in response. The last time his body hadn’t complied with his common sense he’d proposed to her. Seeing how that had turned out, he wasn’t eager to repeat his past mistake of being led astray by his powerful attraction to her.

“I noticed that lunch has arrived,” she said, gesturing to the open balcony doors. She twisted her lips and frowned. “I hope you weren’t waiting too long for me.”

“It just arrived.”

The white lie rolled off his tongue. The truth being that their lunch had been catered shortly after she’d left him.

One thing the hotel prided itself on, and what its affluent patrons paid for, was express and high-quality service. And they'd delivered, so he was content. Better yet, they'd left their lunch in several warming trays.

Amal led the way indoors. "It's a lot," she commented, her eyes bugging at the numerous plates atop the long dining table. Pulling out a chair for herself, she whipped her head toward him when he grabbed the seat beside her.

Surely, she hadn't believed he'd seat himself on the opposite end?

She goggled at him and he stared back at her. It didn't take too long for her to shy away from his direct gaze. She ducked her head and grabbed at a pitcher of iced water. Filling her glass, she hesitated when he held his glass to her. She poured and snuck a glance at him from under her thick black lashes. Her eyes were even more alluring when they were lined with kohl.

He caught himself gawking, but managed to cover his slip-up by gulping at his glass. A good thing, too, because the iced water countered the sparking heat building up in his blood.

"What exactly did you inherit from your father?" Amal asked.

"Farming land," he replied, aware of how tight his voice had become. He sipped at his water, needing a pause to recollect his cool composure. "Acres of it. All fertile, too, and mostly untouched."

It would fetch millions with the right buyer, but he hadn't anticipated the roadblock he faced in claiming the land.

He gritted his teeth and spoke carefully, to avoid revealing the anger simmering below the surface. "There's a clause I have to fulfill before the deed to the land can be signed over to me."

A clause that was quickly blooming to be a thorn in his side.

Amal had her mouth full, but covered it to ask, "What's the clause asking from you?"

Her intrigue was natural. Anyone would've asked the same question. Yet hearing it from her made his whole body tighten with the stirrings of panic. He recognized the sharp teeth of anxiousness gnawing away at his insides, pulping him. Skirting the worst of it, he forced a calm he didn't feel and decided to answer her—because there wasn't a way around it anymore, and it wasn't as though he was sharing anything he should fear…sharing parts of himself as he once had with her. This was platonic. Strictly so. A way to pass the time while they enjoyed another meal together.

"The clause," he began, enunciating carefully around his swell of nerves, "requires me to visit some family here in Addis. My father's second family."

Amal lowered her hands over her plate, the fingertips clutching a piece of naan over some garlic hummus slackening and the bread plopping onto her plate forgotten. She blinked several times, opened her mouth, snapped it shut, and then just stared like he'd sprouted an extra head.

So much for keeping it platonic. It was getting personal—and fast.

Because you're making it personal.

He grudgingly admitted that he was. But it wasn't news to her. Not really. She'd known about his father's other family before amnesia had struck and wiped her adult memories—or so she'd told him.

He narrowed his eyes at the lurking doubt. Doubt he snuffed out quickly, because it wouldn't be like Amal to trick him. She'd always been forthcoming, and he sensed that part of her hadn't been affected by the amnesia. If she said she didn't remember, then she didn't remember.

"I didn't know," she said, her tone breathy with shock.

Acknowledging her genuine surprise, Manny replied, "My mother never spoke of it. Your grandmother knew. She was one of the few people who did."

He paused, wondering if he should tell her everything or keep the past fixed firmly in the dark.

You have nothing to hide; just tell her.

It was true. He didn't want her rejection making decisions for him. What better way to prove that he'd moved past his love for her than by sharing how they'd come to love each other?

"You knew, too," he said. "I told you a couple of years back."

"You came to Hargeisa?" She frowned, her brow wrinkling with consternation. "I don't remember."

"No, I didn't come home until my father passed."

Back then he hadn't had time to visit over the summers between school years. All the money he'd saved from working part-time had gone into his livelihood. The full-ride college scholarship hadn't covered all his living costs, and plane tickets hadn't been cheap.

"We used to speak on the phone. And sometimes, when our timing was right, we'd video-chat."

Amal's face was transformed, her smile changing the gloomy cloud of unease hanging over her. "We did?" she breathed.

Manny tensed his muscles, felt his body locking into its usual defensive mode. Her small but sunny smile wouldn't undo him. Not that he didn't enjoy the memory of their conversations…

What he hadn't told her was that some days he hadn't been able to bear going without hearing her voice. That if he hadn't been obliged to work he would have given anything to talk to her for a little longer. Many times his need for Amal had nearly driven him to drop his life in the States and return to the life he'd once had in Hargeisa. It would have been simpler, true. But he wouldn't care so long as he could be close to Amal.

But that's changed. You've changed, he reminded himself.

"I don't remember that either," she said, her smile vanishing as her lips trembled. The gloom came thundering back, enveloping her. She looked the portrait of sadness. "I—I'm sorry."

"Don't apologize. It wasn't like you wanted to forget."

Manny pushed his plate away. He'd barely touched anything on it. The fava bean dish, so similar to Somali *ful*, looked unappetizing suddenly, and he knew his diminished appetite had more to do with his sour mood than the quality of the meal. Full of misery, he couldn't stomach anything else.

Noticing Amal hadn't made progress in her meal either roused his sympathy for her. They'd both be eating if he hadn't gone into the territory of their past. He'd ruined their lunch.

He'd promised his mother he'd look out for Amal, and he was doing a shabby job of it.

"I should be the one asking for forgiveness," he said. "I shouldn't have brought up my troubles."

The inheritance and the disruptive clause requiring Manny to meet with his father's second wife and children was his problem—not Amal's.

She shook her head sharply, right after he spoke. "I'm glad you told me," she said, her face filled with more concern. "What are you going to do? About the clause."

"If I want the land, I'll have to meet them."

"Will you?" she asked.

He shrugged, feeling no better after it. "I haven't decided," he confessed, his voice gruff with indecision. And, anyways, there was one more roadblock… "If I choose to meet my half-siblings and stepmother, I'll have to hire a private investigator first."

"You don't know where they live?"

Amal had connected the dots on her own. Her eyes doubling in size told him enough about how she felt. She was shocked that he didn't know where they resided. Of course she would be! Amal cared for her family, and even though it was down to only her two brothers and her father, she likely couldn't imagine not knowing their whereabouts. For her, the idea of family being strangers was perturbing.

He narrowed his eyes, seeing what he already knew written across her face. "I've never met them."

He'd told her once before, but saying it a second time was far harder. When he'd shared his family secret with her the first time it had been after they'd re-established their friendship. By that point they'd spoken often and, on his part, he'd felt the beginnings of love for her.

Sharing the pain of coming second to his father had felt natural. He had known Amal wouldn't judge him. And she hadn't—even when she'd attempted to get him to reach out to his father and mend the broken father-son bond. She had never forced his hand. Never pushed her unwavering value of family onto him. With her, he had trusted that his thoughts and heart were safe.

At least he had thought she understood.

He set his jaw, mulling over her later rejection, tripping on the flaring hurt it still inflamed in him. She hadn't been able to accept his indifference toward his father's death. And he hadn't been willing to settle on ending his grudge without the promise of her love.

None of that mattered now. He wouldn't commit the same mistake again. He couldn't chance his sanity a second time.

"A private investigator would help me track them down."

Manny pushed himself up to stand, compelled to change position. He couldn't sit there under the microscope of her discerning gaze. Amal had a knack of bringing to light the secrets in him. And he didn't want to regret telling her something he wasn't prepared to share.

"I'll hire an investigative firm. Then it'll be a matter of what I do when they're found. I'm not sure I want to meet them—especially after all this time. We've lived separate lives." And why ruin the unspoken arrangement they had? "I'll have to consider my choice very carefully," he said.

Amal swiped her fingertips over a napkin and shifted in her seat to fully face him. "Does your mother know?"

"She doesn't," he answered, adding, "And I'd prefer you didn't tell her."

"I won't," she promised.

He nodded. "I appreciate your discretion." Looking at the sumptuous feast before them, he said, "It's safe to say I wasn't as hungry as I thought I was. I'll head out and leave you to finish your lunch."

Amal parted her lips, looking for all the world like she had something to say to him, but then she closed her luscious mouth and bobbed her head.

With her silent permission, Manny strode away from her. He didn't stop to look back, just focused on reaching his suite next door and being far away from Amal's catastrophic influence on his emotions.

CHAPTER FIVE

"You look ready to run."

Manny made the observation the next day, after watching Amal discreetly. She had been distant at breakfast… aloof during the car ride to the hospital. Now she looked as washed-out as the walls in the large private room they'd been immediately escorted to once he had given her name. Ashen with fear of the unknown and unexpected.

He knew it because he'd seen himself appear just as leery before. Right after she'd rejected his proposal. He hadn't been able to trust anyone. The distrust had extended to all his choices. For weeks he'd questioned the simplest decisions that had once been easy. Working out of his home had been his only option until he'd been able to look at himself without wanting to punch out a mirror.

He still didn't know what angered him most: the fact that he had acted so pathetically following Amal's rejection, or that he'd allowed himself to love so fiercely at all. Because he *had* loved her. So very much. Enough to go against his characteristic behavior and buy a crazy expensive diamond that had been nowhere near her worth to him.

She'd done that to him.

Only her.

Now, seeing her close her eyes, breathe shallowly and generally appear distressed, galvanized him into action.

He switched seats, sealing the space between them. Nudging her with his leg rewarded him with her eyes opening and her attention falling on him. She even gasped lightly, taken aback. Clearly she hadn't expected him to make direct contact, to be as near to her as he was now.

"Did you hear me?" he asked, surprising himself as he pushed his face closer to hers. "Take deeper, fuller breaths. It'll help."

She did as he advised. Soon her breathing had evened out and a rosiness had returned to her complexion. If he could get her to maintain this improvement when the doctor arrived they'd be solid.

"Remember to ask questions," he said.

Her thigh was close enough for him to imagine her body's sweet warmth. His arms weighed heavily with the desire to hold her. Comfort her with contact. Very personal contact. The kind of contact he couldn't allow himself to indulge in respectfully.

Clearing his throat lightly, he suggested, "Squeeze any information you believe to be helpful from this opportunity. Grasp it for what it could be worth."

"I don't think the doctor will be telling me anything new."

"Then you'll walk away with a peace of mind and zero regrets."

She gifted him a small smile. "I guess I have no choice but to see it through..."

The pitch of her voice at the end was a last-ditch effort to leave the five-hundred-dollars-a-night hospital room before the doctor joined them. But Manny saw it—he saw *her*—and acknowledged her unspoken fear of disappointment.

"You always have choices, Amal." Her name rolled off his tongue, gruff with his fascination for her. "If you want to leave, I won't stop you."

"Even if this visit might be good for me?"

He shoved his nerves down with a forced swallow. "Yes," he said at last, "because having a choice is your fundamental right. If I didn't give you that—if you felt like you'd been brought here and held against your own will—you'd never forgive me for it. Perhaps even resent me for it."

"I wouldn't..." she demurred.

"You would."

He held firm to that conviction, remembering how, given the choice to be with him, she'd spurned his love instead. Somewhere, that Amal was locked away in the woman before him. For all he knew she was prowling beneath the surface of amnesia, lurking ever closer and ready to strike him at his weakest and most unsuspecting moment.

One day I'll let my guard down...

And that was the possibility that froze his muscles and cooled the sizzling desire in him to a manageable, albeit uncomfortable state. He had to be careful. One slip and he'd be kissing goodbye to what he viewed her amnesia as: a get-out-of-jail-free card. To be more specific, a chance to dodge the awkward debrief they should have had after his marriage proposal and her rejection.

It had been like this yesterday, too. Right after he'd enlightened her about his father's second family. He'd been edgy around her. Nervous that she'd recall her rejection of him and push him away again. Make him feel he wasn't worthy of her. Not that he felt he was, but he'd hoped he wasn't a lost cause to her either.

In a twisted way, he found himself aligning Amal with his father. Like his father, she seemed to have judged him as beneath her. He'd come second in affection to his father and, similarly, Amal didn't see him as worth her love. She hadn't desired to bind herself to him. And yet, despite the fierce bitterness in him, he couldn't bring himself to hate her. Not the way he hated his father.

Amal shifting beside him planted him in the present once more.

"I believe you'd talk to me and successfully convince me to stay. Just like you talked me into coming to Addis Ababa," she said.

Amal's oud perfume grew stronger when she leaned into him. The sweet balsamic notes of her choice of fragrance curled under his nose. She was close enough for him to count the few and nearly imperceptible brown freckles sprinkling her cheeks.

She touched his forearm and the muscles under her lightly pressing fingertips bunched and flexed. Manny reacted defensively, isolating the parts of him that were most affected and shutting them down as best he could. In short, he transformed himself into a living statue. He breathed, but he felt as minimally as possible, and he fought back against the sensual attack.

She licked her lips, whether consciously or not he didn't know, but he couldn't stop ogling her slickly glossed mouth. Her dusky pink lips screamed sweet innocence to him as much as they made him want to lean in and satisfy his darkly obsessive pining.

One kiss, he vowed. One kiss and he'd be cured of his craving for her.

"Mansur..." she said breathily, invitingly.

"Amal..." He growled her name low, losing total control for a blinding, bewildering few seconds.

The brisk knock on the door pried them apart. A second and a heartbeat more and they'd have been locking lips. He knew it to be a fact. Neither of them had demonstrated restraint. And he'd seen it: her echoing desire. He wouldn't have faced resistance in stealing a kiss.

The knocking that had halted what might have been either their salvation or their destruction started up again.

For a moment, Manny forgot where they were. Right—the hospital room. White walls and periwinkle wainscoting. A large bow window, with picturesque views of Addis Ababa and a shelf where an abundance of Delft blue vases and freshly plucked and trimmed floral arrangements were placed. Not to mention plentiful chairs, a sixty-five-inch wall-mounted television, and luxury gold silk jacquard bedsheets draping the state-of-the-art hospital bed.

"Come in," he called, facing away from Amal in the nick of time.

The door opened and in breezed the neurosurgeon, a diminutive woman whose rosy brown skin was closer in shade to Amal's. She instantly homed in on her patient. "Hello, Ms. Khalid. I understand you're here to discuss a head injury resulting in a concussion and a subsequent case of retrograde amnesia." She glanced at Manny. "Your husband?" she asked.

"No," they answered in unison.

"Very well, Ms. Khalid," she said, referring to her clipboard. "Then, with your permission, would you like me to proceed with the check-up and consultation with your companion or alone?"

He wanted to stay, but he could sense Amal's fraction of a hesitation.

Standing, he said, "That's fine. I'll be waiting nearby. I want to grab a coffee anyways."

"Mansur..." Amal began softly, but recognizably not urgently wanting to counteract his decision.

He'd made the right call to excuse himself. That was good enough for him.

"I'll return once you're finished."

He walked away from her, past the neurosurgeon who would hopefully live up to her professional reputation, and out of the hospital room.

"Would you like me to call for your husband?" asked the nurse who had helped guide Amal back to the private hospital room, officially making her the second person to make that assumption in the span of an hour.

Amal opened her mouth to correct the nurse and call Mansur her friend, but discovered herself fumbling with that description. Because it wasn't entirely true. They weren't *friends*.

She still knew little about him and, although he'd shown that they had history, and she technically knew they had shared a childhood, it wasn't enough. At least not for her.

But the nurse was staring at her like she was a crazy person, and Amal had to tell her something or risk her catching flies with her gaping jaw.

"He's a…f-friend," she stammered.

She blamed the jitters on the experience of being in the MRI machine. The awful, teeth-grinding battering sound as the machine powered on in its high-resolution imaging had left an indelible stain on her mind. She shuddered as cold, slimy fear pooled in her stomach. So far, it was one experience in Addis she didn't wish to relive again anytime soon.

The nurse nodded. "I'll let your friend know you're done." She left then, and Amal was alone.

She hadn't realized how empty the lavish hospital room could feel. Really more of a suite than a room, it had a brightly lit wood-paneled alcove as a coat room, a washroom with a glass-walled shower, a plush sofa, and even a small crystal chandelier.

Amal caught a glimpse of herself in the mirror above the blue-and-gold geometrically patterned sink. Grasping the edges of the basin, she leaned in to examine her reflection. Either the bright white lighting in the room had washed her complexion out, or the pressure of having so many firsts—first travel, first flight, almost first kiss—was to blame.

Amal touched her fingertips to her lips and fluttered her eyes shut. It *had* nearly happened. She hadn't imagined it. Her quivering mouth and thundering heart wouldn't let her forget.

She dropped her fingers from her mouth as a knock on the closed bathroom door pulled her attention from her reflection.

"Amal?" Mansur's low voice sounded from the other side. "I just wanted to let you know that I'm here, but take your time."

He'd barely crossed the spacious room when she flung the door open, her cheeks aflame and her body lit with the need to be closer to him. She hadn't known it could be such a thrill to have a crush. Couldn't remember if she'd ever felt this way around him before. No, that was a lie. She recalled having a crush on him as a young girl. Had memories of being glued to his side when they'd play together.

But that didn't come close to how she felt about him now. The sharp pull of attraction sliced at her more cruelly with each passing moment, and it was only her second day of being near him. She imagined the need in her for Mansur would transform into a driving pain as time passed.

Amal watched him turn around, his expression breaking from its usual impassive look.

His eyes widening was the first indication she had that something was wrong.

In her haste to see him she'd upset her headscarf. The silky veil had loosened to reveal her curly fringe. She blushed harder. Her rich brown skin warmed, but there would be no evidence of her embarrassment for him to witness. And yet he must know she was flustered by her mistake.

He whirled away from her.

Amal worked without a mirror. She'd been wrapping her headscarf most of her life, and not even amnesia could stop her hands from working quickly and effortlessly to cover her head.

Looking modest again, she called his name. "Mansur?"

Given the all-clear, he flicked an assessing look over his shoulder before he realized she was ready for him now, though her cheeks still burned, the heat creeping to her collarbone.

"The nurse said you were ready," he explained, an apologetic look in his eyes. "I didn't mean to barge in."

"I told her to call you," she said.

He stared, and then asked, "How did it go?"

The rough edge to his voice rubbed her sensitized nerves and frazzled her even more. She didn't think anyone could sound so…so sexy. She could close her eyes and hear him talk all day long—but then he'd think she was crazy.

Then he'd know how you feel about him.

And she couldn't allow that. For so many reasons. The top motivator being that Mansur had no life in Hargeisa. He'd built one in America and soon he'd leave her. And she didn't want to be left mending the pieces of a broken heart. It wasn't like she hadn't had that experience only recently.

Just like that, her thoughts were redirected from Mansur to her father.

Her father hadn't come to visit her except for that first day she'd got out of the hospital. And even then it hadn't been to ensure her well-being, but to ask for money. Again.

She blinked rapidly, forcing the stinging from her eyes. She didn't dare cry in front of Mansur. He had his own family problems. And he'd been considerate enough to avoid burdening her with his troubles. She should do the same and spare him the misery her father continued to cause within her.

Realizing Mansur awaited her reply, she said, "The doctor is reviewing the scans. I was instructed to wait for the rest of the consultation."

"Do you want me to leave?" he asked, his gaze boring into her.

She knew that if she said yes, he'd leave. But she didn't want him leaving her again. She had the strong sense that she could use him as a buffer if the neurosurgeon returned with bad news.

"I'd like you to stay, please."

"I'll stay, then," he said.

They resumed their seats, sitting close together again, and Amal couldn't help but notice him tapping his fingers on his thighs. He looked good in one of his suits again. Polished and immaculate and powerful. Mansur commanded the room with his presence alone, and she felt a mix of envy and admiration. Especially as more childhood memories were resurfacing with each passing day.

He certainly didn't look like the young boy from her past. Older, yes, but the lines on his face told a story. Each furrow and crease spoke of the struggles he must have faced on his own in America. She still couldn't believe that he'd left at seventeen. Amal barely remembered the day, but even after all these years Mama Halima got sorrowful when she thought of her son living apart from her.

Amal had learned to avoid speaking about Mansur, period. Maybe that was why she blurted now, "Do you miss Hargeisa when you're in America?"

Mansur snapped his head to her, a scowl slashing his brows. "Sometimes," he said, frown lines bracketing his downturned mouth. "Why are you asking?"

"I was thinking about your mother." Amal laced her fingers together, staring down at her hands. "She gets sad whenever you're mentioned."

"Who mentions me?"

Taken aback by his snapping question, she looked up and murmured, "I did…a couple of times. But then I learned not to bring you up. I didn't like how upset she'd get."

"I call. Though I suppose not as often as I should—especially not since my father passed," he said gruffly.

His father was clearly still a sore subject. And he had mentioned that to her before they'd left Hargeisa for Addis. She might not have understood why he disliked his father before, but she knew better now, after he'd reminded her of his half-siblings.

Amal still couldn't believe she'd forgotten such an important detail. She hadn't loathed her amnesia more than she had in that moment. It had left her blindly navigating a field full of hidden emotional landmines. If she so much as stepped over a trigger—*bam!* She would lose Mansur to whatever battle he was clearly fighting internally.

She'd seen how he had left her in a hurry yesterday. Without his having to explicitly say so, it had been obvious he was stressed from having to decide whether he should meet with his half-siblings and stepmother.

A part of her was curious as to whether he'd settled on a decision. But she wasn't going to ask and pick at those scabbing wounds on him. Just like she avoided mentioning him to Mama Halima, she would tread cautiously where his other family was concerned.

"I'll have to call more often." He grasped his knees and tipped his head toward her once more. "Thanks for letting me know."

Amal flashed a smile, feeling a little more heartened

now. "I can't blame you if you don't. You're busy. I barely find time to catch up with Bashir and Abdulkadir. It's hard for us to find a time where we're all free."

"They've grown up," Mansur remarked, a small grin pulling at his lips. "I remember when they'd follow us everywhere. Follow *you*, actually. They worshipped their big sister."

"Only because I found the best trees to climb and the best games to play."

He smiled wider. "Right…how could I forget?"

"I'm recalling more of my childhood, and it's nice. I feel less of a disconnect, and it gives me hope that I'll fully regain what I've lost."

"Is that how you view it? As a loss?"

"By definition amnesia *is* a loss—of memories."

It wasn't what he'd meant, though, and Amal knew that. She realized her deflection tactic wouldn't work when he stared, waiting for a better answer.

Giving in, she said, "It feels like I've lost a part of myself, yes."

And she didn't think that was an exaggeration either. She *had* lost several pieces of herself. Her memories were bundled with her personality. She didn't know if she was making the same mistakes, and if she was less of herself for doing it.

"And if you can't regain all your memories? What then?" he asked.

She rolled her shoulders. "I haven't thought that far ahead."

"Guess we both have decisions to make," he surmised.

Amal saw an opening and went for it, her intrigue overpowering her. That and the fact she'd done enough squirming in the hot seat. She figured it was his turn.

"Have you made yours yet?"

"No," he said. "Though I'm considering driving out to survey the land."

"You haven't seen it yet?" she asked, sucking in her lips when he appraised her quietly. She dredged up the courage to say, "I thought you were going to sell it. I assumed you'd seen it."

"I've had surveyors take measurements and photos. Everything I'd need for a sale once the deed is in my name. But of course, there's the clause I'll have to fulfill if I wish to claim my inheritance."

She thought over what he'd said. "Will it make a difference if you see the land?"

"I'm not confident it will. It might." He pushed back, sitting upright once more. His movements were fluid and graceful. No one would believe he was troubled by his decision, even when he gave it voice. "I'm only hoping that one way or another I'll settle on a decision."

"And be able to live with it?" she said, filling in what he hadn't expressed but what his statement implied.

She understood more perfectly than most, being in the situation she was in. Coming to Addis Ababa had been a tough decision for her—albeit one she'd made quickly, thanks to Mansur. She wasn't certain she'd remain thankful once the doctor joined them and completed the consultation, but Amal couldn't see herself blaming him for inspiring her to join him on his journey.

She'd come because she'd wanted to. She'd *had* to, for her peace of mind.

"I was thinking maybe you'd like to come with me?" He folded his arms, and there was a gruffness in his voice as he continued, "I'll leave after we're done here, but if you'd like me to drop you off at the hotel I can arrange for that."

He wanted her to go along? Amal had trouble wrapping

her head around his request. She saw he was in earnest, though. All she had to do was agree and they'd be leaving the hospital together, heading out on a new adventure to see his inheritance.

"Okay," she said, not needing to think too long on it after the initial shock had worn off. "Why not? I'd like to see more of the city."

"Actually, it's not in Addis," he informed her.

"That's fine."

She beamed then, as the reality set in that she would be spending the remainder of the day with him. True, Mansur made her nervous. He unsettled her with his commanding gaze and his frank manner of speech, and yet she'd be lying if she said there wasn't a thrill in her heady attraction to him. She felt like she'd swallowed bubbles and they were popping non-stop inside of her. She felt as if she could walk on air when he gave her a rare smile or a laugh. It was an exhilarating experience in and of itself.

"Then it's settled," he said smoothly, smiling. "We're going on a road trip."

"I know it's not a trip for fun, and that this is crucial to your decision-making, but I can't help but be excited," she admitted shyly.

"Amal..."

Mansur was staring at her, his focus so painfully sharp it felt like he touched her. He'd done it before, when he'd first seen her at his mother's home. But back then it had been like he was looking at a stranger. He hadn't expected to see her in that moment.

This time it's different.

He looked at her like he was truly seeing her. Like when they'd almost kissed earlier.

"Amal," he said again, "I don't want you locking up that excitement on my behalf."

"I won't."

"Good," he rasped.

The doctor entered, and she was moving like a woman determined to conquer what had to be a long day and a lengthy schedule. Somewhere on that clipboard she carried were the results of Amal's MRI scan.

"Ms. Khalid," she said by way of greeting, and dipped her chin to Mansur. "I have to ask again: are you all right with your visitor sitting in on your consultation?"

"Yes," Amal replied, sparing Mansur a smile. "I'd like for my friend to stay."

Amal didn't know where that had come from, but Mansur's eyes widened with unconcealed surprise. He didn't correct her, but turned his gaze to the doctor. Amal did the same, though she was worried about what he thought.

She forced herself to pay attention to what the doctor had to say, even though her mind would've strayed to Mansur.

Did he not agree?

Could they not be friends?

They had been once, long ago, as children. He didn't have to know about her attraction to him, and they didn't have to talk about why he looked like he wanted to kiss her, too. Because suddenly there was something she wanted more than a kiss.

His friendship.

She hadn't been open about her fears surrounding her amnesia with anyone but him. For the first time since waking up in the hospital, confused and unsure about her identity, she was dead set on retaining the small and fragile peace she'd gotten while sharing her feelings and thoughts with him.

Whatever happened, she wanted him to know that they could be friends.

CHAPTER SIX

AN HOUR LATER they were on the road, heading away from the hospital and the bustling metropolis of Addis Ababa. As promised, Mansur was driving them to view the land he was due to inherit under the terms of his father's will.

Amal wished she could enjoy the sights blurring past as he revved the fancy sports car, but she was lost in her thoughts. A part of her still hadn't left the hospital. Like a nightmare, she was stuck in that expensively furnished room, with the doctor before her and Mansur at her side, listening to her bleak prognosis for the amnesia.

"I'm sorry, but there's not much more we can do," the doctor had said. *"I will suggest that psychotherapy, specifically cognitive behavioral therapy, could be of help. We do have a few psychiatrists on staff. Does that sound like something you'd be interested in, Ms. Khalid?"*

She hadn't given an answer, and Mansur had done the talking, asking for time to consider the option and herding her out of the hospital.

She appreciated what he'd done. If she'd remained in that hospital room for one more minute—well, she wasn't sure she'd be coping as decently as she was at the moment. And that was saying a lot, considering how numb she felt.

"Amal?"

She was spooked by the sound of her name. She hadn't

forgotten Mansur was with her, but her reaction was a testament to how deeply she'd slipped into her depressed mind.

Pasting on a smile, she said, "I can't believe we're not out of the city yet. Addis is far larger than Hargeisa."

"By several square miles," Mansur said, his eyes straying from the road every so often. He had his hands loosely on the steering wheel, his posture relaxed, but his face was all hard angles and no-nonsense. "We can postpone the trip. I don't mind pushing it back a day or two."

"I feel fine," she said, realizing what he was hinting at.

"No, you're not." Before she could argue, he said, "And that's okay. I just don't want you feeling like you have to come with me. If you need time—the rest of the day—that's all right with me."

Amal sat in a stupor, the ultra-comfy leather car seat soaking up her tension as she weakened under the weight of it. His concern had her eyes prickling with familiar heat. A display of waterworks was exactly what she'd been trying to avoid—which was why she was thankful for Mansur's deft thinking in whisking her out of the hospital and away from the presence of the second doctor bearing unpleasant news about her amnesia.

Why is he being so nice?

As if it wasn't only a day before that he'd told his mother he couldn't help them.

Couldn't help you, *you mean*, she corrected, lamenting. *He can't reverse the amnesia. No one can.*

Finally, she managed to get her tongue off the roof of her mouth. "It's a lot to take in. I think I set my expectations higher than I should have."

"Do you regret coming? Because you shouldn't."

His hands moved up the steering wheel, his fingers no longer lax in their grip. He revved the engine, too, making the car grumble as he switched lanes and gunned it past several cars.

The freeway here was as lawless as the traffic in Somaliland. Hargeisa had one traffic light, and navigating the roads was the stuff of a traffic engineer's nightmares. But for someone who didn't regularly drive in no-holds-barred traffic, Mansur grasped the wheel like a race car pro.

"You took a chance. It might not have panned out the way you hoped, but there has to be some comfort from hearing what the neurosurgeon had to say."

He spoke with his eyes focused on the road. Though he didn't need to be looking at her for his words to touch her. Mansur's sonorous voice reverberated inside the car, the space in the luxury vehicle feeling so much smaller suddenly.

"And she did mention there being proven research into the psychotherapy she suggested. It could be of help to you."

Amal shook her head, plunging further into a bottomless pool of despair. "Something tells me cognitive behavioral therapy won't be readily found in Hargeisa."

Mental health wasn't a topic broached in Somaliland—or Somalia. Everyone knew it existed; they just avoided labeling it for fear of ostracization. And those who did suffer mentally and emotionally were hidden by their loved ones and ignored by the rest of society. Even the doctor in Somaliland had looked at her like she was plagued by demons and not suffering the effect of a head injury and brain trauma.

"I won't find any help of that sort back home," she sneered.

"Then take up the doctor's offer and utilize the psychiatry department in the hospital." He glanced askance at her as he made the suggestion.

"I'd have to stay longer in Addis," Amal countered, not even bothering to muffle her sulky tone.

"If you're worried about accommodation, the hotel suite is yours until you're ready to leave the city and head home. It'll come with a meal plan, too. And, as you've enjoyed the lunch there, you'll know the hotel caters a host of delicious meals, both locally and internationally inspired." Mansur nailed his sales pitch with a crooked smile.

She allowed him to dazzle her with his good looks and his generosity, even if she was still unclear why he was being so gentle with her. Again, she wondered whether his actions were a direct result of Mama Halima's wishes. Amal wouldn't put it past Mansur's mother. She was small, but her maternal instincts were fierce. Halima cared for Amal and, despite his lack of visits, Mansur was still her son, and he was acting like it now. It wasn't far-fetched to suspect that his change of attitude resulted from his mother's prodding.

"Thanks," she said, sweetening her tone because it wasn't his fault at all. "Only I hadn't planned to stay."

"Much like me," he echoed.

She nodded. "Like you, I figured that my visit to Addis would be short. That after I saw the doctor I'd be free to go home to Hargeisa."

"And you still can—" he said, stopping short when he had to brake hard. He leaned on the horn for the truck that had cut them off so dangerously. Shaking his head, he growled, "I forgot how it's car-eat-car in this part of the world."

"But it is beautiful," she remarked, gazing out at the sights she could spy as the freeway rode up an incline. "Is that the famous Meskel Square?"

She pointed toward a glimpse of bumper-to-bumper traffic at a barren crossroads. The freeway was congested with traffic, but it wasn't anywhere as busy as Meskel Square.

There had to be hundreds of cars there, narrowly swerving by each other. Her eyes were crossed from watching them.

"Yeah—and that'd be Addis Mercato. Famed for its coffee." Mansur pointed out his window.

She leaned into his side, peering out for a peek at the open-air marketplace she'd read about in her hotel suite. She hadn't only looked up Mansur on the Internet. Traveling out of Hargeisa for the first time had her curious, wanting to get to know more about the city she was temporarily in.

"You could stay," he said, his voice nearer, lower and huskier.

Amal pulled back hastily, realizing how close she'd come to him. She carried his scent even after creating a space between them, his musky cologne tinged with a woodsy essence teasing her nose.

"What about your father's land?" It would be *his* land if he decided to go through with meeting his blended family.

"Like I said, we could postpone." He'd said "we", like he intended to bring her along whether they went today or some other day.

Amal didn't want him to stall on such an important decision. She understood that he wasn't warming to the idea of meeting his father's second wife, but the nameless and faceless woman was still Mansur's stepmother—his *ayo*. In Somaliland it was normal for men to have multiple wives—up to four—and, unlike mental health problems, it wasn't social death to have half-siblings in this manner.

Mansur was treating it unusually harshly. She had the sense that there was more to his hesitation and frustration when it came to his father and his second family, and more of his emotions invested in his perception of them than he might even realize.

They weren't discussing him, though, and she was reminded of that when he drummed his fingers over the steering wheel and asked, "Why is it so important that you remember?"

"It'd be nice to know what I was like," she replied, having had time to settle on an answer for that exact question.

She swallowed thickly, her breathing growing shallow and her body flushing with heat from rising stress. She scratched her fingernails up and down the pads of her palms, the nervous twitch similar to Mansur's drumming fingers. It was nice to know she had company in her discomfort.

"I mean, I know what I was like as a kid now—but that changes as you grow, doesn't it? I used to bite my nails to the quick—I recall that—but I haven't had the urge to do it as an adult."

"You'll have to thank my mother for that." Mansur's profile couldn't hide his small grin. "She got you off the habit—first with gloves and then, when that didn't work, she resorted to a bitter-tasting nail polish and hid the polish remover where neither of us could find it. And I *know* it was bitter because you had me take a lick one day." He broke off with a short but mirthful chuckle. "That was the last day I accepted a dare from you."

Amal's laughter bubbled out of her, first it was a giggle, and then she doubled over at the image of Mansur licking her fingernail and tasting the polish because she'd dared him. She laughed so hard the tears she'd kept at bay up to that point leaked out on their own. She wiped them away and laughed again, looking at him through the blur of her tears and discovering his grin had widened.

"It wasn't funny, believe me." He puckered his lips and wrinkled his nose. "I don't think I've ever tasted anything so bitter to this day."

Amal heard him and she pealed into more laughter. She

laughed, and laughed, and laughed. Clutching her now painful sides, she begged, "No more."

"Surrendering, are you?" Mansur teased. "I guess we'll call it even."

She readily agreed, her giggles coming in smaller waves and fits now. And although the laughter had subsided, hoarseness from it lingered in her voice as she wiped at her eyes and said, "I think I'm starting to remember that incident."

And she was. The memory was crystallizing like magic. Now if only Mansur could help unlock her adult memories… Gripped by the notion, she looked at him, and grew shy when his stare met hers.

"What is it?" he asked.

"It's silly," she began, "but I've had this idea. Though it's a little crazy, it might work." She lifted a shoulder in her uncertainty as to how he'd react.

Mansur nudged his chin at her. "Tell me."

"What if you could share some more memories with me?"

It wasn't her imagination that he stiffened, but his voice was deceptively calm when he spoke. "Your adult memories? I'm not sure I'll be of any help there," he said with a raised brow. "I wasn't around, if you catch my drift."

"Not in person, maybe," she said, remembering what he'd revealed in the hotel, when he'd told her about his half-siblings and stepmother. "But you mentioned we would talk, though, and video-chat sometimes."

He flexed his fingers on the wheel, accelerating faster on the snaking freeway. "And you think that'll help."

"Why not? You heard the doctor," she said.

And he had—he'd been standing right there with her when the neurosurgeon had spoken about the talking therapy that might help unlock memories sealed by the amnesia.

"You're right—but I'm pretty certain the doctor mentioned how reducing stress and elevating the mood of the patient were a key part of the therapy, if you choose to undertake it."

"Yes—and she also said memory recall exercises were most effective when patients could connect with persons who share similar memories. Like family and friends...or acquaintances who were once neighbors and remain family friends of a sort."

That roused a smile from him. "And we're the latter category?" he said, piecing together her sound logic.

Amal grinned, glad to see him following along. "Yes, we are. What do you say? Will you help me?"

She pushed down the squirming bashfulness that would have had her retracting her request. She couldn't allow this opportunity to learn more about herself to slip from her fingers. Mansur could be the key she'd been looking for all along. The key to her still-missing memories.

"All right," he said. "What do you want to know?"

Amal rounded in her seat to face him and placed her cheek in her hand. "What did we talk about—aside from you telling me about your father's second family?"

Manny managed to hold Amal off from her interrogation, stalling her until they reached their destination—at which point she became temporarily distracted by the view of their new location.

Almost as soon as she was out of the car, she shot off exploring. He hurried to trail her.

"Careful," he said briskly, catching Amal as she flailed to right her balance.

When she was steady, she smiled his way. "We're not dressed to hike up a mountain."

"A hill," he corrected, but he agreed. "I'm sorry, I should

have put some forethought into the geographical differences out here in the country."

He partly blamed his clamoring need to distance her as far from the hospital and the upsetting consultation as possible, and partly the emotions that came along with the inheritance itself. He'd been caught up in his head and hadn't taken the necessary precautions.

Amal reminded him of his mistake as she winced and forced him to stop as she checked on her foot. Her ballet flats were worn and mired with dust and dirt. They were clearly well-loved, but they weren't the footwear he'd have chosen for her at this moment.

He had the sudden urge to carry her up the hill in his arms. Flexing his biceps, he thought about it as she shook her shoe and muttered, "Not sure how a pebble got in there," before placing it back on her foot and beaming up at him.

Making a hasty choice, he crouched before her, his back toward her.

Amal's soft gasp reached his ears. "No, I couldn't," she said immediately, swatting at him from behind, and insisting, "I can walk up the hill on my own."

"Hop on, Amal."

He wasn't budging until she did. One of them would win, and he was determined to see this through. Though it was a good thing he wasn't facing her. He was blushing.

"Mansur, I couldn't," she said. She sounded uncertain, though.

"It's Manny—and I'd feel less guilty about bringing you here in those shoes if you climbed on." He glanced back and watched a war of emotions take place on her open-book expression.

And then she nodded, sighing. "Fine."

She climbed on him easily, her warm, soft weight covering his back, and leaned on him entirely when he swept her up and stood with her. She yelped and squeezed her arms tight around his shoulders. Her thighs clamped around his waist and her skirt rode up her toned, smooth legs.

Manny kept his hands locked under her knees, even when his eyes drifted to the sultry deep brown of her calves and ankles. Thankfully the challenge of keeping her safely on his back while climbing uphill kept him occupied and away from wandering thoughts.

"It's a paradise," she breathed into his ear when he crested the hilltop.

Manny couldn't agree more. The beauty of the panoramic scene was jaw-dropping, a one-of-a-kind experience. In his ear again, Amal lightly gasped her admiration for the views at the top of the lookout.

"Are those lakes?" she asked.

"Yes, and they're famous to the area."

He pointed to the two crater lakes the hill bisected, one on either side of them. Amal made cute noises of surprise when he explained how day tours were conducted out of Addis for tourists to experience the natural lakes in all their glory.

Beyond that, there were humble thatch-roofed homes, and tilled and untilled farmland on the hillside. It was an idyllic pastoral scene. Better yet, they were alone in enjoying the sight. No tourists in view.

"I'm relieved I didn't let you talk me into returning to the hotel," she said.

He laughed low, feeling the same relief she spoke of.

"Are any of those farmlands yours?" she wondered, her lips brushing the tip of his ear. He suspected it was accidental because she pulled back after that, and stammered, "Th-That is if you decide to claim the land."

"Not according to the directions. My land should be on the other side of this hill."

He hitched her higher on his back, his hands locking tight around her flexed legs, his fingers mapping out the softness that her clothing hid from him. Amal's curves looked divine, and they felt it, too.

Controlling his voice, knowing it might reveal his lustful thoughts, he murmured, "Why do I get the feeling you're more excited to see this land than I am?"

"Aren't you? I can only imagine what you could do with— Wait…how many acres did you say?"

Mansur had told her in the car when they'd begun passing farmsteads on their way to their destination. He'd followed the map and the precise directions of the surveyors he'd hired to scout out the land.

Reminding her now, he said, "Forty."

She whistled, the sharp noise a contrast to her soft awe. "That's plenty of land. One might even argue it's too much land for one man."

"If I sold it, it might be to a company."

There was foreign agribusiness in the area that struck deals with shady government officials in Ethiopia. Families lost their homes overnight as farms that rightfully belonged to them had their deeds stolen and resold to mega-corporations, driving small family farmers both out of business and out of their homes.

"Then again, I might keep it and find a new purpose for it."

"Like…?"

He'd given this some consideration, and he craned his neck to watch the happy surprise play out on her face when he replied. "I thought I could parcel the lands into smaller sections. Lease out those sections to local farmers. Their rent could come out of a small share of their good crop for the season."

He shrugged and her arms rose with the gesture, her

hands creeping closer to his neck and the leaping pulse at the base of his throat.

Swallowing around the latest flush of desire warming him from head to toe, he said, "I'd have to give it more thought, of course, but it's an idea."

"A brilliant one! It'd be awfully generous of you, Mansur."

Basking in the shower of her praise, he resurfaced momentarily to grumble, "'Generous' is a leap. I'd just be doing business. And business isn't always...*nice*."

He knew that, having fought tooth and claw to get his CEO-ship. His presidency was the result of his blood, sweat and tears. He'd had his supporters in the company, but also his fair share of dissenters in board members, higher management, and investors. For nearly two years he'd had to prove his mettle as a potential president and CEO candidate. Not everyone had been thrilled to have a young, overly ambitious foreigner in the running.

Some days had been hard; those were the days he'd felt most like giving in. It had been during that time he'd reconnected with Amal. She'd readily become his confidante and main supporter. After each of their conversations he'd felt ready to take the next day on, and the next, until the day he sat at the helm of his company.

"No, you're right. Not all business is neat and kind," she was saying. "And of all people I should know."

She meant the corruption of the Somaliland government that had shut down the beneficial operation of building her hospital.

Manny tightened his lips, his fingers squeezing her legs. He knew what it was like. Being judged and found unworthy. His father had done it to him and to his mother. He'd almost endured it again before he'd secured his position as CEO. And Amal had done it to him, too, when she had refused his marriage proposal. Coming second or, worse, last to someone always hurt.

He tamped down the hot bile flaming through his chest and creeping up his throat. Torn was what he was—between wanting to be closer to her and pushing her away for good. She called them friends, but they couldn't be—not when he had this damning attraction for her. It put him in a bind, because he knew how good her friendship had been to him. And her love? Her love had been his salvation. For a brief moment, when he'd thought he had her heart, he'd felt saved from his black anger for his father. She'd made him feel wanted and loved.

"Sometimes it's a long, grueling climb to the top of the hill."

He walked to the edge of the hilltop, hoisting her higher on his back and preparing for the more arduous trip downhill.

Before he could worry about taking his first step, though, Amal wriggled in his hold. "I can walk down," she said.

Her soft breath puffed in his ear and sparked delightful tingles all through him. When she shifted again, his whole body compressed into a hot, tight coil, wired to snap at any moment. Afraid of what he'd do or say if he insisted on holding her to him, Manny loosened his hands around her legs.

She slid down his back, her hands coming off him last.

Manny turned to her and nudged his chin down the hill. "Are you sure?" He dragged his eyes to her flats, peeking out from under her long, dark skirt. "I don't mind carrying you."

Actually, it was probably best he didn't volunteer again, what with how he buzzed from his desire for her.

Amal answered him by plunging forward, leading the

way. She managed to get a few paces ahead before he unrooted his feet and caught up with her.

"See?" she goaded, grinning. "I can walk on my own. Not that I'm not grateful for the ride."

She angled her head away from him—blushing, no doubt. She didn't have to turn red for him to know her tells. Besides, his face was flushed as well, from the memory of carrying her, of touching her more intimately than he ever had before. And he wasn't counting their rare rough play as children, when he hadn't known what it was like to love and be loved by her.

But he knew better now.

Apparently not enough to walk away from her, he thought. Any sane man would be running for the hills by now, but not him. Even though he saw nothing but heartache at the end of the path he was willingly taking with her. She might remember his failed proposal and push him away again, or she might not ever remember and then he'd be forced to live a lie with her.

He didn't even want to consider *telling* her what had happened that night, a year ago.

As if hearing his thoughts, Amal said sweetly, "Now will you tell me more about what we used to talk about over the phone and on video-chat? Did we always talk about your run for CEO, or did we manage to get around to talking about other things?"

"Other things?" Mansur repeated.

Amal bumped against his hand as she sidestepped a jagged rock wedged in the earth. She gave him some room after the danger to her feet had passed them by and smiled up at his wary face. He wore the same expression as when she'd asked him to divulge his memories of her. And yet, despite his obvious reluctance, he hadn't refused outright.

Maybe your luck's run out.

She hoped not—desperately so. Thus far she'd learned that Mansur had shared his professional struggles with her. He'd fought to be CEO, and she had learned she'd been there in spirit, right alongside him.

"Other things like life outside of our respective careers," she explained. "Didn't we talk about anything else?" Suddenly she wondered if their relationship had been only that. Built on their similar career paths. Their talk all shop. She shivered at the iciness of that possibility, feeling a frown overtaking her face.

Mansur clearly saw it, too, lowering his eyes to her mouth before flicking them up a heartbeat later.

"Sometimes, yes. We spoke about our dreams outside of our jobs," he said, his voice gravelly with what she was sure he left unspoken. "I wanted to travel more. Cut my hours and see the world. Give back where I could."

Amal's heart gave a squeeze, and her smile returned full force. "Did I ever mention I'd love to travel, too? Because if I didn't, I do."

"Actually, you did." He slung her a half-smile. "That hasn't changed. You talked about seeing as much of the world as possible when we were younger. And that was before I ever dreamed to call America my second home."

"You consider Hargeisa your first home?"

"I do," he said, nodding and pursing his lips. He looked to be giving his next words some thought before he spoke again. "I might not desire living there at the moment, but someday I'd like to return for more frequent visits. Maybe even build a home close to my mother, so I'll have an excuse to make the long flight over."

"I'm glad I still want to travel," she said. "I don't always feel certain of my emotions and thoughts anymore." Then she looked to him and asked, "What else?"

He rubbed his beard—a nervous tic she realized. She was worried that he'd finally shut the door to her inquisitiveness. So he pleasantly surprised her when he said, "We spoke about my family, and yours."

At the mention of her family, Amal grew both hot and terribly cold.

"Bashir was often giving you a headache, waffling about his schooling. He's always had a good head on his shoulders, and a big heart, so it's no shock he switched from business to medicine. He'll make a great doctor."

"Pharmacist," she corrected, smiling warmly. "Last I spoke with him, he wanted to be a pharmacist."

"A great pharmacist, then. I have no doubt." Manny lowered his hand from his jaw. "And Abdulkadir is happy running his travel agency? I take it that hasn't changed."

"Yes, he's very happy," she replied. She spoke often enough to Abdulkadir to know he was doing well, financially and physically. "Both my brothers are doing well, and it's eased a burden off my chest that I may or may not have felt before the amnesia."

"You always worried about them," Mansur said.

Amal blinked fast, her eyes pinching, hot with quick tears. She wiped them quickly, gasping a laugh. "I'm sorry. I don't know what's come over me."

Mansur's hand on her forearm stilled her. She turned to him. Their bodies were mere inches apart. She could take a step forward and their chests would be touching. Amal had felt what that was like when he'd carried her uphill on his back. It had taken every bit of control to keep herself from squirming when his hands were on her, her front to his back. Now she warmed again, just like before, flushing all over at the naughty part of her that wanted to recreate those electrifying sensations once more.

She wasn't crying now.

"You care for your family a lot. That part of you hasn't and won't likely ever change." He dropped his hand from her. "It's not something to be ashamed of either…something to feel sorry over." He paused, and then said, "I envy that in you. And I know that you caring for my mom makes my heart rest easier when I can't be by her side myself. So, thank you."

She shook her head, stopping when she glimpsed his stern look. He wasn't going to accept any more of her self-deprecation it seemed, so she gave up. "You're welcome," she whispered, and knew that he heard her.

They walked in silence, continuing to the base of the hill.

When they got down, Amal steeled her nerves and asked, "Did I speak about my father?" Her voice barely a whisper when she asked.

Mansur gazed deep into her eyes before he dipped his head.

That opened a floodgate for her. "He visited me right after I came home from the hospital." Amal paced forward, then wound back to his side and peered up at him. "Your mother would've thrown him out, but I asked her to let him in to see me. I thought that he had traveled to Hargeisa when he'd heard I was in the hospital. Abdulkadir had seen him, and warned me like your mother. But I didn't listen. I shouldn't have let him in."

She sucked in a breath, realizing she was speaking faster than she was allowing herself to get air. Only suddenly it felt like she had to get this off her chest. But she hadn't even told Mama Halima what had happened fully…the shame had been too great.

Why tell all this to Mansur?

Because he'd leave for America sooner rather than later. She wouldn't have to deal with his pitying looks.

"What did he do?"

Mansur's voice was eerily calm. The quiet before the destructive storm. When she tightened her lips and turned her head to the side he didn't let her off the hook easily.

"Amal, tell me. What did your father do to you?"

He'd broken her heart without so much as touching a hair on her head.

"He… He asked for money as usual." There. She'd said it, *finally*.

Moving to mold his big, warm hand to her cheek, he rasped, "He isn't worth your thoughts, Amal. Put him out of mind."

"He's my father," she said, pulling free of his hand and missing his touch as she took more steps to distance herself from him. An arm's length away from him now, she was able to think coherently, even as her voice trembled with the tears blurring her vision. "He has a right to ask for help, even if his timing wasn't opportune."

"Then why are you upset? What's the problem, Amal?"

Mansur kept a respectful distance, but his clenched jaw and fists hinted at the anger he'd leashed on her behalf. She knew he hadn't been close to his father, and that it had to do with him having had a second wife and family, but she didn't need him conflating his contentious memories of his father with hers.

"He didn't stay after I'd transferred the money to his account." She had used her phone, and as soon as he'd had what he wanted her father had been in a rush to leave.

"Where is he now?" Mansur's tone curled into a low growl.

She imagined that if her father had been with them now, Mansur wouldn't have held back in pummeling him. As impressive as his control was, he looked ready to do some serious damage on something—or someone. She hadn't pictured him as capable of violence until that very moment.

"Far from us," she said, sighing and pinching the bridge of her nose. "He should be in Mogadishu. He has family there. A brother and sister I've never met. He wants to start a business. That's why he asked for the money." Luckily, she'd had some to spare. "It's like I told you…his request for money wasn't what troubled me."

"It was realizing that was all he wanted from you," he gritted, baring his teeth.

Amal flinched, her eyes squeezing tight as she soaked in more calming breaths. Hearing Mansur voice aloud how she felt about her father's cut-and-run attitude had knocked the wind out of her. Now she caught her breath, opened her eyes and confronted his simmering ire for her father.

"Don't be angry with him. I should have known better." She lifted her heavy shoulders, the shrug doing nothing to rid her of the sadness this conversation had wrought. "He didn't stay to raise us, and he didn't visit regularly either. I just couldn't help but hope. Or maybe the amnesia made me vulnerable—" She broke off with a head shake and turned to walk on before she remained mired in the past.

Mansur caught up quickly, bumping into her hand this time—purposely, she realized, when he grumbled, "I like your hope."

She had liked it, too—before she'd awakened to hopelessness.

As they walked forward to view Mansur's inheritance Amal began to wish something crazy: for her amnesia to rid her of her hope, because it wasn't doing her any good. That included hoping for her father to have a change of heart, and for Mansur to want to stay longer with his mother.

And with me, she thought with a sinking heart.

CHAPTER SEVEN

MANNY STARED LONG and hard at the spring-green untilled pasture before him. His mind was rich with ideas of what he could do with the inheritance if it ever became his. That didn't last long when he glimpsed Amal's subtle frown and the stifled frustration in her enticingly dark eyes.

He shrugged out of his suit jacket and dropped it to the ground, crouching to spread it out as a makeshift blanket. Amal noticed him only after he called her.

"Amal?"

She looked down to him, confusion deepening her frown. Then the light of realization went off in her eyes and she sat down beside him, sharing the jacket he'd thoughtfully set down without a peep of protest. It was the second sign that something was off. The first being her moody expression.

He knew it was bad when she said softly, "It's really beautiful. You should meet your family and then do what you proposed about leasing sections of farmland to local farmers."

It was her tone that broke him. Flat. Listless. *Hopeless*, he concluded, with a shiver crawling over his skin.

She sat with her legs under her, her hands in her lap and her posture unnaturally stiff. She didn't even seem aware of his presence—at least not until he nudged her leg with his, just as he'd done at the hospital. Then Amal snapped her head to him, that frown still marring her pretty face. Brows pleated, she looked down to where his thigh bumped her again. She looked adorably perplexed.

He smiled, but masked it when she lifted her head up.

"It's more than I expected," he confessed, looking at the expansive land stretching out before them. "Now I know what all those Romantic and pastoral poets wrote about when they were so in awe of nature. Very picturesque."

"Has it changed your mind?" she asked.

He was pleased that she'd latched on to his lure. As long as she wasn't in her own head, she was safe from the sorrow he knew she had to be entertaining. He knew because he'd done something similar after she'd rejected him. The only difference was that he'd lost Amal and had no one else to lean on. But now, despite her being the source of his pain once, Manny was finding it more difficult with each passing day to remember why he should steer clear from getting any closer to her emotionally…

And physically.

He had to be careful. But surely he could create some comfort for her in the meantime? Even at the risk of throwing himself under her perceptive gaze…

"It might have," he drawled, leaning back on his arms and crossing his legs one atop the other. He felt her watching him as he stared out at the inheritance his father had left him. Thinking of his father had him saying, "I was shocked to learn he'd given me anything."

"Why? He's your father. Aren't you his firstborn?"

"Yes, but there wasn't much love between us. I hadn't seen him for years."

And Manny had preferred it that way. He'd left at seventeen and never looked back to see himself as a boy, flailing wildly—and embarrassingly so—for his father's attention.

He had made himself a new man. Sloughed free of the skin of the insecure teenage boy he'd been when he had pulled himself out from under his mother's skirts.

As much as he appreciated his mother, staying with her would have never brought him the peace his profession now gave him. He stood on his own two feet, his history nowhere near as important as his present and future. That was where all his possibilities lay—before him, not behind.

Amal shifted to face him more, her knee touching his outer thigh, their contact re-established accidentally. She looked down at the same time as he did, but neither of them made a move to break the contact.

"When was the last time you saw him?" Amal asked.

"Shortly after I left for America," he said.

"Mansur, that's fifteen years!"

Amal's aghast look reined in his retort. He had to remember that she was viewing him through the filter of her high value on family.

"I'm aware of my age," he grumbled, "and I can do the math myself." But then he hissed in a breath at the hurt blooming on her face. Trying again, he said, "There's a reason I kept away from him. It's personal…something I'd rather not touch on."

He convinced himself the lump in his throat was from the anger he muffled, but the truth was much more pathetic.

His eyes smarted as he looked off to the side, away from both the farmland he was due to inherit and Amal. "He wasn't a very good father, Amal. Not much different than your dad. He paid my mother's bills and brought us the occasional gift from Addis when he'd visit, but that was it. Certainly it wasn't enough to make him father of the year."

"But, Mansur, he was still your father," she urged.

He saw her breath hitch when he looked to her suddenly.

"I don't want to talk about him anymore. As for seeing his family here in Addis—I'll continue to think on it."

And hopefully have a decision by the time the investigative firm searching for his father's second family got back to him.

Standing, he looked down to her and offered a hand. "It's time we head back."

She tipped her head up to the sky, her hand shielding her eyes from the sun now lowering from its zenith in the sky. "Guess it'll be late when we reach Addis Ababa."

"If we leave now, we might catch the sunset," he said.

"It won't start."

Mansur slipped free of the steering wheel and stepped from the car out to her. He crouched down by the car and looked under it. After a few minutes he stood and wiped his hands on a tissue he'd pulled from his pants pocket.

"We're leaking fuel. If I had to guess, the gas tank was punctured by road debris. This country terrain is a lot rougher than the city streets. Even rougher than I predicted. I should have accounted for it."

"Are we stuck here?"

Amal's insides churned at the possibility. Being trapped out here with him, just the two of them, after everything she'd shared about her father—no! They had to find a way back to Addis Ababa.

Mansur scowled, the fierce look stopping her protest short, withering her tongue, halting whatever she'd planned to say.

"Amal, I'm not risking driving a car with a leaking fuel tank."

"But—"

He gave her a hard look that brooked no argument. Then he leaned against the hood and fiddled on his phone. Taking the opportunity to study him from behind, Amal glowered at Mansur's back and then poked out her tongue.

He chose that moment to look back at her and he froze, his hand clutching the phone to his ear and his face slackening at her childish antics.

She blushed, happy when he had to speak to whoever was on the line. It saved her from his questions.

Amal hunkered down and took her own peek beneath the car. The pungent smell of fuel struck her first, and then she saw the small but growing puddle of inky oil under the car. She'd known Mansur wasn't lying about something so serious, but seeing it was truly believing it. And in this case she had to accept they were stranded for the time being.

Amal stood and brushed at her skirts. She rounded the car to where Mansur was, at the front, sitting on the hood now, speaking warmly on the phone. It amazed her how unfazed he was by their predicament.

"Half an hour is fine," he said, smiling and nodding. "We'll see you then. Bye."

Amal coughed lightly, which garnered his attention. It wasn't her fault, a breeze had kicked up the dust, but she was curious as to what he'd meant by seeing someone. Who was he expecting?

Not holding her in suspense for much longer, he patted the space beside him on the hood. "Might as well have a seat and get comfortable. I've called for rescue, but it'll be a little while before they reach us."

"Who's rescuing us?" she asked, sliding up to sit beside him.

"A friend."

Amal shrank in on herself at his succinct but obvious response. He'd sounded comfortable, talking to this friend of his. And they were obviously close enough that he felt he could rely on this person's assistance now. She hated to admit it, but she was jealous. Envy for Mansur's friend crept over her chest like heartburn. She wanted his trust, too. From what he'd told her, she'd had it once. Clearly the amnesia had changed that—otherwise wouldn't they be closer now?

"Are we friends?" Amal barely heard her own question, softly spoken as it was.

Mansur had heard her, though. He tipped his head to her, his brows furrowing. "Where did that come from?"

"Are we?" she asked again, urgency raising her voice. "I know we must have been once, but are we still friends?"

Did he still consider her a friend?

"I have few friends—even fewer these days, with my work schedule being what it is."

Mansur rolled his sleeves higher, the muscles of his forearms bunching. His face was devoid of any telling emotions. And yet she couldn't shake the feeling he was evading eye contact for a reason.

She opened her mouth, closing it when he spoke first.

"You're a family friend, so…yes," he said.

"Is that all?"

She could've slapped a hand over her mouth, disbelieving her own ears. Had she really just asked him that? *Oh, no!*

Before she could explain her lapse of sanity to him, Mansur chuckled. His laughter was surprising, and a bit unsettling given the situation. Especially as she couldn't tell whether he was laughing at her or not. Maybe he thought she was having a good joke. She hoped it was that. The idea of having to explain herself posed a daunting challenge.

"Why are you questioning our relationship?" he asked, once his humor wore off.

"Not questioning. I'm only curious." And she hoped he'd indulge her intrigue.

"We didn't speak for a long time, Amal. Not until you called me a couple of years ago. Then we started speaking again. Before that we both lived our lives. Chased our studies and our professional aspirations." He inclined his head slowly, his face softer in a blink. "I do consider you a friend or I wouldn't have asked you to come here with me."

"I thought you did that for your mother. Mama Halima can be persuasive."

Mansur smiled crookedly. "That she can—and yet she wouldn't have twisted my arm into helping you if I hadn't wanted to. And besides, I'd be stuck out here all on my own if I'd left you behind."

Amal gripped her knees tighter, her knuckles popping white against her skin. He was joking—she understood that—but her grandmother had told her once that every joke had a nugget of truth embedded in it. What it sounded like to her was that she was a convenient companion. If he hadn't already had this inheritance business in Addis Ababa he wouldn't have given her the time of day. He'd be back in America already, far, far away from her and her problems as an amnesiac.

Licking her lips slowly, watching his eyes dip to her mouth for a fraction, Amal sucked in a shaky breath and felt flames ignite in her veins. Those flames were soon fanned furiously into a wildfire. The need to kiss him smacked her dead center in the chest. She had experienced something similar in the hospital. And, given the way he was looking at her, she didn't think he'd stop her from leaning in for a kiss this time either.

The only difference now was the part of her that nagged, telling her she'd be making a mistake. Kissing him would leave her wanting more, she was sure of it. Her bones ached from the push-and-pull battle waging in her.

"This friend of yours…she lives in Addis Ababa?" Amal

squelched the desire to lean in and grab onto him, pull his face closer and taste his mouth. Redirecting her thoughts elsewhere helped immensely.

"She?" He gave her one of his long looks and then, glancing around their surroundings, said, "Yes, we've worked together."

"She works in the same field as you? In construction and engineering?"

"No," he said simply.

Amal didn't like the short, safe answer for a number of reasons. One, it felt like he was hiding something, and two, she didn't have any confidence that she held his trust. Not as a friend, despite what he said.

"You must be close," she remarked, side-eyeing him.

"We've worked as business partners before." He peered up at the cloudless blue sky, squinting. "I measure a person by how they conduct themselves professionally."

She did much the same in her line of work. Some clients were shady, finding loopholes in order to wiggle out of contracts *after* construction was completed. Her amnesia would've ruined her business, too, if she hadn't had a loyal staff around her. Her office manager Iman had stepped up, even without Amal's explicit request. That was real friendship.

Amal's heart swelled with a mix of pride and happiness for her staff. "I know what you mean," she said, and she met his eyes.

"I knew you would." He gave her another small smile. His phone vibrated, and he drew it out of his pocket, eyeing it for a solid minute before a stormy frown clouded his features. "I have to take this," he announced, slipping off the hood and striding from her at a clipped pace.

He put some distance between them before he placed the phone to his ear and Amal watched him pace as he spoke, his words swept up with the kick of a breeze. The blue sky was looking slightly gray now.

She looked around, tired of watching him and wondering what kind of call had delivered such intense urgency into him. A squeeze from her gut warned that it couldn't be anything good, though she dredged up the hope that it wasn't bad news.

For his sake, she thought, her heart panging for him.

When he returned, Mansur didn't leave her guessing.

"Sorry about that. It was the investigative firm I hired." He clenched his jaw, a muscle leaping high in his cheek because of whatever he'd just learned.

She could only come to one conclusion, and she wasn't sure of how to react. "They found your family?" She framed it as a query. No point in making assumptions.

Mansur's curt nod told her she was right on the money.

"But it's not good news?" she asked softly, and studied his curling lips and furled brows. "Are they not in Addis Ababa?" She couldn't think of what else might have caused his displeasure. "Wait—are they not in Ethiopia?"

"They're in Addis," he said, grumbling. "That's not the problem. I just hadn't expected to hear back so soon." He sighed. "The call caught me off guard. I had hoped to prepare a little more before I heard any word from the investigators."

Amal was silent, speechless. She had gotten the sense he was dreading the decision about meeting with his father's second wife and family. Only she hadn't thought he was so affected by it. It made him seem…*normal*, honestly. Given his wealth and immeasurable successes, she'd assumed he had everything under control. Every facet of his life. And what he couldn't control he'd easily wrangle into submission.

He's human.

Of course he was. She'd built him up in her mind as something other… *Untouchable.*

Clouds scuttled across the once-clear sky. She tried not to interpret them as an omen, even as forbidding as they looked when they passed shadows over the earth. She focused on Mansur and his troubled expression. He looked ready to split at the seams. *Him!* She hadn't thought anything could shake his stalwart composure. But here he was, pacing in front of her, plainly disturbed by the call he'd received from the private investigators into his blended family in Addis Ababa.

"What will you do?"

"I haven't made a decision yet, but I've asked for the report to be sent to me from the firm." He stopped finally, swiveling to face her and folding his arms. There seemed to be a new resolution dawning in him. It was palpable in his strong, even tone. "I won't do anything until I know what I'll be dealing with."

"And who you'll be meeting," she said, finishing his thought. She was doing that a lot lately. It felt nice, knowing they were on the same wavelength.

"You agree?" He sounded a little taken aback when he asked the question.

"It's smart to be cautious. Never hurts to do a little research. Might even save you some grief later down the road," said Amal.

Mansur bobbed his head slowly, returning the smile she gave him. He climbed up beside her on the hood and leaned back, stretching out. He looked at her with a silent invitation in his eyes. Amal followed his lead, lying beside him, the windshield at their backs. It was pleasant, staring up at the sky and divining images in the clouds that speckled the heavens.

"It really is peaceful here." She sighed happily and

closed her eyes. "No traffic. No noise pollution. A perfect retreat from the real world."

"Maybe we should both look into being farmers."

Amal snorted a laugh at his suggestion, pealing out into giggles when his sonorous laughter mingled with hers. She watched him turning onto his side, his hand propped under his head, and it compelled her into mirroring him. She found it hard to avoid looking at his mouth when he spoke.

"I was thinking about your hospital. If you're looking for funding..." He trailed off, the offer speaking for itself.

"Why do you want to help? It's not like you'll be in Hargeisa again anytime soon."

"I won't, but I like to put my resources to good use where I can."

"I know," she muttered, realizing that she'd divulged more than she cared to about her snooping online. Somehow it was hard to keep secrets around Mansur. Next to impossible to smother her true feelings. Sighing, she said, "I looked you up online."

"What did you learn?" he inquired, not appearing upset by her news.

"You donate to several charities. Also, you're very generous with your money when it comes to helping start-up companies."

"And...?"

"And your success and philanthropy haven't gone unnoticed. Getting on the *40 under 40* is quite the accomplishment," she said. "I'm shocked it hasn't gone to your head."

"How so?" he wondered.

"Most millionaires would be lapping up the glory in front of the media. But you're not most millionaires."

"Couldn't find many pictures of me?" he guessed teasingly.

Amal pursed her lips, oscillating between whether to

put the brakes on her interrogation or to continue chipping away at him.

This might be the last time you get to speak to Mansur about this. He'll leave for America and you'll never have this opportunity again.

Sufficiently motivated, she pressed on. "Why is that?"

"Why aren't there many pictures of me?" He raised a shoulder, his shrug full of mystery. "I like my anonymity."

Clearly seeing that it wasn't enough, he sighed heavily and flopped onto his back once more, his hands interlacing over his stomach, arms bunching and flexing with his restless shifting.

"I'm not a famous actor or musician, or a revered journalist or politician. It's true, I'm the face of a multi-billion-dollar company, but I'm also just a man who likes to work hard for his rewards. Being the CEO of Aetna hasn't changed me beyond the fact that I've got more power to help the helpless and to move the company in a progressive direction. It's exciting to work with billionaire hoteliers, shipping magnates and steel moguls, but it's just as thrilling to set aside time to connect with local communities and the non-profit social organizations linked to them."

He tucked his arms under his head, a faraway look in his eyes.

"Not all of those organizations get a fair shake. No one should feel left behind. No one should feel as though they come second on someone's priority list."

Amal thought of Mansur's father, and she knew without a doubting bone in her body that he had to be thinking about him, too. It had her thinking about her father, too, and his last visit. About the visceral sense of abandonment that he'd left her with when he'd walked away from her again.

He hadn't wanted her as a daughter. Not when her mother had died, nor when her grandmother had passed.

She was his family when he desired money from her—that was all. It was a difficult truth to swallow, and it choked her even now, when she should be able to move on.

She rested flat on her back once more and blinked up at the sky, bottling her depression.

"Amal?" Mansur's voice slipped into her ear, his minty breath washing over the side of her face.

She turned her head, blinking slowly to avoid crying. "Yes?"

"Thanks for coming along with me."

Amal smiled, her lips trembling from the strenuous effort not to cry and from being so close to him and holding back. "What are friends for?"

Mansur looked away and she forced herself not to read anything into it. Especially when his hand brushed against her side and she lowered her hand to touch the back of his. She expelled the breath she hadn't known she was holding, feeling a measure of relief pouring through her.

The moment was burst by the sound of a distant aircraft. Amal didn't give it much thought until the noise couldn't be ignored. The dot that was a helicopter grew bigger and bigger, until it filled the sky only a hundred feet from them, before passing over the hill and Mansur's sports car and moving further on.

An icy pool of dread manifested itself in her insides. "Is that—?" She stopped short when it became obvious that Mansur couldn't hear her over the aircraft's whirring blades.

He sat up and turned to follow the chopper with narrowed eyes, a hand going to his face to protect his eyes from the dust and debris being swept up into the air.

Coughing lightly, Amal sat up too and watched the helicopter slowly sway and descend, settling on the road a safe stretch from them, yet within walking distance.

She panicked and looked to Mansur again. "Are we riding in *that*?" She couldn't believe him. After knowing how shaky she'd been on his luxury plane, now *this*? She was shaking her head already, sensing what was coming. "No, no, no… I can't."

"We have no choice." He leaned in to speak directly into her ear. "It's the only way back to Addis. The *quickest* way, Amal. I'm sorry."

She was crushed by his rationale. Of course, he was speaking and acting from a place of reason. And, as scary as the thought of taking the helicopter was, she had to be reasonable. In a car, their rescuer would have to drive three hours out of Addis Ababa and another three back, and by then it would be plenty dark. This way they'd be back at their hotel before the sun switched hemispheres.

"Coming?" Mansur held out a hand to her after he'd slid off the car hood.

Amal grasped it, and with his assistance soon had her feet on ground. But he didn't release her readily, walking hand in hand with her to greet their unorthodox rescuer.

He's a millionaire! I guess he's not above displays of wealth and power.

Amal discovered she wasn't upset by the outcome. And her fear didn't feel so sharp as they neared the chopper. She looked down to their connected hands as Mansur took the lead, and realized it was because she had him with her. He wouldn't hurt her. It didn't matter that she didn't fully remember him, or that he wasn't committed to calling her a friend. Not even her worry that his mother was controlling his strings could blind her to the fact that she knew he would see to her safety.

It wasn't like Mama Halima had told him to take Amal's hand.

He was doing this all on his own whim.

Smiling, she glanced up to the helicopter just as the door opened and a sharply suited man launched himself out.

Amal couldn't help but lean into Mansur, squeezing his hand and catching his attention. He slowed, and then leaned down to hear her accusation. "Is that your friend?" she asked.

He smirked, a mischievous glint in his eyes. "That's him."

She gawped, recalling her jealousy and how it had been focused on a fictitious woman she'd believed to be his friend. Not a woman after all. She wondered why he hadn't corrected her—and then she realized he'd been enjoying himself at her expense.

"Y-You didn't correct me," she stammered.

"I guess I didn't."

Swatting his arm when he laughed, she grumbled with heated cheeks, "You should have told me."

"I'm sorry." He squeezed her hand back. "Forgive me?"

Before she had the chance to reply, having already forgiven him, Amal noticed that they had been joined by their valiant rescuer—who was most definitely *not* a woman. The man hurried to them, a headset firmly on his head and his hands holding two extra pairs.

Following Mansur's lead, she accepted a headset and adjusted it over her ears, putting the microphone near to her mouth. She jumped when the stranger's voice came booming through the headphones, with very little background interference.

"I didn't think I'd ever need to save *you*, Manny."

His brusque laugh cracked like thunder through her headset.

"And deprive myself of the chance to see you pilot that thing? Never."

Mansur clasped the other man's hand. They drew in

for a hug, clapped each other on the back and pulled apart, leaving nothing but her introduction.

"Amal," Mansur said, his voice caressing her name, and his touch landing on the small of her back, unwinding tendrils of heat through her blood, "meet my friend Hakeem Ahmet, owner of the hotel we're staying at. We worked together when my firm built it."

That was news! Amal hadn't known he'd had a hand in building their hotel. Now she was wondering if they'd ever spoken of *that* over the phone, and if she'd forgotten. Stifling the urge to question him, she smiled at Hakeem and accepted the hand he offered her.

Once the introductions were complete, Hakeem jerked a thumb over his shoulder at the helicopter. "Ready to hit the skies?"

"Ready?" Mansur asked her, his voice humming through her ears and stroking secret parts of her—her heart included.

She couldn't find her voice, so she bobbed her head more energetically than she'd ever believed she would, considering how deathly afraid she was of riding in a helicopter.

But then Mansur pulled her close and said, "I got you."

She looked long and deep into his eyes, believing he *did* have her.

And she had him for now.

For how long, though?

CHAPTER EIGHT

THEY'D NEVER MADE it to Addis Ababa.

On Mansur's orders, Hakeem had flown them to the nearby Harar Meda Airport, also the main base of the Ethiopian Air Force. A little unnerved, and plenty confused, there Amal had learned of Mansur's plan for the two of them. He'd had a car ready to drive them to nearby Bishoftu—a breathtaking resort town with not two, but *five* crater lakes highlighting the forest-rich valleys.

She couldn't get enough of the town's natural beauty, its charming stone buildings and the friendly, welcoming faces of the townspeople. The mellow air influenced the other tourists as well, and she didn't encounter any of the pushy sort while exploring the resort with Mansur. Carved into the valley, the town's roads and smaller corridors wound up and down, giving her legs plenty of exercise.

Never had she felt so revitalized. Where Addis Ababa had enlivened her, Bishoftu cleansed her soul and gave it a hearty scrub that left her feeling lighter in spirit and pleasanter in mood.

Now, three restful nights and days later, Amal mewled and gave a yawn of contentment. She stretched her body over the chaise longue on the sun-drenched balcony of her room. The luxury hotel Mansur had chosen for their stay looked out over one of the crater lakes. Her room faced the textured green bowl of a valley and its glassy lake water. Bright white patches of sunlight mirrored off the lake's serene surface as the sun climbed higher in the sky, a testament to another peaceful day in this paradise of a town.

Amal burrowed deeper into her cushioned seat, not wanting to move anytime soon. And, with no concrete itinerary for the day, she could probably get away with it...

What she wanted to do was dive into her journal and get her morning writing in. She'd begun writing again, journaling her thoughts. In particular she had taken to writing outside, where she could enjoy the resort's scenic vista.

Amal was reading over her daily entry when sleep blanketed her. The air held just the right temperature, and the mix of the warm embrace of sunlight and the cool passes of a breeze lulled her. Her lids drooped closed. The journal in her hands listed toward her face—and the *thwap* of the book smacking her forehead jerked her awake.

She scrambled up in the seat as a low, heart-racing chuckle rumbling from behind her rivaled the dull pain where the journal had made contact with her face. She burned with a blush, feeling its searing heat doubled by the golden-white sunrays beaming over the balcony patio.

She had company—and she knew exactly who it was.

Without turning, she said, "I didn't hear you knock."

"You gave me your extra key," he said.

And she had—a couple days earlier. She had a key to his room, as well. Mansur had suggested the trade.

"In case we lock ourselves out. Keeping keys in separate rooms could come in handy then," he'd said, his reasoning perfectly sound as usual.

Mansur stepped into her line of vision. He had drinks in his hands—one she presumed was hers. *Ah.* So that was why he'd come to her. Now she thought about it, bathing in the sun had left her with a scratchy dryness in her throat. His drinks were well-timed.

"I suppose I can forgive you for not knocking," she sassed, with a grin.

She accepted the glass from his hand and gulped half the chilled mango juice.

Noticing he was watching her, she lowered her glass and tipped her head to the side. "What is it?" she asked. Because he had a look in his eyes that said he had something to tell her.

"I thought we could walk by the lake again," he said, though she had the sense that wasn't what he wanted to say at all.

They'd walked all over the resort, acquainting themselves with most of Bishoftu. But Amal liked their walks by Lake Hora the best.

"I'd like to visit the flamingos." The avian wildlife at Lake Hora was plentiful along the sloping footpath edging the green valley. "I can take more pictures for Mama Halima and everyone back at my firm. They'd like to see Bishoftu."

He bobbed his head. Staring down at his glass, he took a hasty sip and then traced his finger along the rim, looking more lost with each passing heartbeat. Finally, he said, "I'm thinking of heading back to Addis."

"You've made a decision?" she asked, drawing her legs around, feeling her bare feet kissing the natural stone tiling of the balcony.

He sat close, on the other chaise longue. His dark curly head lifted up at her movement.

Amal had to remember what it was like to breathe normally when his brooding eyes focused on her. She found her voice, though, and continued her train of thought. "Are you going to meet your family, then?"

"Not my family, really—but, yes."

She ignored what he'd said, but respected his unspoken wish and didn't mention them as being his "family" when she spoke next. "Is that why you're leaving? You've called them and made plans to meet?"

"No, not yet." He scowled down at his drink, grumbling, "I should leave, though—before I change my mind."

Amal was at a loss for words. She knew the depth of anguish this decision had wrought in him. Had sensed it without him telling her and giving her a play-by-play of his turmoil. And he deserved her outpouring of silent sympathy. Yet a part of her questioned why he insisted on holding this grudge of his. His father was gone.

He had three half-sisters—he'd told her himself, after reading the full report from the private investigators. Knowing that she probably wouldn't have turned out anywhere near as decent without her own brothers, Amal couldn't fully grasp why he was repelling this opportunity to connect with this extended family of his. Because they *were* his family—whether he liked it or not.

Despite not wanting to affect his decision-making, Amal heard herself saying, "It'll be that much harder on you if you go in with that chip on your shoulder." She spoke softly, gently, hoping he wouldn't take her advice and twist malice into it. She really was only advising him from the heart.

Mansur understood that she, too, hadn't had the best of relationships with her father. In fact, Amal didn't have much of a relationship with him at all. It hadn't stopped her from trying. And she was fighting the natural pull toward hatred. She didn't want to hold grudges. It only pushed people away.

She wished he could see that. That it did more damage than good in the long run.

"Give them a chance first, and then judge the experience," she said with a heavy heart.

He was silent for so long she worried she'd overstepped. But then he raised his head and curled his lips into a ghost of a smile. A shadow of one, really. It disappeared as soon as she saw it.

"I'll try. No promises." But then he screwed his brows together and said, "I'm not going there to make friends, Amal. I'll be doing this for the inheritance."

"Why do you think your father even put that clause in his will?" She'd thought of asking that question many times since learning about his inheritance.

"To torture me?" he guessed. Shrugging, he shook his head and set his glass of mango juice on the ground. There was a new pair of flashy, expensive-looking kicks on his feet. "I've considered it long and hard, and I have yet to think up a good reason."

"Have you tried putting yourself in his shoes?"

Mansur frowned anew. "I didn't know him, Amal. Wouldn't even begin to understand his sadistic thinking." His eyes narrowed and his jaw hardened, his face chiseled with his rising annoyance.

Seeing that he'd like to change the subject matter, and hoping to lighten the mood, Amal rounded back to his departure. "When are you leaving for Addis Ababa?"

"This evening."

"We'll be able to sneak in one more lakeside walk," she said, happy they'd be making the trip back. She figured it was about time. They couldn't hide out here forever.

Mansur had had their luggage delivered from Addis Ababa hours after they'd arrived in Bishoftu that first day, but they had unfinished business back in the capital—the both of them. She had to figure out whether she wanted to accept psychotherapy at the hospital, and Mansur had to see his family.

Amal gulped down the rest of her mango juice and, gripping the journal on her lap, beamed. “Okay, I’m ready for our last day in Bishoftu if you are.”

“Amal, I’ll be going back by myself.”

Taken aback by his comment, she blurted, “What? No… I have to go back to Addis, too.”

“Yes, but there’s no rush for you to head back.” He spread out his hands, his tone imploring. “You can stay here. Enjoy the town and the flamingoes and the lakes, and all the services the resort offers.”

Amal shot up, her journal clutched to her pounding chest and her hand grasping her empty glass tightly. She couldn’t believe her ears! Was he truly planning on leaving her behind?

“Let me explain…”

Mansur stood slowly, sighing and raking his fingers through his curls before swiping his palm over his beard. A nervous energy clamored off him. It made her jumpy, too.

“I didn’t bring you to Ethiopia to be bogged down by my problems. I want you to stay here and relax, make the most of your time away from Hargeisa. Treat it as a vacation. *Stay*, Amal.”

“I won’t,” she snapped, furious suddenly that he’d expect her to want to remain here all alone. *Abandoned*, she thought sourly.

He couldn’t possibly imagine she’d be happy to stay on in Bishoftu without him. After she’d spent every day with him. She wouldn’t be able to look at the resort or walk through the town without thinking of him. A punishment—that was what it would be.

“I want to come with you,” she said, and stiffened her lip for an argument.

"Why?" Mansur asked, sounding ragged with fatigue.

Amal thought quickly on her feet. "You were with me at the hospital. I'd like to return the favor."

"That… You don't need to do that," he said.

"I do—because I don't like feeling as though I owe you."

"You don't owe me anything," he stressed, baring some teeth now. Exasperation drew creases around his eyes and frown lines along his forehead.

"Why? Because you've done your mother a favor by helping me? By remaining at my side while I'm away from her?" Amal pouted, frustration pouring out of her. She'd had her doubts, and he hadn't quelled them entirely, and now that incertitude directed her outpouring of emotion. "You can block me from joining you to see your family, but I'm coming to Addis Ababa with you. You can't refuse me that."

"They're not my family," he said quietly, his scowl making a reappearance. But then he jerked a nod and relented. "All right, we're going back to Addis together. Now, can we take that walk before we find something new to argue about?"

She didn't think he was joking. If they remained like this they probably would find a new topic to squabble over. Maybe the fact that he was adamant in not accepting his father's second family. Amal didn't want that. She hadn't liked raising her voice, and Mansur looked troubled by it, too.

"Do you still want to take that walk with me?" he asked.

She did. Nodding, she said, "It sounds better than fighting."

He managed a smile and turned for the balcony door. "A truce, then?"

"A truce," she agreed happily, trailing him.

* * *

Amal had expected a walk around the lake, but Mansur had something extra planned.

"A boat?"

She took the hand he offered her when she crested a ditch and climbed down to his level on the thin strip of beach. He didn't pull his hand away and, like he had with the helicopter, guided her over to the boat awaiting them.

A skinny young man stood in the boat, long paddles in his hands.

"I thought this last visit should be the most memorable." Mansur guided her to the lakeshore, his eyes hidden by his shades but a smile twitching over his lips. "I promise it won't be as nerve-racking as the plane and the helicopter."

"Speak for yourself," she muttered, queasiness rippling through her at the sight of the murky lake water. It had looked so serene from afar. But knowing she'd be riding a boat over it had changed her pleasant view of it. Gulping, she said, "I don't know how to swim."

Mansur gestured to the orange float vests on the beach. "That's what the life jackets are for. And I'll jump in and rescue you if you do take a dip in the lake."

He gave her hand a comforting squeeze, and she tightened her fingers on his and peered up. "Promise?" she asked.

He released her hand, stooped to grab a life jacket and opened it out to her. "Promise."

Satisfied with his vow, Amal turned her back to him and had his help slipping on the life jacket. A flutter of attraction pulsed through her when his hands brushed her arms. It didn't last long because he had to get his own life jacket. She watched as he strapped himself into the vest and shrugged out of his sneakers.

Catching her raised brows, he explained, "They're worth enough that I'd rather not hunt for another limited pair."

"Should I leave mine, too?" She wiggled a wedge sandal at him, and burned hotter with desire when his eyes lingered on her feet.

She swore his voice had gotten thicker when he said, "Yeah, probably… Just to be safe."

Shoes off, they walked barefoot into the lake and he helped her up the boat's in-built staircase. Once they were inside, the boat operator pushed them from the shallow, grounding waters of the shore to the deeper bowl of the lake.

Amal craned her neck all around for the new perspective of the lake. "Mansur, it's lovely!"

"I knew you'd like it," he said, his own gaze sweeping the lake and the valley. "Reminds me of an oasis, or what I would think one would look like."

"Being here in Bishoftu has me longing for more adventure." Amal sighed wistfully, knowing her heart would yearn for this special place once they left. "I'm going to miss it," she said, melancholy wavering in her tone. "It's going to have a place in my heart forever. As far as memories go, it's one of the best I'll have, since my amnesia has yet to gift me any of my adult memories."

"I'm happy you'll remember this for a long time."

He'd switched to Somali. Amal understood why, as the boat operator had to understand English. How else had Mansur booked the trip out on the lake? And especially given what he went on to say.

"It's my way of thanking you—for being family to my mother in my absence, for coming out to view my potential inheritance, and for reminding me what I've missed out on by not returning home sooner."

Amal absorbed his words, let them rest in her heart for a

moment, before she dared to ask, "Will you miss me when you go back to America?"

"I'll miss our conversations. It's been nice to have someone to talk to."

"Just nice?" she asked.

It was more than "nice" for her. She finally felt as if someone understood her. She had told Mansur a lot. About her father. About her fear of not regaining her memories. She'd also nearly kissed him—twice. And he'd looked like he had wanted to do the same to her.

If she'd been braver, she might have tested out the theory one more time. Only this time actually made contact and shared her first kiss with him. But they had an audience. She peeked over at the boat operator and stifled a sigh. Ultimately, she should be happy not to be alone with Mansur. She couldn't expect him to remain with her much longer. And, if she was being honest with herself, she wouldn't settle for anything else.

A long-distance relationship *was* a possibility. They could start chatting over the phone again, and video-calling. Eventually that would run its course, though, and she'd yearn for more. She'd want him beside her, and it wasn't fair for him to be forced into a position to choose.

Like he'd ever pick you over his career.

And she didn't want that. Not one bit! He had worked hard for what he had, and he deserved every bit of success and every dollar to his name. She wouldn't want Mansur to make *her* choose either, between her job and him. Because she certainly wasn't willing to pack up and move to America. She loved living in Hargeisa. Hadn't dreamt of leaving Somaliland or abandoning her company.

And amnesia hadn't affected her desire to have a family of her own someday. She had childhood memories of longing for that very same thing. But now she felt ready for it. For love, marriage, and raising children.

Sadly, Mansur couldn't give her that. And she wanted all of him, so she'd best learn to live without him starting now.

"You're right, though. It is nice," she said with a tiny smile.

She looked out over the lake again and pulled out her phone, snapping photos. Ribbons of sunlight shimmered on the lake surface as the boat carved its path toward the lake's center. Like the sunlight, Mansur wasn't something she could hold on to. And she wouldn't add to his plate of worries.

With what she hoped was a clear voice, she said, "Whatever happens in Addis, remember that there's hope and light and positivity in every experience."

Mansur hummed noncommittally. "Your optimism is nice, too."

Amal glanced at him. "What's nice is being here with you and knowing that you'll consider what I have to say. Just…don't make any hasty actions. Go in with an open heart, like I did. It wasn't as though I wanted to come to Addis Ababa in the first place. But I heard you out, and I liked what you said. It's why I'm here."

"This is different—" he began sullenly, but stopped when she sucked in a shuddery breath. Pausing, he gave her a thoughtful, warmer look before he added, "I said I would try, didn't I? And I will. But there's history I can't ignore."

Knowing it was the best she'd get for now, Amal eased off. "That's good enough," she remarked.

It was a start. And she hoped that if she couldn't have Mansur, at least he'd be open to reconnecting with his family. They didn't both have to have tragic relationships with their fathers. He still had hope. He just had to see that he did.

CHAPTER NINE

"THIS SHOULD BE IT." Amal paused in front of a florist's shop.

Mansur dragged his feet, dread slowing him. They were in Addis Ababa again, in the heart of its large and famed open-air marketplace. Addis Mercato was teeming with energy. Stores and stalls were all open for business. Hawkers called out loudly to garner attention to their wares.

After following the directions that the private investigators had emailed to him, Mansur had been able to lead him and Amal to their final destination.

And it was this quaint-looking shop.

Above the entrance was a green-and-white-striped awning, sun-bleached of its original vibrancy and yet clinging to its welcoming charm. At least, his beautiful companion thought so. Amal's face held an innocent glee while she waited for his slower, hesitant strides to eat up the short distance to her.

The swooping in Manny's stomach sharpened with every step now. And he'd just about locked every muscle and clamped down on a bile-ridden spasm from his gut when Amal said, "It's open."

Of course it was. He couldn't avoid this any longer, then.

Get this over with. That had been the mantra he'd chanted inwardly as soon as they had parked the car and traversed into the Mercato. His chance for excuses gone, he had no choice but to accomplish what they'd come to do here. Thankfully, he had one recourse—and she was smiling at him, her hope searing blindingly into his embittered core.

Amal.

He was happy she'd talked him into bringing her along. She was friendly support. Someone in his corner, he hoped. And so far he hadn't gone wrong in allowing her closer to him. Amal had shown nothing but kindness and patience when he'd revealed his indecision about meeting the family he had worked hard to pretend didn't exist.

One thing was for certain: after this meeting he could no longer disregard his half-siblings and stepmother.

You win. Scowling, Manny aimed his concession to the heavens, where he imagined his father was laughing it up. He closed his eyes and swore he heard the laughter—a brushing memory of the roaring mirth that had often emanated from his father at the smallest of jokes. Funny… He couldn't recall many memories of his father. Pleasant ones or otherwise. His father hadn't stuck around long enough for Mansur to hold on to more than a few memories. And time had sanded away the rest.

He opened his eyes and found Amal watching him. What would she be thinking? That he was allowing this meeting to undo him. Was she judging him? He hoped not. Last time she had, she'd left him broken-hearted.

"We could come back," she said softly, touching her fingertips to the back of his hand.

Mansur relaxed. No, he was wrong. Amal *wasn't* judging him. This was different than when he'd proposed to her. She wasn't pushing him away now.

Not yet—but she will once she realizes you can't let go of your grudge.

The malicious thought snaked through his mind but,

clenching his jaw, feeling the ticking cheek muscle react to the swell of his agitation, he did what he did best: pretended everything was all right.

As for this "family" of his—a quick hello should suffice in satisfying the clause that blocked him from inheriting the land.

Nothing more, nothing less.

"After you," Manny said, more brusquely than he'd have liked.

Opening the door for Amal, he watched her hesitate, her eyes tracking his face. Her lips parted slightly, as if she thought to say something, but then, thinking against it, she looked away and walked inside. He trailed her, with weighty unease bearing down on his shoulders.

The shop was slightly warmer than room temperature. An appropriate space for the showy, tropical flowers on display. He imagined the plants requiring cooler climes were housed in the back of the spacious retail area.

"They're lovely..." Amal breathed her awe, gravitating to the closest shelf of potted flowers. She pulled in close to the flowers, inhaled and sneezed delicately.

"Careful. You might be allergic," he warned.

She blinked her watering eyes, sneezed once more, and laughed. "Maybe I am. But they smell so good. It's hard not to take a sniff."

Manny believed he'd be able to control himself. He was already imagining walking out of the shop, messaging his lawyers, and letting them know he'd done his part in fulfilling the clause blocking his land inheritance.

"Nervous?" Amal whispered.

She'd drifted back to his side, and Manny looked down at her, folding his arms. "I'd like this over with, to be honest."

Before he could interpret her sad smile, he heard footsteps approaching.

A tall, fair-skinned man pushed through the back door. He had a smile affixed to his youthful, clean-shaven face, and his eyes bounded from Amal to Manny. As he neared them he dried his hands on his black waist apron, where the shop name, Imperial Flowers, was emblazoned alongside a calla lily.

"Good morning. How can I help you?" His subtly accented English was crisp and clear and polite.

"I'm here to see Zoya Ali."

The friendly expression on the young man's face broke with his confusion. "Do you have an appointment?"

"No," he replied, watching the other man's bafflement intensify.

It was the truth, though. His half-sister Zoya *wasn't* expecting Manny to be here for some good old-fashioned family time, courtesy of their bullheaded father.

I'm close, though. Nearly done with this charade.

He didn't see it as anything else.

"I don't have a standing appointment, no, but she'll want to see me," he clarified.

It was a total bluff. He had no clue what Zoya would think once she knew he occupied her shop.

Frowning now, the young man darted his narrowing eyes to Amal. But he spoke to Manny when he asked, "What did you say your name was, sir?"

"Mansur Ali. I'm her half-brother."

That proclamation cracked like thunder through the shop.

The young man snapped his jaw shut, but the whites of his eyes continued to bulge with shock. "I'll go tell her. Please wait here."

He swiveled and headed for the door he'd come through.

"I don't think he expected that," Amal murmured.

No, and neither will my half-sister, Manny thought grimly, shoving aside the odd trickle of concern for the woman he'd come to meet. Misplaced emotions would only further complicate this situation. All he had to remember was that this was a means to an end. If he could keep that as his focus, he'd come out of this unscathed.

Amal neared him, her fingertips on his arm unwarranted but welcome. "You can do this," she said, her voice unwavering, filled with stalwart confidence. She had enough for them both, and he could feel it seeping into him from the simple connection she'd made. Grateful for her presence again, he gave her the briefest of smiles as a reply.

Their stares simultaneously veered to the shop's back door as it swung open again, nearly crashing into the wall from the force. The willowy woman who hurried out took one look at him and froze in her spirited tracks. She gawked just like the young man. He hovered behind her closely.

Manny could have sliced the tension in the room with a knife. It sat in the air, thick and annoying. But it came in handy. Giving him the time to size up this half-sister of his.

Zoya was nearly as tall as he was. It made it easier for him to look her in the eyes, unearth what she could possibly be thinking now he stood before her.

She was pretty, in a cute kind of way. Her eyes were an identical shade to his, and they shared the same narrowly tapered nose. But her skin was a pinkish beige-brown, her face was wider, and her cheeks were rounded.

He knew she was three years younger than him, making her Amal's age. And Manny also understood from the private investigators' exhaustive dossier that Zoya had studied horticulture in college, and gone straight from school into opening a now thriving florist business. She was doing well, having had the lease on her marketplace location for close on five years.

He knew *about* her. But he didn't *know* her.

Amal's touch hadn't left his arm and he concentrated on it, longing to clasp her hand under his and be reassured that she was with him through this no matter what happened. That she'd continue to be unjudgmental and generous with her sympathy.

For someone who didn't recall him in adulthood, she excelled at soothing the worst emotions in him.

If they hadn't been standing in his half-sister's shop, Manny might have lingered over the thought that this connection he had to Amal would never disappear. No amnesia or great distance would destroy it. Some deep part of him would always care for her.

But, not fully ready to wrestle what that meant, he concentrated on his half-sister. She was finally addressing him.

"Mansur. Is it really you?" Zoya widened her eyes at his subtle nod.

He tensed, preparing himself for her to throw him out angrily. After all, he was a stranger. A family member, yes, but a strange man who had burst in on her life. For all he knew she hated him and wished he didn't exist.

That theory crumbled when Zoya smiled widely. The smile lifted her round cheeks and revealed two dimples. His body jarred on a flashback, of his father's grizzly bearded face, of the deep dimples that had never been hidden by his thick henna-colored facial hair, and of his wide, contagious smile. That spectral laughter still echoing in Manny's mind from the dislodged memory chipped at his defenses. With one smile, this strange woman had awoken the ghost of his father, and now the phantoms of his past haunted him.

Not a strange woman, but your half-sister.

He resented the truth in that thought.

So what? She bears some resemblance to our father. That doesn't change anything.

And it didn't. Not for him. He was here to fulfill the clause in his father's will. Just as smoothly as he'd walked into Zoya's life he'd be walking out of it, richer by forty acres of farmland.

"How did you find me?" Zoya clapped a hand to her mouth, blinked several times, and then, breathing deeply, lowered her hand and added shakily, "I can't believe it's really you."

Zoya stepped closer, pausing in front of him, her smile tearful but effervescent. And all Manny could think was that she hadn't tossed him out of her shop yet. Small mercy.

"We have to talk," he said.

It wasn't what he'd planned to do. Hardly an in-and-out mission. But now that he saw her he strongly desired to have her comprehend that this was a *one-time scenario*. He didn't need her, or her siblings, or her mother. He didn't want their family.

He had his mother, and maybe Amal again, and that was enough.

Oblivious to what he had planned, Zoya bobbed her head. Her ready agreement was unnerving to him.

"I was thinking the same thing. Should we grab coffee?"

It wasn't a question, really, though she'd phrased it as such. Reaching for the ties of her half-apron, Zoya slipped it off and folded it neatly. The young man, who looked to be about Zoya's age, took the apron from her.

"I'll be back, Salim," she told him.

The man clutched her hand, gave it a squeeze, and said, "I'll be here when you do." Then he stepped through the back door and left them to continue their conversation.

Alone with Zoya now, Manny watched his half-sister's attention flicker to Amal, her smile brightening in its wattage.

That was his cue to introduce them—something he figured he'd have to do, but he didn't relish. After all, this was supposed to be a no-frills meeting. He wasn't trying to establish a relationship with Zoya or her family.

But he couldn't be rude, so he made the introductions.

"This is Amal," he said, his eyes straying from his half-sister to watch their interaction. He needn't have worried. Amal's sunny smile looked anything but uncomfortable.

"Your flower shop is beautiful," Amal said, waving to the shelves full of brightly colored flora.

Zoya touched a hand to her heart and dipped her head in gratitude. "It comes from a place of labor and love, so it makes me happy to hear you think so, Amal. My fiancé, Salim, is a great support. He helps me run the business. Without him, it wouldn't be nearly as beautiful as you say."

"You've both done an excellent job. You should be proud."

Amal's compliments to Zoya chafed Manny. He struggled to comprehend what was happening. He didn't want Amal to be making friends with Zoya. He wanted to wash his hands clean of this moment in the very, *very* near future.

Firing daggers at her, he watched as Amal barely turned her head to regard his glowering look. A look he'd hoped would communicate his growing agitation. But Amal was riveted as Zoya pointed out some of her favorite flowers to her.

"About that coffee…" he interjected, his gaze snapping from Amal to Zoya.

"Will you be coming with us, too?" Zoya asked Amal. "If you haven't tried the coffee in Addis Ababa yet, then you're in for a treat."

"I'd love to taste Ethiopian coffee," Amal said.

Manny was glad they were finally moving out of Zoya's shop and getting nearer to the end of this meeting. Though even as they walked through the Mercato in search of a café where Amal could taste authentic Ethiopian coffee, Manny couldn't get rid of his prickly intuition that there was yet another obstacle ahead of him before his elusive inheritance.

And her name was Amal.

Amal's muffled squeal made the quest for coffee worth it. That was what he told himself when she took her first sip of traditionally brewed Ethiopian coffee and exclaimed, "This is delicious!"

Having already sampled what Addis Ababa had to offer coffee-wise, he wasn't as affected—and yet even he grudgingly admitted that Zoya hadn't exaggerated the good cup that could be found in this run-of-the-mill restaurant. No advertisements promoted the tasty, freshly ground beans. Any normal patron would be going in blind. But they had his half-sister.

Lucky us.

There was a bitter flavor to his thinking—more bitter than his black coffee.

Unaffected by his off-putting mood, Amal and Zoya gabbed over their coffee. Their excitement might have been contagious if he'd allowed himself to listen. So he'd tuned them out for the greater part of it, only finally tuning in now.

"It's tasty, isn't it?" Zoya was asking with a grin.

Amal nodded vigorously. "I don't have anything to compare it to in Addis Ababa, but I've had cappuccinos in Hargeisa that are good, but not *this* good."

"I've made it my mission to find the best coffee," Zoya told them, including Manny when she smiled his way, "and after nearly five years as a marketplace vendor, I can say this place can't be beat."

Zoya repeated her praise in Amharic, for the hostess of

their coffee ceremony. The hostess murmured her gratitude, also in Amharic.

"I wonder if I can make this at home," Amal said, having emptied her small handle-less cup and waiting for a refill from the fresh green beans that the hostess roasted for them now. "Mama Halima would probably like it."

At the mention of his mother, Zoya looked at him, and Manny grasped the opportunity to tie this meeting up and move on with his life before his half-sister got the idea that he wanted more from her. Like a relationship. Something he absolutely didn't care to establish today.

Or ever, he thought firmly.

"Mansur?" Amal was saying.

She continued to insist on calling him by his given name, and he'd given up correcting her. He liked the way she said his name. But she was the exception.

"Do you think your mother would like some coffee? I think she would."

She was looking to him for an answer. And so was Zoya.

Manny pried his jaws apart to say, "We'll look for a gift for her in the market. Which reminds me—we should be leaving."

"How long are you staying in Addis?"

His half-sister wasn't smiling anymore. What he might have described as wariness masked her expression, concealing what she was really thinking once more.

Manny gritted his teeth and worked through the childish urge to snap that it wasn't her business. She'd merely asked a question of him. One he could handle *sans* adult tantrum.

Flicking a gaze to the restaurant's exit, he said offhandedly, "As my business is concluded, not much longer."

He didn't elaborate on how that "business" was the inheritance left by their father solely to him. But Amal knew what his icy nonchalance hid, and she frowned at his ungracious tone toward Zoya. He'd been concerned that she might form an attachment to the other woman, and now she was proving his suspicions correct.

"You're leaving soon?" his half-sister asked.

"Very soon, hopefully." Manny kept his eyes on Zoya and away from Amal's pointed gaze and the guilt she was already awakening in him.

Zoya's brows knitted with her confusion. "Wouldn't you like to meet my sisters and my mom?"

"I don't have time," he lied.

"Oh..." was her hollow reply.

For a moment the only sound breaking their table's silence was the hostess transferring the roasted darkened beans into a pestle, then the long-handled mortar grinding the beans and scraping the sides of the wooden bowl.

Manny should have known Amal would be the first to rupture it, with her sweet, silvery voice.

"Does your mother make traditional Ethiopian coffee?"

Amal's query held a cheery note that enchanted Manny into looking at her once more. She didn't have eyes for him, though, her attention now secure on Zoya.

"She does," his half-sister said, laughing lightly, "but I can't say it's as good as the cup you've just had. She's tried to teach me, too, but I've never had the patience and dedication required to do it."

"If you don't mind, I'd love to visit sometime."

Her request surprised Zoya as much as him. He sat forward, coffee forgotten, and felt the bitter, roasted flavor clash with the flood of fiery bile leaping from his chest into his throat.

Zoya beat him to a response. "I'd like that, Amal. You're welcome anytime." Pausing, she glanced askance at him. "As are you, Mansur."

He glared at Amal, and she stubbornly stared back at

him, meeting the worst he could fling at her. Something powerful happened then. His mind changed from night to day, and his heart swayed in the span between one heartbeat and the next.

Amal, Amal, Amal.

She'd seeped into his skin and manipulated him, and he couldn't even find it in himself to hold on to his annoyance. Maybe he'd regret it later, when he realized how easily she affected him. Right now he couldn't think beyond what he opened his mouth to ask.

"Would dinner with your family tonight be all right?"

Zoya's brilliant smile burst clear of the clouds of her circumspection. She didn't even seem affected that he'd called her sisters and mother *her* family and not his.

"That'd be perfect!" she exclaimed, her dimples deeper than ever.

She was smiling so brightly it made him feel guilty that he'd upset her in the first place.

Zoya leaned forward in her seat, excitement raising her voice. "They won't believe that you're in Addis and that you're coming for dinner."

"You all know about me, then?" Manny asked.

He had wanted to ask earlier in her shop, when Zoya had initially called him by name. But he'd figured that his father must have told them of him. That they knew about Manny and his mother in Somaliland.

Zoya appeared bemused, though. "Why wouldn't we? Our father—*inna lillahi wa inna ilayhi raji'un*—spoke about you all the time."

Then she surprised him when she grew visibly shy, tucking an errant curl behind her ear and smiling past her apparent nerves.

"I also looked you up. Well, *we* did. My sisters and I… We were curious about you, and all that you have achieved in America." She lowered her voice and looked between him and Amal conspiratorially. "Are you really a millionaire?"

Amal covered her mouth with her hand, but she couldn't completely smother her laughter.

And, despite what he felt about Zoya, he was amused by her wide eyes and genuine need for an answer. "Yes," he said at last, "I'm a millionaire."

Zoya's mouth rounded into a big circle, and her eyes grew even larger with her shock. When the surprise wore off, she apologized.

"It's just I don't meet...*millionaires*..." she hissed the word, cupping her mouth and speaking for their ears alone "...every day, and you're my brother."

Half-brother.

Manny had to bite his tongue to stop himself from correcting her. And there went the temporary lapse in his sour mood.

Raising his cooling coffee to his scowling mouth, he regarded the secretive teasing smile Amal flashed him. She knew what she had done. Exploited his fondness for her. Influenced him into accepting Zoya's dinner invitation. And now she sneaked gloating looks at him, rubbing in her victory.

Ooh, she was clever. Attractive, smart, and wily. And his heart was doing that stupid thing of falling for her again.

You're in love with her.

The truth struck him as suddenly and soundly as his about-face decision to dine with Zoya and her family.

He'd never stopped loving Amal.

CHAPTER TEN

HE SHOULD HAVE canceled dinner with Zoya and her family.

Manny regretted the decision not to as he pulled up outside the restaurant. His hands gripped at ten and two o'clock on the wheel. He wanted nothing more than to do a sharp U-turn and beat it back to the hotel. Break this dinner engagement and leave Addis Ababa and Africa as soon as he was able to get his plane in the air.

You'd be leaving Amal, too.

A good thing. Because he'd just realized—like the fool he was—that he had been deluding himself all along.

You love her—so what?

So what? He couldn't chance loving her again. It was a torturous feeling, wanting her and knowing he wouldn't be able to have her. For that, he'd have to spill his guts. Come clean with her—first about his failed marriage proposal to her. And once Amal remembered she wouldn't desire him. She'd explain why he wasn't enough for her all over again. Why he wasn't worthy.

Besides, they lived in two separate worlds. He couldn't see himself staying in Hargeisa for long. And she wasn't going to leave the life she had in Somaliland.

He'd get through this dinner, see that she was comfortable in her hotel if she chose to do her therapy and remain in Ethiopia alone, and then he would head to his American home. That was if he could even manage to leave the car to meet with Zoya and her family now.

"We can turn back."

Amal's voice pierced the bleak fog painting his thoughts. She had a smile ready for him. Small but encouraging.

"Whatever you choose, Mansur. I don't want you to feel like you have to do this right now."

"Why?" He grated the question. "Why is it important to you that I do this—now or tomorrow or ever?"

She stared at her lap, at her upturned palms that had closed into fists. "I'm grateful I had my grandmother. Without her, I don't know who my brothers and I would be today. And you have Mama Halima. I know that. Your mother is wise, kind, and generous…"

He heard the "but".

"But, knowing that my father didn't want us…it hurt. It *still* hurts." She closed her eyes and breathed slowly, her chest rising and falling with emotion.

Opening her eyes, she turned her head to him and he saw them. The tears shining in them, brighter under the LED lights above their heads in the headliner. Mansur resisted dimming the lights to hide her tears. He didn't like seeing her crying. Never had and never would.

Her voice wavering with her despondence, she said, "I don't want that for you. Zoya seems like a sweet and friendly person. If her family is anything like her, wouldn't you *want* to meet them?"

"I'm here, aren't I?"

What more did she want from him? He had nothing else to give.

She tipped her head up toward the car roof. "I want you to be happy," she said. Then, sniffling, she opened the passenger door, stepped out, and shut the door behind her. He saw her pause before the restaurant, wipe her eyes, and then enter without a backward look.

Through the front glass of the restaurant he saw Zoya approaching Amal. Judging by Zoya's smile, all was right as rain. But his half-sister did look around Amal when she pointed behind her. They had to be talking about him. Probably Zoya was wondering where he was, and whether he'd show his face as he had promised earlier, during their impromptu coffee date.

Manny sat back and watched as Amal disappeared from view with Zoya, who was leading her further into the restaurant, where he couldn't spy on them from his car.

"I want you to be happy."

Did she? Because if she did, wouldn't she have accepted his proposal a year ago? Wouldn't they be married and blissfully sharing a life together at this very moment?

Her amnesia couldn't have changed her that much. Deep down, she still had to be the same person. The same Amal who believed family was irreplaceable and to be cherished no matter what. The Amal who had dreamt of improving the lives of her neighbors and Hargeisa's citizens by building a new hospital with her architectural skills. The Amal who had inspired him to make risky moves that were normally unlike him. With her by his side he'd felt courageous. He'd felt unconquerable.

So far, all this week with her had done was remind him that nothing had changed for him.

Amal was still herself, and he was still the man who just wasn't good enough for her.

"He was right behind me," Amal insisted for the fourth time—or maybe it was the fifth time?

She had lost count after looking around the long table, up and down, at the strangers staring back at her. Mostly strangers. Zoya she knew, and her fiancé Salim she recognized from the flower shop. The others were Zoya's two younger sisters and her mother—Mansur's stepmother.

"I'll look again." Zoya stood and left the table.

Amal watched her leave and faced Zoya's family. *Mansur's family.* It wasn't long before Zoya returned, her downcast eyes and her frown communicating what Amal suspected from the beginning might have happened. Mansur had left. He'd left *her* with his family.

She swallowed some of the iced water in her glass. Their plates were all empty, because they'd thought to wait for Mansur before starting dinner.

But he wasn't here.

"I'm sorry," she said, her gaze tracking over the table, settling on each face before finding Zoya's again. "I didn't..."

She stopped short, feeling the heat of tears pushing from the back of her eyes. If she'd known Mansur would do this, she wouldn't ever have allowed him to drive them here. It made her wonder if she even knew him. Who had she been traveling with this whole while?

A stranger, that was who. A complete and total stranger.

And if this is who he really is I should be glad he's shown me what he's capable of.

She couldn't love a man willing to put his own pride over his family—and that was what it was to her: sheer pride. He was judging these good people solely for their connection to his father. It wasn't the fault of Zoya and her sisters that they shared the same father as Mansur. They hadn't chosen to have him as a half-brother. And yet they were trying to make the best of the situation. They were willing to bring him into their family.

"We could do this some other day?" Zoya suggested,

looking pained and confused by Mansur's absence. Everyone else appeared just as unsettled.

"No," Amal said, looking around and stiffening her jaw. "No," she repeated. "We'll have dinner as planned, if that's all right with you all."

Zoya translated Amal's English into Amharic for her mother, while her fiancé and her sisters understood and agreed to stay. Zoya's mother smiled and nodded, giving her assent as best as she could with the language barrier.

By the time dinner was in full swing Amal would have liked to say she felt much better about her decision to stay and was stubbornly enjoying the dinner that Mansur had so rudely skipped out on. But she couldn't help wondering if he was all right. If she'd pushed him into this for herself more than for him.

The last thing she'd told him was that she wanted him to be happy. And she did. But he hadn't been happy about having this dinner, and he wouldn't have chosen to do it if she hadn't practically forced him into it.

The flavorsome Ethiopian cuisine went unnoticed as her mind got stuck on Mansur. Nobody but Zoya caught on.

The other woman leaned in and whispered, "Are you all right?"

She spoke in thickly accented Somali, and Zoya smiled at Amal's blatant surprise. Amal didn't need to ask who had taught Zoya the language. Her father, of course. But hearing the Somali made her think of Mansur even more. Made her long for her home, where she would be safe from having to worry about her heart and how it had somehow grown inextricably tangled with Mansur's. She was afraid that if she tried to separate her heart from his she'd have nothing left. That it would be worse than coping with her amnesia.

"Go," Zoya urged gently, dropping her voice even lower.

"Go and tell Mansur I said it's fine and that we're not upset with him. Please."

Amal opened her mouth to say she would stay and finish dinner, but she tightened her lips closed when she realized that she didn't want to continue sitting here and pretending everything was all right.

She had to go after Mansur. Make him see reason before he destroyed the good thing that he could have with Zoya and her family.

"Go," Zoya said once more.

Amal nodded, looking around the table and catching the questioning eyes of Zoya's family. She knew Zoya would clean up the mess Mansur had created, and would explain why Amal had had to leave.

With a whispered, "Thanks..." Amal left her seat and hurried for the exit.

She nearly crashed into whoever was opening the door. The apology she'd begun to give stopped short when she saw who it was.

Amal gawked up at Mansur, stunned to see him entering the restaurant. Given that he had been less than enthused about the dinner, and hadn't shown up before their meal started, Amal had assumed he'd abandoned her.

And with her clogged throat she couldn't even tell him how she'd felt.

"I had to park the car elsewhere and I didn't have time to let you know," he explained, his brows furrowing deeper the longer he gazed at her face. "Are you all right?"

"Fine," she squeaked.

Sparing a glance around him, she noticed his car was missing. He'd been finding another place for the car. Of course! He hadn't left her with his family and embarrassed her in front of good people.

She touched a hand to her chest, felt her heart taking

longer to relax. She wanted to bask in the relief of having him here, but she knew that it was one battle won and the war was still being waged.

Looking over her head, Mansur regarded the five people awaiting them with an icy stare. “Did they say anything to you?” His tone was accusatory as he leaped to the erroneous conclusion that his sister and her family had injured her.

“No, they’ve been good to me,” she said.

His head snapped down to her, his scowl focused on her now.

Amal smiled meekly. “You weren’t behind me, and it’s been nearly half an hour. I thought…”

“You thought I’d left?” he deadpanned.

She dipped her head slowly, apologetically. It had been wrong of her to assume the worst in him. That he’d break a promise. That he would leave her all alone. She’d acted on her emotions first, and that wasn’t right.

“I should have known something was keeping you…”

Like scouting for a rare parking space in an overpopulated marketplace.

He gazed intensely at her and she blushed harder for it.

“I’m sorry…” she whispered.

She *was* sorry. She looked it, too. Her lips trembled with her apology and her eyes were dewy with unshed tears.

How many times had she looked ready to cry near him? *Damn.* He was doing a terrible job of making her feel comfortable, making her feel happy, he thought with gritted teeth.

Amal’s eyes widened, and he realized belatedly that he might look like he was too angry to accept her apology.

Unclenching his jaw, he said, “I can see why you thought that. It took much longer than I hoped. It was a mission to find parking.”

And it had been—but he'd also hoped that he might not be lucky and therefore not have to attend the dinner. It would've been the perfect excuse. No parking. No family gathering.

Careful to keep his disappointment from his face, he looked toward where Zoya and her family waited on them. "Is it too late to order?"

Amal's smile, so sunny and full of hope, twisted his heart and sharpened his guilt. She really wanted him to get along with his extended family. When it felt so utterly impossible to him.

She led the way to the table in the back. Half the table was wrapped by booth seating. Zoya and her fiancé made room. It left a spot for him beside Amal.

He studied Amal while she relayed why he'd arrived so late to the party. Zoya brightened at the explanation. He didn't miss the relieved way she gripped her fiancé's hand over the table.

"I'm so happy you're here," Zoya told him once Amal had finished.

She smiled so wide and sunnily he had to fidget under the pressing weight of guilt. Manny wondered whether she'd be smiling anymore if she learned that he hadn't wanted to be here. And that Zoya owed Amal her gratitude for having dragged him along. It was Amal he wanted to make happy. Amal he continued to love hopelessly and unrelentingly.

Zoya introduced her family. "My sisters," she said, and he nodded as she named them.

Their names went over his head. His whole world was narrowing in tunnel vision on the older woman seated across from him. Surrounded by her daughters, she bobbed her head and smiled when Zoya said something in Amharic. But it was the maternal sheen of joy in her eyes that froze him.

He breathed harshly, felt Amal's oud perfume filling his lungs and calming him somewhat. Still, most of that peace of mind slipped out of him when the older woman who looked so much like Zoya moved her mouth rapidly. She stood then, stretching her hands and reaching for him.

His stepmother was waiting on him to return the gesture. Manny eyed her warily. He knew what she wanted, and he didn't require Zoya to translate.

His half-sister did it anyways. "My mother, Mansur. She says that seeing you is something she's wanted for a long time."

Amal prodded him under the table with her leg.

"It's a pleasure," Manny greeted her.

Another discreet nudge from Amal had him lifting his hands.

Zoya's mother seized them, her hands stronger than they appeared. She was small, but stout. Softly rounded from her childbearing years. In a way, she reminded him of his mom. And that thought made him pull his hands away faster than Zoya's mother was expecting.

Under the table, he curled his fists, felt a needling sense of betrayal eclipsing his guilt.

Zoya's mother said something in Amharic.

"My mother thinks you look like our father."

Zoya's translation sucker-punched him in the gut. Manny gripped his knees, his fingers digging into his flesh. The pain was good, though. It kept him from hurtling off the emotional cliff he was staring down.

"You do," Zoya commented.

He felt her stare, his face burning hot.

Zoya's mother spoke again.

A dutiful daughter, Zoya translated. "She says that it's like looking at a younger version of our father."

The hot and cold sensation battering him was a frightening experience. Black and red dots muddied his vision, and he noticed that he wasn't breathing evenly. A lack of oxygen was to blame. Panic would come naturally after that. He had to calm down. *Cool it.* But it was a strain on his overworked senses. He felt like he was shutting down. All because Zoya and her mother believed he resembled his father.

Amal's hand came out of the blue. She touched his arm and compelled him to snap his head toward her. Over the ringing in his ears, he heard her say, "My father tells me I look like my mother. It's a strange feeling, isn't it?" She rounded her eyes at the table, her smile serene. "For everyone, that is. Looking at someone but seeing someone else."

She gave his arm a squeeze and then retracted her comforting touch.

Manny stopped himself from grabbing at her hand. Instead, staring resolutely from Amal to the table laden with food, he said, "We should eat before the meal grows cold."

"Yes, let's eat," Amal piped up.

Her cheerful tone dispelled the oppressive silence that rose up after what he'd said.

Manny concentrated harder than necessary on tearing a piece of *injera* and scooping chicken stew from the communal bowl. He ate fast, filling his mouth, worrying that at any moment he'd be fielding questions and wrestling the dark emotions this meeting with Zoya and her family had brought out in him.

By the time the food was finished, he was ready to call it a night.

"Would you like dessert and coffee, Amal?" Zoya flicked a look at him, too, her eyes inviting and kind.

Manny frowned. He nudged Amal. She closed her open mouth, her smile vanishing as she shared a meaningful look with him. He didn't want her making this dinner longer than it had to be. Satisfied that she wouldn't go against him, he turned his attention back to his doting half-sister to refuse her offer.

"We can't, I'm afraid. I have business to attend to early tomorrow."

"Next time, then," Zoya said readily, her smile polite but tense.

Amal flashed her a weak smile. "Yes, I'm hoping we can meet again."

Manny ground his teeth, annoyance surging up in him. "Let's go," he said to Amal.

Then he surprised them both as he took her hand and pulled her up with him. She went willingly, matching his quick strides to the restaurant's exit.

Outside, he let go of her hand and flexed his fingers, missing her touch already.

"The car's this way."

He guided her across the street from the restaurant. Eager to grow the distance between him and Zoya and her mother and her sisters, Manny walked fast. Every so often he looked back to ensure he hadn't lost Amal. She shadowed him, not once offering any complaint that he moved too quickly. Finally, feeling freer of the heavy weight on his chest, he slowed his pace and fell into step with her.

"You parked far away," she remarked.

"The price of driving to the market and not taking a bus or a cab." He looked down at her when her silence bothered him. "Are you angry?" he asked finally.

No point in beating around the bush. He supposed she wasn't pleased with how he'd left so abruptly, and with not so much as a decent farewell. But what could he have said when he was planning never to meet with Zoya and her family ever again?

Nice meeting you, and enjoy your lives?

It sounded awful enough in his thoughts.

"You're mad," he said, the observation coming out more forceful than he wanted.

Amal peered up at him. "I'm sad."

That brought his steps to a dead halt. She stopped, too. He faced her and stared and stared. At last, he asked, "Why?"

"I forced you into that dinner. I shouldn't have." She lowered her head, sighing. "I had hoped it would be easy for you, once you met them, but I can see I was wrong. And it's not your fault." She raised her eyes to him, imploring. "You were in a tough position, and you handled it a lot better than I could've wished for."

She didn't need to say it. He heard it clearly: she had anticipated an angry outburst from him in the middle of the dinner.

Was he really so transparent about his discomfort?

Manny scoffed lightly. *Who am I kidding?* He'd been ready to leap out of his skin all through dinner. He'd breathed easier with each step that had carried him further from the restaurant and the memory of the dinner he hadn't wanted to be at.

Amal started forward and Manny mirrored her.

"What you said in there, about your father saying you look like your mother..." He trailed off and gave her the opportunity to decide whether she wanted to share anymore or leave it there.

Amal being better than him, though, smiled—albeit with a sad tinge—and nodded. "It's true. He used to say it a lot when I was younger." Her throat rippled with emotion and her voice was softened by it. "When my mother was alive."

"You remember?"

He'd asked her something similar when she had revealed her personal motivation to build a hospital in Hargeisa.

Amal had told him that her childhood memories were returning at a hopeful pace. It was many of her adult memories that remained a blur.

All the better for him, he'd thought at first. Now, though, after spending five days with her, and realizing that he still held a torch for this fierce-spirited and gorgeous woman, Manny acknowledged that her memory loss of his failed marriage proposal wasn't as comforting to him any longer.

"My memories are patchy, of course," Amal was saying.

She mesmerized him, and so his mind blanked as he listened to her.

She sighed again, softly, her voice catching. "It was hard to endure the comparison later."

After her mother had died, she meant.

"Naturally," he rumbled.

"And then he said it again when he visited me after I came home from the hospital."

Manny's body and thoughts were at a disconnect, because he reached for her and stopped them both.

"Mansur…?"

His name fluttered from her mouth, her eyes round and the streetlight not masking her curiosity. At least the sadness was gone in her surprise. But he wanted to ensure it stayed gone. She'd been downcast for longer than he should've permitted. He loved her easy smiles and her contagious joy for the simplest things.

He loved *her*.

"He shouldn't have said it."

She shrugged. "It was difficult to hear it, but I don't remember her clearly. I have pictures, but he knew her. He loved my mother. And maybe at some point he even cared for me and my brothers, because he didn't have to worry about the heartache that comes with losing a loved one."

Amal grasped his hand over her wrist and squeezed. "We can't help who we look like."

"Still, he shouldn't have said it," Manny growled, and Amal dropped her hand, letting him hold her.

Before he knew it she was stepping into him, her free arm wrapping around his shoulder as she sprang up onto her tiptoes. He leaned down into her hug. Clutching Amal felt so good. She made the world come to a standstill for his sake. With a groan, he sank his nose into her headscarf, the hijab smelling of the sweet musk of her favored oud.

She melted into him. He felt her go almost boneless and meld their bodies into the perfect fit. The happy mewl she made so close to his ear was not of his imagining.

It took Herculean strength to draw back from her initiated embrace. Staring down into her dark eyes, Manny was at a loss for words. All that blared through his mind was the urge to confess his love to her.

I love you. I love you. I love you, Amal.

She looked at him with intent, too. Could she possibly be feeling the same way? Could they somehow make this work like they hadn't a year ago? Did she care for him, too? Did she love him?

Amal blinked and her smile returned. "Could we talk more at the hotel? I don't want this to end."

No, he didn't either.

She slipped her hand into his when he loosened his grasp on her wrist and got them walking again.

Manny followed her with a lighter heart and a hope for their love that came rushing back to him.

CHAPTER ELEVEN

AMAL STARED AT her hand, playing over how it had felt holding Mansur's—how *right* everything had been—as they'd walked hand in hand back to his car and driven to their hotel. Now they were in his suite together, and he was in the kitchen preparing tea.

They weren't ending the night quite yet. She was more than happy to spend longer with him. To salvage what she'd ruined for him tonight.

The dinner had been disastrous.

She hadn't walked away from it feeling good about orchestrating the whole thing. All she'd done was make Mansur feel worse, and his feeling bad made her hurt awfully.

But as he strode out of the kitchen, carrying a tray with a tea set, he looked less like he had the world crushing his shoulders.

Amal sat up and smiled. "You should have called me to help you."

"You're in my suite. That makes you the guest."

Mansur settled the tray atop the coffee table and sat beside her on the two-seater sofa.

"Are you sure you don't want me to order dessert? I can't help but feel I've deprived you of it tonight."

Her heart felt extraordinarily full at his words. After

messing up as she had tonight, how could he still be so *nice* to her?

"I'm sorry," she blurted, watching him pour tea and creamer and add sugar to their cups.

Amal accepted the cup and saucer he offered her, but she stared at him, waiting for his response.

After he'd sipped at his tea, he lowered his cup and looked at her with guarded eyes. "I chose to go. I'm an adult, Amal. Perfectly capable of making my own decisions. I could've easily refused."

But he hadn't, and that meant a lot to her. The fact that he hadn't slammed the door on his half-sisters and stepmother gave her an inkling of hope that one day he would be willing to embrace them as family. In her eyes, tonight had spoken for his character. He wasn't holding a grudge; he was wounded by his lack of a relationship with his father.

She understood where he was coming from.

Her father hadn't cared to be in her life or her brothers'. His father had taken on a second family and, somewhere along the way, lost that irreplaceable parental bond with the son from his first marriage.

Amal drank her tea, slipping deeper into her thoughts. They would've mired her in sinking sand if Mansur hadn't spoken up.

"I should be the one apologizing," he said. His voice was deep and even. Though not cool and devoid of emotion entirely. Something heated flashed through his surprising statement.

Snapping her head up, Amal stammered, "Wh-Why would you have to apologize?"

Her cheeks warmed the longer he watched her quietly. She shook her head, countering the blush that crept from her face to her neck. He had nothing to be sorry for. The blame was entirely her own.

"My manners weren't exactly something to write home about," he said.

She closed her mouth, finding no comforting words. It was true. He had been abrupt near the end of their dinner. Probably at his wits' end, though, so she'd excused and forgiven him.

As he looked like he had more to say, Amal turned to face him, their legs closer, their bodies less than an arm's length apart. All she had to do to touch him was have the courage to reach out.

Her hands clenched tighter around her fragile and prettily painted teacup. Now wasn't the time to ogle him. With a great measure of control, she concentrated on his words and not his wonderfully handsome face. It was the hardest thing she had to do tonight.

"It was difficult, I have to admit. Restraining myself from walking out the minute I set foot in the restaurant. The second I sat down." He drained his teacup and placed it on the tray, his eyes fixed there as he continued. "Obviously, I didn't want to be there. Even less so after Zoya's mother said I looked like *him*."

Zoya's mother had made the comment harmlessly. She hadn't considered that her stepson might not have had the best of relationships with his father. It was tragic, really, on both sides. For Mansur to have to hear it, and for Zoya and her family to be blamed for it.

Amal sucked in her lips, afraid that if she spoke now she'd stifle his candor. She hadn't witnessed this side of Mansur when he spoke of his father. Every other time there had been a shield up. A distant look in his eyes and a resentful aura around him. Now his shoulders sagged, and he appeared overburdened with emotions and by his past.

"Do you know, when I became CEO I called my father?

The call didn't go through, though. Wrong number. He must have changed it."

He leaned forward, forearms resting on his legs, hands clasped together, and one of his legs bouncing in his agitation. He probably didn't even realize what he was doing. What he was revealing to her with his actions.

"You were the first to know, and my mother had learned of the news of my promotion, too. But I hadn't called her; you'd told her. I called *him*, though." He took a cleansing but noisy breath through his nose. "I don't know why I did, but I did." He shook his head and scoffed. "My point is, I don't want anything from Zoya Ali or her family."

Amal didn't have to hear anymore. She understood, loud and clear. He didn't want this other family he'd found in Addis Ababa. Just like he'd learned not to want or expect anything from his father. Mansur had proved that by building his career, making his name, working for his fortune. He could take care of himself. He had his own back. And he'd taken care of his mother far better than his father ever had.

And hadn't she done something similar? She'd worked hard to provide a good life for her grandmother when she'd been alive, and now for her brothers. Putting Bashir through his schooling and seeing Abdulkadir thrive in his own business meant the whole world to her. They were her family.

"It's likely they feel the same. I'm just an intruder. Someone they feel obliged to be kind to," he said, his voice dull and unfeeling. "And I'm not one to impose where I'm not wanted."

When he finally looked at her it was with that wary reserve she'd grown accustomed to seeing whenever they discussed his father. Amal saw it for what it was now. Fear. She froze at the sight of it. Even blinked. Because she wasn't certain she'd read him correctly. But, no, it was still there.

He's scared.

Amal didn't understand. Was he scared of *her*? Why?

Why would he be afraid of me?

Mansur, of all people…afraid of *her*?

The longer she swam in the bottomless pools of his brown eyes, the more emotions she saw. Unadulterated panic and bashful regret that he'd said too much. The fear that she'd push him away after he spoke unfiltered and from the heart.

As if I ever could.

Without thinking on it too much, Amal brought her hand to his arm. Mansur tensed under her palm, and yet he didn't brush her touch away. Taking it to be a positive sign, she inched closer, leaning in and giving his arm the lightest squeeze.

"I used to wait on my father, too. I don't remember too much right now, but I get the sense that I've been waiting on him for most my life, and it still feels like I'm in queue sometimes."

"Hope…" he grumbled.

She smiled, understanding. "Yeah, hope. I think one day I'll give up on it, but it's always there."

"Maybe now's the time to make a pact. To keep each other from hoping again."

"No, I don't want to give up on hope. And neither should you."

Amal slid her hand to his. He reached his fingers for her and took her hand. Their palms kissed, their fingers interlocked, and Mansur stared down at their joined hands.

When he opened his mouth next, he sounded less bleak. "There's something I've been meaning to tell you, Amal."

I'm in love with you. Again.

The words were right there. Along with the truth of their past.

Looking up at her was a mistake. Manny lost his train of thought. He lost his nerve.

A blush warmed his face, and his body was filled with a contrast of emotions, both positive and negative. Joy that she hadn't been chased off by what he'd said of his father. Anxiousness to move on and reveal his love. Hope that she'd want him after he unveiled his failure of a marriage proposal to her. And distress over what her reaction might be once she knew his true feelings for her.

"Tell me," she urged softly, her hand gentle in his.

I loved you, and I haven't stopped loving you.

Her warm brown eyes promised him all the trust and confidence in the world.

But I messed up, and you rejected me, and I don't think I'll ever be good enough for you.

It wouldn't be the first time he'd fallen short of expectations. With his father, though, he should've known. He should have stopped trying. Should have maintained the wall he'd built, brick by brick, after discovering his father had married a second woman and had other children. Zoya and her sisters. He never should have wanted more from his father. But he had. And, if he were being brutally honest with himself, a part of him was still that stupid little boy who was waiting on his dad.

With Amal, though, it wasn't too late. Manny still had a chance.

Still, he'd tucked away this frightening love for her. Had nearly convinced himself that he wouldn't give his heart to her or anyone else. Wouldn't repeat his mistake. And yet here he was, painfully tempted to tell her. Seconds and heartbeats from claiming his love for her again.

"Back in Hargeisa, you wondered who was watching out for me in America..."

He forced himself not to break eye contact with her. Vulnerability wasn't his style. But Amal had made him want to risk it after his father had chosen to divide his attention and love between two wives and two families.

"I remember," she said with a small grin. "I haven't hit my head again."

No, she hadn't. His gaze alighted on the side of her head. He'd first spied the scar when her headscarf had slipped in the hospital. It had been a brief moment. An infinitesimally small fraction of time. But the sight of it had made him ache as if it were his own wound.

It was a miracle that he hadn't realized he was in love with her in that very moment. When he had struggled to set her pain apart from his own. They were one. Always had been, for him, and always would be no matter what happened from this point forward.

Sucking in a fortifying breath, he exhaled with a subtle shudder and said, "And I told you no one. I wasn't lying."

He'd pushed everyone away. Other than when he had to attend a social event for business, as the new face of the company, Manny made it a point to block his schedule from intrusions. As for dating…he'd stopped in college, when his romances had floundered because he'd placed his career ahead of the few women he had dated. Then Amal had come into his life again. And for the first time in a long while he'd allowed someone in.

"I made a choice." He tightened his hold on her hand, afraid that she would slip away from him. "I decided to be alone. I didn't want anyone by my side. But you changed that."

You changed me.

Manny swallowed. His voice was hoarser when he said, "You called one day to check on me. It wasn't expected." He smiled wistfully at the memory. "Actually, I was in the middle of crushing our competition in the market, and I'd caught the eye of our chairman for the soon-to-be vacated position of CEO. The board wanted a change. I'd made splashes in the industry. I had my head in the game…"

And then he hadn't. Amal had called, and he'd got wrapped up with hearing her sweet voice. Her concern for him had astounded Manny. Besides his mother, he hadn't thought anyone else worried about him.

He'd fallen in love with her slowly. Eventually Amal had told him she loved him first. Then he'd gone to see her with a ring and his heart, hoping she'd accept both.

The rest is history, he thought mournfully.

Only it wasn't. Not for him. It felt very real right now, holding her hand, looking into her eyes, feeling squeamish in his building anticipation of the truth.

"We talked every day. You supported me. I had someone in my corner. Someone I cared very deeply about."

He flicked his gaze to where she'd raised her hand to her temple and her scar. Manny released her other hand and brushed her fingers aside to see the scar for himself. She shouldn't feel like she had to hide it from him. He'd take her anyway. Because he loved her, and he wouldn't ever live in a reality where he didn't feel his heart would burst with longing for her.

"Does it really not hurt?" he asked. He recalled she'd said it had not, but it didn't dampen his concern for her.

"No, though it tingles and throbs sometimes. It's healed nicely enough."

Her soft sigh puffed out and warmed his hand as he cupped her cheek. Amal leaned into his palm, and his heart thudded harder when she closed her eyes and smiled freely and happily at him.

"I hate that you don't remember…"

She fluttered her eyes open. "Since I came to Addis I'm feeling the urge to have to recall everything less."

Relief poured through him. "You're happier?"

"I am," she agreed.

She'd decided for him. Manny knew what path he was going to take—nerves be damned. It didn't matter whether she wanted him or not. He just had to let her know.

Standing abruptly, watching her mouth form a surprised O, he asked in a husky, urgent tone, "Wait here for me?"

At her smallest of nods, he left her for his bedroom.

Amal couldn't remain sitting.

She was up and moving when Mansur returned.

He looked more alert than he had all night. Except for when he'd appeared like a caged animal in the restaurant with his half-sisters and stepmother.

Almost immediately she noted that he was holding something in one of his fists.

"Amal, I said I had something to tell you, but I should have said I have something to *show* you."

She hurried to meet him halfway, bumping her leg painfully against the corner of the coffee table.

"Easy," Mansur said quickly, closing the gap between them and taking her hand. He was staring at her with such open and raw concern. It wasn't the first time either. Only this time Amal felt a change in the air. There was something more to his movements now. And she couldn't help but worry whether it spelled doom for them.

Amal had thought that *maybe* they were making progress finally. She liked Mansur; she knew that. He was attractive. She was crushing on him. But now she wondered if it could be more…

He made her heart race, her mouth dry, and her body hum pleasantly with the pull to be near him. Whatever he was doing to her, it was powerful and sacred, and she had never yearned to explore anything more in her life. And yet she couldn't stifle the fear that what he had to show her was going to end her hope.

"What do you want to show me?" she asked.

If he was going to crush her with disappointment, she couldn't see a better reason not to rip off the bandage and get this over and done with.

Mansur held up his closed fist between them. "Before I show you, I have something to say."

"Mansur…" She trailed off breathlessly. She couldn't help it. His eyes held a gleaming intent and purposefulness that was single-mindedly locked on her. None of his other gazes compared to this. Whatever he had to tell her, Amal realized now that it was serious and noteworthy.

Maybe even life-changing, she thought with a skip of a heartbeat.

"I didn't come to Hargeisa knowing that I'd be with you like this," he began.

Amal gulped, fighting the urge to flee out of the room.

"My mother left me a cryptic voicemail and I arrived blindly, afraid that something terrible had happened." His eyes darted to the scar he'd caressed on her temple earlier. "Only to discover something *had* happened, and I hadn't been there for you."

Amal freed the breath she'd been holding unknowingly.

Mansur opened his palm to reveal a small black box. Before she could wrap her mind around what it could be, he opened it.

Amal gasped, touching quivering fingertips to her mouth. It was a proper reaction to the ring nestled inside. Not just any ring, but a sparkly band with the biggest and most lustrous diamond she'd ever seen. And the diamond was…*heart-shaped*!

She didn't think she'd seen anything so magnificent in

all her life—and that was saying a lot, given all she had seen in Addis Ababa and Bishoftu.

Thanks to Mansur.

Amal looked up and found he'd concealed his emotions from her once again. He could've been a perfectly chiseled statue. But then he blinked, and suddenly the cracks in his facade were clear to her. He couldn't hide the trepidation or the fear from her. Not now that they were writ plainly on his face. That face she could love forever.

Love? Am I in love with him?

It would make sense. She thought of him unendingly in his absence. And in his presence she felt complete. Whole.

Was it crazy of her to want to kiss him?

"Is it mine?" She heard her voice…how it squeaked with her nerves.

"It is," he said, slinging her a tremulous smile. Then, taking it out of the box, he grasped the ring between his fingers and held out his free hand. "May I?" he asked.

The touch of uncharacteristic shyness in his low, husky tone was new to her. She nearly gave him her trembling hand, but there was so much to ask him. Enough to keep her from giving in to the natural instinct to have him slip that ring on her finger.

Pressing her hands flat over her racing heart, she asked, "How is it mine, though?"

And had he planned this from the start?

Mansur's change in expression from warm hope to confusion told her that it wasn't likely. But surely he didn't think it was sensible of her to accept his proposal? Even if he hadn't actually said the words and asked her to marry him. The ring spoke for him.

"Is there something you're not telling me?" she asked.

Her question stirred him into hanging his head. "I wanted to marry you once."

Amal's mouth popped open. Shock made it hard to breathe. Oxygen sawed in and out of her flaring nostrils and gaping mouth.

"I came to ask you in person, after my father's funeral," he confessed softly, continuing as if he *hadn't* rocked her world off its axis.

"You did?" she choked, part-gasp, part-exclamation. "I don't remember."

"I'm aware of that."

The bitter sting to his tone wasn't her imagining. Mansur lifted his head, his thumb absentmindedly stroking at the diamond ring she hadn't accepted from him.

He'd wanted her? She struggled with that fact in her mind. Her heart was another matter. It throbbed from the overload of joy. Mansur desired her enough to propose not once, but *twice*.

She'd always believed in fate. Her grandmother used to tell her some people were destined to be together. Maybe it was like that for her and Mansur? Maybe they belonged to each other, no matter the odds?

No matter her amnesia, she hoped.

"Amal, there is something else." Mansur stopped moving his thumb over the ring and groaned lightly. "I don't even know where to begin."

"Anywhere," she breathed.

What else had she forgotten—and why did he look ready to suffer a breakdown?

When he didn't speak, she begged, "Manny, tell me."

Maybe it was her plea that did the trick. Or perhaps he reacted to his nickname.

"When I proposed to you…you refused."

Mansur pulled in closer to her. Their eyes were trained on one another unblinkingly at this point. As if he commanded her to watch as he devastated her with the awful truth she suddenly and fiercely wanted to erase from *his* memories, too.

"You rejected my proposal, Amal."

She'd rejected him?

"You told me you loved me, and I knew it was all I needed to hear to propose."

Mansur bared his teeth now, his voice rough and pairing well with his tormented expression. But he was beautiful even when he was tortured by a past that clearly hadn't been pleasant.

"I never act without knowing the end goal, but with you it was different. *You* were different. I thought..." he said, then stopped and shook his head. "I wanted to believe our love was ready for a future together."

Amal staggered away from him. Mansur didn't stop or follow her. All recognizable emotion had seeped from his features. His face was as cold and lifeless as stone by the time she'd created a sizable gap between them.

Gasping, she asked, "I rejected you?"

He jerked a nod.

"Why?" And when he didn't answer she raised her voice, pleading, "Why would I do that?"

Tears pinched the corners of her eyes. Why had she let go of the man she loved? Because she now knew, irrefutably, that she loved this man.

She loved Mansur.

"You didn't like the way I handled myself after I'd arrived too late to attend my father's funeral. I told you that I didn't care to be there. I wasn't as polite and thankful as I should have been to those friends and family members who had visited my mother to pay their final respects. But most of all you saw that I'd hurt my mother with my attitude. You called me out for it, Amal, and it was deserved.

But instead of backing away, and giving you time to cool off, I made the mistake of proposing at the wrong time."

He paused, chest heaving, eyes narrowed, his face cruelly inscrutable.

"Maybe it was for the best, after all."

The finality in what he'd said broke her. Amal was ready to be sick all over the floor. She hadn't even felt this sick on his plane. The room was spinning for her and she stumbled back.

Mansur was there when her knees gave out. He held her up and steered her to the sofa. Seating her first, he left and returned with a cool glass of water. Amal guzzled half of it down and he had to ease her up and help her drink the other half more slowly.

He waited and watched until her breathing had evened before he said, "I apologize for not telling you earlier."

She understood why he hadn't. It was his past, too. And, unlike her, he recalled it—and vividly, if his emotional display was anything to go by. Being who he was, Amal knew it had to be difficult for him to be that open. His stoic expression was his way of maintaining the control he'd felt he lost. But he couldn't hide from her—not now. Not ever again.

"Do you have questions?" he asked.

Naturally she did. But first… "I need to think," she replied.

"Okay," he said, not sounding at all as if it were all right. He stood and helped her to her feet, saying, "I'll walk you back to your suite. Unless you'd like to stay longer?"

"No," she said, and was pained to see the snapping flash of relief on his face.

Seeing that he didn't want her with him would have to be taken into consideration when she gave him her final answer. Even though she told herself that it had to be shock.

They needed to process their reactions, the truth of his marriage proposal and her rejection of his love on their own.

Still, she didn't want to leave him.

Yet she had no choice now that he was guiding her out of his suite and they were walking to hers.

At her door, Amal fumbled to find her keycard. When she did, it slipped from her nerveless fingers and dropped to the carpeted floor. Mansur got to it first, holding it out to her.

"There is one more thing..." he said.

She looked at him more closely, hopeful that it wouldn't end like this tonight.

"Yes?"

He pulled the ring box from his pocket. "I don't want to hold on to it anymore." And when she didn't budge, he rasped, "Please take the ring."

His plea broke her. She took the small box and held it close, hoping he would see that she only needed time to think over all he'd shared with her.

He nudged his chin at the door. "Good night, Amal."

"Good night, Mansur."

She wished to linger, but she remembered how relieved he'd appeared to be when she'd said she was leaving his suite. It was enough to snap her mouth closed and let him leave.

Fighting tears, she opened her door and stepped over the threshold. Curiosity gained the better of her and she peeked to catch one more look at him. Too late. She was watching his back and his hasty retreat to his own sanctuary next door.

Tomorrow, she prayed.

Tomorrow they'd fix this and somehow be happy.

CHAPTER TWELVE

HE'D HAD ONLY a rough go at sleep.

Unsurprising, when all he'd been able to do was replay what had taken place in his hotel room.

By the time sunrise glowed through his suite, Manny had packed his luggage and was getting off the phone after arranging to have his jet fueled for the long flight home.

Before he left, though, he had one last stop to make—and it wasn't to Amal's room.

He stepped off the elevator and into Hakeem's penthouse at the hotel. His friend was there to greet him.

"You're leaving, then?" Hakeem asked as he led him to the living area. "And what about your woman?"

"She's not *my* anything," Manny gritted, the painful reminder of last night all too fresh in his mind.

She'd refused to give him her hand again. And even though she had said she would use their time apart to think alone, he wasn't holding any hope that her heart had changed about him.

Amal didn't love him. All that remained was for her to let him down gently. He had to accept that and leave before he acted more foolishly than he already had.

"Sorry," Manny muttered when he saw Hakeem's frown. He hadn't meant to snap at his friend. It wasn't

Hakeem's fault that, once more, he'd fallen short of Amal's expectations.

The fact that she didn't want him was all on Manny. No one else. She found him lacking. To her, he must be defective on some grounds.

Or she'd be wearing my ring now.

Manny focused on the lurking concern in Hakeem's eyes. "She'll be staying in Addis longer than me. I'd appreciate it if you could look out for her."

It was the best he could muster in this state. Ready to fall apart at the seams, he certainly didn't want to do it in front of Amal, and yet he'd promised his mother he'd watch over her.

He trusted Hakeem to do it in his place. The billionaire hotelier had his faults, true. He was a playboy and a committed bachelor who had the wealth to fly all over the world and do as he pleased, but he was also a good and loyal friend. Trustworthy.

Hakeem nodded. "I'll do my best. Does she know about this arrangement you have planned or are you bargaining on me telling her?"

"She knows you, and I trust you. That's enough."

"I won't force my company on her."

Jealousy shafted through him at the thought of Hakeem and Amal spending time together and growing closer. With a growl, he said, "You'll ensure her comfort and security and that her means of transportation to the hospital will be covered—that's all."

By no means did he want Hakeem muscling in on his territory.

But she's not mine, and she doesn't want me.

Still, it didn't mean he had to deal with Hakeem and Amal becoming a couple. Hakeem was his friend, and Amal was the woman who'd always have his heart. Wasn't it enough that he'd suffered losing her a second time? Lost out on his second chance with her?

That justification wasn't sitting well with him, so he cooled his jealous rage and remembered the other reason he'd come up to see Hakeem.

"I'll be heading to the airport now. I know we were to have had talks of a new hotel in Abu Dhabi..."

Ahead of him in his thinking, Hakeem nodded. "No worries. I'll message you when you land. Anything else?"

Manny had been getting to that. "You know I've been dealing with an inheritance...?"

"I do," his friend said.

"And you know that I've been considering selling it from the start? Well, I've had a change of heart. At least for now, the land will remain in my care."

Hakeem frowned, crossing his arms. "And there's no way to talk you into selling it to me?"

Manny knew his friend had an interest in the property. Hakeem had contacts in the agribusiness industry, and he rubbed elbows with politicians whenever he had to. But Manny couldn't be certain that Hakeem wouldn't go and sell to the wrong people. Amal's praise when he'd suggested helping local farmers still echoed in his mind. It had egged him on into announcing this final decision on his father's inheritance.

"I've made up my mind," he said, with sturdy conviction.

Unruffled, Hakeem lowered his arms, sighed and smiled. "You've changed. Who do I have to curse or thank for that?"

Manny clenched his teeth and glared.

His friend merely laughed at him. "Relax, bro. I think I've got my answer anyways." Then, more solemnly, Hakeem asked, "Are you sure you don't want to tell her yourself?"

"No, it's for the best."

Besides, he had the strange sense that, despite her negative reaction last evening, Amal would somehow try to stop him leaving. Of course it wouldn't be the first time he held such a grandiose notion that she cared for him…

Instead of deluding himself, he looked Hakeem in the eye and told him, "She won't mind. It's not like we've been in each other's lives for very long anyways."

Hakeem shrugged. "As long as you're happy, I'm cool."

"So you'll do as I asked?" He didn't want to have to beg, but he'd do it if it meant Amal would remain safe and sound in Addis Ababa.

Hakeem readily offered his hand.

Manny gripped it tightly before they pulled together into a brief hug.

"Yeah," Hakeem drawled, grinning when they pulled back, "I'll watch out for your girl."

Manny didn't even correct him a second time.

"What do you mean, he's left?"

Amal couldn't have heard Hakeem correctly. Surely Mansur's billionaire friend was playing a joke on her.

But Hakeem said, "You just missed him. He's paid for a month in advance for your room, and your meals will be catered from the hotel's two-star Michelin restaurant—"

"He's left?" Her interjection was fraught with her nerves. Normally, she wouldn't be rude, but interrupting Hakeem was the least of her problems.

Hakeem smiled benevolently across the table from her. They'd met out in the massive gardens at the back of the hotel. Now they sat on the patio overlooking the manicured green lawn, gleaming flagstone paths, fountains and perfectly trimmed hedges. A priceless, once-in-a-lifetime view that meant nothing to her in that instant.

Pressing both her hands on the glass table, she cried, "He can't have left me!"

Not when they had so much to discuss.

It had started an hour ago, when Amal had called at Mansur's door and gotten no answer. Immediately she'd worried, and had asked after him at Reception. When they wouldn't circumvent their privacy policy for her, she'd demanded to speak to the hotel's owner, Mansur's friend Hakeem Ahmet.

Now she placed her hopes on him.

"Please, if there's a way I could speak to him…"

Hakeem had had his shades fixed in place up to that point, but now he pulled them up to his head. "I did get a call from him. Apparently, there's been a need to check over his plane's engine. I could put another call through to see if he's still stalled at the airport…"

Amal heard a "but" coming.

Sure enough, Hakeem said, "But he made it very clear he didn't want you to know of his departure in advance. He's my friend, and I have his trust. I don't mean to lose it."

Sagging back into her chair, she knew exactly why Mansur hadn't wanted to tell her. She touched the ring on her finger, watching as Hakeem's narrowing gaze fell there, his face smoothed of any telling emotion.

She had to convince him to betray Mansur's trust—just this once.

"I love him, Hakeem. I need him to know that before he goes."

What chance would she get once he was in the air and bound for America? She pressed her trembling lips together, her eyes heated from the tears she wasn't ready to cry.

"Okay, you sold me," said Hakeem, after too long a pause. Chuckling when she gasped her joy, he told her, "He'll hate me for it for a bit, but I'm no monster. I won't stop you from making Manny see that he's in love with you, the stubborn fool."

Hearing that Mansur loved her was all the incentive she needed. She had to be with him. Had to let him know that she loved him, too, and that it wasn't too late for that future together he'd spoken of so tenderly.

"Do you think you could stop his plane from leaving?" She didn't know where she'd got the idea that Hakeem could do that, but she had to try. And he *was* a billionaire.

"I could try," he said with an impish grin.

"I thought we were wheels up shortly?"

That was Manny's response when the pilot interrupted his plans to shower to inform him of yet another unscheduled delay. First the engine, now this…

Apologizing profusely, the pilot promised they'd be in the air as soon as possible. It wasn't what Manny wanted to hear. Given why he was leaving so suddenly, he didn't wish for any reason to linger and tempt himself to go hunting for the source of his anguish.

Banishing thoughts of Amal from his mind for what had to be the tenth time in that hour alone, Manny dressed in haste. He headed to the front of the plane to see for himself what the delay was.

He found it quickly.

Or she found him.

"Amal…" he breathed, his disbelief vanishing after a few heartbeats. He forced a frown instead of revealing the immense pleasure sparking through him at the sight of her. "What are you doing here?" He didn't have to ask, but gruffly he wondered, "Are you the reason the pilot has delayed take-off?"

She nodded. "I had to do something when I heard you hadn't left Addis yet."

It took him another moment before he grumbled, "Hakeem?" But he couldn't bring himself to be annoyed. Seeing Amal had made that impossible. "What are you doing here?" he asked. And then, in the very next breath, he growled, "You shouldn't have come."

"I had to."

Amal sat primly on a leather sofa in the lounge area, her hands in her lap, her fingers fidgeting. The diamond on her finger was hard to miss.

Manny didn't know what to make of seeing her wearing his ring. Especially after his tumultuous night thinking of how he had failed yet again in making her love him. And then there was the terrible choice he'd made to leave her in Addis…

His voice noticeably rougher, he asked, "Why? We said everything that needed to be said."

"*You* did, Mansur. I haven't given you my answer yet, remember?"

Of course he hadn't forgotten. And that was why she was here. She must want to return his engagement ring. End this one-sided love of his once and for all.

Steeling his spine, reminding himself that he'd survived the first heartbreak and would make it through this one as well, Manny dipped his chin for her to continue. To deliver the killing blow.

"I've decided I want the ring," she said.

Okay… He hadn't been prepared for that. Not one bit.

He blew out an unsteady breath. "Keep it, then. Or fling it in the Indian Ocean if you want. It's yours. Do whatever you wish."

"And if I prefer to have it remain on my finger?"

He hardened his jaw, felt his heart wavering on a reply. What could he tell her? That nothing would please him more than for her to do as she said? For his flashy yet traditional token of affection to stay wrapped around her finger?

"If it makes you happy," he said at last.

Amal lifted her hand, her fingers caressing the white gold band inlaid with tiny diamonds. She did it so lovingly he almost unrooted his feet and moved to be nearer to her. At the last second he stopped himself.

"Do you care about my happiness?" she asked.

He couldn't think of anything that mattered more.

"Yes," he snapped, annoyed with himself for even answering. For giving her more ammunition to wound him with. This wasn't going to end the way he'd dreamed. He was too grounded in reality to try to hope.

"And if I said my happiness isn't tied to this ring?"

She found his eyes again, her stare bold but not confrontational. The teasing warmth in her gaze stirred him forward.

He slid one foot closer, and then the other. His heart was leaping up higher and higher, and it had to be in his throat as he rasped, "Then what would make you happy?"

"You."

She said it so simply it brought him to a halt. He widened his eyes at her and then scowled, refusing to believe her.

"You don't want me. You've seen the way I treat my family. I always thought you'd made a mistake, rejecting me, but you didn't, Amal. I'm not a good man. It's kind of you to lie, but you don't have to pretend."

"It's true, though! Nothing and no one could make me happier. I've realized that this past week. Spending time with you, traveling with you, going to the hospital with you…all of it is a happy blur that I'll cherish for the rest of my life," she said when he shook his head sharply.

Amal touched her hands to her chest and smiled.

"These are the memories I'd hate to lose. I know I hurt

you by rejecting your proposal in the past. I see that." Her bottom lip trembled visibly. "And if I could turn back time I'd change it. I swear. I'd do anything. And it's because I love you."

There they were. The words he'd dreamt of hearing for too long.

"And I know you love me," Amal said, her voice catching as she asked, "Unless I'm wrong? *Am* I, Mansur? Am I wrong in thinking that you love me?"

"But my family..." he argued.

"You and your family will find a way to heal and be together one day. I know you will."

"What if I can't?" Manny raised his voice. Not quite a shout, but close. He snarled low and thumped his fists against his thighs. "What then? If I can't love them, if I remain cold and distant, will you care for me then?"

Would she continue to love him as vehemently as she'd declared in that moment?

"My love for you will be unchanged. I swear it."

He... He believed her.

The fight ebbed out of him. Tired, and wanting her comfort, Manny went to her. He dropped to his knees slowly, crumpling before her in awe at how she'd tamed his doubts. How she'd slayed his heartbreak.

Amal framed his face with her soft hands and repeated the words that had calmed the rage in his heart. "I love you, Mansur. I came because I wanted to see your love for me for myself. I couldn't let you leave without knowing that I'd done everything—even begged a billionaire—to stop your plane and keep you with me."

"And if I still plan to leave?" he asked hoarsely.

She beamed, blinding him with her beauty.

"Then I shall have to demand that you take me along.

Wherever you go, you must promise I'll be there, right by your side, and you will be by mine."

He laughed softly. The mirth caught him by surprise, but Amal easily added her laughter to his.

When their laughter had subsided, he wondered, "Where did you get the idea that you love me?" Then a thought occurred to him. "Did you get your memories back?" That would explain a lot.

"That's not it. I still don't recall those memories." Holding his face and bringing hers closer, she whispered, "But I knew the instant I couldn't bring myself to take off your ring. And, if you'll let me, I'd like to make new memories with you. Starting with this one."

She kissed him. Her lips touched his softly, curiously. She experimented with pressure and with strokes. And he was a happy test subject.

Manny had always thought he'd initiate any intimacy first, but he should've known that Amal would amaze him. She always had and she always would.

He warmed quickly to their kiss, his experience kicking in and his need for her driving him to take over. Amal gladly followed, and their panting soon filling the air as he reared up and pressed her back to the sofa. They kissed until they had to give in to their breathlessness and pull apart.

He looked at Amal and found no frosty reception from her. The exact opposite, in fact, as she smiled and giggled.

"I've thought about that kiss for a long while," she admitted.

He laughed huskily. "Same."

"Mansur," she said then, "ask me to marry you again."

By coming to him in this eleventh hour Amal had taken a risk with her heart, too. She had put herself on the line for him, not knowing whether he'd abandon her again, and she had issues with that. Issues she'd been willing to contend with for him.

He saw that now. Loved her even more for it.

She loved him enough to take a chance on being heartbroken. And now she was asking him to take a second leap of faith with her.

Without needing to think it over anymore, Manny took her hand and kissed the diamond on her finger. "Amal Khalid, I love you. Will you marry me?"

She pulled him up for another brain-melting, heart-stopping kiss.

It was all the answer he needed.

EPILOGUE

Eighteen months later

"Do you miss Hargeisa?"

Amal gasped softly as her husband's rumbling question came from behind her. He'd snuck up on her. She had left him working in his home office, fully expecting they would have breakfast together a little later. But Mansur had found her. And now he had her in his arms, and she didn't know a better place to be.

They were standing on their master bedroom's balcony. The view of his American city—and hers now—was breathtakingly beautiful. Pittsburgh was her home because it was his. And yet he was right to ask. A piece of her heart would always remain in Hargeisa. Naturally she missed her other home.

"We could move up our flight. Head back a little earlier." Mansur kissed her temple, his lips gentle on her long-healed scar.

Amal hummed teasingly, thinking over his proposal. "I wouldn't mind that. It'd be nice to share our news with everyone earlier."

"Done. I'll buy the tickets tonight." He palmed her swelling belly, smirking. "I'm surprised you haven't revealed the secret yet and told my mother—or your office manager, Iman."

She laughed. "I'm not that bad with keeping secrets. I think the amnesia's taught me to appreciate every moment, that's all."

"Afraid you'll forget our baby? You'll forget me?"

She whirled in his arms and touched his beard, loving the feel of the coarse curls under her palm. Since he'd discovered she liked stroking it he'd been growing his beard, and it was thicker and wilder than ever. It was just one of the ways he pleased her.

"Never," she breathed. "I'd never forget you."

He placed a kiss in her palm and asked, "How is the firm doing?"

She'd left her architectural firm in the combined hands of Iman and her team of talented and capable technologists. They reported to her regularly, so she still had a hand in the numerous projects flooding in.

The influx of business was all thanks to Mansur funding the hospital she'd dreamed of for Hargeisa long before her amnesia, and long before he'd ever thought to propose marriage to her. She'd argued for him to keep his millions, but he'd said, "My money is yours—just as my heart is yours," and she had found she couldn't refuse him.

Now the hospital was built, and more lives were being saved than ever.

"It's going great…and my living here hasn't affected business," she replied.

"Good," he said, kissing her cheek and tickling her with his beard.

Amal snuggled closer to his chest. She thought of how they'd come to be here. Playing the events back in her head again as she sometimes liked to do.

Right after he'd proposed to her again—and very successfully that time—Mansur and she had discussed their living arrangements. It had been decided that they'd live part-time in America and part-time in Hargeisa. But mostly America, because Amal had known it would be easier on him and his company.

They'd married in Hargeisa shortly after their return from Addis Ababa. The wedding had been lavish and large as Mansur hadn't budged about spending money on her. In the end it hadn't mattered. Amal and Mansur had celebrated their love with their family and friends.

Then Mansur had left for America and filed for a spousal visa. While he'd been away from her Amal had kept busy, journaling and having talk therapy with a psychologist in Addis Ababa over video sessions. She'd since stopped therapy, but she was still journaling.

She was at peace with her amnesia now. It was a part of her. She didn't recall all her memories. And she wasn't certain she ever would. But, given all the memories she was making day in and day out with Mansur, Amal found herself less inclined to care about those lost memories.

She was happy—and had been even happier when her visa had been approved and she'd been able to fly over and start her life with Mansur in their American home.

She'd been away from Hargeisa for six months now, and already a lot had changed. She was managing her firm remotely and learning on the go. Meanwhile, Mansur was doing extremely well, juggling married life, his demanding position as CEO of the company, and his most recent building project with Hakeem—a five-star over-the-top luxurious hotel in Abu Dhabi.

And finally, happiest of all, they were expecting their first child in five months.

"What about Zoya?" she asked, curious about her good-natured sister-in-law. "How is she? And Salim, her sisters and her mother?"

Manny smiled. "The flower farm is thriving on our father's land. Everyone's pitching in to help Zoya—my stepmother included. And apparently she's totally booked for several seasons in advance for leasing out the rest of the farmland."

"Is it that popular with the local farmers?"

"Very. They're happy a big company hasn't moved in to displace their farmsteads and their homes." He paused, and then said, "I'm glad I had the sense to sign over the land to Zoya. She's done more with it than I ever could have."

Amal kissed his chest, right over his heart. "You're forgetting she wouldn't have been able to do anything if it were not for you."

Manny chuckled. "I suppose that's true."

"It is," she chirped, beaming up at him with a mix of pride and love.

She couldn't believe this was the same man who had been certain that he couldn't have an amicable relationship with his half-sisters and stepmother. To see him at peace with himself...she didn't think anything in the world could be so pleasing. Not even the wondrous sunrise view of the Liberty Bridge and the Mon River from his million-dollar home.

Amal went on tiptoes and touched her lips to his bearded jaw. Manny didn't let her go and leaned down to give her what she desired. A kiss that warmed her soul.

"What do you think your mom will say once she learns she's to be a grandmother?" she asked.

He gave her a toothy smile. "I imagine she'll be less shocked than when she learned I'd contacted my stepmother and half-sisters and given them my land inheritance."

"I still can't believe you hadn't told her anything."

“I’d hoped not to upset her.” He laughed breezily. “Though Zoya’s certainly won my mother over now, with her regular deliveries of coffee.”

“Stop, or you’ll make me want a cup.” She’d had to cut her intake of the delicious Ethiopian brew drastically since learning she was an expectant mother. And Manny, being the doting husband that he was, had gone as far as to abstain from his regular caffeine jolts, too, for her sake.

She couldn’t love him more—and yet she did.

Amal stared deep into his eyes and knew she could stand there snuggling in his arms and looking at him forever. “I’m glad it all worked out for the best,” she said.

“Even better than I could’ve dreamed it would,” he murmured against her lips, and he kissed her slow and sweet and nearly robbed her of breath.

But not before she asked him, “Have I mentioned how much I love you?”

“Only every day. You’ll never let me forget, will you?”

“No, not ever,” she vowed with a smile, kissing him again.

And she never did.

* * * * *

MILLS & BOON

Coming next month

RECLAIMING THE PRINCE'S HEART
Rebecca Winters

Rini was hooked up to an IV and one of the nursing staff was checking his vital signs. After a while Luna could tell he was coming to because he moved his strong legs and turned his head to the other side of the pillow.

She moved to the other side of his bed to be close to him. Without thinking, she whispered, "Jeu carezel tei, Rini," in her native language. It meant I love you.

Suddenly he opened those translucent gray eyes she'd thought she'd never see again. They stared at her without recognition. She assumed it was because he was still sedated. "Ti discurras rumantch?"

Her heart turned over because he'd heard her outpouring of love and understood. He'd just asked her if she spoke Romansh. That was the strange language no one understood?

"Gea." Yes, yes, yes.

"How come no one else can communicate? Where am I? I've been going insane that no one understands me. But you do. Why? Do you know me?"

His questions were fired one after another. The last question shocked her, but now was not the time to try and understand what was going on.

"I know you very well." Her voice shook. "Your name is Rini and I'm your wife, Luna."

An incredulous expression entered his intelligent eyes. "Impossible! I've never been married."

Help. Something was terribly wrong. Don't panic, Luna. "Thank heaven you're alive and that I've found you. You're in a hospital in Rezana, Slovenia. I'm going to take you home. A helicopter is on the way."

At that moment Carlo appeared at the door. He motioned her to come out in the hall. Her gaze shot back to her precious husband who was so disoriented, she realized he was still under the effects of the anesthetic. "I have to leave you for a few minutes."

"You can't go. No one else understands me." He sounded utterly frantic. It wrenched her heart.

"I promise I'll see you in a few minutes. Trust me."

Continue reading

RECLAIMING THE PRINCE'S HEART

Rebecca Winters

Available next month

www.millsandboon.co.uk